MARY —
ALL THE BEST TO
YOU!
TOM
COMBS

HARD TO BREATHE

A Drake Cody Suspense-Thriller
Book 2

Tom Combs

Evoke Publishing

Hard to Breathe

This is a work of fiction. All of the characters, organizations, and events portrayed in this novel are either products of the author's imagination or used fictitiously.

Published in the United States by Evoke Publishing

Author website: www.tom-combs.com
Email: tcombsauthor@gmail.com

ISBN-13: 978-0-9903360-3-7
ISBN-10: 0-9903360-3-4

Dedication

Donald J. Combs

The gift of a loving father is a joy forever
Gone but will never be forgotten

and

For twenty-five years I've worked the front lines of U.S. emergency care alongside police, fire/rescue, paramedics, EMTs, nurses, fellow doctors, technicians, air rescue crews, and the many others who respond when illness, trauma or tragedy strike. I dedicate this book to them – the special people committed to helping others when needed most.

Chapter 1

Memorial Hospital ER, 6:16 p.m.

Dr. Drake Cody grabbed a new patient record out of the Emergency Room chart rack. As usual, patients filled every bay of the Twin Cities' biggest and busiest ER. The hallways overflowed with patients, staff, and the clamor of voices, overhead pages, and phones.

He scanned the chart as he dodged down the hall toward patient room twenty-five.

Thirty-three year old female, married, Caucasian. Chief complaint – facial injuries. History – tripped on stairs.

Drake pulled back the curtain and stepped into the exam room.

The slim, dark-haired woman seated on the exam bed wore diamond earrings. Designer jeans showed below the hospital gown. The skin around her left eye was purple and swollen. Her lower lip was puffy, and a jagged horizontal gash gaped on her chin beneath her lip.

"I'm Dr. Cody. Sorry for the wait."

The woman raised her head, looked at him with her non-injured eye, then lowered her gaze. Despite her injuries, her loveliness struck him. With her delicate features and olive skin, she looked enough like his wife to be her sister.

A tall, mid-thirties man stood up from the bedside chair.

"I'm Dan Ogren." He extended a hand, executing a motivational speaker's shake and eye contact. "You can call me Dan. You probably recognize the name. My dad served on the hospital board for more than twenty years. I'm on it now."

Drake recognized the name but not from knowledge of who sat on the hospital board. The ads for Ogren Automotive were everywhere. The Ogren dealerships' marketing avoided the screaming pitches typical of others in auto sales. Their commercials and billboards featured good-looking, stylish Dan “the man” Ogren posed next to luxury vehicles in upscale settings around the Twin Cities.

Today Dan Ogren wore an Armani workout suit, and his wavy, blond hair looked artfully styled. His deep tan stood out in the Minnesota December.

The ads had not fully conveyed the man's striking physical presence—he had the size and lean muscularity of a pro athlete, with metallic blue eyes and the handsome Scandinavian features common to the area. Drake smelled alcohol.

“My Beth took a tumble on the stairs. Just a dumb accident. Can you fix it? I don't want a scar.”

Drake's “bad vibe” sensor gave a twitch.

“Sorry you were hurt,” Drake said as he bent to the injured woman. “We need to make sure you're going to be okay.”

She met his eyes then looked away.

“Can you tell me what happened? Did you lose consciousness?”

“You can call her Beth,” the husband said. “She fell on the stairs like I told you. Her chin is messed up the worst—”

“Please, it's best if she tells me.” Drake bent again to the injured woman. “Can I call you Beth?”

She nodded.

“Can you tell me what happened?”

She swiveled her head towards her husband.

“Answer. You heard the man.” His words were curt. As he turned back to Drake, he flashed his smile again.

“I fell on the steps.” She kept her eyes down. “I didn't get knocked out. I already told the nurse all this.”

“Sorry about the repetition,” Drake said. “Do you have pain in your neck? Can you see out of that eye? Any other areas hurting?” He stacked the questions together to observe her ability to process and respond. It would help him assess his concern about head injury.

“I can take the pain and I can see.” She raised her chin and pointed. “This big cut goes all the way into my mouth. That's why he brought me here.”

Drake examined the wound. She winced slightly.

“Sorry. I know it hurts but I can help you with this.”

The wound would require stitches inside the mouth, a stitch buried in the deep tissues, and several more on the chin. Even if she did not need X-rays or other tests, the repair of the complex laceration would take some time.

The noise and bustle of the ER sounded through the curtain to the hallway. They were a doctor short, the ER was already jammed, and on a Sunday evening it would get worse. The time-consuming facial repair meant more patients piling up in the waiting room. The main worry with people having to wait was not convenience or patient survey scores. It was providing timely treatment for patients who might worsen due to the wait. The ER staff turned themselves inside-out trying to make sure that didn’t happen.

But none of those concerns were what triggered Drake's flaring unease and the growing tightness in his neck and shoulders. His years of medical training and the violence he’d witnessed behind bars and barbed wire had him convinced of one thing.

Beth Ogren had been beaten.

He continued his exam of the injured woman.

“I couldn't believe we had to wait.” Dan's tone emphasized the specialness of 'we'. “Damn busy place. I guess you have good job security.” He laughed as he leaned back with hands behind his head and legs extended.

Drake said nothing.

“My dad donated the money for the hospice unit upstairs. And a lot more. We've been supporting this hospital for decades. I put on a charity golf tournament every year. Haven't seen you there. Are you a player?”

The words and behavior were not those of a man concerned about his wife after an accident.

Dan's entitled manner and breezy bullshit caused Drake's body to coil like a compressed spring.

He didn't have indisputable proof, but in his gut, he was certain.

He wanted to drive his fist into the man's face.

The abusers who admitted what they'd done, claimed their victims “made them” lose their “bad” tempers. Yet somehow they never lost their temper with anyone bigger, stronger, or tougher—or when there were witnesses. The darkest period in Drake's life had proved to him that such violent cowards were not rare.

He completed Beth's examination. Thankfully, she did not have evidence of additional injury.

"You're sure you can fix her face?" Dan lounged with his legs outstretched and hands behind his head. "Maybe you can toss in an extra stitch and tighten up things. She's a beauty now, but she's not getting any younger." Again Dan laughed alone.

If Drake were a dog, his fur would be on end and his fangs bared.

He'd dealt with some whose brutality justifiably kept them locked away. Drake sensed that underneath Dan Ogren's handsome businessman exterior, similar cruelty hid.

A fierce urge to lay hands on Ogren gripped Drake.

"I'm sorry," he bent to Beth's eye level, "I need to step away for a moment. You're safe. We'll take care of you."

Drake had lost control before with others who'd victimized the defenseless. It had torn his life apart.

He let out a big breath as he escaped into the hall. His hands trembled.

Chapter 2

Drake took another deep breath. He toweled off the water he'd splashed onto his face from the corridor sink.

He knew in his gut Ogren had beaten his wife. *Bastard.*

A wealthy businessman who sat on the hospital's all-powerful board—guilty of domestic abuse. And his victim afraid to tell the truth.

Drake knew too well how the system worked—and how badly it failed.

"Dr. Cody!" Halfway down the hall, an orderly and security guard rolled a patient gurney up against the wall.

"We got trouble," the orderly called out as he locked the rolling bed's wheels. "A mean one."

During busy times the hallways became patient care areas. The guard's body blocked Drake's view of the new patient.

A scrawny arm lashed out from the cart. The orderly raised a hand to his ear. "Ouch."

The security guard stepped forward and again the arm flailed.

Drake hustled to assist.

A skeletally-gaunt, unshaven, and wild-eyed old man in a soiled robe and underpants crouched on his knees on the cart. A shock of white hair stood up over snarling features. He looked poised to strike again.

"I think he's gonna need to be restrained," the orderly said. "The paramedics had another run so he was a quick drop-off." He handed Drake the nursing home transfer and the paramedics' transfer sheet.

Drake read the handwritten paragraph of nursing home information: "Alzheimer's. Non-verbal. Aggressive today. Hitting caregivers. Normally nice."

The paramedics' sheet showed a fast pulse but otherwise normal vital signs.

"I'll get help to hold him down," the guard said. "Can you drug him?"

"Hold on a second," Drake said.

Agitated elderly patients sometimes needed to be held down and injected with a strong sedative to keep them from hurting themselves or others. Drake hated the terror these struggles caused the patients and restrained them only as a last resort.

As he turned back to the patient, he spied Dan Ogren standing in the doorway of his wife's room, arms folded, looking irritated. When he noted Drake's gaze, his phony smile reappeared. The car dealer tapped his wrist as if indicating a watch.

Sorry for the delay, Danny-boy. You'll get taken care of sooner than you'd like. Drake put Dan Ogren out of his mind and focused on his elderly patient.

The nursing home's report noted "usually nice."

What had triggered today's change?

In a glance, Drake took in the pinpoint pupils, the trembling jaw. Agitation. Anger. Fear. Something else?

He's hurting.

He stepped closer. This man was someone's father, brother, friend, husband—now unable to speak, helpless, and dependent on others.

Drake tried to capture the man's gaze. Wild eyes skipped about but kept coming back to Drake's, then finally held.

Drake nodded as he maintained eye contact. "I know you're in pain. Let me help you."

He moved close. A sinewy arm shot out and clamped on Drake's upper arm, the talon-like fingers digging into the thickness of his bicep. The orderly and guard started forward.

Drake froze them with a shake of his head.

He kept his arm limp, ignoring the discomfort. The musty, sour smell of age and illness intruded.

"I'm a doctor. I can help." He held out his free hand as if approaching a growling dog.

The man's frown softened.

He gently laid his hand on his patient's leg. The pincer-grip on his arm tightened but no blow followed. The patient's stringy muscles were knotted, his forearm a bundle of stretched tendons. The odor of soiled human and age now stronger.

Drake looked for a telling sign: facial swelling from an abscessed tooth, the redness or swelling of an extremity indicating inflammation or injury.

"We're going to help you, sir."

The man's eyes remained on Drake but the gaze was now less focused.

As the frown softened, the grimace beneath became clear.

So much pain. *What's hurting him?*

He put a hand on the man's shoulder and, speaking softly, eased the patient back on the cart. The man's hand remained but now it felt like the clutch of a frightened child.

He laid his hand on the man's abdomen, gently probing while watching the man's face. Below the navel he found a fullness. The man's eyes flickered and fingernails once again bit into Drake's arm.

Drake's fingers traced a cantaloupe-sized mass. *This is it.*

He spoke over his shoulder to the orderly.

"His bladder is ready to burst. Get me a Foley catheter, please."

No rooms were available, so they guided the cart out of the hallway and into one of the Crash Room bays. The man kept his hold on Drake's arm as the curtain closed.

As the orderly opened the urinary catheter packaging, Drake crouched to the man's level.

"This will be uncomfortable, but then your pain will go away." He nodded. "The pain will go away."

Drake passed the soft tube through the penis and into the bladder. The old man's grip tightened, but he remained still. Urine jetted into the tubing. In less than a minute, more than a liter had collected within the bag.

The man's bladder had been distended to twice its normal size. An enlarged prostate—the enemy of old men—had blocked the outflow of urine.

The fullness in the man's lower abdomen had now disappeared.

The man lay with eyes closed, his features relaxed.

"He doesn't look like the same guy," the orderly said.

“Thanks for getting my attention.” Drake held up a fist and the orderly bumped it while smiling.

Drake's work often gave him the opportunity to perform dramatic interventions on victims of accidents, gunshots, and heart attacks—procedures that saved lives. Those were what many perceived as the glory events in emergency medicine—and they were. But for Drake, recognizing and relieving the suffering of this vulnerable old man gave him the same kind of damn-am-I-lucky-to-have-this-job thrill.

His stomach clenched. The feel-good rush of helping the elderly man nosedived. He swallowed.

Once again the shadow of his past swept over him. His dread flared.

He could lose this.

Someday they’d approach him and it would all be over. They'd tell him he’d been found out. His lies uncovered. They’d learned what he'd done. Who he was.

He'd lose everything.

Chapter 3

5:55 p.m., WCCY newsroom

Before the evening news went live, Tina Watt looked over the news director's red-ink slashes and handwritten additions to her lead story. *Is he serious?*

As he strode past, she raised a hand. "Excuse me, Ned."

"What do you want?" The balding director frowned.

"These changes you made—"

"Yeah?"

"I covered the original story. I interviewed Dr. Cody, the ER staff, the police, and the man who was arrested." She held up the sheet. "This is big news on the doctor's history, but some of your other content isn't right. I think you forgot—"

"I didn't forget anything, sunshine." He scowled. "We're on in less than a minute. Just read what I wrote."

"But it's not accurate. This is sensationalized and biased."

"Listen. You're new and your numbers are good so far. The local yokels think you're exotic." She knew he was referring to her being black. "But I'm the news director." He pointed a finger at her. "Read what I tell you and look good doing it. Remember that and you'll do fine, pretty girl."

He turned away

She flushed hot. *Ass!*

After three months in Minneapolis as an on-air reporter, the six-o'clock anchor spot was a great opportunity. But irresponsible reporting was not what she had signed on for.

The set technician called out. "We're on in five, in four..."

The cameras swung to her at the anchor desk. She took a settling breath as she slid her original story copy next to the director's red-inked sheet. The lights flooded to full, the heat immediate.

"...in two, in one. We're live!"

The camera light went red. She turned on her smile.

"This is Tina Watt coming to you from our downtown Minneapolis studio with WCCY's six o'clock news. Our top story involves breaking news on the violent emergency room confrontation that occurred at Memorial Hospital ER two months ago. As we reported at that time, a Minneapolis resident (*the red ink edit read "an unemployed person of color"*) sustained a broken nose and rib injuries (*the red ink read "horrific and life-threatening injuries"*), while being seen as a patient in the ER. Mr. Quentin Jackson was arrested and charged with assault.

"Mr. Jackson alleged that the ER physician, Dr. Drake Cody, assaulted him without provocation, and that police beat him thereafter. The hospital, police, and witness accounts identified that Mr. Jackson had struck a nurse when she refused him drugs and then attacked Dr. Cody when he intervened. Mr. Jackson (*director's copy: "the assaulted individual"*), whose booking photo is shown here"—the image of a black male with a swollen, deformed nose appeared—"was arrested and charged with assault. Community leaders joined in challenging police and hospital accounts. Mr. Jackson (*director's copy: "The abused citizen"*) was subsequently released and charges dropped.

"In breaking news today, WCCY has learned that the ER physician involved, Dr. Drake Cody, has a previous conviction for felony assault. At the age of sixteen, he was found guilty of aggravated assault by an Ohio juvenile court. An inquiry to the State Medical Board today revealed that neither the conviction nor Dr. Cody's time spent incarcerated in an Ohio facility for violent juvenile offenders was reported in his Minnesota medical license application.

"Hours ago, Mr. Jackson's attorney announced their intent to file civil suits in Hennepin County alleging assault, racial discrimination, and damages. Memorial Medical Center, the Minneapolis police department, and the university are reported to be among those to be named, along with Dr. Drake Cody. Our reporter spoke with Mr. Jackson's attorney, Edina-based personal injury lawyer, Barry Ward."

The back screen filled with a slim, blond man in an expensive suit. He spoke into a microphone pointed at his clean-shaven chin.

"Additionally, we will be filing complaints with the Minnesota Board of Medicine and the American Hospital Association. What happened is an outrage. My client, an ill black man in need of treatment, sought care and was subjected to a horrific beating. The charges against my client were a cover-up. Dr. Drake Cody is clearly a violent man."

The attorney stared into the lens. "Who is the victim and who is the criminal here? In civil court, we will be seeking ten million dollars in damages. I know the fair people of Minnesota want to see justice done. "

This was where the director's red ink cross-outs indicated the report should end. A brutalized victim and clear inference of the doctor's guilt, with the hot-button issues of race, class difference, and high dollar damages at center stage.

Massive hype and trial by media—a ratings bonanza.

Tina had only recently earned the anchor chair for the six p.m. broadcasts and weekend ten p.m.'s. If she stopped now, she might survive the story as she'd reported it. She decided in a blink.

"Dr. Cody's conviction occurred when he was sixteen years old. His sentence was commuted by a state of Ohio mandate after four months served. The criminal record was sealed, but details leaked, triggering today's report.

"Mr. Jackson also has a criminal record. His felony convictions include drug trafficking, gang-affiliated crime, and assault. He spent two years in Stillwater prison. WCCY will be following these developments and will continue to present the latest and most accurate news on events as they unfold."

Tina sensed the laser-heat emanating from the crimson face of the news director.

She didn't care. Her parents had raised her to be someone with integrity—not a brainless talking head. *Pretty girl this, you classless ratings shill.*

The rest of the broadcast slipped by with the weather forecast predicting more brutally cold temps and the ho-hum of a mid-December sports night.

Tina gave her sign-off. "WCCY, we keep you informed. Be safe."

The lights dimmed and she pivoted on her chair. The director was in her face before she'd completed her next breath. He reeked of garlic and cigarettes.

She felt a spray of spittle as he hissed. “You arrogant bitch! If you ever ignore my instructions again—”

“Get out of my face—now.” Tina kept her voice low but inside she raged. “Your manipulation of the story was shameful. Ratings matter, but so does journalistic responsibility. I'm taking this up with management.”

The director rocked back, wide-eyed.

“I *am* management,” he yelled. “I'm the news director of this station! You got that?” He looked about as if expecting support from the stunned station crew.

At that moment a shaft of pain ripped through Tina's lower abdomen. She gasped.

“I'm not going to take shit from some newbie talking-head,” the director yelled.

The pain doubled and took Tina's breath. She fell back into the chair, clutching at her waist.

The director froze with his mouth open.

“What the hell?” He bent toward her.

Perspiration drenched her and the pain rocketed past anything in her experience. Panic flooded and she lurched to her feet. Sound faded as if someone had turned down the volume knob. Her vision blurred.

God, no!

She pitched forward as blackness engulfed her.

Chapter 4

Drake scrubbed his hands in the Crash Room sink. His elderly patient slept.

"Should I park him in the hall?" the orderly asked.

"Yes, thanks. He's got to be exhausted." Drake dried his hands with a paper towel. "I'll take care of the paperwork when it's ready." He tossed the towel into the receptacle as he exited the Crash Room.

Patti, the ER charge nurse, stepped out of an exam room with her hand on the shoulder of a stooped gray-haired lady. Discharge papers protruded from the woman's purse.

"We're always here if you need us, Gladys. Take care."

The woman clasped both hands around Patti's, then moved toward the exit.

Charge nurse responsibilities included patient placement, staff supervision, and general oversight of ER patient care. The pressure-packed job made herding cats look easy. His friend, Patti, handled the task with seemingly unlimited energy and a ready smile.

Drake caught her eye.

He approached close, then lowered his voice. "Room twenty-five is an abuse victim. A nasty laceration, but she's stable. She says she fell."

Patti sighed and shook her head.

"The husband is in there. I want to get him out of there and see if she'll talk, but he's the hovering, controlling type. I haven't confronted him yet." He paused. "I'll be notifying Minneapolis police. Grab me when they get here. This will be worse than usual. The guy is on the hospital board."

Patti's eyes went wide.

"And please call in the domestic abuse advocate for the patient. And can you get a tech to set up for a complex laceration repair in there straight away?"

A yell sounded.

Drake looked over his shoulder. Paramedics were wheeling a huge, bearded guy wearing only a blaze orange hunting hat and undershorts into one of the psych rooms. More patients were now parked in the hallway.

"Triage is swamped, too," Patti said. "And I assume you know we're a doctor short all evening."

The events of several weeks back still cast a dense shadow. Drake and his colleagues' research breakthrough had resulted in a nightmare. Greed and the astronomical value of drug D-44 had attracted ruthless, brutal attention.

He and his family had survived but were still recovering. Drake's two closest friends had been horribly injured—Rizz in a wheelchair with paralysis, and Jon transferred to a rehabilitation hospital in Duluth after being near death.

Apart from his worries for their health, their absence had created a staffing hole. With two top emergency medicine resident physicians out of action, the remaining doctors were working long hours seven days a week.

The physician shortage impacted the whole department.

"How are you holding up?" Patti asked. "You've been—"

The shrill electronic bleat of the "doctor to the radio" signal intruded overhead, indicating that paramedics were racing toward the ER with one or more critical patients.

Patti shrugged. "Having fun yet?" She pivoted toward the Crash Room.

Drake sliced through the busy hall to the radio room. He grabbed the transmit microphone.

"Doctor Cody here."

"Ambulance 7-1-9 three minutes out. Thirty-one-year old black female with onset of abdominal pain and collapse. Unconscious, protecting airway, pulse 130s. Can't get a blood pressure. Can't get an IV. She's got nothing for veins. Color is bad. Two minutes out. Over."

"10-4. Crash room three. Out." Drake knew the paramedics in 7-1-9. A rock-solid team. They'd shared all they knew. With an unconscious patient, there'd be no further information to help.

Drake's eyes found the ER station secretary, who stood ready with headset in place.

"Med Team Stat, Crash Room 3," he said. As he moved toward the Crash Room, he heard her "Medical Team Stat" call announced three times overhead.

Drake entered the Crash Room. White linens, electronic monitors, and stainless steel instruments surrounded each of the four patient beds. The Life Clock positioned above the bed in bay 3 had been triggered, and red numerals flashed the minutes and seconds since the paramedics' call.

Patients triaged to the Crash Room were fighting for their lives, and Drake and the ER team understood the stakes. Ambulance 719 was bringing in someone for whom each instant without critical intervention brought them closer to death.

Diagnostic possibilities raced through his head—what had struck down the young woman?

When people collapsed and life was draining from them like fluid from an overturned bottle, there was rarely time for definitive "tests."

Lifesaving steps had to be initiated immediately, with physician intuition often the only guide—delay meant death.

Nurses, emergency medical technicians, a respiratory therapist, and lab and radiology techs scrambled into the Crash Room and began to prepare. A heat lamp was directed at the white linen sheets that would soon support their patient. Drake spoke to the team as he pulled on a surgical gown.

"Thirty-year-old female, abdominal pain, collapsed and in shock. Protecting airway but minimally responsive. No IV so far." He slipped on a mask, then grabbed a central venous access tray from the wall-mounted shelves. "Get two units O-negative blood here now. Try for an arm vein but I'll insert a central IV line if you can't get one immediately." Drake nodded to the respiratory therapist. "Support breathing and have a tube ready if I need to intubate."

Drake tore open the central line pack as he processed what was known. The history, scant as it was, pointed the way. Young female, acute abdominal pain, collapse, and shock…

The doors exploded open as crew 719 rammed the cart into the Crash Room. One paramedic held an oxygen mask and bag over the patient's mouth. The second spoke, his expression grim. "Still breathing. Lungs clear. Heart rate 130 on the monitor, but we just lost her pulse. She's crashing."

Drake pulled back the airway mask. A young black woman, though her color now a deathly gray. They swiftly transferred her to the bed as the techs cut away her clothing. Drake felt for a pulse in her neck—only the faintest flutter. He put a finger on the skin beneath her eye, exposing the tissue beneath her lower lid. What should have been a ruddy reddish color showed nearly white. Her flesh was ice. He picked up a lilac-tinged scent—perfume? His gloved hand palpated her abdomen—a faint wince showed on her face when he pressed.

He glimpsed the life clock—3 min 04 secs had elapsed since the paramedics' radio call.

"Dr. Cody, her veins are nothing." The nurse held an IV needle in her gloved hand. "Can't get an IV."

The patient needed fluids and blood now.

"Get saline, two units of blood, and pressure bags ready for my central line. Get me four more units of O-negative blood." The nurses prepared the liter bags of clear fluid and the smaller dark scarlet blood bags, their movements practiced and deft. "Place a Foley in her bladder, then someone run her urine to the lab for a pregnancy test. Stand by in the lab and call the result back the second it's known."

Drake knew the look of imminent death, and this patient had it. *She's bleeding to death internally.*

He inserted a hollow four-inch needle attached to a syringe into the patient's upper chest. He exerted slight traction on the plunger of the syringe as he advanced the needle beneath the collarbone. He used his knowledge of anatomy and surface landmarks to guide the needle toward the large but invisible subclavian vein lying adjacent to the lung and major artery.

The plunger's resistance gave way, and the dark purple of venous blood filled the syringe. He'd entered the target.

Holding the needle fixed, he removed the syringe. Warm blood welled out the needle's hub and over his gloved fingers. He fed the guide wire through the hollow needle into the large vein. He then removed the needle and threaded the large, plastic IV catheter over the wire and into the vein. He removed the wire and secured the catheter with a single fast stitch.

The nurses connected the blood and fluid IV lines to the catheter ports. Blood and fluids rushed through the catheter into the patient's body.

"Keep blood and fluids wide open," Drake said. The IV bags were being squeezed to speed the flow of blood and fluid through the catheter into what Drake believed was the patient's nearly empty system.

The life clock clicked and the red numerals showed: 5 min 14 secs. *Hold on, lady. Hold on.*

"Heart rate 130. I can feel a pulse now," the paramedic said.

The patient moaned and a grimace twisted her features.

"Versed for sedation—2 milligrams slow push now," Drake said.

"Heart rate 125 and pulse is stronger." The nurse puffed the BP cuff and listened. "Blood pressure 80."

The unit secretary stuck her head in the door. "The urine pregnancy test is positive. Hemoglobin seven." She waited.

Both results fit Drake's working diagnosis—a ruptured tubal pregnancy. Pregnancies outside the uterus expand until they rupture the surrounding tissues and blood vessels. Once ruptured, the bleeding does not stop. Without surgery, death is a certainty.

Their patient needed the operating room. Her only chance was to have her belly opened up and the bleeding vessels tied off.

"Please call the on-call OB/GYN doc, and wait on the line until you get them."

The secretary nodded as she pivoted toward her desk.

"Patti, call the OR. Preliminary diagnosis—ruptured ectopic pregnancy with shock," Drake said. "Tell them we'll be on the run. I'm going to intubate her so she'll be ready for surgery."

Drake picked up the light-equipped laryngoscope and inserted the blade of the device into the patient's mouth. She gagged slightly, but Drake was able to see deep into her throat, viewing the white, shutter-like vocal cords. He slipped the plastic ET tube between the open cords and into her trachea. He nodded to the respiratory therapist, who was already securing the tube. The patient's airway was now protected and they could breathe for her.

The OB/GYN surgeon would need to operate immediately—there was no time for additional testing. The runaway bleeding needed to be stopped—now.

"Dr. Cody, I have the on-call doctor." The secretary held a remote phone. "It's Dr. Stone."

Yes! Dr. Julie Stone was rock-solid. Drake craned his head, and the secretary held the phone to his ear, allowing him to keep his bloodied gloves free as he spoke.

"Julie, I've got an emergent OR case. Looks like a ruptured ectopic pregnancy. She's dying. Thirty-year-old. Abdominal pain and collapse. Positive pregnancy test. Hemoglobin seven. I've got a large bore central IV and we're jamming blood and fluids. She's intubated and ready for the OR. She doesn't have much time. Can you take her?"

It would take trust for Dr. Stone to take this dying patient to the OR based solely on Drake's assessment.

If he was wrong, the patient would die. If he was correct, surgery provided the only way to save the patient's life.

"Sounds right, Drake. Make sure we have plenty of blood available, and get her to the OR. I'm on the third floor but on my way." She disconnected.

Drake was still gut-tight and sweating, but he felt a flush of hope.

Dr. Julie Stone and the OR team would give his patient every chance.

Chapter 5

Drake stripped off his gloves and gown. He washed his hands in the Crash Room sink, then splashed water onto his face and the back of his neck. The protective gear, high-intensity lights, and pressure always caused a sweat.

Now it would be the OB/GYN surgeon facing the heat. It would be touch and go.

If Julie opened the woman's belly and found the problem was other than a ruptured ectopic pregnancy, it could mean disaster. A shadow of doubt rippled through Drake's mind.

No. He trusted his call.

As he wiped his face with a paper towel, someone cleared their throat. He turned. Stuart Kline, the hospital's new CEO, stood before him.

A ballerina in toe-shoes and a tutu would have surprised Drake less.

"Dr. Cody." Kline was a fiftyish, fit-appearing guy—very much the blow-combed, attention-to-his-appearance type. His cream-colored linen suit couldn't be more out of place in the setting. He and Drake had never talked personally. Kline had come to the top hospital spot from the university business operations department a few months ago.

The CEO did not introduce himself or extend a hand.

"You're giving the wife of Dan Ogren the best of care, right?"

What? Drake said nothing as he crumpled the towel and threw it into the trash.

"Dr. Cody. Yes, you're the one who's done some promising research for the university—correct?"

"I'm involved in research. But it's private. It's not for the university."

"Hmmm. So you say."

So I say? Yes, I say.

Orderlies gathered the mess from the numerous drapes, blood and fluid bags, medications, and instruments that had been used to resuscitate the near-death patient. As usual after such action, the Crash Room bay looked like a bomb had gone off.

Kline did not appear to notice their surroundings. He stood, staring at Drake with his arms folded on his chest as if waiting for Drake to plead his case. "In my previous position, I oversaw most of the research-related business for the university."

"I'm busy taking care of patients right now," Drake said. *Why is he here*? Who cares what he did for the university?

"That's why I'm here. Dan Ogren and his father, Dan Senior, are special friends of the hospital. Dan is a Board member." Kline pursed his lips. "It's important that he and his wife receive the very best care." He glanced about, seeming to notice the blood and medical debris for the first time. He clasped his hands to his chest as if to avoid being soiled.

We should try and give patients the best care? What a novel idea! Drake hoped his growing annoyance did not show.

"We provide every ER patient the best care we possibly can," Drake said.

Kline shrugged. "I received a call from Dan a number of minutes ago. Apparently, you'd told them you'd be back in a minute. It had already been twelve minutes when he called me. I arrive and she still has not been cared for." He shook his head. "Totally unacceptable."

Dan "the man" Ogren had called the CEO after twelve minutes? And Kline had raced in? Drake's expectations about the upcoming confrontation worsened. Dan Ogren was seriously connected. And the new CEO of the hospital clearly knew nothing about emergency care.

"A nurse updated the patient and her husband that I was caring for a critical patient. Did he tell you that?"

"I also heard you chose to spend time taking care of a crazy old man while the Ogrens waited." Kline frowned. "Mrs. Dan Ogren is a special patient. You need to hop to it."

A *special* patient. Really? What are the rest of the patients?

Drake had overheard doctors' lounge mutterings that the new CEO focused solely on the "bottom line" and knew nothing about taking care of patients. Many said that without Jim Torrins' efforts as chief medical officer, the hospital would have already run aground.

Bashing the CEO occurred in virtually every hospital, but Kline had, in less than a minute, convinced Drake that in his case the gripes were on target.

"And I expect to be updated on the status of Dan's wife." Kline straightened his tie in the mirror above the scrub sink.

"Dan Ogren and his wife are in the department and both will receive appropriate attention," Drake said.

Kline gave a dismissive nod. He picked his way out of the Crash Room, veering wide around the untidy remnants of patient care.

Patient privacy law demanded that Drake share nothing about Beth Ogren's condition or care with a non-medical person such as Kline. Drake would not give him one word of update. No doubt the meddling CEO would hear plenty after the impending collision occurred.

Drake paused at the counter just outside the Crash Room, wrestling with what he faced—a wealthy businessman, friend of the hospital's CEO, and hospital board member, had beaten his wife.

A report of suspected abuse against such a powerful figure wouldn't assure justice or the victim's safety, but the man's lawyers would certainly investigate Drake's past. His throat tightened.

Not reporting was the safest course for him but...

Ideally, he would wait to call the police until he'd repaired Beth Ogren's injuries and had spoken with her alone. Reality made ideal a dream—neither he nor the police had the luxury. When abusers detected suspicion, they often took their victim and left the ER—even with care incomplete. ER staff had no authority to stop them.

Dan Ogren would sense something soon. The police needed time to get to the ER before he could leave.

He dialed the number from memory. As it rang, he sighed. Dan would get the attention he deserved. And Drake would be put dead center in the powerful man's gunsight.

"This is Dr. Drake Cody from Memorial Hospital ER. I'm calling to file a report of suspected domestic abuse with injuries," Drake said. "Occurred in Minneapolis, the Kenwood neighborhood." He waited as they routed the call.

An intimidated wife/victim denying assault and a wealthy, influential abuser. Would the law protect Beth Ogren and deliver justice to her powerful husband?

Drake's experience made him doubt that would happen. His instincts called for him to do more.

He'd followed those instincts before and dealt out justice directly to people like Dan. It had destroyed the people he'd loved most and spiraled his life into darkness.

He had to abide by the law, despite the wounds its failings had inflicted on him.

"Yes. Memorial ER. Dr. Cody here. Did you get the information?" He listened. "Have the officers ask for the charge nurse at the triage desk. She'll get me and I'll update them before they go in. Let them know this will be a high-profile case." He hung up, then rubbed his neck.

This would not go easy. It would not go easy at all.

Chapter 6

Drake stood masked and gowned at Beth Ogren's bedside. Her face lay framed by sterile drapes and centered in the surgical light. A tech had cleaned the wound and set up the plastic surgery instrument tray with the suture types Drake had requested. Beth's husband remained sprawled on the chair with his hands behind his head.

"Dan, you need to go to the waiting room." Drake began to put on his surgical gloves.

"I'll stay here," Dan said.

"You being in the room increases the risk of infection, and it can be distracting for me to make sure you don't feel ill or faint. I'd really appreciate it if you'd step out."

Dan Ogren's eyes narrowed as he looked at Drake. "I've been sewn up before and people stayed in the room. And blood doesn't bother me. I'm not leaving." An animal-wary glint showed in his eyes.

"It's different seeing a loved one's injury. I once had a surgeon pass out when I was sewing up his child." There was some truth to what Drake said, but primarily he wanted Dan gone so he could talk to the injured wife alone.

"I'm not going to pass out. I'll stay here. Did the CEO talk to you? He's a friend of mine."

"If you won't leave, let me know if you feel sick or light-headed. And please let Beth answer my questions herself."

The look Dan directed Drake's way was not that of a concerned husband.

The cunning bastard knew Drake had not bought the phony nice-guy act. Beth Ogren would not be talking to anyone alone.

It was best to repair Beth's face before triggering the showdown that loomed. If Drake pushed the confrontation now, Dan might take his wife and leave, her care incomplete.

Beth's injuries were not life-threatening—this time—but the laceration needed expert care.

"Beth, the first step is for me to numb the area." Drake picked up the syringe loaded with local anesthetic, keeping it off to the side and out of Beth's view. "Do you want me to tell you what I'm doing as we go or not? I'll warn you of possible discomfort either way."

"Tell me," she said. Her eyes were closed.

He adjusted the blue surgical drapes, framing her chin.

"I'm going to hold your lower lip. Let me know right away if you feel pain." He grasped her lower lip and pulled it gently forward. "You'll feel a pinch inside your mouth, a bit like you've probably felt at the dentist."

Drake introduced the needle in the lowest point of the gutter inside the mouth between the lower teeth and the lip. "You might feel a burning sensation." He advanced the needle, then injected a small amount of local anesthetic around the nerve serving the chin and lower lip.

"While we give the anesthetic a moment to work, let me tell you about your injuries. A peri-orbital hematoma, basically a nasty black eye. The swelling and maroon color is from blood that has collected under the skin. The eye itself is okay. It will heal completely. You have no broken bones, but your face and jaw are badly bruised. The laceration I'm going to repair is from where the inside of your mouth smashed against your lower teeth. Your teeth cut through the inside of your mouth and out through the skin. I know it looks scary, but I've repaired a lot of these. You'll heal."

She gave a tight nod.

"I don't want a scar on her," Dan said.

"Deep wounds heal by scarring." Drake said. "What my repair does is make the amount of scar and its visibility as minimal as possible. The instructions and follow-up will also address this. If after healing it is bothersome, there are things that can be done."

Drake lightly touched the needle to her chin. No response. He repeated the maneuver several times all around the wound.

"Let me know right away if you have any discomfort."

She nodded, still with her eyes closed.

Drake worked quickly as he initiated the three-layer closure. First he placed four stitches on the inside of Beth's mouth, closing the inner laceration. He then changed into new sterile gloves.

"What time did you get injured, Beth?" Drake asked.

"This morning," she said.

Out of the corner of his eye, Drake saw Dan sit forward.

"No. She's wrong. It was just before we came," Dan said.

Drake placed one absorbable suture in the deep tissue, which pulled together and aligned the edges of the facial wound.

"Which was it, Beth?" Drake asked. Dan hadn't brought her to the ER until late afternoon. Enough time for a drunk to sleep it off.

"Like he said." Her eyes were now closed tightly.

"Yeah. She was confused," Dan said.

Drake placed five fine-gauge sutures, aligning the skin wound in a smooth even line. If it did not become infected, the wound would heal with minimal scarring.

"All done. Do you want to sit up?" Drake said.

She nodded. Drake helped her to the sitting position.

"It didn't hurt," she said sounding surprised.

"You did great."

He turned to her husband. "Dan, I'd like you to leave for a moment."

"I'm not leaving." The big man took his hands from behind his head and sat up straight.

"Beth, can you ask Dan to leave for a moment?"

She looked at Dan then back to Drake. She shook her head.

Drake sighed.

"Dan, I'd prefer you leave, but if you won't, please don't interrupt."

"I'll talk whenever I want to." Dan's good-guy act was long gone.

Beth's eyes darted. She looked as if she wanted to run.

"You're safe, Beth. We can help. Tell me who hurt you," Drake said.

Dan jumped to his feet.

"What the hell are you saying?" He stood close enough that the smell cologne and alcohol was strong. "I told you she fell down the stairs."

Drake ignored him.

"Beth, who hurt you?"

She kept her eyes down.

"It's like he said. I fell." She glanced toward Dan. He gave a barely perceptible nod. Her eyes went to the floor. "I tripped on the stairs."

Drake sighed.

So sad and ugly. The bastard had her.

Drake slid back on the rolling stool. "I don't believe either of you."

He looked from one to the other. Beth would not meet his gaze. Dan directed a "you're a dead man" look his way.

The look would probably have intimidated someone who hadn't survived the Scioto Furnace State Facility for Violent Juvenile Offenders.

"The injuries don't fit with a fall on the stairs," Drake said.

"You're full of shit," Dan said. "Get me the CEO. Call Kline. Now."

Drake focused on Beth.

"You have slight bruising around your neck. You also have what are called petechiae—dozens of tiny spots on the whites and skin around your eye. They occur when someone is choked. The pressure causes pinpoint bleeding." Drake sighed again. "Also, your eye and mouth wounds fit with being struck with a fist. Unfortunately, my job makes me an expert on injuries that occur when people hurt each other."

Dan took a step toward Drake, his face crimson, fists clenched.

"Don't be stupid," Drake said, remaining seated. Getting to his feet might provoke the violence he desperately wanted—but had to avoid. Nothing would be as satisfying as kicking Dan's ass. The wife-beater had no idea how close to snapping Drake felt. "Don't make things worse for yourself, Ogren. The police will be here any minute."

"Listen to me, Doc." Dan's tone had changed with the mention of the police. "You can still undo this. We can make this work. I guarantee you don't want to do this. If you let the police know you were mistaken, I can make it very worthwhile."

"Not happening." Drake shook his head. *How much crap had this jerk bought himself out of?*

Ogren's face twisted, his eyes hate-filled. "If you do this, you'll regret it. I'm not playing. You and yours—call it off or you're dead."

In the jungle that had been the Scioto Furnace, Drake had faced threats like this. His survival had demanded violent response. What he'd had to do crept around the boundaries of his conscience like a foul and bloodied beast.

“Quit talking, Ogren. It's done.”

Drake had other patients who needed care. Dan Ogren had earned what the police would do. He deserved worse.

“Beth, a domestic abuse counselor will talk to you about your safety. She’s a person who's been where you are.” Drake took her hand in his and looked her in the eye. “Be honest with the police and listen to the counselor. Otherwise, things will only get worse. You're in real danger.”

A tear rolled down Beth's cheek. The bruised, cut, and swollen sections of face were like puzzle pieces that did not match the loveliness of her uninjured features. Once more, her resemblance to Rachelle struck him.

Another innocent victimized by others. Sadness and anger competed in Drake's head. “Don't let yourself be hurt anymore. Let us help you.” Dan yanked Beth's arm from Drake's hand.

“Get your hands off her. This is bullshit.” He stuck a finger in Drake's face. “You're done in this hospital, boy. I'll destroy you.”

Ogren brushed against him as if to intimidate. Drake grit his teeth and did not engage. His fists remained clenched as he spoke.

“Beth, you have five stitches on your chin that will need to be removed in four days. The other stitches will dissolve. After the police and the counselor, the nurse will go over everything with you. Any questions, just ask them to get me. You need to have someone stay with you tonight as a precaution for head injury. Do you have someone?”

"I'll be staying with her, asshole," Ogren said.

Drake ignored him. He knew where Dan Ogren would likely be staying.

“Beth, if you need us, we're here. Always.”

Drake exited the room with the empty feeling of one who hadn’t done enough.

Chapter 7

Memorial Hospital, Medical records department, 6:18 p.m.

"Let me show you how, Dr. Rizzini." The medical coding specialist bent but held her body arched away from Rizz and his wheelchair. Her fingers skimmed over the desktop computer's keys. She hit the last key, then straightened while retreating to the edge of the cubicle. "Depending on what you want to review, just change the dates or the desired report parameters. Make sense?"

He looked up. She couldn't meet his eyes.

"Thanks. You're the best." Rizz advanced the wheelchair, and she edged further away.

Rizz's fingers skipped over the keyboard, his upper extremities fully functional. A clinical record appeared on the screen. "I'll holler if I need help."

The coder backed out of the cubicle. Her posture eased as she got clear. She'd tried to look relaxed, but it was plain to him that his "condition" made her uncomfortable.

It had been almost two months since the crazed woman's bullet had trashed his spinal cord. He was paralyzed and insensate from the mid-chest down. *Insensate*—a medical term no one else used. The inability to perceive sensation, to feel. The loss of movement was straightforward—and brutal. The loss of feeling was something he could never have imagined.

He looked over his shoulder. Only a skeleton crew remained in Medical Records evenings and nights. He slipped the flask from his lap bag and slugged down a swallow of vodka. The liquid heat slid down his throat.

Reading people had always been one of his special gifts. The coder's effort to hide her discomfort was obvious to him. Similarly, in the ER, he saw through the artifice and attempted deceptions of drug-seekers, malingerers, or others with a hidden agenda. More importantly, he was able to sense the real medical issues in patients who didn't intentionally mislead but unconsciously minimized symptoms due to denial—or exaggerated them due to anxiety or fear their concern would be ignored.

For physicians, interpreting what patients were trying to communicate posed the greatest challenge in diagnosing their problems.

Rizz's ability served him well in the patient-flooded ER—no one could see, evaluate, and treat ER patients faster.

Drake could read patients as well as Rizz, but no one could "treat 'em and street 'em" as fast. It was an ability he prided himself on. He had helped more than his share.

His ability had also served him in the other great passion that had driven his life—at least until the bullet struck.

Up to then, he could generally tell within two minutes whether a woman he had interest in would be up for the casual sexual intimacy and partying that typified his notion of a relationship.

Now he didn't know if he would ever help a patient or be with a woman again.

The bad part of his "gift" for truth was that he could not bullshit himself. Every rationalization or excuse he tried to construct for his selfishness and other failings stood out as the bullshit it was.

Was there anything more pitiful than a man who could not fool himself?

He uncapped the flask and took another drink. He had a decent buzz going. Imported, ninety-five-proof anesthesia.

Since the shooting, he hadn't been able to do much beyond desk work and therapy. The twin six-inch titanium struts placed in his shattered spine were now fully anchored. He'd worked hard at strengthening his upper body and learning to care for himself. Other than working out, he'd spent a lot of time either medicated or drinking. There'd been no change in his paralysis.

"Don't be in a hurry." That's what the therapists said.

Hurry? To where? At least his restrictions had been eased. Initially they'd said no lifting more than ten pounds.

"So I can't piss without help." He'd rolled out that tired joke. Might have been funny if he could piss. Instead he had to catheterize himself every six hours. An exercise in plumbing that he could not feel at all. The care team had responded to his sad joke with rueful smiles.

He wasn't allowed to take care of patients in the ER. And no sex. They hadn't said that. They didn't have to.

His moose-in-rut obsession with sex had led to his current state. Now, more than ever, the wonders of women filled his waking thoughts. His nighttime sexual dreams were the highlight of his post-injured life. Would the dreams fade as his nerve-damaged body withered?

A troubling memory of Faith. Faith Reinhorst Malar—the wife of Jon, his kind-hearted and innocent friend. She'd been straight-up wicked—twisted and wrong but a sexual rush beyond anything.

He'd had magic times with so many women—but never a married one. Now the memory that hung was Faith and his unforgivable betrayal of Jon.

She'd set up the whole thing. Played him for the selfish, sex-hound that he was and then blackmailed him to turn over the D-44 research.

Weak and selfish—and he couldn't fool himself that he was anything else.

Some called him a hero for jumping in front of Drake's family and taking the bullet. *Yeah, right.* He was no hero.

He faced the computer. He'd never reviewed the operating room report describing the damage to his spinal cord. He'd held onto the post-surgical comments of the neurosurgeon, which offered a glimmer of hope. He feared the report he was about to look at might extinguish that glimmer.

The old medical saying was that a physician who treats himself has a fool for a doctor and a patient. But Rizz had treated himself—with Drake's worried assistance.

They'd treated a condition that had no accepted treatment.

Immediately after his surgery, Rizz had convinced an anguished Drake to deliver a full dose of their experimental spinal injury drug D-44.

The billion-dollar potential of D-44 had driven Jon's wife Faith to deceit, caused her murder, and attracted rogue agents of the pharmaceutical industry to the Twin Cities. Greed and violence had left Rizz in a wheelchair and almost killed Jon.

D-44's value remained, but Drake, Jon and Rizz now faced major legal challenges to their ownership of the drug.

Rizz loved money and indulging in the best of things, but it was now the healing potential of the drug that he valued. The possibility of an injured spinal cord healing—the pie-in-the-sky dream that had driven Drake through his years of fanatical effort—was now Rizz's all-consuming hope.

In their research, a small weight striking the animal's exposed spinal cord had left no visible abnormality but had resulted in irreversible paralysis. The cat's spinal cord became devitalized from the impact—and paralysis was permanent. *Devitalized*—another word that only medical people used. It meant without life.

Paralysis following spinal injury rarely resolved—very rarely. Following Rizz's surgery, the neurosurgeon had said that most who had an injury like Rizz would never get anything back. They'd remain totally paralyzed forever. But then the surgeon had said something about hope, and Rizz, in his post-anesthesia fog, had clamped onto those words.

When treated with Drake's D-44, the spinal-cord-injured cats, especially the little black and white one, had improved dramatically. This was so startling that Rizz had not initially believed it.

Now he believed in D-44 desperately. D-44 might help him regain movement if—and only if—his spinal cord had not been severed.

If the cord had been completely severed or was missing portions of its length, his chance for recovery approached zero. Even with D-44.

He feared the report at his fingertips would reveal such destruction.

He scrolled through the operative report, down to the key portion. He steeled himself with another deep swallow from his flask.

"...the spinal canal is violated at the level of the tenth thoracic vertebra in the wake of the projectile's transit. The spinal cord..." Rizz swallowed hard and his chest tightened. "...is contused. The myelin sheath has a small defect and local clot is evident." Rizz's heart thudded, his breath came hard. A sheath disruption could heal. "The cord is markedly bruised and appears devitalized..." Devitalized—he'd known there had to be at least that much damage, but reading it made his stomach sink. A drop of sweat trickled down his forehead. His hands had gone cold.

"...but there is no evidence of tissue loss or evidence that the cord has been severed."

Rizz let out the breath he had not known he was holding. He dropped his head to his hands. Yes. Yes. Yes.

Rizz's cord had suffered a greater injury than their cats but "no evidence of tissue loss or evidence that the cord has been severed."

He felt like he would slide out of his chair and form a puddle on the floor.

He might heal.

When? Every day of paralysis scared him.

In their research, the spinal-cord-injured cats had taken close to two months before any sign of recovery. It had been almost two months since Rizz had been shot, and nothing suggested D-44 had made any difference.

Maybe with time, Rizz would regain some movement. Perhaps his cock would become something more than an unfeeling conduit for urine. Things might get better. If they didn't? He wiped at his eyes.

D-44 was unproven and completely untested in humans. Rizz knew the risks and didn't care. The drug increased his chance to alter the "forever" prognosis for his cord injury. The first three weeks after the drug, he'd had headaches and been sicker than ever in his life. He'd lied to Drake and hidden his symptoms. There'd be no more D-44 forthcoming if his cautious friend knew of the adverse effects.

Drake considered the use of the powerful, unproven drug a deadly gamble. Rizz knew Drake would guilt himself forever if the drug caused Rizz's death. And it could.

None of that changed Rizz's mind. He wanted another dose of D-44 and he wanted it soon.

The risk did not matter. Drake's misgivings and possible guilt did not matter. The improved chance for recovery—no matter how slim—was the only thing that mattered.

His cell phone rang.

"Dr. Michael Rizzini here."

He listened for a moment.

"TV news. No. Why?" He listened. "What? Ohio? Yeah, that's where Drake's from." As he listened further, his mouth went dry.

He disconnected and his arms fell limp to the chair. Drake a convicted felon? His caring friend a criminal?

The image flashed of Drake when he'd taken down the big drug-abuser who'd assaulted Patti in the ER. He'd been a different person.

Was that guy capable of having committed a crime? Rizz sighed.

Drake had looked like he could kill.

Chapter 8

After the confrontation with Ogren, Drake went straight to the Crash Room. He rubbed the knotted muscles of his neck. It had been difficult, but he'd done a decent job holding onto the reins. Ogren deserved to have his ass kicked—and worse.

Drake took a huge breath then turned on the water at the scrub sink. He splashed cool water on his face, half-expecting steam to rise from his skin.

Dan Ogren was a bully. The word really didn't fit. It trivialized. Abusers like him terrorized and subjected those weaker to lives of fear and misery.

Under the provisions of a new Minnesota law, when police responded to a report of suspected domestic abuse and injuries were present, the abuser went to jail—even if the victim denied assault. Drake's report should result in Dan Ogren being arrested and taken to jail.

Drake rested his hands on the sink as the water ran. He'd handled the situation the way he was supposed to.

He couldn't afford to deal with the abusers the way his instincts called for—the way a part of him hungered for.

Would Dan Ogren's money and influence protect him? The thought sickened him. Drake turned off the water and stood for a moment, arms braced and head hung. Why did he feel as if he hadn't done enough?

He detected the hint of lilac—a trace of his anchorwoman patient's perfume somehow still hung in the Crash room. It had not been long and she would still be in the OR. She'd been so close to death. He hoped she'd pull through.

He straightened and reached for a towel. There were patients who needed him.

"Tell me it's crap, Drake. What the hell, man?"

Drake turned. Rizz sat at the entry of the Crash Room with his hands on the struts of his wheelchair. Had he sounded angry?

"What do you mean?" Drake said.

"The news. Is it for real?"

Yes, definitely angry. "The news is here?" Drake said. Had the media learned about Dan Ogren already? Drake hadn't thought about the media response. It would be a big story.

"I'm talking about the television news," Rizz said.

"My patient. The anchorwoman?" Drake's gut went cold. Had she died? *No!*

Rizz cocked his head. "Don't you know?"

"Damn, Rizz. Know what?" Drake's mouth went dry. Something bad had brought Rizz to him. The seconds stretched as the buzzes, ringing, and bustle of the crowded ER filled the void.

"You were the lead story on the channel eight news. They reported you had a felony assault conviction and spent time locked up in Ohio when you were sixteen. The story is racing through the hospital. It's gotta be bullshit. Right?"

The ER sounds disappeared. An air-hiss roar filled Drake's ears. Each beat of his heart slammed his chest.

He scanned the glass wall of the Crash Room. Nurses, paramedics, techs, orderlies, and others were looking though the glass. His friends—his ER teammates—their faces puzzled, doubting, worried.

His secret had been discovered.

His throat clenched and his stomach plunged. What he'd feared for so long. *No. No. No.*

He'd been found out. His legs went weak. He turned and crumpled into the chair next to the sink.

He needed air—the wind had been knocked out of him. *God, no!*

The wrecking ball of his past would destroy his life. Rachelle, the kids, his mother, his friends—everyone who counted on him. All his dreams.

One day—really just minutes. Fourteen years ago.

He put his face in his hands. Trying to think—to analyze—to figure a way out. His mind blank. Beyond blank—a void. As if an explosion had blown his thoughts and feelings to nothingness.

He dropped his hands. It was out. His record. His lies.

"You okay, Drake?" Rizz had rolled to within arm's reach. Anger gone. Concern in its place.

"I'm so unokay, I can't even think." He could hardly breathe.

"Son of a bitch, Drake," Rizz said. "Can I help? What should we do?"

Drake knew only one way to get by—his strategy since the death of the person who'd meant most to him.

His family, his studies, his patients, the research, exercise—he never stopped. The guilt, doubt and memories would catch him if he stopped.

"Only one thing for me to do." Drake spread his hands in a gesture encompassing the ER. "My shift doesn't end for hours, and there are patients who need me. I'm still a doctor tonight." *Will this be my last shift?*

Rizz extended a hand. Drake grasped it, his friend's grip intense. Rizz stared up from his wheelchair into Drake's eyes.

"It's not over," Rizz said. "It ain't a done deal, and I'm not going to take this sitting down." He looked at his wheelchair. "Figuratively speaking." He shrugged, smiled, and then cupped his other hand around their clasp. "It's not easy finding a partner who makes me look so good in comparison."

Drake would have laughed if the situation weren't fall-to-his-knees bleak. "You're the ultimate smart-ass."

"Damn right, brother. Don't forget that. The smartest ass around. Starting now, I'm putting this ass in gear to make sure I don't end up having to teach some other guy all I've taught you. I've got a big investment, and it hasn't paid for shit yet." Moisture welled in the eyes of Drake's wheelchair-bound, crazy, loyal, and courageous friend.

The waterworks were trying to take over Drake's eyes as well.

"You've taught me about modesty," Drake said. "You have none."

Neither was able to smile.

"Thank you, Rizz. Thanks for everything."

Drake released Rizz's hand and headed for the patient chart rack.

Chapter 9

Townhouse

"I'm sorry, Dr. Cody is busy with a patient." The ER unit coordinator sounded harried over the phone.

"Please tell him his wife called," Rachelle said.

"You can try back later, but it's crazy now." A din of voices and ringing phones sounded in the background.

"Okay. Thank you." *Sure, thank you, ER—for nothing.*

Rachelle hung up the wall phone in the kitchen of their rundown rental townhouse. Rachelle tried not to hate the ER, but it kept Drake away from her and the kids night and day. She could not imagine any lover or addiction that could claim him as completely. Or leave her more on her own. She draped a hand over the thick scar on her neck.

Drake was unavailable as usual. Should she call the police about what had happened?

Their jerk of a neighbor had grabbed their seven-year-old son when an errant slap-shot tennis ball had struck the man's fancy car. He'd shaken Shane and sworn at him.

Shane had run to Rachelle white-faced and trembling. Little Kristin had burst into tears as Shane told Rachelle what had happened.

Rachelle grit her teeth. Almost two hours later, and her anger remained.

What should she do?

Drake needed to know— Wait. How would he react? Maybe she shouldn't tell him?

Yes, she should.

Goodness! Could she be more indecisive?

The trauma counselors from Minneapolis Children's hospital had said that the best thing for the children's recovery from the trauma of the kidnapping was to carry on normal activity.

Normal? Rachelle wondered if things would ever be normal again.

Kristin broke into tears several times a day.

Shane's eyes seemed too wary and hard for a seven-year-old. Recently he'd hurt an older boy who'd caused Kristin to cry. It appeared to have been innocent teasing, but Shane had to be dragged off the bigger boy.

Shane never mentioned the kidnapping, but he thrashed and cried out in the night.

None of them had forgotten what had happened.

Anytime the kids were out of her sight, Rachelle's nerves sizzled like frying bacon.

She'd survived her hospitalization and the skin grafts of her burned hands and wrists without taking anything beyond Tylenol or ibuprofen. She could handle pain.

Fear and worry were what tormented her. Yet somehow she'd held off using any of her post-traumatic-stress medication or panic attack pills since their nightmare.

Her life sometimes seemed like a string of diagnoses—PTSD, anxiety, depression, panic attacks. Ever since her childhood, the doctors had been throwing different drugs at her to "help." The ones currently prescribed were to be taken only "as needed."

Would she ever be beyond the need?

Up until today she'd been doing well.

Hiring Kaye to help had made a huge difference. The retired ER nurse lived nearby and helped out whenever needed.

Kaye and the kids had a mutual love affair, and her care of Rachelle's burns and skin grafts had been expert. The solid sixty-six-year-old did not seem to know fear or worry. Being around her no-nonsense, handle-whatever-comes attitude had been good for them all.

Kaye had left to visit an out-of-town relative three days earlier. Her absence revealed how dependent on her Rachelle had become.

Blackness showed beyond the curtains of the kitchen window facing the unlit alley. The circle-tube fluorescent over the kitchen table threw trembling yellowish light.

This place, this room. Memories.

Her breathing sped up. A tightness grew in her throat—the feeling that warned of the attacks that struck her like fast-rising storms.

She'd checked the new locks and security system three times already. The alarm light still showed green. The audio monitor in the kids' room sounded an uninterrupted hiss. They were asleep.

Breathe easy. We're safe. We're safe.

Earlier she'd been able to calm Shane and Kristin.

Even during the worst of what they'd survived, Shane had fought hard to avoid showing fear. Then, as now, Rachelle did not have to see their fear—she felt it like heat radiating off molten steel.

Little ones should not have to be so brave.

"That neighbor behaved badly. But he won't hurt you. I promise." She'd pulled her children tight. "It's hard for us because of what happened before." She met their eyes. "That woman. The one who hurt us. She's gone. She can't ever hurt us again. We're all okay. Nothing to worry about." She'd forced a smile.

No worries, Rachelle? Why do you think of using the pills on the upper shelf several times every day? Why do you crave their numbing escape?

A mother needs to protect her babies and help them feel safe.

Try to carry on like normal.

She looked at the cabinet where her pills were.

Chapter 10

CEO Stuart Kline approached his BMW in the hospital lot. He hunched in his winter coat while still worrying that some nasty crud from the ER may have contaminated his custom-tailored suit.

Small wonder Dan Ogren did not like having to wait in that place. Kline clicked his door open, then climbed in. The auto-start had his vehicle comfortable despite the evening's bitter cold.

He entered a number on his cell phone.

If things worked out, he'd soon be free of the hospital for good. He didn't like sick, smelly, or noisy. He hated dealing with demanding physicians and pissed-off nurses. Worse was being anywhere near sick people or their families. He had others to keep patients and their families away from him, but even the thought of sick people bothered him.

More significantly, the biggest money in the medical business was found even more removed from actual patients. That's where he wanted to be—getting rich while far away from sick people and those who took care of them.

His connection clicked.

"Afton Tait, university counsel."

"Tait, Stuart Kline here. What have you heard?"

"I'm holding the position draft in my hands right now. It's eyes-only to a few of the top university brass and the legal team members. There'll be some fine-tuning, but the main positions are decided."

Afton Tait had provided legal input on an issue while Kline was head of the university's patent and intellectual property revenues department. Tait was a junior member of the university's legal staff, but Kline had sensed they shared ambition.

They both spelled ambition M-O-N-E-Y.

"And?" Kline asked.

"The legal opinion is that the university is in a no-lose position. There's no downside to making a grab for the drug. There'd be little to no penalty if somehow the doctors prevail but potentially millions for the university if the courts rule our way." He paused. "The attorney who handled all the doctors' legal work was the wife of one of the doctors. She filed false documents identifying her as the owner of the research. She signed a contract selling the drug to the Swiss firm and took partial payment. She died before handing over the drug. Because she never filed the intellectual property protection documentation for the drug and research, the doctors' ownership is vulnerable to the university's claim."

"She screwed them and tried to cash in for herself," Kline said. "The protection they thought was in place for their research was not."

"Correct. She left them wide open. It's the legal team's opinion that two of the doctors—let me see here—Michael Rizzini and Jon Malar, have no defensible claim. They were in the residency program, had signed the university's standard intellectual property waiver, and accepted educational credit for their involvement in the research. The lab space is university property, which also favors the board's claim.

"The only person anyone is worried about is the third doctor, Drake Cody. Even without the formal documents, he still has a solid claim. He refused any educational credit, never signed the university's intellectual property waiver, paid rent for the lab space, and is the principal investigator of record. On the other hand, he is enrolled in a university residency program. Given the compromised paperwork, the belief is that his claim is vulnerable." The attorney paused. "Worst-case scenario is a court case—it would take years. The university's team of attorneys versus a young, debt-burdened doctor currently in the news as a convicted criminal."

Kline nodded, "I'm going to do everything I can to play up his criminal record and discredit him. I know it doesn't impact directly on his ownership claim, but it should affect public opinion. The timing is perfect." The news about Drake Cody's juvenile assault conviction seemed almost too good to be true.

The attorney continued, "At the end of the discussion, the chief financial officer provided estimates of the revenue potential for the drug. If the drug ends up with FDA approval, it will bring in billions. The motion to claim D-44 for the university carried easily."

"It makes total sense. The money is huge," Kline said. "What's our next step?"

"We, that is, the university as a public entity working for the good of the citizens, will raid the lab and seize the research."

"And Ingersen Pharmaceutical's claim?" Kline said. The Swiss pharmaceutical firm was Kline's other benefactor in his scheme. He knew where they stood.

"The most likely scenario is we arbitrate an agreement with them where the university gets a percentage of any downstream revenues, like the standard arrangements you dealt with in Patent and Intellectual Property Revenue. Overall, that's the best course, regardless. The Swiss have the resources and expertise to oversee the development and regulatory approvals for the drug while also absorbing the costs. If the drug gets to market, there'll be big money for all."

Kline felt his smile stretch wide. Things were developing almost exactly as he'd figured. When he'd learned of the doctors' misfiled legal work, he'd approached the university with the suggestion to make a grab for the drug.

He'd dealt with the Swiss pharmaceutical firm before, so he'd had a good idea of how they would proceed. And he'd known how to reach out to them through back channels.

He'd positioned himself as a middleman for both entities.

"Excellent," Kline said. "When will the university move?"

"Soon, but that was left as need-to-know," Tait said.

"Contact me when it's going to happen."

"And my money?" Tait asked.

"When the university has the D-44 synthesis info and the drug in hand, you'll be paid," Kline said. He ended the connection then jammed a fist in the air.

He felt like he was floating. Like he'd just hit the longest, best drive of his life. Like he'd won the lottery.

His position managing the university's patent and intellectual property revenues had educated him to the astronomical dollars in pharmaceuticals. Each year, more than fifty individual drugs had sales over two billion dollars each. The top drug had raked in more than thirteen billion—one drug with sales of more than thirteen billion dollars in a single year!

And that did not take into account how new drugs entering a company's pipeline influenced stock prices. The profits and impact on stock value led pharmaceutical companies to invest huge sums of money in experimental drugs with breakthrough potential.

Drake Cody's D-44 was such a drug.

Kline's scheme for cutting himself in for a piece of the wealth was progressing even better than he'd hoped.

Too bad for Drake Cody and his naive young doctor buddies. As Kline had learned, most doctors knew science and how to care for patients but were idiots about the real business of medicine. When Kline had ordered Drake Cody to speed up service to Dan Ogren and his wife, he'd sensed the doctor's irritation. So many of these doctors thought they were special because they took care of patients and saved lives.

There was a hell of a lot more to the medical business than that.

Kline put the car in gear, still smiling at his prospects.

The university, the Swiss firm, and one clever individual named Stuart Kline were going to make one hell of a lot of money.

Chapter 11

Rizz rolled his wheelchair into the hospital's physician-on-call sleeping room. He'd never had the chance to be in a call room this early in the evening. For most of his nights in the hospital over the past four years, he was so busy his head had never hit the pillow.

He needed privacy to place a phone call he dreaded. A call that would decide his future with Jon. And much more.

He'd avoided Jon since everything went to hell. They'd both been patients in the ICU at the same time, but even as they'd improved Rizz couldn't face Jon.

Should he confess to the friend he'd wronged or continue with the deception and lies?

Rizz's actions had helped set in motion the events that had devastated Drake's family, almost killed Jon, and left their claim to D-44 in jeopardy.

No one would have predicted Jon's survival two months earlier when he arrived in the ER with gunshot wounds to the chest.

The wounds had put him into prolonged shock. Somehow Drake and the nurses and doctors of Memorial Hospital had saved him. The question that remained—could his brain and body recover?

Jon continued outpatient rehabilitation in his home city of Duluth.

Reports were that Jon's physical recovery continued, but his mental state suffered. Literally an Eagle Scout and choirboy, Jon had formed an unlikely trio with Rizz and Drake. Three very different guys whose unique friendship had been forged in the blast furnace of emergency medicine training.

Rizz had initially figured Jon had to be a phony to act so nice. He'd learned his kindheartedness was genuine. He'd come to envy his friend's selfless and cynicism-free view of life.

Rizz entered the number to Dr. Jon Malar's family home.

No way could Jon be the same person after all that he'd endured—the agony of his near-lethal injuries, the pain and humiliation of his wife's betrayal and wanton infidelity. Drake had hinted that a deep shadow had fallen over their friend's sunny worldview. Up until the very end, he'd been blindly and hopelessly in love with Faith.

Faith's betrayal had also put at risk the opportunity to cash in on D-44 financially. That wouldn't matter to Jon. He didn't care about money, and besides, his wife's death had made him heir to millions.

"Hello, Malar residence."

"Mrs. Malar, this is Michael Rizzini. Is Jon able to speak on the phone?"

"I'm sorry. He won't take any calls."

"It's important. Please."

"I don't think he'll want to talk. He's had our basement level remodeled and he pretty much lives down there now." Her voice broke. "He barely even speaks to his dad or me."

"Tell him it's Rizz and it involves Drake."

A pause.

"I'll try," she said.

As the seconds ticked past, Rizz considered being honest. Would Jon knowing that Rizz had been one of Faith's many sex partners help anything?

Hi, Jon. Wanted to call and let you know I screwed your wife, submitted to blackmail, and almost handed over our research to pharmaceutical industry predators. My wandering cock and selfishness contributed to your wife's murder, your near-death, the suffering of Drake's family, and my paralysis. Wondering if you could help me out with something?

No. Now was not the time for honesty. To get what was needed, he'd focus on Jon's affection for Drake.

"Hello." Jon's voice sounded flat.

"Hi, Jon. It's Rizz. I should have called sooner."

Silence.

Shit, does he already know?

“How you doing, brother?” Rizz asked.

“I'm alive.” No emotion. Volunteering nothing.

“Sorry you've gone through so much.”

“It's not your fault.”

Rizz mouth went dry. *If you only knew.*

“I'm calling about Drake,” Rizz said.

“The news story? An assault conviction?” The first hint of emotion. “I don't believe it.”

“Drake told me it's true.”

“Had to be a reason.”

“Doesn't matter, Jon. They'll take his license.”

“What do you mean?”

“The Minnesota state medical board.”

“They can't do that.” He sounded angry.

Can't? Jon's statements were off target. Residual damage? Depression?

He'd been a brilliant guy. This was not like him.

“Jon, Drake lied in all his applications. He hid a felony assault conviction. They have solid grounds.”

“It's not right. Drake is the best.” Jon sounded like a fretful child.

“Unless something changes, Drake is going to lose his medical license and maybe even the rights to D-44. That's why I called. We need to help him.”

“Damn it.” Jon's voice was shrill. “I can't help anyone.”

Jon never cursed and did not whine. He definitely wasn't himself.

“You're wrong, Jon. You can help.”

“I'm not good for anything now. Don't call me.”

“Listen to me. Please. Don't hang up. For Drake. He needs you. Give me one minute. Okay?” Rizz held his breath with the phone pressed tight to his ear...

Chapter 12

Jim Torrins paced the carpet of his paneled office. The administrative offices were deserted and dark except for his desk lamp. He hadn't been in the hospital after midnight since his days as a practicing physician. He missed taking care of patients, but after thirty-three years of being on call, sleeping through the night was incredible.

As the hospital's President of Medical Affairs, uninterrupted sleep was the only desirable thing about the job these days.

His position assured that every day he faced problems, unhappy people, and disapproval. Staff confrontations, claims of malpractice, pressure-cooker emotions, and complaints of all kinds came his way. Patients, their families, medical staff, business operations, and even board members directed problems to him. As head of Medical Affairs, he was the lightning rod for anybody who was dissatisfied or angry.

He prided himself on objectivity and balance. He knew some people thought he was a cold fish and not a strong backer of the medical staff. Many thought administrators had it easy. *I wish it were true.*

He was a realist, and that was requirement number one for the job. His wife kidded that he loved to suffer. Lately he wondered if she was right.

Recent troubles included a SWAT team target shot dead in the hospital parking lot and three of the hospital's best ER doctors wounded. Adding to those problems was the useless new CEO, a threatened nurses' strike, and a quarterly financial report showing the hospital operating deep in the red.

All of these issues impacted Jim as president of Medical Affairs. The CEO held the ultimate responsibility for most of the issues, but unfortunately the CEO was Stuart Kline. Jim sighed. He was proud of the hospital and the care it delivered. He did not want to see it fail.

And today things had worsened.

Drake Cody exposed on TV news as a convicted felon. Assault no less. Jim had not believed it initially but now knew it to be true.

For most of Drake Cody's time at Memorial Hospital, he'd been a clinically excellent, low-profile member of the emergency medicine resident staff who also had a strong commitment to research. Then came the incident with the drug-seeker who'd assaulted an ER nurse. Shortly thereafter, the hospital was again in the news when pharmaceutical industry criminals tried to steal the promising research Drake had developed. Drake and his colleagues Jon Malar and Michael Rizzini had been shot, and the quiet young doctor had nearly lost his family. Terrible misfortune.

Today's report revealed that Drake Cody's history of attracting trouble had started years before.

The TV broadcast had thrust Drake's previous incident with the drug-seeking, assault-charged ER patient back to the forefront. Negative media attention, medical staff problems, financial woes, and legal action—the hospital was in deep trouble.

And Drake Cody—disaster.

He had to know what the discovery of his criminal record meant. Clearly, he'd falsified all his documentation throughout his career in medicine. The state medical board—already beleaguered—looked bad once again.

Jim didn't see any way Drake wouldn't lose his license and career. A real shame. The young doctor had the gift.

Jim's cell beeped a text message alert. He pulled his phone then eyed it.

where are you? he read. Jim sighed. Kline, the annoying CEO. Jim's cross to bear.

Jim texted, *my office.*

stay there. see you in 5 min

Kline in the hospital on a Sunday night? Why?

Jim had little hope the man would be useful. The guy hadn't proved useful for anything in his initial months on the job.

Kline's appointment to the CEO position still mystified Jim. Had the hospital Board all been drunk? Why had the university contingent been so keen on him getting the spot? Had to have been the guy's reputation for financial results. Leadership skills or a focus on patient care had clearly not been selling points.

***

Stuart Kline entered Jim's office.

Kline wore casual clothes, but was the kind of guy who never looked casual. In his button-down shirt and pants, he looked like a department store mannequin. Stiff and posed. Hair just so. As if his outfit were missing a tennis sweater tied around his neck.

"Let's move to my office," Kline said.

"No reason to move." Jim said. "What do you need?"

Kline looked at the chair in front of Jim's desk but remained standing.

Jim knew Kline's office setup. The desk was gargantuan and his chair elevated—a transparent ploy that assured the CEO would be higher than anyone sitting in front of him. Petty manipulation 101.

"Do you know you have a criminal on the medical staff?" Kline's words were an indictment. "The news broadcast his record. And now we'll be facing civil suits because of your Dr. Drake Cody assaulting that black guy. We need to cut all ties with him. He's bad news."

"I'm aware of the news story." Jim gave silent thanks for his ability to deal with idiots without blowing his stack. "And the incident in the ER you refer to was not Drake Cody assaulting anyone. He defended an ER nurse who was assaulted. Saying otherwise is irresponsible."

"That's what people are saying." Kline shrugged.

"No, Kline. That's what the lawyer for the man who demanded drugs and struck one of our nurses said." Jim raised his voice about once every six months. Kline in his short tenure had altered that pattern.

"You may not be aware of what else your Dr. Drake Cody has done," Kline said.

"I know he led a successful resuscitation of a news anchorperson this evening. Is that what you're referring to?"

"He messed up again in the ER. You need to get rid of him immediately."

"What are you talking about?"

“This is my second trip to the hospital today. Earlier, I had to go to the ER to assure Dan Ogren received appropriate treatment.”

“Dan Ogren made a turn for the worse?”

Kline looked blank for a moment. “Not Dan, senior. Young Dan came to the ER with his wife. She'd had a fall. Dan called me because they were being ignored.”

“I don't believe that,” Jim said.

“Drake Cody made the Ogrens wait. That alone should get him sacked, but it gets way worse.” Kline shook his head. “After I left, Drake Cody called the police on Dan. Dan brought his wife in after an accident, but Drake Cody claimed Dan had beat her up. Dan Ogren, son of Dan Ogren, senior. The Ogrens are huge contributors to the hospital and young Dan is on the board.”

Jim felt his jaw drop. Jim knew and respected Dan Ogren, senior. He'd also met Dan, junior. When “Big Dan” started to get sick, Dan, Jr. took his place on the hospital board.

“Young Dan is a friend of mine,” Kline said. “He's a member at Crossed Wings. We almost won the club’s two-man best-ball event last year.”

Kline sounded like a high school freshman talking about the varsity star.

Dan Ogren, senior had been a special guy. A self-made man. Became a giant success. Owned several car dealerships. Served on the hospital board for many years. Strokes and dementia had hit him hard. Now he was profoundly incapacitated and no longer able to communicate. A sad thing.

Dan Ogren, the younger, had taken the reins of the Ogren automotive empire. He'd been a college hockey star, a playboy type forever but married sometime in the past few years. Society page stuff. Jim didn't know much else about him, other than that his Dan “the man” dealership ads were everywhere.

“You need to make sure this mistake with Dan and his wife is taken care of.” Kline straightened his collar and sniffed. “And get rid of Drake Cody.” He exited the office.

Jim shook his head. What a buffoon. The guy knew nothing about patient care or caregivers. Heck, his background was accounting and finance. Anyone leading a hospital should have firsthand experience in patient care. But Kline's deficiencies were more fundamental than that. Something was "off" with the guy.

Kline's patent and intellectual property position had created big revenue for the university. The big money experience of that job must have influenced the Memorial Hospital board. Jim could not see anything else to recommend him.

Cody's filing of a suspected domestic abuse report on Ogren was news to Jim. If Drake Cody suspected Dan Ogren of abuse, there had to be merit. Nonetheless, such an arrest was bad news. More trouble for the hospital. And more trouble for Drake Cody. *Unreal.*

Jim didn't know the details surrounding Drake's juvenile assault conviction, but it couldn't be good.

And less than two months ago, Drake happens to be the guy nearest a huge, drug-seeking patient who assaults a nurse. Drake responds righteously and is damned.

Days later, Drake, his family, and his closest friends are nearly killed as ruthless criminals try to steal their experimental drug.

Today Drake picks up a chart and it turns out to be the wife of one of the Twin Cities richest, best-known figures, and there's reason to suspect she's a victim of abuse.

Drake Cody was proving to be the ultimate shit magnet.

The unlucky ER physician in the news again. And Memorial Hospital with him.

Jim took a deep breath. It looked like one of Memorial Hospital's best physicians would have his career ended any day. And Jim realized the gravity of the other threats the hospital faced.

He picked up the phone. Time to start circling the wagons.

And why did I become an administrator?

Chapter 13

Early a.m.

Drake scanned the ER patients "to be seen" rack. Finally empty.

There were still plenty of patients in the department, but they'd all been seen and were in various stages of care: receiving medication, IV fluids, awaiting labs, or repeat assessment. Two patients on psychiatric holds as risks to themselves were awaiting the always scarce locked psych unit beds they needed. Several other patients awaited admission to rooms that always seemed to take hours to make ready. Three intoxicated folks whose injuries had been repaired were being watched until they were safe for discharge.

These rare quiet periods allowed members of the ER team to do things they deferred in the busier times—eat, drink fluids, or visit the bathroom. It also provided a chance to catch up on documentation or talk with co-workers.

With the evening's earlier reveal of Drake's criminal record, he didn't feel like conversation. He wished there were more patients to occupy his mind and block his worries.

The ER phone sounded. The unit secretary answered.

"Memorial Hospital ER, unit coordinator speaking." She paused. "Yes." Another slightly longer pause. "Okay. Will do." She hung up then looked around, raising a finger when he caught her eye. He went to the counter.

"That was Dr. Torrins," she said softly. "He wants you in his office in ten minutes."

Drake's mouth went dry. He kept his face from showing what he felt.

"Sure thing. Thanks." Report to the hospital's head of Medical Affairs in ten minutes. Shit. It's happening.

"Laura." His ER partner on this night shift, Dr. Laura Vonser looked up from the health records computer screen. "I'm going to slip out of the department for a few minutes. Okay?"

"No problem, Drake. Got it covered." She turned back to the display.

"I'll grab any codes and run back if I get a flight." Drake had the beeper as the assigned doctor for any Air Care rescue helicopter calls.

Laura gave a thumbs up.

Drake escaped down the hall. He swiped his ID card to access the sliding doors linking the ER to the main hospital. He wanted to run.

His lies had caught up to him. His head thrashed like a blender on high, and he was struggling to keep the cover on.

Was this the end of his medical career?

There was nothing he could do.

He entered the northwest stairwell. Exertion calmed him. Challenging his body had long been the way he kept the reins on his mind.

He started running up the stairs, two at a time.

He focused on his breathing.

He passed the first landing, then the next, and kept on. As his muscles began to burn, he accelerated. *Years of worry. A dream with a foundation in quicksand. I'm screwed. Finished.*

Now he took one step at a time but increased his pace. The floors passed. A good job on the ectopic. Hope she makes it. Will she be one of the last patients I ever take care of? What about Beth Ogren—will my report protect her?

He reached the eighth and top floor, his breathing now deep and rapid. He turned and began to race down. His footsteps sounded like a trip hammer as he virtually free-fell between landings. He flew past the fifth floor, focusing on the stairs, his problems gone.

Too late he saw the door on four open and someone step onto the landing. Full brakes. *Shit!*

A blur of auburn hair, fair skin, and a white coat as he impacted. Somehow he wrapped his arms around the person and avoided launching them down the stairs. Momentum slammed them against the wall and Drake's healing shoulder twinged. They fell awkwardly to the floor with Drake able to cushion the person's fall with his body.

His collision victim's size, shape, and fragrance registered. He'd almost destroyed a young woman. She lay on top of him, still wrapped in his arms. He was breathing hard and adrenaline-stoked. He could have seriously injured her.

The woman's body lay pressed against him. She raised her head.

Dr. Julie Stone's delicate features registered surprise.

"Julie, are you okay?" His face burned in embarrassment.

Her face softened with recognition as she shook her head.

"Felt like I got hit by a train. What was the hurry?"

"I was just getting exercise. I'm so sorry."

She seemed to collect herself as she shifted to a sitting position. "I'm okay. Actually I'd planned to drop by the ER to talk with you."

Julie, an always friendly colleague he admired but didn't know well, wore an expression he could not read.

Her brows knitted and her mouth opened slightly before her face broke into a smile. "Oh, my bad. I left you hanging. I was going to drop by to tell you and your crew that our patient is doing great."

Relief washed over him. He'd been holding his breath in fear that the young anchorwoman would die. "Thank God."

She laughed. The sound was startling, like the ringing of a tapped crystal glass.

"From your expression, it appears you didn't trust I was going to do well in the OR," she said.

"Oh, gosh, no. I'm sorry. I—"

"I'm kidding you, Drake." She smiled. "I'm thrilled she made it. Is there anything better? Great job, Doctor." She laughed again and raised a hand. Drake high-fived her.

His tortured worry eased for an instant. His patient was doing well.

"You do great work in the ER, but your stairwell skills are horse-shit." She stared at him for an instant then burst out laughing again.

He began to laugh as well. He had no reason to laugh but couldn't stop.

They sat on the landing with backs leaned against the wall, laughing.

Nothing in his life was funny right now. A dread meeting with the president of medical affairs in minutes. His record revealed. Everything at risk.

But he had this moment. Their patient doing well.

He laughed so hard he couldn't catch his breath.

In five minutes it could all be over.

***

Drake swiped his ID on the access pad to the administrative offices. The lock clicked and he entered.

The glow from Dr. Torrins' office was the only light visible in the administrative offices wing. The air smelled of new carpet and fresh paint. Drake knocked on the partially open door.

"Come in and close the door, Drake."

Drake closed the door. His stomach churned.

Torrins sat with his hands resting flat on his desk in the cone of light from a tiny lamp. The rest of the office was shadow.

Torrins looked at him, his expression serious. "First off, I want to say 'good job' on the ruptured ectopic patient. Sounds like strong work."

"Paramedics and everyone in the ER came through big. Julie Stone raced her to the OR. I just heard that the patient is out of surgery and looking good," Drake said. In this setting he did not experience the thrill he'd felt with Julie.

"Excellent. A good save." Torrins' tone did not match his words.

In modern healthcare, great saves and outstanding performance were expected. The administrator had not summoned Drake to cheer a good case.

As the hospital's President of Medical Affairs, Dr. Jim Torrins had the benefit of his administrative position—no night work. His 1:25 a.m. call to the ER and request to meet was beyond unusual.

The typically buttoned-down administrator had his tie off and collar loosened.

Ever since Drake had learned of the news broadcast, he'd been waiting for the ax to fall, dreading what he'd feared every day for years. The wrecking ball of his past would slam into his life—their lives. Rachelle, the kids, his mother, his friends—everyone who counted on him.

All because of what had happened one day— in just two or three minutes—more than fourteen years ago.

The question that would destroy him had first appeared on his medical school application. And again and again in the years since. He had it memorized:

Have there ever been any criminal charges filed against you? This includes whether the charges were misdemeanor, gross misdemeanor, or felony. This also includes any offenses which have been expunged or otherwise removed from your record by executive pardon. Misrepresentation of answers will result in revocation of privileges and the fullest permissible professional and legal action.

The language had left no wiggle room. In that first moment while applying to medical school, he had to either flat-out lie or his dream of working as a physician would end before it ever started.

The years of pre-med effort and study. Working in addition to school, yet still having to get every loan possible to complete his college degree and apply to medical school. A massive gamble on being accepted, knowing most were turned away.

He wanted it. He'd sacrificed years for it. He believed in his heart it was what he was meant to do.

After all the time, effort, and hope, he'd come to that question on the application form—the most important document in his life. He knew what an honest answer would do.

After the first lie, there was no going back.

His annual medical license renewal, hospital staff privileges, malpractice insurance, and medical research documentation all contained the same straight-between-the-eyes inquiry.

Drake had responded with a lie each time.

Torrins cleared his throat. “Drake, the hospital's media relations department received a call from a Tribune reporter this afternoon seeking a response on your record. I assured risk management, legal, and anyone who would listen that it had to be crap.” He rested his elbows on the desk. “Then the story broke on TV.” He took off his rimless glasses, then rubbed his eyes. “Damn, Drake.”

“I was sixteen. Juvenile court, the record was sealed.” The words sounded pitiful to his own ears.

Fear of discovery had influenced everything he'd done for more than a decade—their move from Cincinnati to Minneapolis, his limited social interactions, and his fear and distrust of police and the legal system.

He'd not let even Rizz, Jon, or Patti know of his troubled history.

"The facts are the facts." Torrins looked to be in pain. "The state Medical Board knows. The woman you saved had just broadcast the news to the fourteenth-largest metropolis in the country. You falsified your records—you know the consequences."

Drake had kept things hidden for years. Now in a flash it was everywhere.

Torrins continued, "The broadcast also said that the patient that hit Patti, the guy you... er, restrained, intends to file civil suits. Not just against you but the county, the Medical board, the hospital, and the medical school. The Tribune will print the story in the morning."

Drake's mouth had gone dry. His stomach a knot.

Torrins shook his head. "The reality that a physician restrained a drug-trafficking, abusive gang member who struck a nurse becomes the tale of a criminally violent doctor who beat up a hard-luck, inner-city black patient who came to the ER seeking help. You know the media culture in this town. The narrative they'll choose to report is a given."

"The guy is bad news. You know that."

"What I know doesn't matter. This threatens the hospital, Drake. In a matter of months, we've faced more violence and controversy than in the past decade. And you've been a part of it all. I know you didn't directly cause it, but your past changes everything. The public will give a doctor the benefit of a doubt. But not if he's a convicted violent felon who falsified his record."

"I should have never even been arrested. They assaulted my brother."

"I don't doubt that, but we can't re-try your case." Torrins held his hands open. "The fact is you're a convicted felon and you lied about it." He dropped his hands and met Drake's eyes. "You're as good a doctor as there is on our staff. You may be as good as any I've known." He shook his head. "I've spent the last few hours dealing with this. Seeing how I can keep the ER staffed. Figuring if I can help you. I don't even want to get into the Dan Ogren situation now."

He took off his glasses then rubbed his eyes. He replaced them and sighed. "I'll keep you working as long as I can, but I believe your medical career is going to end, Drake. Do you understand? Done."

Strength drained from Drake like water wrung from a sponge. His shoulders slumped.

The wrecking ball had struck.

Chapter 14

Drake pulled his old Dodge into the crumbling asphalt parking lot of the Northeast Minneapolis rental complex. A lone parking light illuminated the front side of the worn, multi-unit townhouse construction. The nightmare Rachelle and the children endured had started here.

He wanted to get them out of here. On a resident's pay and with his mountain of debt, he couldn't afford anywhere else. The way things looked now, he had no idea when he might be able to provide them better.

He parked in the lot near the door to 2121 Sumpter, Unit C. It was 2:55 a.m. Another wicked-cold night.

He sat for a moment, trying to get his mind around the problems he faced. In the ER, he often had to care for multiple critical patients at the same time. He had to determine who could be saved and among them who needed attention first—the process known as triage. Treating the most critical first resulted in the best possible outcomes.

He needed to perform triage on his out-of-control life. The urgent problems were many, and he could only do what he could do. Rachelle and the kids needed him. The ER and his patients needed him. The research animals needed him. His mother alone in Cincinnati needed him. And his grievously injured friends Jon and Rizz needed him.

Even as things had stood, they all needed more than he'd been able to provide. And now that the secret of his former life had exploded…

He squeezed the steering wheel. *No!*

His work in the ER meant pressure, tragedy, failure, and exposure to terrible suffering.

It also meant working with great people and helping others. He was no Mother Teresa, but nothing matched relieving people's pain, reducing suffering, and saving lives.

Though often visited by death, the ER was more intensely alive than anyplace he'd ever been. Every shift, patients, their families, and caregivers displayed courage, toughness, and class. The stakes in the ER were the highest, the struggles profound, and the emotions life-or-death intense. It was harder than anything he'd ever done. And more meaningful.

He loved it. But soon it would be gone.

Working as an emergency physician had been his path to providing for all who counted on him. In just months, his specialty training would have been completed and he'd have started making good money.

He leaned his forehead on the steering wheel.

The state medical board would take his medical license. They'd end his dream.

How would he take care of those who needed him?

His self-pitying thoughts grated like the squeal of a microphone's feedback. He shook his head.

Get over it, wimp. Quit whining.

He felt embarrassed for himself.

Every day in the ER, he cared for patients whose situations made him look like a lottery winner.

Great health, his family, all his gifts—a lucky guy.

He'd have to find a new way to take care of everyone. He could do that.

But damn, oh damn would he miss the crazy magic of ER.

The sprawling rental complex lay in darkness. No activity. It often struck him how in the night, while most of the city slept, the ER pulsed with desperate action.

He revisited the evening's shift. The young TV anchorwoman. She'd lost her pregnancy but not her life. They'd done good work.

Dr. Julie Stone rocked. Being responsible for someone's life or death was heavy stuff. And she'd come through. It had been special to share that with her.

And the Ogrens. Would Drake's reporting of Dan Ogren to the police make a difference? He thought of the injuries she'd suffered and the self-absorbed smugness of her rich, powerful husband. Drake felt a special level of contempt for those who hurt women or children. He could not shake his unease that Dan Ogren, despite his money and position, was no different than the predators Drake had dealt with when locked up. Had he done enough? At least having Dan in a cell tonight assured she was safe for now.

Whatever amount of time Drake had left working in the ER, he'd double his commitment to the vow he made before every shift. *I'll give all I've got and care for every person the best I can.* It sounded too corny to ever share with anyone else, but he meant it. It helped him stay on target no matter how rocky things became.

In the time he had remaining, there was no way he'd cave in to political or personal pressure. The new CEO, Kline, was a twit. And Dan Ogren was an abusive asshole. Screw them.

He got out of the car. The freezing air bit. The night's temperatures were colder than anything Cincinnati would face all year. He took a deep breath. So cold and pure—the frigid air seeming cleaner than any other.

He'd become attached to Minnesota—the lakes, trees, marshland, rivers, and seasons. Within the city there were bald eagles, herons, kingfishers, waterfowl, and all manner of songbird. And good people. Rachelle and the kids loved it, too.

Rachelle—he'd been so busy in the ER until late that he hadn't called her. Or perhaps he'd been avoiding it. She rarely watched TV or listened to the radio. That she had not called the ER suggested she hadn't heard the news. Until very recently, he'd kept his criminal record hidden even from her.

He'd explained the likely consequences if his lies were discovered. She knew their dreams would end.

If the TV report had revealed everything from his history that could hurt them, he might feel some measure of closure.

But it was not everything. The blackest of the shadows would never be gone.

***

Drake opened the door, flicked on the light, then punched the security code into the wall-mounted keypad before the alarm triggered. The home protection company had installed the system on credit with six months interest-free. He locked the door and slid the deadbolt closed. The alarms, deadbolts, reinforced locks, and other security additions were the physical changes made since the kidnapping. Otherwise the two-story unit's worn family room and tired linoleum-floored kitchen were unchanged from when it had happened.

Shane's hockey stick rested in the corner next to Kristin's three-wheeler and helmet.

Other changes were more profound though less visible. While Rachelle's concern for the kids' safety had always been intense, now it consumed her.

The children had also changed. Previously carefree, they now stuck close and repeatedly looked for the presence of Rachelle or Drake.

Drake turned off the light and climbed the stairs. He stepped lightly, trying to minimize the squeaks and groans of the steps. The kids shared the bedroom at the top of the stairs. He smiled as he quietly opened their door. Due to his work hours, middle of the night glimpses were too often his only contact with them for days. The visits, no matter how short, always lifted his spirits.

They were visible in the glow of the night light that four-year-old Kristin needed since what had happened. She lay curled up in a sea of stuffed animals. She slept easily—the night terrors had become less frequent as the weeks went by.

Shane lay curled under blankets and against the wall. His baseball bat rested against the headboard.

They'd both gone through so much.

As Drake pulled the door closed, he experienced a moment of absolute clarity. So many things in his life were unclear—this was not. These little ones were his gifts and his greatest responsibility. No matter what happened, everything else came after.

His phone buzzed. He smothered the ring-tone as he slipped back down the stairs.

He answered in the living room with his hand cupped around the phone. "Drake Cody here."

"Dr. Cody. I'm sorry to call you so late, but I know you worked late." The man's tone soft, his words hesitant. "This is Detective Farley. I'm not sure if you remember me. I work with Detective Aki Yamada."

Not sure if I remember? The young detective had helped save Drake and his family. The policeman's heroism had made all the media.

"Of course. Thank you for all you did."

"Oh, er, you're welcome. You were kind of out of it when we met."

Drake drew a blank. He did not remember the detective other than from media reports. A foggy exchange with Aki as Drake came out of surgery returned. Perhaps Detective Farley had been there?

"You're right. I am a little hazy on having met." He looked at the digital clock on the microwave. "It's after 3 a.m."

"Sorry." The deferential manner continued. "It's a long story, but Detective Yamada and I got assigned to a domestic abuse case tonight. The Dan Ogren case." The detective sounded as if he were apologizing. "I, er, we learned you were involved and, well, the suspect said a lot of stuff. I think he's looking to get you in trouble." He paused.

Drake pictured Dan Ogren and his battered wife. The big man had already made his threats.

"Thanks for the warning. I figure he can't get me into too much trouble from a jail cell."

"That's part of the problem," Farley said.

"What?"

"Ogren's lawyer got a judge out of bed, and an hour later the order came to release him. He's out."

"That's wrong." Drake's stomach roiled.

"Aki told me to inform you. We're doing everything we can."

Drake pictured her battered face. Dan Ogren released already. Drake closed his eyes and gripped the phone hard. *Son of a bitch.*

"Will he be convicted?"

"We just caught the case and don't know much of anything," Farley said. "We were assigned because it's so high profile. We'll update you when we know more but wanted to alert you. It's ugly and already political."

"I have to sleep now but call me on my cell anytime. I'm back on in the ER this afternoon."

"Will do. And doctor?"

"Yes."

"I hope your family and Doctors Malar and Rizzini are doing well."

"Thank you, detective." Drake disconnected.

Dan Ogren out of jail in hours? Normally bail offense hearings weren't possible until the next morning at the earliest. Drake felt sick

Would Ogren dodge justice and continue to hurt others?

Drake's unease grew.

The criminal justice system was an imperfect machine. Too often the guilty went free while the innocent had their lives shredded.

Drake had barely survived.

Chapter 15

Drake undressed in the upstairs hall and put his scrubs in the separate hamper. He slipped open the door to their bedroom. The parking lot light penetrated the shade, leaving the room in a dim glow. He could not see Rachelle among the tousled covers.

He took a step forward. A slim shape lay curled on the floor in the corner alongside the headboard.

"Rachelle?" There was no movement. His stomach clenched as he moved to her. "Rachelle?" He grasped her shoulders.

She raised her head. Her pupils shone large but unfocused. She looked around the shadowed room. She got to her knees. "What happened?" She rubbed her face. Her posture stiffened. She looked up, face blanched. "Drake, oh God, the kids."

"They're okay." He helped her into bed then wrapped his arms around her. "Are you okay? How did you end up on the floor?" Her body trembled.

He held her and felt her muscles slowly loosen. He leaned back and saw tears glisten in her huge dark eyes. Even in sadness her beauty transfixed him. Only she had ever had such an effect on him. Not just her beauty, but something more.

"No, Drake, I'm not okay." Her voice broke.

"What do you mean?"

"My medication." Her eyes went to the floor where she'd been slumped. "I hadn't taken any since before the hospital." She faced him but dodged his gaze. "Something happened today. I was losing it. I took a pill after the kids were asleep. I shouldn't have. It really hit me."

Rachelle and medication. She worried that the medications that were prescribed were little different than the street drugs she'd used in the past. Drake shared her concern. What would be horrible imaginings for most people were memories for her. Mental health issues and medication had been a part of her life since she was a child. Drake understood how "escape" into a drugged consciousness could be preferable to reliving the traumas she'd experienced.

He wrapped his arms around her.

"It all started to come down on me," Rachelle said. "The kids. What they went through. You. Jon. Rizz. Money. Us. Me worrying about worrying. Bad memories. I wanted to turn it off." She looked at him, her silken black hair obscuring much of the thick burn scar of her neck and shoulder. "I took one of the pills." She gripped him tight, her whisper desperate, "I don't want to be like her. God, please don't let me be like her."

Her mother's addiction and its tragic consequences had made Rachelle's journey to adulthood a grim one. She seemed to be blind to her own strength, unable to climb free of all that had come before.

How could she fear being like her mother after the courage and strength she'd shown? He didn't understand what went on inside her head.

Lately, she seemed to be doing better. Drake believed the nightmare they'd survived had made her stronger.

Finding Kaye to help the kids and care for Rachelle's burns and skin graft cares had also helped. The presence of a strong and helpful woman in Rachelle's life was a first. The retired ER nurse's "take care of business" attitude positively affected both Rachelle and the kids.

"What upset you?" He slid his hands to her shoulders. Had she heard the news broadcast about him? No—she'd have said something.

"Oh, er... Let's not talk about it." Rachelle fidgeted.

"Please, tell me." He felt her tension. His need to tell her about the news story and its devastating consequences could wait.

"Okay, but please stay calm."

"What is it?" Her manner had him on edge.

"It's Shane."

"Is he okay?" Drake's throat tightened, everything else forgotten.

"It was the neighbor guy. The end unit. The one with the fancy car he washes all the time."

"The tall guy with the Corvette." Drake nodded. The guy was always alone. Never acknowledged a wave or a nod. "What does he have to do with Shane?" His system had switched to full alert.

The rumble of a train became audible in the distance.

“Late this afternoon, Shane and his friend were playing hockey with a tennis ball on the sidewalk next to the parking lot. I'd just checked on them. Two minutes later, Shane came into the house terrified.”

Drake said nothing. The distant train grew louder. The tracks passed near the edge of the development.

“Their ball hit the guy's car,” Rachelle continued, “and bounced over by his front door. When Shane went to get it, the guy came out and grabbed him. Shook him and yelled in his face.” She paused. “When Shane came to get me he could barely talk. Really scared.”

Drake sat up on the edge of the bed. The digital clock's red numbers blinked to 3:13 a.m. Pressure surged in his head and a wired tightness engaged the muscles of his neck and shoulders.

“Did Shane say what the guy said?”

“He didn't want to, but I told him it was okay, even if it was bad words. He was crying. Said the guy called him the 'F' word. Said he'd 'kick his ass' if he ever got near his car again.”

Drake stood. “How was Shane later?”

“Real quiet and went up to his room. When I went up to check on him, he tried to hide it but he had fresh tears. Asked me to lay with him. That was around seven-thirty. I was so angry. I didn't know what to do.” She took a big breath. “I called the ER a few times, but you were always with someone real sick. I thought about the police but...”

The approaching train's sound was increasing and Drake could feel the faint rumble and throb deep in his chest. No wonder Rachelle had been freaked. He had, as usual, been absent. And his Shane...

Drake bent and pulled on a pair of sweatpants, then slipped on his basketball shoes. A growing heat enveloped him.

“Drake, what are you doing?”

He shook his head. His jaw was set and his movements quick and sure.

“Don't worry. You stay right here.”

The train grew closer, the sound and feel stronger.

He moved down the stairs, fatigue gone. His body coursed with an explosive energy.

He opened the front door and strode shirtless, in untied basketball shoes, onto the walk. The cold was nothing.

The train drew nearer. Drake marched, feeling its growing thunder, to the end unit's front door. He rang the bell three times in succession, then knocked hard.

He waited. His reflexes poised. His vision sharpened and became red tinged as if illuminated by flames. He knocked again.

After some seconds, the door opened partially and the tall, bearded, shaggy-haired resident stood bent at the waist at the foot of an inner adjoining stairway. Drake smelled cigarettes. He wore an open robe and boxer shorts.

"What the hell do you want?" the guy said in a sneering tone with beer breath. "Shit, you aren't even dressed."

Drake snatched both sides of the man's bathrobe collar at the base of the throat in his left hand. He forced the man to a bent position, his grip tight enough to cut off breathing.

Drake spoke over the train. "Did you swear at, threaten, and lay hands on my seven-year-old boy today?" The train's roar increased.

"Well, ah, uhh," the man mumbled as he struggled to stand straight. Drake's grasp was a vise. The man's face reddened and his neck and forehead veins bulged. "They hit my car with the ball," he choked out lamely.

Drake's instinct for violent response flared. Assholes. Where do jerks like this come from? *Goddamn, piece-of-shit assholes.*

He knotted his right hand and drew it back. His heart pounded and his rage hung poised like a cresting wave as he prepared to drive his fist through the bones of the man's face. Harsh lessons from the past flashed. The train's thunder reached its screeching, clattering, and clanging peak. His fist trembled as restraint grappled with the inner voice that screamed for him to deliver justice.

Drake locked his gaze with the now begging eyes. Did the abusive asshole know how close he was to being destroyed? How easily he could die?

Drake pointed his index finger like a gun between the man's eyes. He spoke, his voice hoarse with emotion as he enunciated each word. "If you ever look at, speak to, or in any way disturb my wife or children again, I will snap your worthless, punk-ass spine. Do you read me, asshole?" Drake let the molten rage he felt show in his glare.

The bully twisted his eyes down and away. "Yes. Please, yes," he said with his voice breaking.

Drake threw the man backwards onto the adjoining stairs. The guy scuttled like a crab up a few steps, eyes wide, raising a hand to his throat.

Drake turned and followed the sidewalk back to unit C. The train noise had shifted in frequency and fury as it moved away.

He sat on the cracked and uneven slab of their front stoop with his hands trembling. The frigid air felt as mild as if he'd just stepped out of a sauna. He took a deep breath.

As with Dan Ogren, he'd restrained himself.

Was his rage and urge to react wrong or closer to justice than what would result if he called the police? At least he'd sent the asshole a clear message.

Had Dan Ogren received a warning? Would he hurt his wife again?

Who did the system serve?

He traced a jagged crack in the cold cement of the stoop with the knuckles of his right hand. It sent him back. Another place. An earlier time. A vulnerable person being abused. The one he'd loved beyond all.

Drake had done what he knew was right.

It had ripped their lives apart.

Chapter 16

Cincinnati, Ohio
Drake's childhood

Kevin Cody was born eighteen months after his big brother Drake. In the last minutes and seconds before Kevin's birth, part of his brain didn't get enough oxygen. His mind was good, but the control center for movement had been damaged.

Cerebral palsy.

Kevin's body defied control. Only through iron resolve and grimacing will did Kevin accomplish what was effortless for others.

For him, speech was an agonizing, halting struggle. Walking was a labor of flailing crutches and gravity-defying lurches.

Among Drake's early memories were his mother's words, "You've been given a gift—a blessing. You get to watch over your special brother. That's why God made you so strong."

Kevin fell frequently and visited the ER often. Drake, inseparable from his younger brother, helped with communication and care. Kevin continually suffered bruises, cuts and fractures. He never quit. He never cried.

Drake and Kevin communicated without effort, sharing laughing fits or pain, often without exchanging a word. From earliest childhood, Kevin was the largest and best part of Drake's world.

Episodes of childish cruelty and abuse occurred. Drake dealt harshly with anyone who wronged his brother—even those older and larger.

The small circle of the Cody brothers' contacts and schoolmates knew how cool Kevin was.

Other places, gawking and ignorant comments were the rule.

"I'm j-just t-too g-GOOD lookING! Th-they a-aren'T u-used t-to IT," was Kevin's response. He would flash his contorted grin.

Drake saw all and forgave less. The "talking down" speech and presumption that Kevin was mentally handicapped maddened him.

"You're not talking to a beagle, lady," Drake had snapped at a clinic nurse when he was twelve years old. "He's way smarter than you are." His mother had made him apologize. Drake was not one bit sorry.

Kevin entered seventh grade at the same public junior/senior high where Drake was starting the tenth grade. On their third day, they waited next to the auxiliary parking lot off to the side of the main school building. Their mom would pick them up any minute.

Three slouching twelfth graders with shaved heads stood by a trash dumpster smoking cigarettes and talking loud. They had a bad rep and were given a wide berth. Kids called them skinheads.

"C'mon Kevin, let's wait over there." Drake pointed farther down the lot.

"B-but M-Mom s-said to b-be h-here."

"You're right, but she'll see us. C'mon." Drake put a hand on Kevin's shoulder.

"O-ho-KAY d-DRAKE." Kevin started his ungainly movement away from the dumpster.

"Hey! What the hell is that?" came the shout. "Looks like an almost-human helicopter." Coarse, biting laughter.

Drake slowed, muttering. "Brainless assholes."

"D-Drake, i-it's o-kay."

A second voice now, "What is it? A bird? A plane? No, it's Super-retard!" They howled.

The harsh laughter echoed off the brick walls of the school. Drake's face flushed hot.

"I-it's o-kay D-Drake! C-c'mon!" Kevin worked his crutches, struggling to distance himself from the hyenas. Their braying surged and moved closer.

"Hoo-hoo-hoo. What've we got here? Its retard boy and his keeper," yelled the largest and loudest of the three as they stepped in front of the brothers. "ARYAN" was tattooed on his forearm below a grinning skull with lightning bolts coming out of the eye sockets. He finger-flicked his cigarette, bouncing it with a burst of spark at Drake's feet.

"You getting ready for take-off, retard?" said the vacant-eyed second skinhead.

"I think I'll try out those sticks, spaz boy," said Aryan tattoo.

"Yeah. See if you can fly better than the wiggly retard," sneered the tough-looking third skinhead.

Drake stood on the sidewalk where tree roots had heaved the concrete. A faint drumming started inside his head. The jagged crack and an uneven step-off of the sidewalk lay under his feet. The smell of cigarettes grew stronger.

Kevin stood, crutch-propped and weaving, the skinheads laughing in his face.

Time stretched. Drake's vision tunneled and edges sharpened. The drumming in his head intensified. His face burned as though he was standing too close to an open fire. His reflexes were trip-wired. His body electric.

Aryan stepped forward, grabbed Kevin's right crutch, and yanked, his laughter cruel.

Drake grasped Kevin's shoulders, and smoothly lowered him to the curb. He took the left crutch strut, slipping the reinforced aluminum forearm ring free of Kevin's arm.

Aryan pulled hard on the right crutch, dragging Kevin.

Kevin's eyes pinwheeled, the whites showing large. His face contorted as he resisted. "Nuh-nuh-NO!"

Aryan launched his leg, the sole of his boot driving towards Kevin's face.

The crutch whistled as it sliced through the air. It struck Aryan in the middle of his face with the sound of an ax biting into a hardwood log. Aryan pitched backwards, his nose collapsed and his face a volcano of erupting blood.

Out of the corner of his eye, Drake saw the second skinhead advancing. Drake pivoted, shifted his grip, and drove the crutch, tip first, into the belly of the second aggressor.

The skinhead gave an "Ooofff!" as he jackknifed to the ground, arms hugging gut, legs bicycling in the air.

Drake glimpsed, too late, the third skinhead's incoming punch. The fist struck his face like a thrown brick. A lightning bolt of pain lanced his jaw and the taste of pennies filled his mouth.

He was on his back, away from Kevin. He slid toward unconsciousness, blackness reaching. The puncher straddled his chest and pounded his face.

Clinging to consciousness, Drake drove his hand through the storm of punches and found the attacker's throat. His fingers closed. As the blows rained down, he squeezed.

Rage and instinct fueled his grip, his fingers hydraulic. From his hand the sensation of twigs snapping and he heard a strangled bawl. The punches stopped. The drumming in his head thundered on. His arm supporting a limp weight.

And still he squeezed.

A flapping on his arms, clutching fingers and Kevin's voice cutting through the drumming. “N-NO! D-draAKE! N-noO!”

Drake released his grip, discarding the gurgling body. Turning, he saw the other two skinheads on the ground. He met his brother's wild eyes and wrapped him in a hug as they lay on the cracked sidewalk, Kevin's body quaking with sobs.

Drake held his brother tight to his chest. Pain spiked his jaw with each word. “I've got you, Kevin. We're okay, brother. We're okay.”

***

Drake's broken jaw required a steel plate and screws. He wore an ankle bracelet under house arrest for the three weeks between his discharge from the hospital and the criminal proceedings.

The Aryan tattooed assailant's face would be left with permanent deformity. The attacker that broke Drake's jaw had almost died.

At the trial, Drake's charges read “felony assault with weapon resulting in grievous bodily injury.” The father of the assailant that had broken Drake's jaw was the largest highway construction contractor in the state. Drake's “victims” wore sport coats and ties. Their hair had grown to crew-cut length. Their past records were inadmissible as they were not on trial.

Drake's mother had no money. The novice public defender looked scared, and his voice trembled on the few occasions he spoke at trial. He didn't consider Kevin as a possible witness. He allowed the prosecutor to introduce hearsay reports of Drake's previous "assaults" of those who "kidded" with his brother.

For Drake, it was as if the proceedings were a TV program—it didn't seem real.

The prosecution closed their case with a psychiatrist whose only contact with Drake was a ten-minute interview in a holding cell. Drake later learned that the doctor's only "practice" involved delivering testimony for pay.

The psychiatrist wore a fine suit, wire-rimmed glasses, and a trimmed goatee. "The accused uses a delusional sense of responsibility to legitimize a hunger for brutality. Innocent schoolyard horseplay provides an excuse for him to indulge his lust for violence."

The timid public defender did not even cross-examine.

When the verdict was read, Drake's mother fell to her knees, dropping the rosary she'd clutched throughout the trial. The bespectacled, balding black judge spoke over her quiet tears and the braying sobs and writhing protests of Drake's brother.

"You are convicted of one count of assault with a deadly weapon." He glanced at the trio of alleged victims and then at the rookie public defender. He gave an exaggerated sigh.

"The verdict disturbs me, but based on what transpired in this courtroom," he looked over his glasses at the public defender, "I have no technical grounds to reverse the decision. I must, by mandate, remand the defendant into custody for the minimum sentence allowable: twenty-four months incarceration in an Ohio juvenile correctional institution for violent offenders. I note, for the record, that this result offends my sense of justice." His eyes met Drake's. "I remind the convicted that he has the right of appeal." The gavel struck.

***

Drake entered the Scioto Juvenile Correctional Facility for Violent Offenders in Franklin Furnace County. The "Furnace" had six times the frequency of violent events as the worst of Ohio's adult maximum security prisons.

Drake was a white boy entering an institution that was eighty-five percent minority, overwhelmingly gang affiliated, and a segment of which were criminally insane. He was a lone dog among wolves. Separated from his mother and Kevin, he feared for them and himself. Loneliness and depression extinguished any light in his life. He submerged into a black place, his life nothing more than a grim struggle for survival.

In the Furnace, the weak were mercilessly abused. Only strength protected the victims from the abusers. He'd been forced to savagery. To become someone he was not.

His capacity for violence kept him alive.

He learned to recognize those who enjoyed preying on others. These heartless predators were missing a part of what made others human. They deserved no mercy.

Others who needed help sought him out. He did what he could to protect the weak. Behind bars, turning the other cheek guaranteed further abuse or destruction. Survival meant hurt or be hurt—or, potentially, kill or be killed.

He tried not to, but sometimes he'd think of his brother—worry about him, miss him. The pain of their separation was like a hand held over an open flame.

He was alone, soul-aching sad, worried about what he was becoming. He could not believe any God would create a place like the Furnace or allow the abuse and suffering that occurred there.

He thought of giving up…

The Juvenile Court judge's on-the-record comments had left open a door to action by a pro bono criminal justice oversight group aligned with the University of Cincinnati Law School. It took time, but they secured Drake's freedom.

Four months and seventeen days after being delivered into the hell of the Scioto Furnace, Drake was released for time served.

His release came twenty-one days too late. What he'd done hid in a chasm deep within his mind.

He was released from jail, but his sentence would never end.

Chapter 17

Calhoun Beach Condo, Unit 6A

Dan Ogren rolled over. A quilt as thick as a down jacket covered him. His thoughts moved like wet cement. Memory clicked into place—his weekend of women, drugs, and booze had crashed.

He should never have gone home. He'd been high and screwed to near exhaustion. Beth had started flapping her jaw. He still couldn't believe the trip to the ER had ended up with the police and then jail. Disaster.

After finally getting him free last night, Mesh had insisted Dan not go home. He said Dan needed to stay away from Beth. The little attorney had been pissed and said Dan had screwed up big this time. Dan had to bite his tongue. Mesh was the smartest person Dan had ever met, but the straight-arrow little attorney too often forgot his job was to get Dan out of trouble—not tell him how to live.

Dan had called Clara around midnight and bless her horny little heart, she'd obliged him. As if there'd been any doubt.

He spied the clock. Shit! He'd missed his scheduled court appearance. He'd put himself in even deeper shit. Mesh would be blow-his-stack angry. But if anyone could smooth things over, it was his uptight but smart-as-hell lawyer.

Coming to after a long stretch of booze and drugs always sucked, but today set a new low. Thirty seconds or so of reflection exceeded Dan's typical stretch. He didn't waste time looking backwards. Whatever. *Time to get up and get it on.*

He climbed out of the bed and looked around Clara's room. The huge comforter. Giant pillows. Shag carpeting. Everything puffy. All either pink or white. A poster for the rock group ABBA on the wall. Hadn't they been like a million years ago?

He shook his head.

He'd met Clara at one of the hospital charity affairs a few months back. Beth, clearly the best-looking woman in the place, had been on his arm. When they were introduced to the hospital's “most capable administrative head,” the drab but intense woman had looked at him like a starved dog eying a steak. Not skinny, but she had the lean, slightly hollow-eyed look of a distance runner. Not a beauty, but that worked for him. The princesses and babes think everything is about them.

Women came on to him all the time, but he’d long ago learned to distinguish the duds from those who had that special hunger. The freaky, lonely ones were the best ones to take advantage of. They'd been on the sidelines so long they'd do anything to be in the game.

He'd got her number that night.

A little older than most he used, but so desperately hungry for it.

She got off so hard the first few times he thought she might be having a seizure. And she liked pain.

He'd found himself going back.

A glance out the south-facing window showed Lake Calhoun under a gray sky. The lack of snow left the lake a two-mile sheet of dark glass. Two risk-takers were skating near the middle of the lake's ice.

Shit. That's what he was on—thin ice. Should’ve never gone home to Beth yesterday. All his problems had become more complicated. Never should’ve hit her in the face—but hell if she hadn't asked for it.

And now he'd missed the court appearance that Mesh said he absolutely must not miss.

Screw him. That's what Dan paid him for. Last night Mesh hadn't got him free of the police for hours. Then he'd acted like Dan should kiss his ass because he'd done his job.

Dan walked into the bathroom. Fluffy white rug, white porcelain, and everything else lime green. Smelled like Lysol. He raised the toilet seat, hung out his member, then loosed his stream. He delivered a jet like a fire hose. He got a kick out of standing next to the eunuchs in public restrooms, hanging his hose out and unleashing a torrent. Some dudes got so shook their sphincters locked. They'd fidget, eyes averted, then zip up and leave as if they'd completed their business.

He thought of Kline. The day they'd first met at the country club they'd used adjacent urinals after a round of golf. Kline had leaned over and stared. From day one, the guy had been like one of the rich, old jock-sniffers who hung around when Dan had been a university hockey star.

Kline walked around the country club like a big man. Treated the caddies like shit. Always talking about big money deals. Dan didn't like him, but Kline was good at things Dan was not. He understood accounting, had contacts, and knew how to move money around. He could get things done. A bit like Mesh but without the hang-ups. The hotshot CEO Kline had definitely failed Dan in the ER yesterday. His business advice had been for shit as well.

Dan opened Clara's medicine cabinet and scanned labels. Nothing good. No uppers, sedatives, or narcotics. A bunch of antibiotics.

He turned on the shower. As the water warmed he caught his naked image in the mirror. No surprise that the wenches couldn't get enough of him. One incredible stud.

Almost from the start, Clara had talked all drama-voiced about their "relationship." How their love would overcome everything.

She might be a medical whiz, but in other ways she was dense as dirt.

On the positive side, she bought into the importance of not being seen together or letting their "relationship" be known. She thought it could be an issue with her job. Most of his sex cows couldn't wait to tell their friends. Or worse, be seen with him in public. He treated them all like shit, but it had never stopped him from finding others who were eager to let him do whatever he wanted.

He'd had a continuous hard-on since high school. Women made themselves available and he took them. Most he didn't have to do a thing—they were all over him. Some he charmed, some he got stupid drunk, and some he took against their will. There was an endless supply and like the song said, "Ever since the first I had, the worst I had was good." Like the autos he sold, they'd all get you from point A to B, but style, performance, and features could make for a better ride. He liked riding them all.

When he met Beth it had been different. There was something about her that he had to have. He'd read part of an article in a magazine lately. It talked about special pheromones, the angle of a chick's hips, their cycle, and some kind of link between the DNA of potential mates. Primal stuff that left a guy primed—damn near helpless. Whatever it was, that's what he'd had for Beth. He'd been a stallion in rut. He had to have her. And she'd said it had to be marriage. Somehow it had made sense.

She was prime, but she wasn't enough. He'd been screwing around on her almost from the start. An incredible babe at home and more whenever he wanted it—a perfect set-up.

For his recreational screwing, he'd learned that it worked best to get in, get the freak show on, then clear out. His "screw and dump" pattern took care of his needs and had kept Beth from suspecting.

But lately she'd finally started to catch on.

With Clara's commitment to discretion and can't-get-enough sexual appetite, he'd found himself returning. He'd used her for almost two months now. Not exclusively, but regularly. On a couple of visits he'd even shared some of his personal business with her. He'd never done that before, but this woman was smart and could be trusted to keep her mouth shut.

He stepped into the shower. Fuzzy sponges, blue soap, and a dandruff shampoo sat on the shelf.

He showered, wrapped a towel around his waist, and returned to the bedroom. As he pulled on his pants, his phone vibrated. He pulled it from the pocket. Mesh. And it looked like he'd missed eleven other calls from him. *Shit, lecture time.*

"Yep," Dan answered.

"Son of a bitch, Dan. Where are you? You missed the bail appearance. You idiot. The judge—"

"Did you take care of it?"

"Oh, geez. Are you for real? Did I—"

"Save the sermon, Mesh. Am I cleared?"

"I got you a release without bail until trial. Don't know how. The judge is one of—"

"Meet me at the Normandale Sports Club. Bring your racquetball gear. Forty-five minutes."

"Are you serious? Do you have any idea—"

"Meet me at the club. You can tell me what we need to do next." He disconnected.

Mesh—the smartest guy ever. Indispensable. But he thought he could bitch at Dan and tell him what to do. No one could do that.

That's how yesterday had gone to shit. Dan had made the mistake of returning home—very high and smelling of strange. Beth had got in his face.

She'd gone into full bitch-mode. Stupid to have hit her in the face—he knew better. But damn if it hadn't felt good.

He glanced out the window over the dark expanse of ice. His problems swirled. He tried to figure out what role to play. How to act. Every day he laid out a script. He directed himself in the movie that was his life. But the roles kept getting more complicated.

Mesh would have to come up with a way to dodge the domestic abuse charge.

Beth wouldn't dare testify against him. He'd taken care of that.

Dan slipped on his clean shirt. He always carried a bag of clothes in the trunk of his car—his "getting it on" travel bag. He liked the feel of his muscles and the way he filled out the custom-tailored shirt. Forty-one years old but still rock-hard.

Domestic abuse—what bullshit. Would it all come down to this damn doctor?

This ER doc, this Dr. Drake Cody, trying to be a hero. Even banged up, Beth was a babe. The doc thought he was rescuing a damsel in distress. Dan knew he'd misplayed his role, but even so the doctor gave off a strange vibe. If they'd been playing hockey, Dan sensed the gloves would have come off. The guy looked pretty sturdy, but hell, he was a doctor. Those guys were always play-by-the-rules types.

For sure, the doctor hadn't recognized how he stacked up in the real world compared to Dan. He hadn't been open to being bought and wasn't smart enough to be scared.

There had to be a way to deal with this guy—one way or the other, there always was.

Chapter 18

Townhouse, a.m.

Drake woke to Rachelle standing at the foot of the bed. The room glowed with the orange-tinted glow of daylight penetrating the shade. Rarely did he sleep through Rachelle arising. He looked at the clock. Whoa! Almost 10:30 a.m. He'd been out for almost seven hours. For him practically a coma. What day was it? What time did he need to be in the ER? Those were always his waking thoughts. Was that right?

He'd not yet shared with Rachelle the brutal news of his record being discovered. After Drake's visit to the asshole neighbor, they'd both dropped off to sleep. He hated to have to share the news. It would not lighten her load.

"The kids have eaten," she said. "Can I get you something? When do you have to leave?"

"I can grab some cereal."

She wore jeans and an old jersey, and her hair was draped over the right side of her neck. She looked beautiful.

"Shane seems good this morning," she said.

Clearly she had not seen a newspaper or heard the news.

"You did a good job with him. You're a special mom."

She smiled.

"I have to leave in a minute." He rubbed his face. "Rachelle, please sit down."

She sat next to him, looking concerned. He took her hands in his.

"The media discovered my record." Her eyes widened and her hands clenched. "It was the headline story on yesterday's six o'clock TV news." He shook his head. "The assault conviction. My time locked up. The fact that I didn't report it. I'm sure it's in the paper today."

Her jaw dropped and she paled.

"What will it mean?" Her voice a whisper.

"We'll be all right." Drake put an arm around her "Things will change, but we'll be all right."

She freed herself and faced him.

"But will you be a doctor? I thought—"

"The president of Medical Affairs says I'll lose my license." Drake shrugged, pretending a casualness he did not remotely feel. "I'm a smart guy and hardworking. I'll get other work. Don't worry." He forced a smile.

"No, Drake." Her voice rose. "Don't you dare pretend this is nothing." She stood and faced him. "You've worked so hard. It means so much to you. You take care of people. It's who you are." Her eyes were filling.

"It's okay, really—" His voice broke.

She pulled him to his feet then hugged him fiercely. He bent his head and buried his face against her hair and the scarred skin of her neck.

The reality of his work as a doctor ending—the loss. Her tears wet his chest.

He tightened his arms around her and hung on.

***

County Morgue, late a.m.

The squeak of Drake's soles echoed. The county morgue's 1950s stone and terrazzo hallways reminded him of the Catholic school he'd attended as a child. He opened the double door to the examining theater, and the saxophone wail of Foreigner's rock-classic "Urgent" reverberated from within.

The meat-locker cool temperature never changed here. The tang of formalin dominated but could not fully cover the scent of dead flesh and putrefaction. It was like the efforts of some hygiene-challenged ER patients who sprayed on perfume or cologne by the ounce.

Dr. Kip Dronen's Einstein-wild hair bobbed to the music as his skeletal physique hunched over a corpse on the stainless steel autopsy table. As Drake approached from behind, the white-coated pathologist reared back and air-drummed to the music, using a scalpel and surgical scissors.

Drake hit the stop button on the iTunes player. The dying echo left Kip frozen. He whirled, frowning at Drake through oversized wire-rimmed glasses.

"Damn it, man! That is one of the best alto sax riffs ever. Have you no respect? Son of a bitch—I was feeling it." Kip's surgical mask hung around his neck unfastened. His always high-pitched voice had ascended to a whine—for him a common occurrence.

"Sorry, Kip. I was afraid I'd startle you if I'd tapped you on the shoulder."

"Good point. That would have been dangerous, ER." Kip mimed a slow-motion, slashing karate move toward Drake while still holding the instruments. "Reflexes like a cat. I'd have written up your cause of death as "messed with a ninja-level pathologist." Kip grinned at his own cleverness.

The naked corpse of an obese, elderly white male lay on the table with a standard Y-incision exposing the viscera. Kip flipped the surgical scissors onto the metal instrument tray. The clank echoed in the now silent vault.

"Why are you here, ER?"

"I need your help."

"The burden of genius." Kip shrugged his coat-hanger shoulders. "What do you need?"

"Have you—"

"Wait. Did I tell you yet?" He waved the scalpel, speaking fast. "My report, "Neuromuscular Blockade and Pseudo-Drowning" was accepted by The Journal of Pathology. I nailed the cover article in the most prestigious journal in the field." He laughed—a helium-high screech. "I owe you for that, ER. I rocked the pathology world with my work on that soggy wench."

Drake fought to tolerate Kip's inappropriate manner. The "soggy wench" had been Faith, the wife of Drake's friend, Jon Malar. Jon had been deeply and blindly in love with Faith. Her betrayal of him and her subsequent murder had triggered tragedy and ugliness. Jon remained far from recovered physically or psychologically.

For Kip, Faith Reinhorst Malar's murder was nothing more than a challenging intellectual exercise. The profane, emotionally-defective pathologist lived for the study of death.

"You don't look excited for me, ER. Cover article is big time."

"Kip, I'm in serious trouble."

"Deep shit, huh?"

"I have a felony assault record and I lied about it. Now it's been discovered. Torrins says the state Medical Board will take my license."

"A record. Yeah, I heard the news. You're a criminal. Went primal on some guys." He cocked his head. "They'd take your license for that?" He paused. "Yeah, I suppose they would." He shrugged. "What's that got to do with me?"

"Nothing. I came to you for help with a patient."

"A live patient?" The scrawny pathologist's expression soured. "I don't do live patients. When they're no longer alive, and that happens to all of them eventually, that's where I come in. I find people much easier to understand when they're dead."

"All I need is lab work. I can't use the hospital. The tests have to be off the record. I'll bring you the blood. You run the tests and give me the results."

"Golly, that's all? Would you like fries with your order of secret medical tests?" Kip frowned. "What's going on? Sounds like it's too late for you, but I plan on keeping my medical license."

"Trust me. It's nothing unethical." *Or is it?* Regardless, Kip wouldn't be at risk.

"What if your patient ends up messed up—or dead? What would happen to me if that happens?"

"Geez, Kip." Drake pushed the thought of death or bad outcomes out of his head. "I wouldn't use our friendship to put you at risk."

"Friendship?" Kip's eyes widened. "No shit?"

For one of the first times ever, Kip looked moved. Had the notion of friendship touched the social misfit?

"Okay. What the hell, I'll run your tests." He raised a finger. "Two conditions: one—if anything scientifically significant develops, I get to publish it. And two—this friendship shit does not mean I'm going to prom with you." He honked out a laugh.

"Thank you, Kip."

"You're up to something funky." He pointed a finger at Drake. "I'm intrigued."

"It's best that you don't know," Drake said.

“A secret patient—hmmm, I've already got some ideas.” He wagged his eyebrows. “I'll figure it out soon enough. It's what I do.” He hit the play button with a gloved baby finger, then turned back to the corpse as the music roared.

Chapter 19

Racquetball court three
Normandale Racquet & Sports Club

Dan put on his racquetball glove. He leaned against the glass rear wall of the court and stretched. Even after four days of booze, women and drugs, he felt like he could kick ass. From his earliest experiences with drinking and drugs, he'd found his body handled excess well.

A counselor Dan had been forced to see as part of a deal Mesh had worked out to avoid a DUI had told him his ability to drink alcohol without getting a hangover was a bad thing—said it favored abuse. The guy was an idiot. *Not getting hangovers a bad thing? Ridiculous.*

He saw Mesh approach, then enter the court through the door in the glass. Mesh held his racket in one hand and protective eye-wear in the other. His sharp nose, dark eyes, and hyper-alert manner reminded Dan of a bird. Dark hair, baby-faced with a soft voice, Mesh had a black belt in self-control. Fit and wiry, he stood no more than five-foot-seven. A mild-mannered, little guy, but in legal wrangling and getting Dan out of trouble, he punched like a heavyweight.

Mesh didn't look friendly right now.

Dan would have to play things right to get the most out of him. His standard act with Mesh was as a fun-loving, prone-to-screw-ups friend who greatly appreciated the attorney's help. It always worked.

"Thanks for handling the bail deal," Dan said.

Mesh pointed his racket at Dan. "You compromised everything by missing the hearing." His jaw clenched. "By the time you hadn't answered by my fifth phone call this morning, I knew you were screwing up again. We barely dodged a contempt citation. I got a bailiff to bring a note to the judge's chambers. Total luck it was Judge Elling. He's not a supporter of the new domestic violence law. Knows your dad. I told him you were ill, the charge was a mistake, and that you were not a risk. He cancelled your hearing. Incredible luck. A contempt citation would have been bad news. You endangered everything and left me hanging, asshole."

"Okay. I was lucky. You saved me," Dan said. Mesh was pissed off. The attorney could get away with a lot because Dan needed him but he better watch his mouth. "How do we dodge this wife-beating crap?"

"Crap? Are you for real? This is big-time serious." Mesh shook his head, then looked Dan in the eye. "Are you already high? I can't even tell anymore."

"Screw you. Let's play." Dan stepped to serve position. "I'm ready to pound something."

Mesh muttered something as he put on his protective eye gear and readied to receive.

Dan ripped a serve to Mesh's backhand, the explosion of the ball's impact echoing like a gunshot in the enclosed, parquet-floored court. Mesh got to the serve, hitting a ceiling shot that moved Dan to the back wall. Dan took it off the wall, snapping a low corner shot. Mesh lunged to his right, shoes squeaking. He somehow got his racket on the ball. The weak return came to Dan's forehand. He used his length and power to rifle a slam cross-court two inches off the floor. Mesh dove, racket outstretched, but the ball skipped past in a blur.

"Hell, yes!" Dan yelled and pumped a fist.

Mesh jumped to his feet then threw his racket overhand off the back wall. It ricocheted, missing Dan's head by an inch before clattering to the floor.

"Damn. Lighten up. It was just the first point," Dan said.

"Do you really think I give a shit about this meaningless game?" Red-faced, Mesh strode forward and pushed a hand into Dan's chest. "You jerk! You don't even show up at court and leave me taking care of your shit. Then you act like it's nothing. They say you beat her."

"Whoa. Settle down. I get it. It looks bad. But you're going to pull some legal magic out of your ass and—"

"No, I'm not!" Mesh ripped his eye guard off and glared at Dan. "This is not one of your bimbo cases or beat-downs of some drunk. This is assault of your wife, with injuries and a doctor's report." He shoved Dan in the chest. "If it's true, you deserve to have your ass kicked."

Incredibly, he shoved Dan again.

Dan grabbed the smaller man's arms. He looked down at him. Mesh had never acted like this. Anyone else pushing Dan would have their face stomped on.

"Well, effing boo-hoo, little man. I get it. I'm in trouble, but excuse me for not pissing my pants." He tightened the grip of his powerful hands on Mesh's arms and drove him against the sidewall. "Push me again and I'm going to kick your ass."

"Great idea. Now you insult and threaten the person who has saved your ass over and over. You ungrateful bastard." Mesh's arms went limp in Dan's hands and he slid to the floor, his back against the wall. "I'm so sick of taking care of your shit."

It couldn't be denied. Mesh had covered Dan's ass for years. Rape claims, minor arrests, guys he'd kicked the shit out of, and all the business stuff. All sorts of badness. But Dan paid him well and Mesh cashed his checks straightaway. His job was to take care of trouble—not tell Dan how to live his life.

The problem was Mesh was wound too tight. He had a conscience that got in the way. He'd bailed Dan out of a lot of jams, but his disapproving daddy act irritated. Several times Dan had controlled an urge to kick the little man's ass, but he hadn't let on. He couldn't afford to let his mask slip now.

He needed Mesh. The guy could see several steps ahead of everyone else and always made the moves that worked out best. The smartest guy ever.

How did he need to play it to keep Mesh on board?

Dan slid down on the floor next to the attorney. He picked up his racket and rested the strings against his forehead.

"I'm sorry I messed up, my friend. You know me—I'm a screw-up. Thanks for helping me. I'm listening, Mesh. Tell me what you want me to do."

Mesh looked at him.

Dan nodded, putting on his practiced apologetic and appreciative expression.

“I don't see a way out, Dan. You're going to lose everything. With the prenuptial and what you've done with the business—” Mesh paused. “You understand what's at stake, right?”

“Lay it out for me. You know I'm not good with this stuff.” Playing dumb almost always helped. Mesh liked being the smart guy.

“Here's how I see it.” Mesh straightened. “If you're convicted of any domestic abuse charge, even a misdemeanor, your prenuptial agreement is void. That leaves all your assets, including your inheritance, vulnerable in a divorce. Beth could clean you out. Additionally, with the prenup voided, even the filing of a divorce action will expose your and Ogren Automotive's financial records. Reviewers would see everything. Do you understand?”

“Spell it out.”

Mesh rubbed his forehead. “If you're convicted and she divorces you, without the prenuptial the divorce court will review all assets. They'll see what you've done with the business money. I warned you. Your financial dealings would guarantee a conviction for tax evasion and embezzlement. You'd spend years in a white-collar correctional facility with Madoff, Petters, and the like. It would mean bankruptcy for Ogren Automotive. Even without divorce, the shit you've done business-wise has the company on the edge. We have less than six months to come up with enough money to make the books right.”

“Can't you head it off?”

“If you're convicted of domestic assault and she files for divorce, you'll lose everything. There's nothing I can do.”

“You've always found a way.” Combining Mesh's brains, high-level contacts, and Dan’s well-directed payoffs had never yet failed. Also being Big Dan Ogren's son still meant something to a lot of powerful people. “Beth won't say anything. I made sure of that.”

Mesh raised both hands as if to stop traffic. “Don't say anything more about that.” He shook his head. “If you hurt her that's sick. I don't want to know.”

“Attorney-client privilege covers what I say,” Dan said. Despite a lifetime of brushes with the law, Dan still didn’t know a lot about the legal system, but he knew this.

"Don't play lawyer," Mesh said. He ran a hand over his scalp. "There's no reason for us to discuss anything further. I need to tell you something you're probably not going to like."

"Damn, Mesh. That's the way women usually start bitch-sessions."

"Okay. I'll be direct." Mesh looked Dan in the eye. "I've wrestled with this, but now I'm sure—I can't do this anymore. I'm removing myself as your counsel. You need to find someone else to represent you."

What the hell?

"No way." Dan shook the racket. "No effing way. You can't bail on me. I won't let you." The self-righteous, gutless little prick.

"It's best for both of us. I'll still take care of the business, but you need an attorney who specializes in domestic abuse defense, and I—"

"No. You're my attorney." Dan extended the racket, putting it under Mesh's chin and forcing his head toward him. "I'm not asking. I'm telling."

Mesh played by the rules, but one time in order to get Dan clear, they hadn't. Dan had made sure he had Mesh's involvement documented. Subsequently he'd subtly let Mesh know it. "I'm not giving you a choice."

"Or else what?" Mesh said.

"You know." Dan shifted the racket to Mesh's throat. "Don't make me go there."

Mesh didn't play dumb convincingly. His eyes flashed. He'd lose his license to practice law. He understood Dan's threat.

Mesh had been loyal. He probably figured he and Dan were friends. That acting job had been one of Dan's longest running and most important.

Mesh didn't want to defend Dan but too bad. What Mesh wanted or deserved meant nothing. He lowered the racket.

"Besides being an asshole you just don't get it, do you?" Mesh said. "There's nothing I can do for you. It doesn't matter what I say. It doesn't matter what you say. If the doctor testifies her injuries are due to abuse, you'll be convicted. If Beth says you hurt her, you'll be convicted. From there on it's unstoppable. If Beth divorces you, it's all a done deal." Mesh tapped a finger against his temple. "Can you get that into your twisted head?"

Shit! Yeah—unfortunately he could. Mesh had never steered him wrong. The picture his on-top-of-everything attorney painted was grim.

If he got convicted and Beth divorced him, he'd lose the dealerships, his property, and his wealth. Even worse, he'd lose his sport screwing, drugs, and booze—his life. He'd go to jail.

He'd totally blown it this time.

Mesh was the only one he trusted to defend him. The guy always looked ten steps ahead. He outsmarted everyone. *I need him.* He put a hand on Mesh's shoulder.

"Mesh, I trust you. You're the smartest guy I know. And my best friend. You're my guy. You have to stay with me. Please."

Mesh looked tortured. He'd always looked out for Dan. Had never abandoned him no matter how justified. The little guy was a slave to loyalty, conscience, and responsibility. Dan knew he'd hit all the right notes.

And Mesh knew the threat to get him disbarred was real.

"Will you listen to me and do what I say?" Mesh said.

"Yes. You have my word."

"You have to understand going in that I don't see a way out. I think you'll be convicted of at least a misdemeanor. The best we can hope for is damage control."

"There's gotta be something," Dan said.

"Something has come up but it won't be useful in court," Mesh said. "The doctor who reported you has been in the news. He had an assault conviction in the past."

Dan had sensed there was something about the doctor.

"That's got to help," Dan said.

"I expect not. It's trouble for him but it does you no good. He was a licensed physician in good standing when he cared for Beth. There's no way his testimony could be excluded. Conversely, his assault record will not be admissible."

"What if he didn't testify?" Dan said.

"The prosecution would have to use the written medical ER record. Those are brief and focus on the medical aspects. Without the doctor on the stand, it's a much weaker case. His testimony is key. The prosecution will make sure he's on the stand. They'll subpoena him if necessary."

Dan had tried to buy the doctor off in the ER—no way. Could he be stopped from testifying?

Mesh already seemed beaten. Wimping out. Giving up on the case because of the damn ER doctor...

Something Clara had said jumped into his mind. It had seemed just another of her "out there" comments at the time. Trying to impress him with her intelligence, always chirping about being smarter than all the doctors—as if he cared. But she was really smart. All the hospital people had said so.

He thought about what she'd said.

According to the smartest guy he'd ever known, he was on the path to losing everything. Clara's words pointed the way to an intense gamble. Did he have any alternatives?

Maybe Clara had more to offer than getting his rocks off?

Dan would not give up the life he had.

Bold steps. He'd do whatever it took.

Chapter 20

RV campground, late morning

"Can you have her call me as soon as she's out of court? It's urgent." Beth listened, then nodded—the movement caused pain. "Thank you." She disconnected from the attorney's secretary.

Beth had ditched her personal cell phone and bought the prepaid disposable at Walmart. She knew Dan could use her personal cell phone to track her. She set down the prepaid and began to pace along the forty-foot luxury recreational vehicle's carpeted length.

Last night after the ER had been miserable. Even with the pills. Today she hurt worse. And her face—scary.

She didn't want to look in the mirror again. Her left eye was purple and almost swollen shut. Her lower lip was fat and beneath it six black stitches held her chin together. Her tongue ran over the stitches and damaged tissue inside her mouth. It tasted like blood.

The doctor had said she should be with someone for forty-eight hours. She couldn't do it.

She opened the freezer of the RV. She'd been applying bags of frozen peas to her chin and eye. A goofy sounding suggestion from the ER doctor but it worked. The frozen vegetables molded around her injuries and soothed. She held the bag of peas to her chin. The RV had everything a house did. So strange for this to be her sanctuary. Thoughts of what Dan had engaged in here in his "party barge" were enough to make her ill.

Where else would she go? Her mother lived in Wisconsin, and Beth didn't have many friends—or any that she wasn't too ashamed to see.

After the ER she'd stayed overnight with Katrina. They were both volunteers at the Animal Rescue center. Katrina was like Beth—what Dan sneeringly called an "animal freak."

Katrina had volunteered her home for longer, but Beth couldn't impose.

Most importantly, Katrina was taking care of Kidder. Beth could trust Katrina. She understood what the puppy meant to Beth. Beth had “rescued” the flop-eared setter-mix puppy from the pound. Truth was, the four-month-old puppy had rescued Beth.

The thought of what Dan had done caused a rush of horror and loathing to pass through her.

The domestic abuse counselor in the ER had shared the typical reactions of abuse victims. What Beth had thought was sick and unique, she learned was predictable and common. Shame. Guilt. Anxiety. Isolation. The counselor had laid out her feelings as if she'd been living in Beth's skin.

Beth had Katrina bring her “home” early in the a.m. Before getting out of the car, she’d checked to make sure Dan's vehicle was not there. As she gathered up what she needed, she'd spied the keys to the RV hanging in the kitchen. In the moment it had made sense. She could stay almost anywhere—all she needed was a parking spot and an outlet. The luxury appointed rig was warm and comfortable. Beth's farm-girl background made handling the vehicle no problem.

Leaving Kidder had hurt, but Beth recognized she was not up to taking care of anyone beyond herself. The task she had in front of her would take all she had.

Dan had written off the RV as a marketing expense for Ogren Automotive. The business bought tickets for the University of Minnesota and the Twin Cities' professional sports teams. Dan, with his degenerate hangers-on—and God knew how many women—made the vehicle a fixture at sporting events, concerts, and even the state fair. He wrote off all his decadence as “work-related.” Beth had attended a couple of events when they were first married, but the drinking and decadence had been too much.

She knew now that Dan had no doubt been thrilled when she'd left him on his own. *Bastard.*

In hindsight it jumped out at her. From shortly after the wedding, he used work obligations and other responsibilities as excuses.

After too long a time, she realized the RV was one part of a life of alcohol, drugs, and women. She'd been so trusting—so stupid!

For the longest time she'd fooled herself.

He was the best-looking man she'd ever seen. And he could turn on the charm. She'd believed he loved her and had been happy to marry him.

Now it was obvious. He couldn't love. His charm was an act—a sales job. Fun-loving Dan Ogren. That was his pose. The real Dan Ogren—narcissistic, a sexual fanatic, selfish, cruel, an abuser of alcohol and drugs—had so many fooled. He'd kept getting worse—or maybe he just hadn't cared enough to hide it anymore?

Along with her pain and anger came shame. She was ashamed that she let herself be humiliated and beaten. Yesterday's abuse was the worst but not the first. He'd always been careful not to leave marks. His apologies were as phony as his charm. She'd heard the "never again" lies before.

And, as the counselor had shared, his bogus remorse was one more example of an abuser's standard pattern.

It had taken all she could muster to call the attorney. Her emotions surged—sadness, shame, anger.

How had she ended up so pathetic?

Beth wished the attorney would call back. She had to follow the plan before she turned coward.

She looked out the window. The wooded campground lay in Dayton, a township on the edge of the Twin Cities' suburbs. She'd called and the fellow who managed it said they'd technically closed for the season. He'd said that if she took responsibility for getting the big vehicle out if a snowstorm hit, she was welcome.

Bare-limbed maples and oaks extended to a huge marsh. Acres of golden cattails bent and riffled in the frozen marshland surrounding the island of leafless hardwoods and high ground that formed the park. The manager lived in a farmhouse a quarter mile down the road.

Just Beth in the ten-acre campground on the outskirts of the metro. She'd never felt more alone.

She shifted the bag of frozen peas to her eye. Never again, Dan.

Never again.

***

It had been just over twenty-four hours earlier that Dan had come home after another of his all-nighters. He led off with a transparent lie—the kind of feeble story she'd fooled herself into accepting so many other times. Work and a meeting downtown. Had a couple of drinks. Time got away from him. He'd been worried he might be close to the legal limit so didn't want to chance driving. He'd slept at the club.

"Sorry, should have called, " he said then tried to hug her.

Bloodshot eyes, the odor of alcohol and sex—he'd gotten so casual he came home smelling of it. He was still high.

Her memory pinned each of the next moments.

"I'm not an idiot," she said. She had been—but no longer.

"What do you mean?" His mock confusion was pitifully unconvincing.

"You're a cheating, lying, drunken prick. You disgust me." The words felt good.

His head snapped upright and the curtain closed on his innocence act. His eyes blazed. The flipped-switch shift to rage she'd seen so many times had occurred. She tensed.

She knew what would happen if she said more. *I must get free of him!*

He turned for the stairs.

"You're sick." Somehow the words came out of her. "A pervert. A limp-dick who can't have sex unless you hurt—"

He spun and had her by the throat pinned against the wall in an instant. He snarled, the tendons in his neck taut, and a vein on his forehead standing out like a hose.

"Shut up, bitch." His breath foul and hot. "Shut up and I'll let it go."

She could not breathe, her throat in a vise, his strength terrifying. As the hellish seconds passed, she could see his wheels turning. The myth of anger that he couldn't control, once again calculating how much he could get away with. His hand relaxed and her feet touched the floor. Trying to act as if he were letting her off easy while she knew it was about not leaving evidence. He hadn't left a mark. *Brutal bastard!*

She gasped, bent over, a hand to her throat.

"Answer this," she said her voice cracked and weak.

Dan stood over her with raised eyebrows, open-mouthed that she dared to speak.

"How is it possible that a worthless coward like you is the son of a *man* like Big Dan Ogren?"

Her vision flashed red in an explosion of pain and light. Another blow struck. Her face was in agony. The taste of blood filled her mouth.

On the floor, fetal-curled with her arms over her head, the wait was endless. Her battered daze cleared. The attack had ended. He'd hurt her bad this time.

It had to end.

Chapter 21

North Minneapolis

Drake slowed as he approached the two-story, weathered-brick building. The university chemical storehouse in Minneapolis's north side lay surrounded by decaying blacktop. A wire fence separated the lot from high-rise complexes containing hundreds of subsidized housing units. The low-income, high-crime neighborhood and the distance from the main campus made rental space cheap.

After shots had rung out on a pitch-black night several weeks earlier, Dr. Jon Malar's near-lifeless body had been found sprawled on the asphalt. The police's initial thought had been a robbery victim. That assessment had almost cost Drake's friend his life.

The first floor of the building held little-used offices. The second floor housed the space Drake, Rizz and Jon had used as their laboratory for the past four years.

Drake parked near the separate entrance to the stairwell leading to the lab. He opened the car door and the December cold gripped him. He stepped out, then locked the door.

Drake looked at the asphalt and swallowed hard. Was Jon's blood still part of the discolored, crumbling asphalt? Jon had survived, but his healing remained incomplete. Would Jon ever recover from the damage the bullets and emotional trauma his wife's greed and betrayal had inflicted on him?

Their miracle drug—the breakthrough that had been Drake's long-held dream—had triggered treachery, misery, and death.

But Drake was not giving up. The drug showed promise in treating one of humankind's cruelest afflictions. Rizz's paralysis made Drake's hopes for what D-44 might do both desperate and personal.

He unlocked the building's outer door, then climbed the stairs to the second level. The steel door out of the stairwell was heavy and fire-resistant. It shut behind him with a soft clank. Countless times over the past four years, Drake had followed this path.

Until a few months ago, his efforts had yielded nothing. That had changed. Even now, despite all the tragedy, entering the lab lifted him.

The sunlight streaming through the multi-paned windows revealed high ceilings, a warped parquet floor, and several slate-topped work tables. The walls were crisscrossed with exposed pipes and ductwork. It wasn't fancy, but the space accommodated the cat kennels, lab equipment, and other needs of their research activities.

The cats sensed Drake. The cedar shavings in their kennels rustled, and a yowl greeted him. He crouched to look into the first of the five occupied kennels stacked along the wall. The little black-and-white cat meowed. FloJo, his current and forever favorite.

Drake's world had been sent spinning by the smooth-furred, undersized cat.

***

Lab, Four months earlier

"Rizz, are you sure this cat's deficit met protocol?" Drake opened the research log book.

"Absolutely." Rizz continued putting away equipment. "That's specimen D4, female, 2.1 kilograms, fully med-checked. You performed the procedure at 0730 hours, forty-eight days ago. I confirmed zero motor function at 1930 hours that evening, then infused study drug D-44 at 2100 hours." He mock-bowed. "I am a slave to protocol, research master."

Drake shook his head looking at the records. "I can't believe what I'm seeing." He indicated the smallish black-and-white cat. "She has function."

Rizz cocked his head. "No shit?"

Drake's examination of the cat revealed movement—a slight twitch of the tail and claw extension on a hind foot. For a spinal cord injured animal, it was as if she'd done a back flip. Could it be real?

“I hope it's not a technical error.” Drake checked the healed incision midway down the cat's back. He rubbed the cat’s forehead with a fingertip.

“Not likely,” Rizz said. “Your surgical skills might be even better than mine. Whatever screwed up, it probably wasn't your technique. And it wasn't me. It's something else.” He went back to gathering his gear.

“I'll review the data trail and video records. If there's an error, it means this little one went through surgery for nothing.”

“Don't beat yourself up,” Rizz said with a shrug. “Remember these kitties were headed for the great catnip field in the sky before we gave them a last chance to help their human buddies.”

Drake obtained the research animals from the to-be-euthanized queue at the city's Animal Humane Society facility. The cats he selected would've otherwise been put to sleep within hours. But it still troubled him. Sometimes they appeared in his dreams.

His exposure to the human suffering caused by spinal cord injury overrode his misgivings. He took care of patients—scared, injured people he spoke with and touched. He looked into their eyes. It was his heartrending responsibility to tell them they were paralyzed.

Then he had to confess that no treatment existed. On each occasion it was a struggle for him not to break down.

Up until now, the four years of research effort had resulted in a solid animal research model for creating and testing spinal cord injury—nothing more. The drugs Drake had developed and tested showed no benefit. With each failure, his doubts grew.

But this night, everything felt different. Could this cat’s astounding improvement be real?

Drake slipped his hands under the drape, lifting the little black-and-white cat and placing her, as if made of crystal, into one of the kennels along the wall.

Rizz stopped his cleanup and looked across the table. “Drake, you knew going in that the odds against success were ridiculous. There's never been a treatment that helps spinal cord injury. Never.” His expression lightened. “Whatever. You're the biochemist and principal investigator, while Jon and I get research credit just for being Igors to your Dr. Drakenstein genius.” He affected a hunched back and claw-handed posture.

Drake looked at the cage where he'd just placed the black-and-white cat. "I have to try."

"Hey, I respect that, partner, but just keeping it real. This is the ultimate long shot. Pfizer, Genentech, and all the giant pharmaceutical labs have been trying to develop a drug that treats spinal cord injury for a long time. Newsflash—they haven't come up with one. When the spinal cord goes down, it stays down." He stuffed a last item into his backpack.

"I won't quit."

"No," Rizz said, eyeing him. "You won't." He looked at his watch. "But I will—at least for today. I'm meeting someone a hell of a lot better looking than you or these cats."

"Rizz, why not wait? I can double-check this pretty quick." Drake picked up the test drug vial. The vial's protocol label read D-44. Could it be the miracle he dreamed of?

Rizz slipped a backpack strap over his shoulder. "Dude, it's party-time. All work and no play—"

"If my review shows no errors, I'm gonna be super jacked. Keep your phone handy. I'll call you."

"Don't bother." Rizz gave a backhanded wave as he passed the cages heading for the door. "I can wait. Later." He pulled the lab door closed behind him.

Drake shook his head. Rizz had ceased believing.

Drake dared to believe. He tried to control his excitement, dreading the disappointment of a technical error. He turned to the data records and computer with surging anticipation.

The lab's overhead lighting hummed. He smelled the mix of the cats and the fresh cedar shavings used as bedding. He heard the soft, quick paw pounces of the untested animals and a soft mewing from the upper cages. He began to bounce his leg as he reviewed Rizz's documentation of the cat's pre-drug paralysis. His leg stopped. Rizz had not made an error—the animal's findings were complete.

Drake soared inside as he accessed the video file.

The screen flickered. The images revealing his surgical treatment of the black-and-white cat were clear.

His technique was without flaw. The experimental record left no doubt. There were no errors. His mind emptied and warmth flooded him.

He carefully closed the laptop, slid it forward with both hands, and stepped back from the slate-topped table.

He felt as if he might float away, static charged, his scalp tingling. In his dreams of a breakthrough he jumped into the air, screaming his joy. Tonight he placed both hands over his face and slumped to the floor with his back against the ancient iron radiator. The unyielding flanges dug into his back. He heard the scattered soft mewing, the ticking clock, the hammering of his heart.

He looked up and out the upper panes of the streaked and vine-latticed windows to a brilliant full moon. Absolute confirmation would require repeat trials. But inside he knew.

It was real.

***

Present time

Drake cleaned and freshened the bedding, replenished the food, and topped off the water for FloJo and each of the four remaining cats. He'd come to enjoy the scent of the cedar shavings and well-cared-for animals. He examined each animal and documented any return of nerve function. FloJo's recovery continued. She could now stand and take steps. The four cats treated with D-44 after FloJo had also shown improvement, demonstrating subtler signs of recovery.

Their success defied all odds. It was like a couple of guys in a garage developing a breakthrough in computer technology. Improbable but real—no experimental treatment for spinal cord injury had ever shown such promise.

Beyond that, Rizz's self-treatment with D-44 had occurred at least ten years ahead of when, if all testing went well, human testing would have been allowed. The risks were profound. So far none of the cats had shown any ill effects, but it was too early to presume safety, and none of the cats had ever been given a second dose.

The repeat dose Rizz so aggressively sought would be another giant leap into a dangerous unknown. Besides which, they had to keep use of D-44 secret. Drake had Kip lined up to provide screening lab tests, but generally the first human subject would be watched continuously and tested exhaustively. They were doing neither of those things with Rizz.

There was no doubt that a drug this powerful could sicken or kill. Drake remained filled with misgivings, but Rizz had no hesitation.

Did Drake have the right to withhold a second dose because of his fears?

Rizz understood the stakes better than anyone. But if Rizz suffered adverse effects or died, Drake's already burdened conscience would make him a victim as well. They were in this together. He stared at the locked medication refrigerator.

They faced another D-44 crisis—challenge to their ownership. With Rizz's paralysis and the likelihood of Drake losing his career, they'd need money. D-44's potential value was so great some had been willing to kill for it. Now it was uncertain if Drake, Rizz, and Jon had the legal right to sell it.

Acting as their attorney, Jon's wife had not only failed to safeguard their intellectual property rights, but she'd falsified documents and signed a contract selling D-44 to a Swiss pharmaceutical corporation. Thankfully, she'd delivered nothing more than research data before her death.

The Swiss firm believed it had a legal claim.

The university's patent office posed another, perhaps greater threat.

Drake, Rizz, and Jon had trusted Faith to handle the legalities. Now they had to deal with the disaster her criminal behavior had wrought.

Business and intellectual property law were not areas Drake held expertise in. He was a physician and medical researcher. He did know enough to recognize that defeating both a giant multinational corporation and a massive university in court was a long shot—and would be hugely expensive.

Could the law be trusted to protect their rightful ownership of D-44 in the end? Drake's experience with the courts and "justice" left him queasy with distrust.

They could lose everything. He ran his hands through his hair and took deep breaths. The laboratory's exposed pipes and radiators clanked and knocked in the background. What should he do?

He had to look several uncertain steps ahead. The challenge was similar to the critical thinking that guided him in the dynamic of treating crashing patients—if this response then that, if that response then this, and so on. The variables were unpredictable and constantly changing. The objective in the Crash Room was singular and never in doubt—the impact on the patient's well-being guided every decision.

What should guide his decisions with D-44?

He stepped over to the window. The sun lit the crumbled asphalt surface of the parking lot below.

After a moment he turned, went to the medication refrigerator, then unlocked it. He surveyed the contents.

It would take all they had.

Chapter 22

2:40 p.m.

Drake headed down the hospital corridor, glad to find it empty. Though the administrative wing rarely had patient or visitor traffic, there was generally staff headed to or from medical records. With news of his criminal history and civil suit spreading throughout the hospital, he preferred to avoid contact. The hospital areas outside of the ER felt like foreign territory—as if he didn't belong.

He opened the oak door to the administrative executive offices. His mouth was dry. He looked at his hands, then clenched and unclenched them to lose the tingly sensation.

Called to the office of the President of Medical Affairs twice in less than twelve hours. He'd been there once in his previous four years of emergency medicine residency training—and that was to learn he'd won an award.

Torrins' text message had reached Drake as he was finishing up at the lab. He'd been summoned to meet Torrins at 2:45 p.m.—fifteen minutes before his ER shift started. The head of Medical Affairs had not shared the reason, but it sure as hell was not an award. Drake's gut clenched. Would he be allowed to work his shift?

This could be the ax falling. Jim Torrins could be planning to tell Drake his career was over, that he could no longer care for patients at Memorial Hospital—or anywhere. Ever.

Drake knocked on the administrator's partially open door.

"Come in, Drake." Torrins sat at his desk. He glanced up then returned his attention to a document on his desk. He held a pen in his hand. "I heard the anchorwoman is doing well. That's good."

“Yes.” Drake would normally acknowledge Dr. Stone, the paramedics, the ER team, and others, but the life saved was not why he'd been summoned. He held his breath.

Torrins kept his head trained on the paper in front of him. The rumpled look he'd evidenced in their middle-of-the-night meeting had disappeared. He wore a pressed white shirt and a red power tie with a gold cravat pin. Every strand of his razor-cut salt-and-pepper hair was in place. His dark pin-striped suit coat hung on a padded hanger along the cherry wood wall. He peered through reading glasses perched low on his nose.

“I've reviewed the Ogren situation and your domestic abuse report. All I have to say on that issue is use your judgment. Despite what Kline and others may believe, it's none of their concern. It's your responsibility as a physician to do what you believe is right—period. Neither I nor anyone else has any business attempting to influence you.”

Torrins signed the document, set the pen down, then looked Drake in the eye.

“The rest of what we will discuss today directly involves the hospital and, unfortunately, falls under my responsibility as president of medical affairs. This,” he indicated the sheet of paper on his desk, “is the closest thing to good news I've got for you. And it isn't much.” He held up the sheet. “This is a temporary continuance of duties release. It allows you to work in the ER, get paid, and keep your license until the Medical Board rules on you next week.” He shook his head. “If it weren't for the fact that the shootings have left us short-staffed in the ER, I don't think I could have gotten even this.” He set the paper aside. “The other news I have for you is bad or worse.”

Drake stood in front of the large desk. The wood-paneled walls and lack of windows made him feel as if he were trapped in a box. The office was warm but his fingers were ice. Memory spiraled back—sixteen years old and standing in front of the judge's bench in Cincinnati juvenile court. Torrins’ expression reminded him of the judge's—pained but resolute.

Drake once again felt helpless.

“Kline wanted you gone yesterday. University risk management thinks you’re radioactive because of the lawsuit threats, and the word is the Medical School will cut all ties to you. My Medical Board contact says your license revocation decision looks open-and-shut." Torrins spread his hands.

It seemed as if the air had left the room. *No!*

He'd known it was coming—he'd always known—but now that it was happening it seemed unreal.

"A history of a felony assault conviction broadcast all over the state and a civil suit alleging racism and assault. The media is in a frenzy. All with Minnesota licensed, University Medical School accredited, residency enrolled, Memorial Hospital employed Dr. Drake Cody dead center." He took off his glasses. "You know the score. What else can the authorities do?"

Drake could still picture the crutch he'd used to protect his brother. He could hear the sound of the aluminum strut whistling thorough the air as he'd swung it. He recalled the feeling in his hands as it had impacted the big skinhead's face. Then his fingers on the throat of the second skinhead, the snapping twigs sensation as the airway fractured and collapsed.

He'd almost killed those who'd attacked his brother so many years earlier. He regretted how badly they'd been hurt, but he didn't accept the legal judgment of guilt. The trial had been a travesty.

"I was sixteen years old. They hurt my brother. I defended him." The court's verdict had nothing to do with the guilt that gnawed deep inside him. Those regrets came from the court of his conscience and had nothing to do with his arrest and conviction.

Torrins' expression softened for a moment, then his administrator's face returned.

"We can't retry your case. You were convicted. It is what it is. I'm sorry. If we had an emergency medicine physician available that could handle what comes into our ER, I'd have been forced to cut you loose immediately." He put his glasses back on. "I'll keep you working as long as I can. The Medical Board meets next week. I'd suggest you make plans."

Drake swallowed. A bitter taste filled his mouth. The floor shifted underneath him. His stomach plummeted and for a moment he was lightheaded.

It was really going to happen. They were going to take being a doctor away from him. *No!*

He'd been forced to kill and had others attempt to kill him. He'd been locked in a place alone among monsters. He'd failed the person closest to him. His mother and his best friend now both suffered paralysis. He'd almost lost Rachelle and the children he loved more than anything. He blinked.

In spite of all that—perhaps because of all that—he felt a hollowness greater than any he could remember.

His life as a doctor had just received a death sentence. The grief struck so hard he didn't know if he could remain upright.

Chapter 23

Clara exited the hospital stairwell after her mid-morning stair workout.

She'd climbed strong despite little sleep. Dan's late-night visit had been unexpected but glorious. The fevered middle-of-the-night workout and shuddering bliss his body provided had made the few hours of sleep she'd got restful. She couldn't get enough of him. She knew he felt the same.

Underneath her lab coat Clara was sweating. She wore a white coat over her workout gear when she slipped to and from the southeast stairwell. It was rare that anyone used those stairs so she was able to run her eight floors up and eight floors down in isolation. Every day she completed the circuit twice—once in mid-morning and again in the afternoon. She pushed herself so hard that sometimes she became light-headed and nauseated. Lately she allowed herself a quarter of a granola bar before each workout.

On the rare days she wasn't at the hospital, she ran outside. Taking off from her Calhoun Beach Club condominium, she would circuit Lake of the Isles, Lake Calhoun, and Lake Harriet. She could punish herself on those days.

It paid off. Dan relished her endurance. She could take a lot and give back in kind. There could be no way his wife could match what Clara could do. She revisited their frantic, almost savage, sex sessions.

God, he was magnificent. And so in love with her!

She wiped her brow as she swiped her ID card to open her private office. As the hospital's clinical information technology head and lab services chief, she ran two departments that each typically required at least one alpha-level performer. She scanned the door-mounted placard:

Clara Zeitman, PhD Clinical Laboratory Science, MS Health Informatics
Chief of Laboratory Services and Health Information Management

Her position and titles were nice, but the absence of the degree that meant everything tormented her.

Every day the shame of their moronic misjudgment raged within her.

Clara opened the door and entered her office, which was windowless but bright white with high-output fluorescent lighting. The air conditioning kept the room in the mid-sixties. The negative air flow left the air sterile and scented with a hint of disinfectant. The computer fans sounded their soft, continuous whirring. She had her keyboard and display screens positioned on the horseshoe-shaped desk such that when she occupied the lone chair she felt as if she were at her personal NASA command center.

The rear wall held a door marked with a biohazard symbol and a sign reading “Laboratory access. No unauthorized personnel”. As head of Laboratory Services, she was the only one authorized to use this entry.

Her science knowledge and commitment to precision made management of the laboratory little challenge. The physician pathologist who was the licensed head of laboratory services knew his stuff but recognized Clara's competence. He left her free to oversee the day-to-day operations. She worked hard to make sure he did very little.

The laboratory staff were highly educated, skilled, and conscientious. The work attracted intelligent and self-motivated people. The lab technologists weren’t her friends, but they feared her disapproval, which worked out better. The lab earned high marks from the physician staff.

Her autonomy in healthcare information technology was even greater. The computer network and display screens allowed her to monitor virtually all activity within the hospital at a glance. In her sixteen years at Memorial, she'd seen the hospital's data management explosion and oversaw the conversion to electronic health records.

As the technology grew, so did her expertise and importance.

It surprised her that the administration did not recognize how dependent the hospital was on her. Even the giant software vendors and support staff were only posturing when they pretended to question the system alterations she suggested. They did what she said.

Most of the administrative and medical personnel had an uneasy alliance with the technology. Even among the IT staff, there was no one who fully understood the intricacies of her network. None of the doctors had anything but a rudimentary grasp. It was beyond them. *Beyond everyone.* When problems arose, they sought out Clara like hikers lost in a hostile wilderness. She was the system's undisputed master.

Clara liked it that way.

Clara had tried to impress Dan with her knowledge and skills. It did not seem to matter to him. In their short but magical time together, she'd come to understand that his love for her transcended their daily lives.

She noted the time. A change into scrubs and a new white coat, then she'd make her visits to the wards and ICUs. Unlike most laboratory and IT people, Clara liked leaving her office and spending time in the hospital patient care areas. She said it helped her do her job better. People were impressed.

The truth was that putting on the white coat and providing information that influenced patient care decisions was the closest she could get to where she deserved to be. She decided to visit the surgical ICU first.

***

As Clara sat at a computer monitor in the nurses' station of the surgical ICU a grating voice arose from behind her. She winced, recognizing the staff physician she hated more than any other.

"Hey lab-girl, how about you get moving on the culture results, huh?" Every time Dr. Bart Rainey opened his mouth, people flinched.

"Hey, you hear me, lab-lady?" the giant surgeon practically hollered as he scanned a chart. "I've been waiting on sensitivities on bed eight's infection forever. What's the hold up?"

"Black Bart," as the nurses secretly called the almost seven-foot-tall, black-haired surgeon, talked to non-doctors like he was addressing lower life forms. He was notorious for having made nurses cry.

He made a special effort to put Clara down in front of others. She had a PhD and requested that people address her as "doctor." Most physicians and hospital personnel did. Bart Rainey scoffed and seemed to take pleasure in demeaning her.

"It's an anaerobic bacteria, Dr. Rainey," Clara said. "Meticulous culture requirements and very slow growth. We'll have the sensitivities as fast as is possible." The fawning manner that her position demanded made her want to retch. "I think meropenem would be the best antibiotic choice pending results. The organism is certain to be multi-resistant."

"Well, little missy, I know it's multi-resistant—that's why I need the sensitivities. Why don't you just get the tests done and leave the thinking and decision-making to those of us who are doctors?"

Clara kept her head hidden behind one of the unit's computer consoles. Her heart pounded in her throat, flame stoked her core. She imagined herself a stick of dynamite with the fuse burning.

The secretary paged Rainey to the phone. Clara sensed his giant mass moving away. He hadn't gotten within five feet of her, yet she could smell the cologne he used to cover the smell of his brutish carcass.

How had such a middle-of-the-road intellect been judged to be the right stuff? *Him and so many others.*

Forty-five medical schools. Forty-five selection committees. Each had said she wasn't good enough. Instead they'd selected cretins like Bart Rainey.

The selection committees were imbecilic, sexist, corrupt bastards. A bitter taste visited her tongue.

Rainey left the nursing station. Her muscles relaxed. One day she would explode on one of these unworthy physician pretenders.

Despite all the years that had passed, her resentment still burned. The fire of her outrage had an endless fuel supply. *Not good enough!*

She'd been valedictorian of both her high school and NYU class. Her I.Q. made MENSA geeks self-conscious. She'd blown the Medical College Admission test out of the water. She'd even volunteered with sick kids at the Children's Hospital during high school and college, documenting the boo-hoo, look-how-caring-I-am crap the selection committees loved.

Her application materials glistened. On paper she'd been the perfect candidate.

Health records, counseling, and her personal problems were all privileged information and by law could not be accessed—or so she'd naively believed.

She'd been granted interviews at every medical school she'd applied to, and that only happened for the very best candidates.

Then the actual visits. She met face-to-face with physicians, psychologists, and counselors. Clara knew just what they wanted to hear. She'd laid it all out for them. There'd been awkward moments but there'd been no doubt in her mind that she ranked among the strongest of applicants.

And then the inexplicable...

After months of waiting, the letters had arrived on medical school letterheads. "We regret to report...," "more qualified candidates than positions...," "Unfortunately...," blah, blah. Rejected by all—even the schools that were not remotely worthy of her.

She'd tried a second year—humiliating as it was. Again the rigged system chose losers.

Dr. "Black Bart" Rainey and others like him proved her point. Assholes or middling intellects that had somehow been judged among "the best and brightest," while she was not.

He'd played on a championship collegiate basketball team. Clara knew that was the difference. Somehow the jock-sniffing old-boys' club thought that meant something.

Selection committees seemed to base their decisions on sex, physical attractiveness, quotas, political correctness, insider favoritism, or their ridiculous notions of character.

As head of Information Technology for the hospital, Claire had access to the data for every physician on the hospital staff. Very few had been anywhere near her as a candidate. She measured herself against Rainey and every MD she met—rarely was it a contest.

Even some of those who seemed decent did not belong. The startling news about that ER doctor, Drake Cody, meant he'd lied on his application. He'd cheated someone such as herself out of their deserved opportunity to be a physician—stolen someone's life dream.

Her failure to become a doctor was a wound that would not heal. The rejections as "not good enough" had affected her like exposure to a lethal dose of radiation. The toxicity had penetrated to her marrow.

Because she hadn't been allowed to obtain the MD title she deserved, she had to take shit from assholes like Bart Rainey.

Because she'd been denied, she had to live forever with the patronizing conceit and condescension of her loathsome parents.

Dr. Carl Zeitman, head of the department of Medicine, international chair of Endocrinology at Duke—her father and a jerk of the first order.

Dr. Freida Zeitman, staff pathologist also at Duke, international bridge champion—Clara's mother and a partner in a marriage of careers and egos that left no room for anything else.

Medicine was the only career worthy of a Zeitman.

Physician, attorney, or scientist were the only careers anyone in her mother's family would accept. Prestige and self-importance were the air her parents breathed.

Her parents' superiority to Clara had been affirmed for them by the medical school rejections. Their condescension and transparently false sympathy continued to this day. Nothing Clara had ever done had made them happier than her failure to equal or surpass them.

They'd used their power and contacts in a way opposite that of other parents. She believed they'd used their influence to keep their daughter *out* of medical school.

She'd been cheated—by her parents, by the medical establishment, by every person with an MD degree that was not her equal.

Bart Rainey. Drake Cody. So many others. They'd all stolen from her.

They owed her. They should pay. She'd started to collect but nowhere near enough—

Her cell phone vibrated. She retrieved it and scanned the number. Dan! Never before had he called her in the daytime.

Last night so special. In trouble he'd reached out to her—her passion erasing his pain. Now a call in the day—their love expanding!

She wondered if Dan could get Bart Rainey thrown off the hospital's staff. Her man had power beyond that of his magnificent body. He'd do anything for her.

He cared more about her than himself.

Their love was like no other...

Chapter 24

Mesh exited the Normandale Racquet Club doors, then stopped and held them open as a young blond woman with Spandex-clad legs and a puffy parka scampered toward him. Her breath fogged in the freezing air. She did not acknowledge him or his manners. He recognized her as she passed. One of many women he'd seen with Dan. He pulled his coat tight as the sub-zero wind chill bit.

Had he convinced Dan? Did Dan believe that an abuse conviction was unavoidable? Did he accept that if Beth divorced him, he'd lose everything and be sent to jail?

Reading Dan had never been easy. He didn't react to things like normal people.

Anyone else would be a quivering mess, but not Dan. He never showed fear. When they'd first met, that was one of the things Mesh had admired.

Mesh beeped his car open and climbed in. He started the car and waited for it to warm up.

"Big Dan" Ogren, Dan's father, had given Mesh a job as a lot boy for Ogren Automotive in high school. He and Dan junior had shared job duties. They were both seventeen, but Dan looked twenty-one. Tall, muscular, a natural athlete and, Mesh felt embarrassed noticing, strikingly handsome. Mesh attended South High School but knew of Dan from media coverage of his hockey stardom at Edina High School.

They'd both lost a parent to cancer four years earlier but had little else in common. Mesh missed his father every day. Dan's loss of his mother didn't seem to affect him at all. It was another of many things that had initially impressed Mesh.

The dealership job involved washing the cars, ferrying new and used vehicles, running parts, cleaning asphalt, hauling tires, and dozens of other tasks.

Mesh's dad, a bookkeeper for Ogren Automotive, had died when Mesh was in grade school. Before the cancer took him, his dad had worked for the man everyone called Big Dan.

After his dad's death, Mesh's mother worked in a dry cleaning shop. Money was tight and Mr. Ogren sometimes helped out. Mesh recognized his kindness. Mesh's job was one more thing Mr. Ogren did for them.

Mesh worked as hard as he could.

Dan screwed off continuously. They were not closely supervised, as the job often involved moving cars from one dealership to another, running parts, or giving rides to customers whose cars were being repaired.

Dan grabbed the driving jobs while Mesh covered by doing the grunt work.

While Mesh took care of the car lot chores, Dan sometimes "borrowed" vehicles and picked up whichever of several girls he was currently seeing. He had sexual adventures in the dealership cars while "on the clock."

Mesh had kissed one girl in his life. Dan had been sexually active since the ninth grade.

Mesh was amazed and envious.

Dan started drinking and smoking weed on the job. Just knowing what Dan was up to made Mesh a nervous wreck.

Dan never showed any stress.

One day Dan gave a repair customer a ride home and didn't return for over two hours. The lot manager confronted him when he returned. Mesh could tell Dan was high but he never blinked. He spun a yarn about the customer insisting he take her to the bank and having to wait for her. They'd been stuck in traffic. He told the manager to call her and confirm. He stared the manager down and the matter was dropped.

Dan later told Mesh what had happened when the lady customer invited him in to her house after the ten-minute drive.

Mesh found it hard to breathe just hearing about things he'd only read about or imagined. Dan just shrugged his shoulders and laughed. Cooler than cool.

Mesh had found everything about Dan compelling. Fearless, unshakable, a star athlete, a woman-killer-—all the things Mesh thought mattered. For years Mesh admired Dan.

Mesh's cell phone rang. Dan's name on the display. He'd likely not left the locker room yet. He liked lounging naked about the showers and whirlpool area. So damn proud of his huge package. Mesh triggered his earpiece. “Yes, Dan.”

“If I get ownership of Ogren Auto before the June payments are due, would that affect my, er, situation. You know, regarding the financial stuff you mentioned?”

“Your father's not *compos mentis*. He can't understand, so he can't participate in a legal action. That's why you have power of attorney. His will is solid—you'll gain ownership through inheritance. Ownership now would give us options but no silver bullet. Besides, there's nothing that can be done to speed it up.”

“What about from the senior home money? It was a buy-in deal, right?”

“When your father dies, ninety percent of his buy-in at Noble Village goes to his estate. Again, there's no way to get that beforehand. Besides, you are already fully debt-leveraged. You can thank listening to Kline for that.”

Kline, the accountant who’d somehow made it to CEO of the hospital. Mesh didn’t think the guy was competent. He’d steered Dan into several deals that had gone belly up—a big part of Dan's losses.

“Business-wise, things have to take their course,” Mesh said. “Your inheritance and the Noble Village money will not be enough to solve your problems. It's already accounted for. If you have more questions, let's meet later. This is not for the phone. I'm headed to a meeting with the finance guys now.”

“Email me an update on where things stand after the meeting.”

Mesh heard a click and the connection ended.

He'd explained all this to Dan several times. The guy wasn't dumb, but nothing about business ever seemed to stick.

Mesh pulled out of the parking lot onto France Avenue. He had fifteen minutes to make the meeting. Ogren Automotive now had an umbrella of six dealerships, a lease company, a parts company, and a finance operation. The business had become huge and administratively complex.

Dan had poor judgment, access to the company's money, and zero discipline. He'd pissed away hundreds of thousands of misappropriated company dollars in drugs, gambling, and ill-advised investments. Mesh had worked hard to pound home the message that even a simple audit of the company would lead to Dan being criminally prosecuted.

Dan had few inhibitions, no scruples, and rarely listened. From the days of the car lot Mesh had been linked to Dan. First it had been due to Dan's magnetism. Later it was obligation. It was a link Mesh wished had never been forged.

***

Homicide/Major Crimes office

Aki Hamada found Farley focused on the computer screen.

"What have you found on Ogren?" Aki asked, as he sat at his desk alongside Farley's.

"Not much for convictions but he's no stranger to trouble. Been arrested and questioned but other than a couple DUIs nothing has ever stuck." Farley turned to Aki. "I have more for you but I have a question. Why did we get assigned this case? The captain said someone higher up requested you. I know it's high profile but it still seems weird."

"Good instincts, partner." Aki rolled his chair closer and lowered his voice. "I'm still on probation following a complaint from last spring. An asshole with a restraining order broke his wife's jaw and got off with nothing. He claimed that after he was released I smashed his head against a car and threatened him. I was there but the weird thing was the bastard fell—just like he said his wife had. So now someone requests me for the Ogren domestic abuse case. Does that make sense?"

"Sounds like a defense attorney's dream," Farley said. "That high-up someone must think you're so good that won't matter."

"Yeah, and OJ never hurt anyone."

Farley cocked his head. "So what gives?"

"There's been outside influence stinking up this case from the start." He paused. "I hate to poison you with my cynical take but consider this. Maybe we weren't picked because we have the best chance of getting Ogren convicted. It might be because we have the worst."

Chapter 25

RV Campground, suburb

The image in the mirror scared Beth. The ER doctor had told her to expect to look and feel worse before starting to improve. She looked hideous. And felt terrible.

Something struck the side of the RV and Beth jumped, her heart in her throat. She crouched and peered out the windows. A dead limb lay against the RV. Her breathing slowed and her hands steadied. The strong wind battered the naked trees and made the cattail marsh to the north ripple and thrash.

The attorney had first connected with Beth two hours earlier. The wait for the lawyer's follow-up call seemed an eternity.

The lawyer had been businesslike and she'd emphasized Beth's safety. She'd advised Beth to avoid any contact with Dan and not to let him or others know her whereabouts. Beth had already removed the battery from her old phone and purchased a replacement on her way to the RV park. Her new phone could not be tracked.

The lawyer recommended they file for a "restraining order" against Dan.

"Abusers often escalate when divorce is threatened," the attorney warned. "Women are killed by abusive husbands every day. A third of the women murdered in the U.S. are killed by their husband or partner." It wasn't the first time she'd heard this.

Beth's voice had cracked as she'd given the okay to file the restraining order against Dan.

The attorney didn't pretend that money didn't matter to her. She'd admitted that the prospect of a big money settlement had appeal. Her retainer was startlingly high and she wanted payment immediately.

After being lied to for so long, the lawyer's honesty held appeal. Beth had emailed the prenuptial document and used PayPal to deliver the pricey retainer. Dan was reckless and loose with money, which had made it easy for Beth to build up a nest egg of her own. The attorney promised to review the prenuptial document, initiate the protective order process, and call Beth back.

Shortly after the initial call, Beth had drifted into a medication-fogged sleep. She'd awakened sweaty and fighting for breath twenty minutes later, with no idea where she was. Awareness had not brought relief.

She counted the minutes as she waited to hear back from the attorney.

Big gusts of wind shook the RV. She trembled inside as her fear and self-doubts grew. Could she do what needed to be done?

***

She jumped as her phone trilled. The number showed "blocked." Beth hit "answer" and held the phone to her ear, afraid to speak.

"Hello? Beth, this is your attorney, Nancy Dudley, getting back to you."

"It didn't show on caller ID."

"Good job. Don't talk to anyone until you know who they are. Later I may instruct you on comments for the media, but for now I recommend you talk only to me. I've got a number of things moving. I've filed for the restraining order, reviewed the prenuptial agreement, and spoken with a contact of mine in the district attorney's office. I know everything feels out of control right now. I wanted to give you an idea of what the future may hold. "

The attorney, similar to the women's advocate in the ER, seemed to know what was happening in Beth's head. Her future? The future scared the hell out of her. She wanted to go to sleep and wake up safe from Dan with her new life ahead.

Dan. Her husband. The man she'd been in love with. The one she'd believed had loved her. An unfeeling animal.

"Can you hold a moment?" the attorney asked.

"Yes." Beth had the urge to hang up. Everything felt out of control. *No!* There could be no going back. She had to follow through.

But she was so very afraid...

She flashed back to lying on the floor after Dan's attack, her head reeling, the taste of blood in her mouth.

She heard him moving. She looked up. He'd connected Kidder's leash to his collar and held her puppy dangling off the ground. Kidder's neck stretched grotesquely and twisted as Dan hung her. Her puppy's eyes bulged, his legs swimming in air as he made horrible choking sounds.

"No!" she screamed. She tried to get up but he placed his foot on her chest, pinning her to the floor.

His eyes locked on hers, his expression flat, his tone matter-of-fact. "You pissed me off. You tell no one. I can do this and more to anyone who needs it." He removed his foot.

She fought to get to her feet but before she could, he flipped her near-dead pup to the floor next to her.

"Did you hear me? Hello? Are you there?" the attorney's voice sounded from the phone.

"I'm sorry." Beth said. "I-I'm here."

"I'm not sure if you heard me. Let me repeat. I reviewed the domestic violence clause in the prenuptial and it's clear-cut. A conviction completely nullifies the agreement. There'd be no limits in the case of divorce."

"I never wanted a prenup," Beth said. "He worried about his father's money."

"Common these days."

"My mother made me put in the violence clause. My grandmother had been a victim. I never knew."

"It's often hidden, perhaps even worse back then," the attorney said. "I spoke with a contact I have in the district attorney's office about the case. Apparently the ER doctor who treated you is a prosecutor's dream—sympathetic and credible. He's in the news for a previous conviction, but it's unlikely that will be admissible or reflect on his testimony for your case. The part we need to improve is your report. You told the doctor and the police that you had fallen. We can correct that. The law recognizes intimidation and extenuating circumstances. I'll arrange for you to amend your statement with the police."

“I don't want to go to the police station. Please.” She wanted to go to sleep and wake up when it was all done.

“We can avoid that,” the lawyer said. “I'll make everything as smooth as possible, but you need to understand what to expect going forward. You'll have to be strong. It's not easy. Many abusers plead out before trial to a minimal offense and are sentenced to anger management classes and little more. Because of the prenuptial and your husband’s wealth, they'll almost certainly fight for a complete wash. That means this case will likely go to trial.”

Each word increased the weight of Beth’s fatigue and pain. Could she go through with it?

Damn him! It had to stop. She took a huge breath. Just a step at a time. One foot in front of the other until things came to an end.

“If he's convicted of even the most minor abuse offense, the prenuptial agreement is void and you're in the position of any other wife seeking divorce. Actually, considerably better,” the attorney said. “Judgments in cases of spousal violence are invariably favorable to the abused. You'd likely be awarded most of his assets.”

Beth knew it was positive news, but it didn't feel like it. How many women had to sit in court and face that humiliation? But it shouldn’t get to that. She hoped it wouldn’t get to that.

Her hands shook. It was all a nightmare.

Tears ran out of her good eye, the other still too swollen. Could she do what needed to be done?

She knew she was not truly alone, but she felt more isolated than ever before in her life.

She'd taken the first step. There could be no turning back. It was as if she'd jumped off a cliff with water far below—now she was plunging through the air in what seemed like a forever fall bracing for the impact.

Chapter 26

An hour into his shift, and Drake hadn't had a spare second. His call to Beth Ogren in the minutes between his grim meeting with Jim Torrins and the beginning of his shift had not been answered. He'd hoped to check on her injury status and encourage her to keep herself safe. U.S. statistics showed three women a day were killed by abusive partners. The unanswered call increased Drake's concern for Beth Ogren's safety.

The incoming stream of patients had him and the rest of the staff running. The noise and nonstop action suited him. It left little time to worry about his disastrous personal predicaments.

In the time he had left, he wanted to fully engage in the work he loved.

He placed a patient chart in the rack for discharge with one hand while grabbing one from the patient-to-be-seen rack with the other. He scanned the paperwork as he headed for the new patient's cubicle.

The meeting with Torrins had his mind spinning.

"Whoa—Dr. Cody? Hold up, please." An unfamiliar, deep voice cut through the ER din from behind.

He turned to find a large man in a charcoal three-piece suit pushing through the corridor towards him. Among the gowns and scrubs of the ER patients and staff, he stood out like a crow in a flock of sparrows. He was about six feet tall, with wide shoulders, a big head, a walrus mustache, and thinning brown hair. An expensive-looking briefcase hung from one oversized hand. He looked to be in his fifties and wore a big smile.

"Do I know you?" Drake could not have forgotten meeting this guy.

"You haven't had the pleasure, Doctor." He held out a business card. "S. Lloyd Anderson. Attorney-at-law, CPA, and arbitrator of all things legal, commerce, and conflict related. You have problems. I find solutions.

The man was as broad as a collegiate lineman and fit-appearing. Underneath bird's nest eyebrows, his eyes were green and lively. The tanned face showed deep creases. The guy could be older than Drake first thought but he radiated energy. His expression suggested he amused himself.

The man extended a hand.

Drake shook the big mitt.

The clothes, ring, and briefcase all spoke of style and the quality. Under it all the guy looked a bit shaggy. His burly dimensions, the eyebrows, the hair on the back of his hands—he looked like a Viking raider who'd undergone a makeover.

"May I?" The attorney raised the briefcase, setting it on the small counter outside an exam room. He opened it. "I know you're busy here, but we're already way behind in protecting your interests." He seemed quite at ease for a non-medical person standing in the hallway of a bustling ER. "Neither of us have time to waste."

The guy reminded Drake of Rizz and rare others he'd met who seemed at home in whatever setting they found themselves. How had he been allowed into the department?

"You've made a mistake," Drake said. "I can't afford an attorney." His awareness of his need for legal help had become greater with each of his issues. As a resident at the end of his many years of training, he had no money and massive debt. "Are you looking for pro bono work?"

"Lord above! Don't even say pro bono around me." Again the self-amused smile. "I charge top dollar and I'm worth it. I'm aware of your problems related to medical licensure, right to practice, and the threatened civil actions against you citing racial discrimination and assault. Additionally, I'm able and eager to represent you and your colleagues in protecting your intellectual property rights to D-44."

What the heck? The attorney had succinctly summarized the issues that threatened to end Drake's dreams. The man's words and manner impressed, but Drake had spoken to him for less than a minute—and had nothing to pay him with. *And how does he know so much?*

The attorney pulled out a sheet of paper then held it out to Drake. "This is quick, but your situation demands immediate action. Please read it over and sign—"

"Wait a minute. I don't know you. I can't pay you. And how do you know so much about me anyway?"

"My apologies. I thought Rizz had informed you. Dr. Michel Rizzini is a good friend. He contacted me. My retainer has been paid. Whatever service you require I'll be compensated for. If you are comfortable having me, I simply need you," he clicked a gold pen and offered it, "to sign this document establishing our attorney-client relationship."

Rizz knew the best and brightest in the cities. Drake trusted his judgment. The fact that Rizz had warned them against using Faith for their legal work echoed. If only they'd listened.

"Doc, you can fire me at any time but I need to get moving on things."

"Who's paying you? Who will I owe?" Rizz always seemed to have money for partying and indulging, but no way did he have big-time attorney retainer bucks.

"Talk to Rizz about that. For now, please just sign. There's no time to waste." He pulled his sleeve back and scanned a Rolex on a furry wrist. "I need to get to work trying to save your ass."

Chapter 27

Quentin Jackson placed a sliver of crack in the glass pipe's bowl. He snapped his lighter, set the product bubbling, and inhaled smooth and long. Too fast and he'd torch his throat. He'd done that once. It had hurt to swallow for two days.

He held the smoke in as each beat of his heart floated his head higher. The rush started there but passed like an electric current throughout his body.

He exhaled long and slow as he rode the rush.

The girl sat cross-legged, smiling as she watched “Scooby-Doo” on the flat screen in his living room.

Her momma had told Q the girl had “Downer Symptom,” and the bitch wasn't even trying to be funny. How messed up are you when you can't even get your kid's medical condition right? Seventeen years old but she looked like twelve. The girl's face was kinda whack but she was always smiling. Her momma had been leaving her with Q since he first sold product to her a while back.

Now all the crack-momma wanted was some supply now and again, and the girl worked for him. She knew how to clean house and cook. She did dishes and washed clothes—just like he had his own maid. And she didn't cost him anything beyond the product he gave her momma. The girl didn't even want to get high. TV and Fruit Loops cereal—she'd smile and be happy.

Best of all, she carried his product whenever he went out to sell or deliver—his very own drug mule. A minor and messed up—she could be caught with twenty pounds of flake and an assault rifle and no way she'd be prosecuted. He wished she'd been around before. She could have saved him from the eighteen months hard-time he'd done in Stillwater for possession with intent.

Q loaded fifty Vicodin tablets into his food processor and flipped it to "grate." He let it chatter and whine until the pills were powder. He kept his drugs, tools, scales, processor and other equipment in a reinforced trunk with a strong lock. He only took his drugs and equipment out to process or prepare for transfer and sale. The rest of the time he kept everything stashed and locked away.

Q hadn't been out in public holding even a single joint since the ER shit went down. He took every precaution. You couldn't do business if you were locked away—and business was very good. With the girl doing all his carrying and his other precautions, he was damn near untouchable.

After Q was arrested in the ER, his attorney had pushed it as a race deal and drummed up pressure. Barry Ward cost plenty but was one smart law-boy. Q had got out in less than twenty-four hours. A few days after that, the charges were dropped. The police and courts were backing off anything that looked racial.

He smiled. Getting the charges dropped had been good, but now it looked like his arrest and the beating he took could pay off big time.

The lawyer had called and said they'd found the ER doctor had a previous assault conviction. The lawyer said both the hospital and university had deep pockets, and they'd want to avoid the bad publicity of a trial. He figured they'd pay plenty to settle. A chance to score some real money. *Hell, yeah!*

The ER dude hadn't been like any doctor he'd seen. No regular white-bread doctor could kick Q's ass.

Q's ribs had finally stopped hurting and his broken nose looked okay now.

The good part was that Q's injuries had scored him a ton of oxys from the doctor who fixed his nose, and then a mess of oxys, Dilaudid, and Vicodin from the clinics and Urgent Care doctors he'd visited while his face looked bad and his ribs were healing up.

He'd visited sixteen different clinics and ERs in the first five days after his injuries and multiple more in the weeks following. He'd milked his injuries to the max, altered the prescriptions for bigger quantities, and then filled them at drugstores all over the city. With all he scored plus his regular sources, he had a huge stash accumulated. He ground up much of the Vicodin and codeine tablets, then tripled the volume by adding synthetic THC, bath salts, and talc. His custom "value-added" product got people off big time and it sold for top dollar. The Dilaudid, oxys, Percocets, and other high-test prescription narcotics were gold right out of the bottle.

Q's chemistry teacher mother hated how he lived. She'd pushed junior scientist experiment kits at him since he was a kid. He'd started getting high big time in eighth grade. Right from the first time, there was nothing he enjoyed more. He liked every kind of high. His appreciation helped him in business. He fashioned some truly righteous product. He hadn't turned out the way she wanted, but too bad.

Some of the street dogs called him Doctor Science. He liked that.

He used a small spatula to remove the powder from the blender and placed it on wax paper.

Hadn't seen his mother in more than two years. After the first few arrests, she didn't even show for the court appearances. She still called him sometimes. *Whatever.*

What mattered was what those on the street thought. His reputation mattered for business, bitches, and keeping from getting ripped off or beat down. Being big and naturally strong usually kept others from messing with him. He avoided getting physical unless someone pissed him off. He was into making money and staying out of jail. But when he needed to, he could get real.

Q hadn't heard from his mother since the ER arrest when his picture had been damn near everywhere. He'd looked high and ass-kicked. Q had planned on tracking the ER doc down and taking care of business. Nobody could do him and walk.

Wayne, a wannabe banger in the neighborhood, had dissed Q about getting his ass done by a doctor. Said Q had been punked.

Q had beat Wayne's face to jelly. No one else had said anything, but the story of the ER doc kicking his ass was still out there.

The ER boy would never know how lucky he was. If not for this chance at a lawsuit pay-off, Dr. Whitebread had been in line to be dealt with.

With the chance to get rich by suing the hospital and everyone else, Q would let it go—for now. He flicked the lighter and took in another load of smoke. Good thoughts rode the rush.

He had a huge supply of top-dollar product, serious lawsuit money coming, and his little Fruit Loops mule keeping him safe from the police.

Things had never been better.

Chapter 28

Rachelle looked around the room at the others participating in the YMCA's course offering, "Women's Self-Defense"—approximately twenty women of various ages, clad in everything from jeans to designer workout attire. The two policewomen instructors looked fit and capable. They carried themselves like people who knew how to defend themselves and others.

One of the instructors opened the course. "Women are assaulted, raped, or killed every day. Ten women are physically assaulted each minute in the US. It is estimated that more than six hundred women are raped each day. Self-defense is a survival tool for women."

That is what Rachelle sought. A similar course she'd taken years earlier had taught her some basic survival guidelines. She'd used them to help her and the children endure their recent kidnapping and abuse.

The instructor was outlining some of the general cautions that Rachelle knew well. Her mind drifted.

Her constant worry was unhealthy, but she couldn't get herself to accept that she and her family were out of danger. It was different for Drake. He tried to reassure her, but he hadn't lived the life she had. Not that he'd had it easy—definitely not. But he was strong and not afraid of anything.

She was not strong and knew terrible things could happen anytime. She'd been visiting a counselor once a week to help control what the therapist called "hypervigilance and threat anxiety."

The counseling, new security system in their home, and this class were things she did to help get over her fears.

Last night she'd caved in and taken one of her pills. She felt ashamed. It would take time and effort to get stronger but she would not give up. Despite last night's lapse, she had improved.

Kristin and Shane were in the Y's adjoining kid-care gym. They were having a good day.

The second instructor took the floor and began discussing threat awareness and response.

Rachelle's action on the evening of the kidnapping was an example of what *not* to do. She and the kids had been locked in the safety of the townhouse when there was an unexpected knock on the door. Rachelle hadn't recognized the lone woman standing on the stoop for the threat she was. If only she had never unlocked that door.

Rachelle shifted and repositioned her leg. She rubbed the back of her thigh where they'd taken the skin for the graft of her burns. It felt sore.

As she listened to the instructor's cautions, more immediate worries intruded. Drake's record had been discovered. He said he would lose his medical license. She didn't see how that could be.

Drake's conviction had been a mistake. They'd let him go free. Didn't that show they knew they'd been wrong?

She'd had hardly any time with him after he'd awakened and shared the bad news. He'd said little. He shut others out when he faced trouble—that was his way. She understood his distrust of the authorities, but he seemed too readily resigned to losing the career that meant so much to him. As if he was giving up without a fight. That was not her Drake Cody.

She'd called Rizz after Drake left.

***

"Rizz, it's Rachelle." She'd never called Rizz before. She'd gripped the kitchen phone like a lifeline. She didn't know what she expected him to do.

"I knew you'd be calling." As usual he sounded like he was joking. "The answer is 'no.' Sorry to break your heart. I won't run off with you."

"You are ridiculous," she said, but he'd made her smile.

"Ha! I may be many things. Correction—I am many things, including handsome, brilliant, and puppy-dog lovable. One thing I am not is ridiculous."

Drake had once told her that if he had to go to war, Rizz was the guy he'd want at his side. He never quit, and if you lost you'd go down laughing.

The situation they were in was not funny. What could Rizz do? Rachelle feared she'd start crying and make a fool of herself. She took a deep breath.

"I'm worried about what will happen to Drake if he can't work in the ER. He's been told the state medical board is going to take his license away next week." The silence showed the message had ended the joking. "Rizz, he's acting like it's unavoidable. Like he's given up. He's talking about finding a new job." Her voice hitched.

"He's in shock," Rizz said. "It had to have been brutal to have this hanging over his head for so long. We're going to fight this. I've already talked with Jon and lined up a lawyer. One who loves to fight Goliaths. He's the best. Jon is paying his fees. I'm on this full-time now, and once Drake's head clears he'll fight. I'm talking about a kick-ass team, Rachelle. We sure as hell aren't giving up."

Rizz sounded like his cocky, screw-the-system self. Thank God for him.

Rachelle suspected his partying and womanizing hid a lonely and damaged man. Yet Rizz had been brave and selfless enough to have taken a bullet to protect her family. And no one could understand what working in the ER meant to Drake better than Rizz.

"Thank you, Rizz," Her voice cracked and tears welled.

"And Rachelle?"

"Yes?" She sniffed.

"Don't worry, I won't tell Drake about you throwing yourself at me."

"You're sick." She said it with a smile.

"Damn right, I'm sick. I'm sick of people messing with Drake. Sick of having been screwed over by a lying, greedy woman. Sick of having to fight for ownership of our drug, and totally sick of being trapped in this effing wheelchair. Know this, Rachelle—me, Drake, Jon, and our attorney will fight this to the end. You have my word."

***

The instructor was answering a question from one of the students. More content that Rachelle knew well.

While talking with Rizz this morning, it had felt like they couldn't lose. In the time since, her doubts had grown.

What would happen to Drake if he lost his work? What would happen to them?

He loved her and the kids, but she knew his work did something for him they couldn't. Sometimes he was dead quiet, and the most she could get out of him was, "It's a work thing." What he meant was a patient thing, worrying about a patient. Other times she could sense a lightness about him, a quiet happiness. She'd learned it meant there'd been a special case—a patient had done well.

In a way, his passion for the ER made her jealous. Did she ever dominate his thoughts as profoundly as his work did?

There was much about Drake she didn't understand. And it went both ways. They'd both grown up with pain—histories that had brought them together but made sharing difficult. Whether he shared or not, he always held it together. Something about this threat seemed different.

Drake had confronted the neighbor who'd terrified Shane. He didn't say what he'd done, but he assured her the man wouldn't bother them again.

He'd been quiet and held her close as they'd both gone to sleep. He held her like that when things were real bad—now she knew he'd been thinking about his record and their future. It meant everything to her when he held her like that—but this time it had scared her.

She knew now the catastrophic threat that loomed over him—over them.

No matter what happened now, no matter what they faced, she would never give up.

If they were threatened, she would fight. She'd fight hard and dirty.

She would never let Drake or the children down. She was not her mother.

Chapter 29

Mesh pulled out of the France Avenue parking lot. The finance meeting had gone as he expected. Ogren Automotive had a major note due in June. Payment would provide the company a bridge to a solid long-term debt position. If they defaulted on the payments, it meant financial disaster. Mesh had labored hard to get Dan to accept that this potential "crash and burn" scenario was unavoidable if Beth filed for divorce with his prenuptial agreement voided.

Dan's misappropriation of funds had escaped detection so far. Luckily, today's meeting had been with lenders who had limited exposure to the overall picture. The multiple branches of Ogren operations resulted in compartmentalization of data. That set up the opportunity for financial manipulation, and the temptation had been too much for Dan to resist. He knew just enough to shift Ogren funds around and funnel plenty his way. But he'd lost a ton of company money that he hadn't replaced.

Trying to persuade or explain complex situations to Dan was like trying to teach a dog arithmetic. His attention span for anything beyond women, sports or getting high was almost nonexistent. Mesh had to spoon-feed critical information to Dan in "Business for Dummies" level emails and phone calls. Dan seemed proud of the fact that he was not a "detail" guy.

The incredible growth and success of the company that had started with Big Dan buying, repairing, and reselling a damaged 1950 Thunderbird was an "only in America" tale of achievement. The business and financial realities of the multi-million-dollar firm were now something that only Mesh fully understood.

In the early days, Ogren Automotive was a small corner dealership on Lake Street. The entire operation had been Big Dan, a handful of mechanics, a few salesmen, a bookkeeper, a secretary, and a few unskilled staff like Mesh and Dan.

Dan had been bad-mouthing his father from Mesh's first day on the job. He'd called him "Big Dumb." Made fun of his clothes, his slight Norwegian accent, and his mechanic's grease-stained hands. He said if he hadn't stumbled on fixing cars he'd still be pulling stones out of a field somewhere in northern Minnesota. Dan resented that his father wasn't as impressed as others were by his high-school hockey stardom. In hockey-crazed Minnesota, players as gifted as Dan were celebrities.

Mesh never understood where the bad feelings came from. Dan' s mother had died of cancer around the same time Mesh lost his dad. Mesh knew how hard it was to lose a parent as a thirteen-year-old boy. Dan never mentioned it.

Despite the put-downs, Mesh suspected that Big Dan's opinion was the only one Dan cared about.

Mesh pulled onto 494 and headed west. Mr. Ogren now lived in a senior care residence just a few miles west. Mesh visited him regularly. The visits were short and sad, as the strokes and dementia had left Big Dan wheelchair-bound and unable to communicate.

Mr. Ogren never had been much of a talker. The big man had showed up at their house on holidays ever since Mesh's father had died. He'd bring gifts, stay less than ten minutes, and speak little. His mother told him that Mr. Ogren had a tough time after his wife died. She said Big Dan had worshipped her. His mother's expression always softened when Big Dan was mentioned.

Mesh took the exit to interstate 35W heading north. There'd still not been any snow and traffic moved well.

Mesh had remained one of Dan's friends after high school, but Mesh wondered if Dan cared for him—or anyone else. Dan had quickly become a star on the University of Minnesota hockey team and was instantly a big man on a very big campus.

On a winter night during their sophomore year at the university, Mesh had a meeting that forever linked him to Dan. He often wondered how his life might have progressed if that link had not been forged.

Dan had been kicked off the university hockey team a week before and nearly expelled. The newspapers and other media identified simply that

Dan had "violated team rules." Mesh had known something of the truth. It was one of a series of troubling incidents. In hindsight, Mesh felt he should have recognized the reality back then, but he had not.

Dan was off the team but still in school. That winter night a blizzard howled. Mesh and his mother were at home in their tiny single-story stucco house near Lake Nokomis.

In his wishful spirals of memory, Mesh yearned to revisit the choice he'd made that evening.

***

Mesh and his mother both got to their feet at the unexpected chime of the doorbell on that evening. The wind drove freezing air into their home as they admitted their unexpected visitor. Mr. Ogren stood massive in a snow-sprinkled great coat. Mesh's mother, covering her surprise, had fussed and apologized for "the mess" of her spotless house. Could she get him coffee?

Mr. Ogren had apologized for showing up unannounced. No thank you to coffee. He took off his snow-laden boots but kept his great coat on. He took off his hat, an orange wool cap, then clenched it in his workingman's hands. Could he speak to Mesh for a bit?

"Of course," his mother said.

The big man nodded to Mesh. "May we speak alone?"

"Yes, sir." Mesh's mouth went dry. "We can talk in the kitchen." His mind raced. *What's this about?*

The tiny kitchen held a wooden table with two chairs. His mother had made macaroni and cheese and boiled hot dogs earlier. The table and counter were clear, but the heat, odor, and steamy air hung.

They sat face-to-face in the yellowish cast of the light fixture hanging above the table. Mr. Ogren's short-cropped hair showed gray, his face deeply lined. The snow on the shoulders of the coat had turned to dew drops.

The silence stretched.

Mr. Ogren took a deep breath. He laid his hands flat on the tabletop then stared at them. He swallowed visibly. Another breath and he looked into Mesh's eyes.

"I need your help." His voice cracked.

"My help, sir?" Fear jolted through Mesh.

The big man looked up. His eyes wet, his chin trembled.

"I'm asking you to watch over Dan." He bent his head. The big man's chest filled and shrunk with great breaths. He looked up. A tear tracked down his cheek. "There's something not-right in my Daniel." He bent, clutching his head in his hands. His shoulders shook.

Mesh's stomach clenched, his throat tight. Mr. Ogren's distress was so intense, Mesh wanted to back away as if he were too near a furnace.

"He doesn't feel like people should." Mr. Ogren spoke into the table, his voice quavering. "He does bad things. He hurts people." He raised his head, looking lost. "I hoped it would change." He picked up the orange cap and twisted in his hands, his voice barely a whisper. "It's gotten worse."

Silence. Mesh's heart felt as if it were being squeezed by a fist.

"I've had psychiatrists and therapists seeing him for years. They give labels but can't help. Dan won't see them anymore." He looked down. "He lost his mother. Perhaps she could have helped him. I've failed him." He stared blankly for a moment.

The man's pain filled the room, displacing everything. Mesh could hardly breathe.

"You're good for him, Mesh. He respects you."

Mesh could not speak.

Big Dan gripped the hat in both hands. The black crescents of grease that Dan derided showed under well-scrubbed nails.

Big Dan met Mesh's eyes, desperation showing. "I know you want to go to law school. Managing my business is getting to be too much for me, and Dan isn't equipped. I want to hire you now. Ogren Automotive will pay your tuition, law school expenses, and a weekly salary. You can grow with the company. I want you to become the attorney and chief administrator someday." He leaned forward. "My offer isn't tied to helping Dan, but it would mean everything to me it if you'd stand by him." The words sounded like a business offer, but Big Dan's breaking voice said it was more. He bowed his head and stared at his hands as they kneaded the hat.

Mesh's breath came hard, his guts in a knot. Big Dan Ogren—this powerful, successful, and generous man—needed his help. Mesh understood what he was asking.

Big Dan continued, his head still bowed, the hat clenched. “Asking you to look out for Dan—that's me as a failure of a father trying to help the boy I love. Offering to pay for your education and hiring you is me recognizing your ability and making a business decision.” He raised his head, his eyes locking onto Mesh’s and pleading. “Will you help me?”

Mesh’s thoughts flew at a hundred miles per hour. Mr. Ogren's revelations about Dan had fit the suspicions that had been growing in Mesh's mind.

Dan was not like other people.

What Mesh had seen as fun, fearless, and tough was something else. There’d been several cases of disturbing behavior—most of which Mesh had only heard about. Dan’s latest offense had gotten him kicked off the hockey team but Mesh suspected only Dan’s status as an athlete and his father’s influence had kept him out of jail.

Dan was messed up.

Mr. Ogren, a good man who’d done so much for Mesh and his mother, had sat waiting for Mesh's answer like a prisoner on trial for his life awaiting the court’s verdict.

Mesh had revisited that moment a thousand times.

On every occasion he wished his response had been different.

Chapter 30

Hennepin County Government Center

Attorney S. Lloyd Anderson rose from the chair in the Hennepin County judge's chambers. He'd left Drake in the ER two hours earlier. As a respected insider in the legal community, he'd used his savvy and contacts to make things happen fast. "Judge, I appreciate you accommodating me on such short notice. I think it will allow us to stop this action before it becomes a circus at trial."

Quentin Jackson's attorney, Barry Ward, seated in the other chair in front of the judge's desk, rolled his eyes.

The judge frowned. "Lloyd, sit down. We're not in court, so you can save the drama. Furthermore I would never allow my court to become a circus." The gray-maned judge had at least fifteen years on Lloyd and more than thirty on the stylish Barry Ward.

Lloyd sat down, his expression unchanged by the reprimand. Inside he kicked himself. Never irritate a judge. "No offense intended, Judge. I apologize. As long as we're plain speaking, I'll cut to the heart. I believe my attorney opponent is not aware of the evidence and witness reports obtained by Minneapolis Police at the time of Mr. Jackson's arrest. If he were, he would not have filed a suit against Dr. Cody." He'd have to be an idiot, and Barry Ward was no idiot. He'd represent anybody for a quick buck, yes. But far from dumb.

"Barry?" the judge said.

The lanky, blond attorney remained at ease. His styled hair, robin's-egg blue suit, and laid-back manner made him the picture of urban cool. "Two days after my client's vicious beating and arrest in the emergency room, the district attorney advised me that the charge against my client had been dropped." He shrugged. "They had so little we never even made it to discovery. The fact that they dropped the charges confirmed they had nothing. Clearly they were in the wrong and were eager to distance themselves from the mistreatment of my client."

"Judge, if I may." Lloyd removed two thin folders and placed them in front of the judge and the plaintiff's attorney. "These folders contain copies of eyewitness accounts provided by two nurses, two doctors, and an ER patient present at the time of the event. They are part of the police record."

The judge leaned his considerable mass forward. "Lloyd, are you presuming to try this case in chambers?" He looked as if he'd just bit into a rotten apple. "You talked of a circus. This—"

"Bear with me, Judge. Please. I know this is irregular, but I assure you it's in the court's interest."

"I'll give you two minutes," the judge said.

The judge and plaintiff's attorney each opened the folders.

"The eyewitness accounts are clear, but there's more." Lloyd slid a laptop out of his briefcase. He opened the laptop and placed it on the desk where both men could see the screen. "I'm sorry there is no audio. This is the hospital's security video. The image is time and date marked. It has not been manipulated." He hit a key.

The screen flickered, then a frozen black-and-white video image appeared. A large black male in a do-rag and Raider's jacket stood in front of a short, slim nurse who appeared to be offering him some papers. They were in a hallway with gurneys and other equipment lining walls interrupted by curtained doorways.

"The location is Memorial Hospital ER. Can you identify your client, Barry? The affidavit identifies him as Quentin Jackson. Street name 'Q'," Lloyd said.

The judge raised a hand. "You're straining propriety here, Lloyd. Where are you going with this? I warned you we will not be trying this case in chambers. Considerable damages and a man's future are involved."

"Exactly, sir. It is my client, Dr. Drake Cody, who is facing devastating damage." Lloyd met the judge's eyes. "Just the filing of this suit has injured his reputation and threatened his professional future. Give me one more minute, and I'm sure you'll agree bringing this case into your courtroom would be a further injustice. "

The judge sighed. He addressed the young attorney.

"Any objections, Barry?""

"Let's see what he has." The blond attorney shrugged, still the picture of ease. "I think Lloyd here might consider dropping law and trying out for community theater." He looked at his fingernails. "And yes, the individual of color in the video, who came to the ER seeking care, is my client. He was upset and near-crazed with pain. And by the way," he glanced at the judge, "if this were court, I'd object to Lloyd identifying my client as 'Q' and referencing a 'street name.' Clearly prejudicial. It's simply a nickname and of no relevance."

"I would sustain that objection." The judge nodded. "Lloyd, you're being granted great leeway. Don't abuse it." He made a go-ahead gesture.

Lloyd started the video.

Quentin Jackson stood in the middle of the corridor with the nurse facing him. Her lips moved.

Quentin reacted, jutting his head forward as he jawed at her. He advanced and his posture became more threatening. His face twisted. The nurse shrank back. She said something and once again offered the papers.

The big man slapped the papers out of her hand, then moved even closer, his posture menacing. The petite nurse now stood backed against the wall, fear on her features.

A sturdily built young man in blue scrubs moved into the field. He wore a smile and had his hands held wide. A stethoscope was draped around his neck. His lips moved, a friendly expression on his face.

Lloyd paused the image. "That is my client, Dr. Drake Cody." He restarted the video.

The big man facing the nurse turned his head to Dr. Cody with his face a snarl. He jawed toward the doctor, then faced the nurse again. Lloyd paused the image again.

"This is Patti Verker, the charge nurse, a fifteen-year veteran of the ER. Her affidavit regarding the incident is in the folder in front of you." He restarted the video.

The agitated big man drew back his hand, then jabbed Patti twice in the chest with his knuckles. She rocked back with the blows, pain evident.

Drake Cody stepped forward and his smile was gone.

The big man pulled his fist back. As it advanced to strike Patti again, the doctor's hand flashed and deflected the blow.

The action then moved very fast on the small screen.

Without hesitation, Quentin Jackson twisted and rifled his fist towards Drake Cody's face.

The doctor slipped the big man's punch and drove a hand into the man's ribs.

The out-of-control patient threw another looping roundhouse. The doctor, fist blurred, beat the punch and buried a blow in the big man's gut. The man doubled forward and Dr. Cody met the man's face with a slashing elbow. Blood erupted from the man's nose.

Dr. Cody then took Patti and moved her clear.

The man gathered himself and lunged. Dr. Cody fired a kick into the man's groin and the attacker dropped. The doctor slipped behind him and wrapped his arms around the man's neck.

The video ended.

Silence.

The judge spoke first. "Barry, I assume you had not seen this."

The young attorney sat forward and blew out a long breath. He shook his head. "No, Judge. Had not."

"Please discuss things with your client," the judge said. "Let me know as soon as you've decided about proceeding."

"My client, yeah." The GQ stylish and smooth attorney had lost his smug visage. He sat stiff and upright, biting his lip with his gaze off to the side.

When he turned back, Lloyd saw worry in Barry Ward's eyes.

Chapter 31

Calhoun Beach condominiums

Clara tore open the two-pound bag of blue nacho corn chips. Dan should arrive before long. A visit before dark—another first.

She removed the plastic lid from the jumbo tub of guacamole then looked out the window at the ice-covered lake. The cold snap that had hit the Twin Cities had turned Lake Calhoun to ice without the influence of wind or snow. The surface was a mirror. Daylight was waning and the scene was an Ansel Adams study in black and white.

She loaded a chip with guacamole, then put it in her mouth. No longer did she feel guilty about her eating. Sometimes it just felt right.

Right now she tingled as she considered how her and Dan's love had blossomed. God, he couldn't stay away from her.

There was more than enough time for her to relax a bit then make herself ready for him. She opened the bag of nachos more fully and filled both hands with the salty blue chips. She sat cross-legged on the sofa, her legs wrapped around the tub of guacamole, and deposited the chips on her scrubs-attired lap. Her "Best of the Nineties" compilation played in the background.

For a while she relaxed and ate, not letting things bother her. Forgetting about Dr. Bart Rainey's humiliation of her. Ignoring the countless slights she'd suffered. And especially not thinking about the greatest injustice of all. She was aware but none of it touched her. Issues roiled beneath but eating provided comfort.

As she chewed she savored the music, the smells, the flavors, the textures. The dry peanut-like odor of the nachos. The solid crunch of the chips as they fractured and ground between her teeth. The citrus and cilantro accent of the smooth, rich guacamole. The taste of the salt, corn, oil, and avocado accompanying the brilliant tactile contrast of crunch versus the buttery-soft dip.

The flavor waned and the smells faded, but she continued to eat. For minutes she loaded, dipped, chewed and swallowed. Something about the food—no, not the food, something about eating. Load the chip, place it in her mouth, her teeth crunching and crushing it to a mash, swallowing.

It was like work, but a gratifying work at which she was incredibly adept.

She'd long ago quit self-analyzing. She'd gotten past the "this is wrong" arrogance of the in-patient eating disorder treatment center her parents had sentenced her to as a teen. Instead she simply ate and erased things later. Not a big deal.

Two-thirds of the family-sized bag of chips and a like portion of the jumbo tub of guacamole had disappeared.

The next song on her collection started. "Magic Man" by Heart. In her mind she changed it to "magic Dan" and almost laughed out loud. In her feeding reverie she'd accepted something. Not accepted—embraced. Dan Ogren's love for her had been her miracle in waiting. His intellect did not match hers, but his magnificent body and his worship of her had changed her. The years of waiting had been worth it. He was the most handsome man she had ever seen. The moment she saw him she'd known she had to have him.

The years of battling her weight and the guilt about the purges—she'd put that behind her years ago. She ate, she purged, she worked out intensely—she'd never felt good about her body, but she knew no one could work Dan's incredible staff harder than she did. She provided him what he needed and he delivered pleasure she'd never imagined possible—her magic man.

Some would say it was wrong because he was married, but his marriage had died long ago. *He made a mistake marrying his ingrate of a wife, but now he's found me!*

What she and Dan had was alive. So very alive. And special. So very special.

She checked the clock. Time to go erase and get ready for him.

She knew what would happen with Dan when he arrived. He was an addict and she was his drug.

***

Dan approached the elevator. The smell of exhaust hung in the Calhoun Beach condominium building's underground garage. The virtually unused rear service elevator went to the sixth floor within fifty feet of Clara's door.

He hit the button and waited.

So many things worked out with this setup. Clara accepted that they couldn't be seen together because of his wife. And she worried about knowledge of their involvement compromising her at the hospital. As far as he could tell, Clara had zero friends—none. That assured she didn't engage in the girlie-girl tell-all about their boyfriends like some of his cock-stops in the past had.

End result—he'd been playing pelvic pogo stick and other carnal sports with her for a few months and nobody knew.

No one had seen them together. No one knew they had anything to do with each other. Perfect.

That's why the idea that had popped into his head seemed possible. A risky gamble with high stakes, but if Clara knew half as much as she said she did, it could work. No one could expect he knew the kinds of things she shared with him.

The doors pinged open. He stepped into the sixth floor hallway

When he didn't have her servicing him, Clara talked nonstop. Syrupy fairy-tale junk about their "magic" love, but also talk about the hospital and her job. How she was smarter and knew more about medicine than most of the doctors on staff. Generally he just tuned it out and left as soon as he'd got his rocks well-and-truly off, but one night after a killer sweat and moan fest, he'd gotten her to turn off her oldies chick-tunes and turn on local radio. They heard a radio report about a death—a suspected murder.

That had started it. Clara had talked about how someone with advanced medical knowledge could kill and get away with it. She'd sounded convincing.

It had stuck in his memory—and popped up today as Mesh had shared his forecast of upcoming doom and gloom.

Dan stood before her door.

Since today's meeting with Mesh, maintaining his lifestyle dominated Dan's thoughts.

He had to beat the domestic assault charge. Nothing else mattered.

He knocked.

Chapter 32

ER

Drake stood in front of the Captain, who was sitting on the bare cot in the otherwise barren psychiatric holding room. The clock showed Drake's night shift—perhaps his last—would end in less than an hour.

"Captain, no one wanted to interfere with your mission," Drake said. "You were climbing on the outer span of the Hennepin Avenue Bridge at three-thirty in the morning, in the freezing cold. You told the police you were looking for a high spot. You had a bottle and smelled of booze. They were afraid for your safety."

The good-natured, schizophrenic and alcoholic homeless man averaged more than forty ER visits a year. The Captain's belief in his role as an intergalactic scout, as well as a truly unfortunate inclination for alcohol, serious trauma, and critical illness made him the most unique of many ER "regulars."

Drake had not seen him since the events on the Mississippi River flats where people had died. The Captain's actions had helped Drake save his family that day.

"Of course I smelled of alcohol, Bones." The Captain's birthdate showed him to be in his forties, though the tall, gaunt man looked to be at least sixty. "Earth's fermented beverages are among your species' finest achievements." The Captain's fixed delusion involved his role as an advance scout for an extraterrestrial civilization checking on Earth's suitability for colonization. He consumed huge amounts of alcohol and had a tolerance beyond any Drake had seen. "I sought a high spot for interference-free communication with my orbiting interstellar drone."

This visit his blood alcohol measured .36%. Most people would be unconscious and require a ventilator. The captain had been climbing on a bridge support high above the Mississippi River.

The Captain resisted all efforts at "improving" his life situation. He roamed the streets of downtown Minneapolis wearing two oversized coats and two hats year-round. The always-friendly Captain posed no risk to anyone, but his vulnerability had spurred Drake to initiate multiple social service interventions in the past.

The intergalactic scout rebuffed the efforts of Drake and the social service professionals to get him sober and off the streets. He responded with smiles and comments such as, "You have not evolved enough to know where value lies. My mission is clear. Some day you may understand."

Currently, less than three hours after his arrival, the Captain demonstrated good balance and clear speech, and his baseline delusional beliefs were as strong as ever. He was not and never had been suicidal—if nothing else, his mission was too important for him to quit.

Drake handed the Captain a bologna sandwich taken from a stash in the emergency department refrigerator.

"If I let you go, do you promise to stay away from heights?" Drake truly cared for the kindhearted man. Mixed among the Captain's delusional ramblings were sage comments and remarkable insights. Drake felt the scruffy street person had an almost mystical gift hidden within his disordered mind.

"Certainly, Bones. My transmissions have been completed for this reporting period." He examined the sandwich. "A manufactured meat product consumable—most delightful. I thank you." He took a large bite.

As the Captain chewed, Drake bent close to the weathered, blue-black skin of the Captain's cheek. A whitish, almost imperceptible four-inch line ran from near his left temple to the corner of his mouth. Drake had repaired the wicked slash wound several weeks earlier. If not for the pigment difference, the scar would have been unnoticeable.

"Your face looks good."

"Thanks to you, Bones." The Captain called all the doctors "Bones"—thought to be of Star Trek origin. "This interstellar explorer salutes you." He raised his sandwich. "I also much appreciate the nutrients. You've achieved a higher plane than most on your planet."

Drake would like to believe the minimal scarring was solely a product of his skills, but the Captain's healing abilities were a known wonder. He'd survived so many life-threatening illnesses and injuries that some suggested he be given an honorary medical school professorship based on the training he'd provided the physicians who treated him.

The man's recuperative abilities were almost otherworldly.

“Thanks for the kind words, Captain, and you're welcome. You can sleep a bit and then the nurses will discharge you. Please take care of yourself, my friend.” Drake held out his hand.

The Captain flashed a big smile. He set his sandwich down on the cot and grasped Drake's hand in a two-handed grip like a minister after Sunday services. As he shook his expression changed. His mouth opened and his eyes widened. He released Drake's hand, then slid off the cot to his feet. He shook his head.

“Bones, your aura has attracted negative energy.”

“No worries, Captain.” Drake patted the man's shoulder. The Captain often shared sayings like the “could-fit-anybody” vagaries printed in newspaper horoscopes. Rizz believed the Captain’s pronouncements to have been prophetic in the past.

The Captain sat forward, his manner grave. “Be careful, Bones. Good intent is not a shield against ill fortune on this planet.”

The Captain couldn’t know that his predictions of “negative energy” had already come to pass. The concern in the homeless man's voice made Drake smile. Regardless of how delusional the Captain might be, his kindness was deep and true.

Few could know the pleasure of connecting with a man such as the Captain. Drake found caring for him, be it life or death, or simply sobering him up and providing a sandwich and friendly word, a special pleasure.

The opportunity to connect with people of all sorts in a deeply human way occurred daily in Drake's work in the ER.

God above—he would miss it.

Chapter 33

Memorial Hospital

Drake pulled his coat tight as the ER doors hissed closed behind him. He'd fallen in love with Minnesota in his four years here, but the winters were insane. The temperature had dropped forty degrees in the twelve hours of his shift. In a rare turn of events, he'd gotten off a few minutes early as his relief had arrived and his patients were managed. Six-fifty a.m., still completely dark and much colder than Cincinnati had ever been.

The air bit at his nostrils and his face stung. He kept his head down and his gloved hands buried in his pockets as he hiked toward the parking lot. The subzero temperatures snatched at his breath and penetrated the thin fabric of his scrub pants as if he were naked. It felt as if he were in the Arctic. Unlike many of the native Minnesotans, Drake was glad that the first snow had yet to arrive—there'd be more than enough and it stayed forever. He speed-walked the block and a half to the Chicago Avenue outdoor lot.

He took off a glove and retrieved his car keys from his jacket pocket, then fit the key in the car door and got in. The old Dodge's upholstery felt icy and crackled like wrapping paper under his weight. The outside of the windshield lay covered by a layer of frost. His breath immediately formed a frozen film on the inside of the glass.

The starter groaned but spun, the engine fired and caught. It ran hard and whined in its coldness. He turned the heater to max but knew it would be a while before any warmth resulted. Glove back on, he climbed out and used the windshield scraper to attack the frost.

Dead tired but his mind raced. Long night—was it his last? The research—he needed to stop by the lab. Damn. He scraped the frost, a harsh "scrack" sounding with each stroke. The outer glass scraped clear, he climbed back into the car.

He flipped the heater fan on and it whirred to life. He set the blower to defrost and a blast of powdery crystals flew into the air above the dash. So cold. Drake used the scraper to shave the light frost from the windshield's interior. Minnesota winters—the price one paid to live in this remarkable place. He put the car in gear.

He drove slowly peering into the swath his headlights cut in the dark, near-deserted streets of downtown Minneapolis. The defroster fought to maintain two portholes in the windshield as his breath fogged the glass in the still freezing car. He crossed Hennepin Avenue, heading for the lab.

He would check on the animals, document their recovery status, take care of their feeding, and be on his way home in less than an hour. He couldn't wait to be with Rachelle and the kids. No matter how screwed other things might be, he had them. A lucky guy.

The frost-free ovals grew above the defroster outflow. The Target Center, then the multi-story parking ramp showed as he snaked along 7th Street. The road angled to the north and a view of the star-sprinkled night sky opened. Crazy cold but so incredibly beautiful. This place had become their home. If he lost his medical career, could they stay?

Drake coughed while simultaneously experiencing a fierce itching sensation on the palms of both hands. His chest tightened and he coughed again. His breath came hard. *What the hell?*

The skin of his palms burned and the itching spread to his scalp and extremities. He pulled off his gloves and pressed them against the cold of the steering wheel. His chest tightened as if being squeezed in a vise. His tongue and lips were rubbery. He pulled to the side of the road ending under a streetlight on the edge of North Minneapolis. He shifted the car into park. *This can't be!*

Years earlier he'd had a profound allergic reaction. Minutes after taking penicillin for an infected tooth he'd begun to itch, fought to breathe, lost all strength, and swelled up like a balloon. Rachelle had called 911. Paramedics had arrived within minutes and treated him with repeated doses of epinephrine. He'd come close to dying.

But this time he was unaware of any exposure—no medication, no food, nothing to trigger a reaction. He struggled to move air. Wheezing and a progressive tightening gripped his chest. His strength melting like butter on a skillet.

Anaphylactic shock—he would die without treatment.

Epinephrine was the treatment—the substance, also known as adrenaline, is the most powerful hormone in the body. It flogs the heart, opens constricted airways, and helps reverse the swelling and nose-diving blood pressure of anaphylactic shock. Drake carried in his glove box a glass ampule of epinephrine and a syringe he'd "borrowed" from the ER. He kept the miracle medicine on hand not just for himself but for use if he came across someone else in need. Bee stings, medication, foods, or other exposures could kill an allergic adult or child in minutes. Epinephrine saved lives—if given in time.

He clawed out his phone and entered 911.

"This is 911 dispatch. Do you have an emergency?"

Drake attempted to speak, "huh hin har..." His tongue thick and clumsy.

He dropped the phone and hoped it hadn't disconnected. He stretched for the glove box, his movements awkward. He hit the rearview mirror with his forehead and glimpsed a face and lips so swollen he would not have recognized himself. His swollen tongue protruded from his mouth like the toe of a boot.

He fumbled open the glove box, then grabbed the small box containing the syringe, needle, and ampule of epinephrine. He opened the box. The fluid in the bullet-sized, glass ampule had frozen. He slumped. The needle and syringe could not draw up or inject the frozen drug. It needed to be introduced directly into the blood.

His thoughts slowed and fuzzed as his blood pressure plunged. He must get the drug into his system.

The itching registered but no longer mattered. The pain in his chest, the plastic feeling of his swollen face, and his difficulty breathing seemed far away. *Whatever.*

Dying and you don't care? His mind had slid into the torpor of shock. *No! Rachelle, the kids.* He fought against the lethargy. He felt himself sliding. The effort too great.

In the blood. I need the epi in my blood. He lifted his head off the steering wheel and removed his keys. Clumsily, he opened the one-inch blade of the penknife on the key ring. He pulled up his sleeve and stabbed the blade into the flesh of his exposed forearm. He angled the blade side-to-side beneath the skin, opening a pocket. The pain intense but meaningless. His grip grew slick with blood and he dropped the key ring. His chest felt as if it were being crushed between two cars. The pain and his air hunger both incredible and far off.

He clutched the bullet-sized ampule of epinephrine then jammed it nose first into the bloody track he'd gouged. He drove its full length under the skin. He raised his forearm and slammed it against the steering wheel. He hit a glancing blow but slammed again and again. Something gave way. As he dragged his forearm over the edge of the steering wheel he sensed the crackle of the ampule. He held his off hand over the wound and opened and closed his fist. *Melt!*

He struggled to breathe, he collapsed to his side. His thoughts trailing off. *Failing. Again. Failing those who need me...*

He'd failed those he loved before. A long time back but it haunted him.

One day—really just one selfish, thoughtless moment. He'd destroyed the ones he loved.

And now no breath, no strength. Others he loved needed him.

He must not fail again.

***

Fourteen years earlier

Anna Cartabiano was new to the school and, unlike the other eleventh-grade girls, knew nothing of Drake's history. She did not know of his conviction or his time behind bars. It was her first day and she shared his study hall.

Silken black hair and huge brown eyes. Flawless skin, fair and glowing. Her lips were rose-colored and full, one cheek dimpling with her smile. Her body was such that he had no words. Breathless in her presence.

Did he mind if she sat with him? He shrugged—speech beyond him. Then they did speak. And she laughed and her eyes flashed.

She'd asked about his classes. Were the teachers nice? Did he like music? She came from Indianapolis. Had he been there?

Then her face clouded. Her expression somber as her gaze shifted over Drake's shoulder. Partially turning, he glimpsed Kevin, who grimaced with the effort of his labored, crutch-flapping struggle across the study hall.

Her wondrous features pained, she whispered, "People like that. Crippled and retarded. It's not fair. I can't stand to look at them. It's just too sad."

At that instant Drake's sideward glance skimmed his brother's. Kevin brightened and made what only Drake could have recognized as a purposeful nod among his mutinous movements. Drake turned away, his back to Kevin and facing Anna, pretending he had not seen his brother.

In the after-image, Drake caught the flash of Kevin's perception and pain. Kevin had read it all in an instant.

Drake heard the slap, tink, slide and grunting utterances of Kevin's challenged trajectory. Veering away—keeping clear. Kevin had absorbed the message in his big brother's actions.

Drake, for the first time ever, had rejected his brother.

Drake did not speak with Kevin after the study hall. He did not ride home with Kevin and their mother that day. He met with Anna instead.

He sensed he'd hurt the person he loved most, but Anna's dizzying appeal overwhelmed his inner voice.

While heading home in the modified Dodge Caravan that Kevin called the "palsy mobile," Drake's mother and brother were broadsided at a highway crossing by a Coca-Cola truck, two minutes from the school.

Their van had run a light, darting onto the highway. The truck driver did not have time to even touch the brakes. The mini-van had been almost ripped in two.

Kevin was pronounced dead at the scene, their mother transported by ambulance in critical condition.

A day later, she regained consciousness in the University of Cincinnati Medical Center's ICU. With consciousness came recall. She'd been distracted behind the wheel. Kevin had been unusually quiet when she picked him up. Minutes later he'd started to weep. Kevin never cried.

In her distress she'd turned to ask what was wrong.

The answer never came.

Their mother's soundless tears had started before she received the other news. Her spine had snapped at chest level and the lower half of her body would never move or feel again.

She'd nodded and given a slight shrug. It seemed she accepted it as penance deserved.

Drake's brother and their mother—one dead, the other paralyzed.

Others thought it an accident—the cruel hand of fate. Drake knew the truth.

He'd rejected his brother, denied him. He'd devastated the person he loved and who loved him most. Kevin, who despite his endless courage, needed Drake's acceptance and love. Drake had failed him.

He must never fail another.

Chapter 34

Memorial Hospital, Administrative offices, 6:57 a.m.

Jim Torrins' desk phone rang. He noted the caller ID, sighed, then raised the phone to his ear.

"Hello."

"This is CEO Kline."

Jim sighed again. What kind of jerk introduces himself to a fellow administrator as CEO?

"Yes, Kline. This is early for you. What's up?"

"Is Drake Cody on in the ER today?"

"Why? What difference—"

"Just answer me. Is he in the ER now?" Kline said.

Yesterday Kline had pushed hard for Drake to be kicked off the hospital staff immediately. Drake's record could be bad for hospital PR, but the domestic abuse report he'd filed on Dan Ogren seemed the true trigger for Kline's hostility.

"Why do you care where Drake is?"

"Just check for me. Now," Kline said.

Jim turned to his computer and pulled up the ER assignment schedule. The schedule was complicated and it took Jim a moment to decipher. "Drake's 'A' shift, which is night, ended a few minutes ago, but he's probably still here. It's rare they get out on time. He's on the schedule for another A shift tonight. Why do you care?"

"Damn it. I thought 'A' meant a day shift. Catch him before he leaves. Make sure he sticks around." Kline spoke fast, even more bossy than usual.

"Why would I do that? He worked all night. He's going to want to get home—maybe after a quick stop at his lab. He's sure to be beat."

“Get down there and stop him. And don't call it ‘his’ lab. That building is university property,” Kline said.

“What's going on?” Why did Drake’s location matter to him?

Kline had come from a university finance position straight to CEO of Memorial Hospital. Unusual. Jim avoided politics, but its odor had trailed Kline's appointment. The stink had grown stronger since. The links among medical providers, educators, and big business were unavoidable but troubling. What was going on?

“Just keep him tied up as long as you can. Understood?”

Slow to anger, priding himself on calm, Jim's patience ended.

“No, it's not understood. What game are you playing?”

There was a long silence.

“It's today.” Kline sounded as if he were referring to a military operation. “This morning.”

“What, Kline? What's this morning?”

“The university legal team and all the intellectual property experts agreed. You'll be helping everyone if you keep Drake away from that lab.”

Intellectual property? The lab?

It hit him. The reason Kline had been so interested in Drake and his research. His previous position with the university's patent office and revenue operations. He was familiar with drug patents and revenues arising from pharmaceutical research.

“Is this what I think?” Jim felt nauseous. Had this been planned all along?

“The university is seizing the contents of the lab this morning.”

“You bastards.” The rough language had jumped off his lips.

“This is way beyond your paygrade, Torrins. Drake Cody's legal documentation is a mess and his claim to the drug is vulnerable. A Swiss pharmaceutical firm has already filed a claim. This is big money. It's better for the university and the citizens of the state to benefit—”

“Spare me, Kline. This is not about the citizens.” Jim felt his restraint falling away.

“The research was done in a university-owned building, the doctors are part of a university-affiliated residency, and Drake Cody's colleagues received educational credit for the research from the medical school, also a part of the university. The attorneys say that the university can claim the research as its own and likely be supported in court. The doctors—"

"What about what's right, Kline? You being involved in such an underhanded scheme doesn't surprise me. But all the others?" Jim knew many in the university and medical school hierarchy—they were good people.

"Screw you, Torrins," Kline's voice loud and shrill, "get down to the ER right now and keep Drake Cody there!"

"CEO Kline, sir. Are you listening, Mr. Boss Man?" Jim found himself on his feet.

"Yes," Kline said.

"Kiss my ass!" Jim slammed the phone down.

He grabbed his suit coat as he raced out of his office.

He hoped he was in time.

Chapter 35

North Minneapolis, roadside, 7:03 a.m.

Drake roused to the sound of his car door opening. Freezing air. Urgent voices.

"Shit, look at the swelling. Gotta be allergic reaction. Grab the epi, amigo."

Drake felt hands on him, his coat unzipped and a stethoscope pressed against his chest.

"Barely moving air. Pulse is fast and weak. He's going down."

A plastic oxygen mask neared his face.

"Holy shit, partner, holy shit! This is Doc Cody."

Drake recognized the medic who bent over him. Nothing shook the rock-solid professional. He looked shaken now.

"His tongue—the swelling. He's losing his airway."

A slight sting in his arm. "Epi's on board."

More epi—yes! The epinephrine from the crushed ampule beneath his skin had slowed the reaction's progression, but he knew he was critical. His thoughts came into focus like boats approaching in fog.

His blood pressure was responding, but his swollen tissues were not. Each breath felt like trying to pull fluid through a too-small straw.

He could not get enough air.

A clinical, detached part of his mind recognized he'd be dead in minutes if this trickle of air ended. Water-boarding without water and it did not relent. He struggled, the paramedics trying to help. He felt the mask over his face and heard the whoosh as they squeezed the bag but the air would not pass.

"His pulse is stronger but his breathing is worse. The swelling is too great. There's no way to get him any air."

The paramedic leaned over him with a laryngoscope and ET airway tube in hand. She pulled back. Her words to her partner a whisper but Drake made it out. “There's no way to get anything in there.” A tube through the mouth, down the throat, and directed between the vocal cords into the trachea would give air a path. Without it—death.

The second medic spoke, his tone grim. “His neck is too swollen for a surgical.” Even cutting a pathway into his trachea, a last-ditch alternative, was not an option. They could do nothing.

At that instant Drake's pathway for air reduced to nothing.

Must breathe. Breathe or die.

He attempted to pull in air, but all passages were blocked.

Panic flared like a struck match.

His world a nightmarish effort to inhale.

Rachelle, the kids. *No!*

“We need to load and go. Bag-breathe him as best you can on the way.”

Drake’s heart hammered, his strength surged in the grip of terror and adrenaline. His mind flashed in total clarity. *I'm going to die.*

The medics started to pull him out of the car.

Drake thrashed, reached out and grabbed the ET tube still in the medic's hand.

“No, Doc.” She held tight. Her expression showed she thought he'd flipped out in desperation and lack of air.

Drake locked eyes, then gestured with his thumb towards his mouth. There was only one chance.

“No way, Doc. Your tongue...” The medic's brow furrowed then her eyes widened. She released the airway.

Drake jammed the tip of the fourteen-inch-long tube between his protruding tongue and the roof of his mouth.

“He's trying to jam the tube in,” she said.

He rested his head against the car seat and drove the tube deeper. No one could see to place the tube—but he could feel. The hard plastic penetrated, gouging between the roof of his mouth and the meat of his massively swollen tongue. He tasted blood. The tip reached his throat. He’d intubated countless patients. He knew the anatomy. His target was the less than one inch diameter access to the vocal cords which sat behind a flap of tissue designed to block anything from entering. His body jerked as he advanced the tube, his gag reflex bucked him like a mule's kick.

He held the tube in a death grip. The inability to draw in air an agony beyond description. Dying!

He summoned strength from a well that plumbed the deepest part of his being. *I will not fail!* He pushed harder. The tube penetrated deep into his throat. Desperately, he forced it deeper. He gagged and bucked as he felt the tube lodge against his clamped vocal cords.

Unless the cords opened and the tube passed into the trachea he would die.

Drake fought the powerful airway reflexes whose sole function was to prevent anything but air from entering the trachea and lungs. He held the tube jammed against the gateway of his vocal cords as the protective reflexes caused him to spasm and jerk as if he'd been tasered. With the last of his strength he fought to draw in a breath. *Please, God!*

Sharp pain and a rush of air. The tube slid forward. He thrashed violently, a fierce cough honking air through the airway. His hands desperately clenching the tube.

His chest pumped like a bellows. *Air. Breathing air!* The relief beyond imagination.

"Hell, yes. He did it! Secure that tube. Whatever happens, do not lose that tube!" Paramedic's hands supported Drake's.

One medic secured the tube, the other placed a stethoscope on his chest.

"Wheezing but moving air. Blood pressure 100 and pulse 130. Let's roll."

"Roger that, partner."

In seconds, Drake lay in the back of the racing ambulance with IV fluids running and the siren screaming.

He could breathe. He had a blood pressure.

The paramedics had him.

He hadn't failed.

Chapter 36

ER, 7:24

Jim Torrins raced down the empty white hospital corridor toward the ER. He swiped his ID card and the automated doors whooshed open. He took a breath, composed himself, then strode toward the main desk. The corridor and Crash Room stood empty and quiet. Dr. Laura Vonser leaned on the central counter with a Styrofoam cup in her hand.

"Laura."

"Hi, Dr. Torrins." She raised the cup, swinging it in a "check it out" arc encompassing the near-empty department. "A nice morning."

"Is Drake still here?"

"No. I got here early and it was quiet like this. He was able to escape on time."

The "doctor to the radio" signal bleated overhead.

"Dang. I shouldn't have said the 'Q' word." Laura set down her cup and headed for the radio.

The signal indicated paramedics needed to advise of an incoming critical patient. Laura covered the twenty feet to the radio closet, then hit the microphone's transmit key.

"Dr. Vonser here."

"Ambulance 725 en route, code 3. Two minutes out. Adult male in anaphylactic shock. Intubated, blood pressure 90, pulse 130s after two doses epinephrine. IV in and saline wide open. Massive facial and airway swelling. Awake, wheezing, sats 90%."

In Torrins' day-to-day administrative work, it was easy to forget the intensity of the life-or-death challenges the ER staff routinely faced. Just hearing the report made his mouth go dry and swallowing difficult.

"Our patient," the paramedic's voice sounded strained, "is Doctor Cody. He was pulseless, in respiratory failure, and minimally responsive when we arrived—damn near dead. Giving 3rd epi now."

"10-4. Crash bay two. Out." Laura flipped the microphone away and turned toward the secretary, who stood with headphone on and finger poised over the paging line. "Med team stat, Crash Bay 2."

The secretary's medical team stat call sounded overhead three times in succession as Laura made her way to and entered the Crash Room.

Jim moved to the back of the Crash Room, his throat tight. How could this be happening? Is there no limit to the bad stuff that can happen to Drake? *Please don't let him die.*

Nurses, techs, and others appeared as Laura ripped back the curtain, exposing the cart and array of monitors and instruments. Jim watched as she turned on the high intensity lights, then pulled on a gown and gloves. The Life clock above the head of the bed ticked off the seconds since the ambulance call.

Jim stood near the foot of the next bay as the practiced ER professionals prepared. Drake Cody in anaphylactic shock—the lethal extreme of allergic reactions. Unreal.

What had Drake done to deserve the waves of disaster that slammed into his life?

The Crash Room doors banged open as the paramedic team rushed the cart in.

Jim's stomach plunged. *My God! Is that him?*

Mottled red skin and a hugely swollen face with the white plastic ET tube extending from the mouth atop a massively swollen tongue. It was like nothing Jim had ever seen.

Laura jumped to Drake's side and leaned close, a hand on his shoulder.

"We've got you, Drake. We've got you."

As horrendous as the scene, as desperate the situation, Jim felt the confidence in the emergency physician's words.

They had Drake.

The ER would keep Drake alive, but there'd be no way he could react to a warning from Jim about the university's plan to steal his breakthrough research. So unfair. Not enough time. If only...

Jim switched gears in an instant. He pulled out his phone. He knew who to call.

***

"We've got you, Drake. We've got you."

Dr. Laura Vonser's words were beautiful. Almost as beautiful as the plastic tube jammed down his throat.

The airway tube. The wonderful, horrible tube.

How did patients stand it? He thought of Jon Malar's days in the ICU. Drake's muscles convulsed as the device triggered another reflex cough. The tube felt like a medieval torture device, but God he loved it. He could breathe!

Dr. Vonser spoke to Mike, one of the ER nurses. "Versed 3 milligrams IV slow."

Mike leaned forward with a syringe.

Drake covered the IV site with his hand and shook his head. He couldn't be drugged now.

Mike looked at Dr. Vonser.

"Are you thinking clearly, Drake?" she asked. "You know the drill. Are you capable of making informed decisions about your care? Do you understand the risks and benefits and what is happening?"

He nodded.

"Okay then. What's the capital of Nova Scotia?"

Drake flipped up his middle finger.

Dr.Vonser and Mike laughed. "Yeah. He's at baseline," she said.

She leaned close to Drake.

"You scared the shit out of a lot of folks, Drake Cody." She nodded toward the hall. A crowd had formed around the Crash Room entry and stretched along its glass wall. She put a hand on his shoulder and squeezed. "No more disasters. Okay?"

The concerned faces of paramedics, nurses, techs, secretaries, housekeeping, and other staff lined the full-length glass partition.

Tears filled his eyes. So lucky to be part of such a special group of people. So lucky to be alive. He wanted to hug the paramedics and everyone else. He raised a hand and gave a thumbs-up.

Smiles flashed and muffled cheers sounded.

***

With each minute, Drake found the act of breathing through the tube easier. He did not have a ventilator. His lungs had opened. The epinephrine and other treatments had reversed the cascade of his deadly allergic reaction.

He could move his tongue now. He put a hand to his face. His skin no longer felt like it was made of vinyl. The swelling was resolving. He'd received steroids, antihistamines, albuterol, and fluids. His blood pressure and thinking had returned to near normal.

Clearer thinking brought awareness. Once again he'd been on the threshold of dying.

What did it mean? Had he thought of his soul? At the critical point he'd felt urgency. He had to fight. Rachelle, the kids, his mother, Rizz, Jon—they needed him. He'd already failed too many people.

He'd been close to dead but he'd not seen a white light. No glimpse of what lay beyond. He'd visited hard memories. Drake had been raised to believe in God but hated much of His handiwork. Why so much horrific suffering? Would Drake have paid for his wavering faith?

Someone stepped from the back of the Crash Room. Jim Torrins pocketed his phone as he approached. Lately the soft-spoken administrator bore nothing but grim news.

Everything had already gone to shit. There couldn't be much more bad news to share. He appreciated that the generally distant Torrins had come to check on him.

Torrins huddled with Laura. Drake overheard parts of their exchange.

"Is he out of the woods?" Torrins asked.

"This should be written up—it's incredible," she said. "Before the squad got there he drove an ampule of frozen epi into his arm, then crushed it so it could be absorbed. Even with that, he had no blood pressure when they got to him. He was unconscious with minimal pulse. They say his swelling was even worse."

"Worse?" Torrins said.

"The paramedics hit him with more epi. His consciousness improved but his airway failed. He was blue and dying. His tongue and tissues were so swollen they had no way to get an airway tube in." She shook her head. "Drake was purple. He grabbed the tube and jammed it through. He blind intubated himself."

"Good God."

"Without the epinephrine ampule or the self-intubation, he'd have died. Heck, now with some luck, we might be able to get the tube out in a few hours," Laura said.

Their talk became background as Drake tried to get his mind right. He'd had a thought before the allergic reaction started but it eluded him now. He almost had it but then it slipped away again—like a word he knew but could not retrieve. What had it been? Something important.

D-44. That was it. A way he could take care of everyone.

Chapter 37

Minneapolis, 7:45 a.m.

The Metro Mobility van turned onto Washington Avenue. Rizz had nearly completed the Courage Center modified vehicle driving course. If necessary, soon he could get his own specially equipped transport. For now, the metro van service worked well, getting him where he needed to go. His transport to the hospital would take less than ten minutes.

His wheelchair was locked down and a restraint ran over his waist area. He was the only passenger.

His head felt fuzzy and his eyes a bit irritated. Unless he got flaming-piss hammered, this was as much of a "hangover" as he ever experienced.

The driver wore a parka and a thick wool hat and mittens. He'd looked to be freezing as he'd loaded Rizz into the van.

"What's your name?"

"My name is Vang." The driver smiled, then looked over his shoulder for an opening in traffic.

"You're Hmong. I'm guessing you came to Minnesota in 1975. Just a kid then, right?"

"How did you know that?" Vang halted his effort to pull into traffic.

"ER doctor magic." Rizz shrugged. "You look Hmong. Your hat and scarf is Hmong weave and color. You seem just a bit too old to be U.S. born. Most people don't remember that the reason the Hmong people had to leave their homeland was because they were fierce U.S. allies. They fought alongside American soldiers. 1975 is when most Hmong families made it to Minnesota."

Vang turned, nodding. "You're pretty smart."

"No argument there." Rizz laughed.

Vang smiled, then turned back to look for an opening. Rizz's cell phone sounded. He retrieved it from his lap bag. "Michael Rizzini here."

"Dr. Rizzini, er, Rizz, Jim Torrins here."

"Jim. What can I do for you?" Rizz made it a point to call all administrators and department heads by their first name. He avoided titles showing deference to any in a position of presumed or actual authority. *Why is Torrins calling me?*

"I'm standing in the Crash Room. Drake Cody is being treated for anaphylactic shock. He—"

"What the—"

"He's stable. But he's intubated."

"Shit! Is—"

"Just listen." Torrins sounded nothing like his usual laid-back self. "Dr. Vonser says he's out of the woods. There's something important you need to know right away."

"Laura's got him? Good." *What's as important as Drake intubated?*

"The university filed an ownership claim on the D-44 research. They're going to seize the contents of your lab." Rizz heard disgust in Torrins' voice.

"Any idea when?" Rizz said. *The greedy, sleazy shitheads!*

"Right now—this morning. Have you got an attorney?"

As of yesterday, they had an attorney. S. Lloyd Anderson had been out last night with Rizz. They'd talked some strategy and had a number of cocktails. Lloyd had speculated about the university claiming the research.

"Jim, if Laura says Drake is good, I'm headed for the lab." The university chemical storehouse building was in north Minneapolis, no more than fifteen minutes away. "Don't mention any of this to Drake. He doesn't need this now."

Rizz stretched forward, his finger just reaching the driver's shoulder.

"Change in plans, Vang. An emergency. Turn left here."

The driver shook his head. "I may get in trouble. I need this job."

"There's $100 in it for you, and I'll take the blame for you going off schedule. It's not far. Turn left here."

The van swung left as Rizz entered the number.

He held the phone to his ear and prayed he got an answer. It had been a late night and they'd enjoyed lots of quality alcohol.

“S. Lloyd Anderson.” The attorney sounded bright and alert.

“Lloyd. It's Rizz. Get to 2114 Jander Avenue right now. I'll meet you there. The university is cleaning out our lab. They're trying to steal D-44.”

Chapter 38

Townhouse, 7:38 a.m.

The kitchen wall phone rang. Rachelle set the bowls of cereal in front of the kids, pivoted, and grabbed the receiver. *Probably another of Drake's "I'll be late" calls.*

"Hello."

"Rachelle, this is Laura Vonser. One of the ER residents. I don't know if you remember me. Drake asked me to call."

Let me guess. He's real busy and won't be home forever. "I remember you. How long?" Rachelle said.

"Excuse me?"

"How long is Drake going to be tied up?" Stop it, Rachelle. You sound like the b-word.

"I'm not sure what you know, but Drake had an allergic reaction this morning. A bad one. He can't talk right now and we'll need to keep him for a while. He didn't want you to worry."

Her gut clenched and her hands went cold. Drake had almost died years back from a reaction to an antibiotic. It had been terrifying.

"Oh my God. Is he okay?" *Who can watch the kids?* "I'm coming right down."

Her tone had risen and she knew she'd talked rapid-fire. The kids looked to her with worry on their faces. *I need to be calm.*

"Rachelle. He's doing well. Everything is getting better. I've got him and won't let him get into trouble. He can't talk right now, but he gave me three messages for you: stay home, let the kids know he's okay, and know he loves you all."

"He's okay? Are you sure?" She fought to keep her breathing in check.

“He's looking better by the minute. I, or maybe even Drake, will call you in a few hours. Okay?”

“Okay... And Laura—thank you and the others for taking care of him. Tell him we love him.”

She hung up and faced the two lost faces. “Daddy is okay. He was a little sick but now he's better. He says he loves you.”

The kids came to her and they all hugged.

“Scary but it's all going to be okay,” she said. Shane and Kristin nodded.

They'd handled the news without tears or panic. That was a good thing.

Perhaps we're getting better.

Chapter 39

University Chemical Storehouse, research lab, 8:10 a.m.

"Vang, pull over right here," Rizz said.

The Project Mobility van pulled to the curb just outside the fenced-in parking lot.

Rizz viewed the pre-World War Two brick structure. The lower level now housed little-used university offices. For the past four years, Drake, Rizz, and Jon had rented a small section of the otherwise deserted second floor as their research lab. At times Drake had practically lived there.

It was here that Drake had developed and tested the drug that looked to be a breakthrough. Rizz had updated S. Lloyd Anderson on what had occurred after.

Greed and D-44's potential had led to betrayal, murder, and violence. Rizz had been left paralyzed, Jon nearly dead, and Drake and his family had been subjected to a nightmare from which they had not fully recovered.

Rizz scanned the lot. Two trucks and a car that didn't belong. The loading dock doors were closed. Nothing had been loaded yet. They had to be stopped!

Rizz checked the time and entered Lloyd's number again.

He rested his other hand on his lap—he felt nothing. His legs might as well be wood. From his chest down, dead weight, like a sandbag fused to his trunk. D-44's promise had led Rizz to inject the experimental, untried-in-humans drug into his own body. He hadn't shared that with Lloyd. No one but he and Drake knew they'd taken that risk.

"S. Lloyd Anderson, attorney."

"Lloyd, I'm here. How long for you?"

"I'm less than ten minutes away and driving like a mad man. What have you got?"

"I see two trucks near the loading dock. Doesn't look like they've loaded yet. I'm just outside the lot. They must be inside."

"Any police or government vehicles?"

"The trucks are probably university. There's a black Lincoln. It's right alongside the trucks. Could be a university vehicle. What do you think?"

"Just watch until I get there. Think about what you want most from the lab. When I get there I'm going to try and stonewall them, but they're probably prepared for that. Realistically, we'll be lucky to lay hands on a few personal things, but even that may be tough. Follow me?"

"We can't let them take the drug." Rizz's hand had slipped into his lap bag and he felt the steely weight of the 38-caliber pistol. Bastards!

D-44 and the research might be the only things of value Drake would have left if he lost his license and his ability to practice as a doctor. Rizz gripped the gun's knurled handle. For him, another dose of D-44 might be the difference between being stuck in this damn chair forever or getting another chance at life.

"Listen to me, Rizz. We do nothing illegal." Lloyd sounded calm. Rizz wasn't. "We salvage what we can today and set up for the legal fight to come."

Rizz disconnected. They were trying to steal Rizz's best chance for recovery. What wouldn't he do to stop that?

Vang had been listening. He turned and faced Rizz.

"These trucks are here to steal from you?"

"Yes."

"Do you need to fight them?"

"The guys in the trucks are just working guys. They're just doing what they're told. It's the assholes who sent them who are the real thieves." Rizz let go of the gun. It was true. The workers were surely just regular employees just doing their jobs with no idea what was going down.

"I can block the trucks with the van." Vang nodded toward the lot's entrance. "They don't get out until you say."

Rizz looked at the man anew. There was some gray in his hair and deep lines around his eyes—he was older than Rizz had initially thought.

Few remembered that the Hmong people had earned their entry to the U.S. through their fierce fighting in support of Americans in the jungles ofSoutheast Asia. Could Vang be old enough to have been one of those fearless allies?

"Thanks, Vang, but no. I don't want you to get in trouble," Rizz said

"Now you say." Vang wore an anxious look. "I in much big trouble already. Ten-minute trip to hospital that I never finish. Boss-man be big angry with Vang." His accent had tripled. He held the scared expression for a moment before his face broke and he laughed.

"I'm bullshitting you." The accent dropped to a trace. He held up his cell phone, still wearing a grin. "I texted dispatch that I have engine trouble and canceled my next pick-up. No worries."

"Nice—you had me." Rizz smiled. Normally he would have laughed but the situation was too grim. His best chance for regaining his life was under threat. "Good stuff, Vang. I love a smart-ass. And thanks for offering to help."

"You tell me to stop them and I'll make it happen. Whatever it takes." The lean man spoke matter of factly, without a hint of fear.

"Stay ready, sir." Rizz met the surprising man's unflinching eyes. "I might need to take you up on your offer to help."

Five minutes passed and the loading dock door lifted. Two guys stood on the dock, one short and old, the other tall and young, both wearing work pants and heavy coats. The younger guy hopped off the dock and moved to the door of the idling truck.

"Okay, Vang. Pull in the lot and nose me up alongside that truck. And put down the window please."

Vang pulled the van close alongside. The young guy looked over, then walked to the van's passenger window. Long hair and no hat or gloves. A Minnesota Wild hockey sweatshirt showed beneath his unzipped jacket.

"Can I help you?" he said looking at Vang then focusing on Rizz. His eyes scanned the wheelchair then looked away.

"I'm Dr. Michael Rizzini. My laboratory is on the second floor," Rizz said. He spied cages on a cart just inside the loading dock. "Those cages are my property. What the hell are you doing?"

The guy made a face and shrugged. "We were told to pick up these animals and the other stuff and transport it. Just a minute." He turned toward the older guy on the dock and yelled, “This guy is a doctor. He says these cages and cats are theirs. You sure you got this right?”

“The university guy upstairs pointed these out. Said he was a lawyer and he seemed sure,” the older guy yelled back.

“Go get him, will ya?” the younger man hollered. “This is messed up.” The kid turned back to Rizz. He shrugged again. “We're getting the guy.”

“You have animals in the kennels?”

“Well, yeah. There's five cats. We're supposed to bring them and the other gear over to the St. Paul campus. There's another crew coming for some of the other stuff. The lawyer-guy said it's all going.”

“Vang, do me a favor. Hop up on the dock and see if there's a little black-and-white cat in one of those cages.”

Vang climbed out of the van and mounted the steps to the dock. He glanced in, then raised a hand with a thumb up.

“Buddy,” Rizz said to the kid, “those are all my cats, but the black-and-white one is my pet.” He raised his voice. “Vang, please bring the cage with the black-and-white cat to the van.” *Hell, if he'd let the bastards take Flo-Jo.*

The young guy shook his head. “Gee, I don't know—”

“Believe me,” said Rizz. “*I* do know.”

Vang slid the cage on the floor behind Rizz.

“Hey, what are you doing?” A tall, heavy-set guy in black-framed glasses and a corduroy sport-coat with elbow patches hollered from the loading dock.

Before Rizz could respond, a red Escalade bucked through the driveway and pulled to a sliding stop alongside the van. Lloyd hopped out of the driver side door, coatless in a jet-black suit with a flame-orange tie.

He took a look, then addressed the elbow-patched dude.

“Any effort to remove items from this facility constitutes robbery and intellectual property theft, and in addition may be prosecutable as corporate espionage.”

He raised his smart-phone camera and panned the area. “Please identify yourself, sir. Do you have any documents supporting your seizure of my clients' property? If you remove anything, I will call the police.”

The guy reached into his pocket and pulled out an envelope. “I have here the deed, the rental agreement, a copy documenting the status of the renters as part of a university medical training program, and the intellectual property waiver that applies. I have an order of seizure signed by the Dean of the Medical School, the university president, and the chief university counsel. We are entirely within our rights to remove university property and materials of research performed by university-affiliated persons." He paused looking smug. "I'm attorney Afton P. Tait, and I'm overseeing this lawful transfer of university holdings. Call the police if you must, but it will accomplish nothing."

"Your assertions are categorically errant, although we will not resolve that in this parking lot. Let me consult with my client." Lloyd moved to the side door of the van then leaned his head in.

"Rizz, I'm afraid getting the police involved right now may hurt our cause. We may look better if we play victim."

"Okay. No cops, but you need to get a few things. He handed Lloyd the list he'd written in the minutes while waiting. "Lloyd, this is Vang." Rizz nodded to the driver. "He's willing to help. Take him with you and get everything on this list."

Lloyd scanned the list then frowned. "This looks like junk."

"Just do it, Lloyd." Stay calm, Rizz. Do not flip out.

"Come on, Rizz." Lloyd read from the list, "Bottle of Wild Turkey, iPad player, two plastic drums, one with wood chips, and one with cat food—"

Rizz's patience disappeared. He clamped a hand on Lloyd's forearm hard enough to draw a surprised look. He snatched the list and pushed it again to Lloyd's chest.

"I'm not asking your opinion, Lloyd. I don't have time to explain. Do whatever you need to, but get this stuff."

Chapter 40

The fluorescent orange Humvee with its “IC-DEAD” custom plates sat idling in the “Police Only” zone under the ER canopy. As Drake climbed out of the ER wheelchair and approached the vehicle, he heard the driving beat of Tom Petty's “Won't Back Down” throbbing at high volume from within the vehicle.

As Drake passed near the front bumper, the horn sounded, causing him to flinch. Medical examiner Kip Dronen’s wild hair and wireless glasses tipped back as the man behind the wheel laughed like a junior high smart ass. Drake shook his head. Referring to forensic pathologist Kip Dronen as eccentric was like saying Genghis Khan was assertive.

The forever “assistant chief” medical examiner and national authority on death was one of the very few people that Drake could come up with to call for a ride.

During his last several hours in the ER, Drake had maintained good vitals as his swelling and other signs of anaphylaxis abated. Laura had removed the breathing tube an hour earlier. Drake's throat hurt and his voice rasped, but his airway remained open. Care for anaphylaxis would typically include admission or at least observation for a longer time, as Drake’s traumatic intubation could cause swelling of the vocal cords later. Laura recommended admission, but Drake refused. She protested, but Drake could tell she understood. He could take care of himself.

They provided him an epinephrine injection kit to replace his old ampule and hypodermic. He promised to seek help immediately if he had any recurrent symptoms.

“Don't let the epi freeze, and try to avoid the need to intubate yourself again—okay?” She'd winked.

Drake had called the morgue and been connected with Kip.

"Shit, ER. Yesterday you're calling me 'friend,' and today I'm supposed to drop everything because you need a ride. If I become a 'good friend,' would that mean I get to give you money?" Kip spoke in his usual whine, but Drake was learning half of it was an act.

"I'm imposing on you again, Kip. If you pick me up, you'd be really helping me out. You're a good man."

Those words had briefly left the pathologist speechless.

Drake opened the illegally parked, gaudy vehicle's door. Kip turned down the tunes.

"Shit, ER, get your ass in here and close that door. It's effing freezing."

Drake did so, though he was not moving like his usual self.

Kip glanced at him, then did a double-take. "Hell, man. You said you needed a ride—it looks like you need an ambulance. What happened to you?"

"Anaphylactic shock." His tongue still felt thick and the words came out a bit slurred.

"When?"

"This morning."

"Wow! The only time I've seen a face like yours is at autopsy. Post-edema dermal redundancy. It's a good look—if you're a Shar-Pei." His teen-girl shrill laugh grated. "And your voice sounds like you've been gargling broken glass."

Drake felt his face. The swelling had receded, and his skin felt slack and loose.

"Yeah. I'm glad I'm okay, too."

"Oh, flog me." Kip clutched his hands to his chest. "Another violation of ER guy and Oprah's touchy-feely laws." He held his wrists extended. "Call the sensitivity police. Cuff me. I confess." He dropped his hands, then frowned. "On second thought, how about just getting over yourself?" He shrugged. "You're alive."

Drake's laugh sprang so fast he startled himself. He'd been playing the tiny violin of self-pity. Anyone other than Kip would have been cooing in sympathy.

Kip had slashed through Drake's whining. Was there anyone else on the planet who would respond like Kip?

Kip looked surprised at Drake's reaction, then smiled.

"That's it, ER. You can't go getting all pissy about a little thing like nearly dying. Shit, we're all drunks on a greasy tightrope in a killer wind. None of us get out of here alive."

Drake laughed even harder despite the pain in his throat. *How bent had he become?* Kip Dronen, possibly the most inappropriate and cynical guy ever—a laugh riot.

Drake fought to stifle his mirth. *Am I high?*

He regained control.

Kip asked for the details of Drake's anaphylactic shock. Drake recounted the morning's events from the time he'd climbed into his frozen car until he was in the back of the ambulance.

"Very cool." Kip sounded envious.

Drake shook his head. Throat raw, face deformed, overall weak, and the memory of the endless, indescribably horrific inability to breathe—at one point he'd been certain he would die. Nothing about it seemed cool.

A hand shook his shoulder. "Hello, earth to ER guy. Hello?"

"Huh? What?"

"Damn, you were gone there for a bit." Kip sighed. "I think your near-death trick left you a bit cloudy."

Drake thought of his laugh attack. And he did feel scattered. Maybe the antihistamines or the steroids? Hell, he'd been in shock. He had good reason to be foggy.

"You're right. I'm a bit slow right now. What did I miss?"

"I asked what you reacted to. What triggered the anaphylaxis?"

"I have no idea. In the past I almost died after exposure to penicillin. Today is a mystery."

"Not good. Maybe you developed an allergy to something in the ER?"

"Probably, but strange that I didn't develop symptoms until I was on my way to the lab."

Kip remained silent.

"They brought my car back to my lot. Can you drop me there?"

"Has anybody checked your car?"

"Security retrieved it. No mention of troubles."

Kip blew out a big breath, then stared at Drake.

"Damn, dude, who are you and what did you do with that reasonably bright ER guy, Drake Cody?" He shook his head.

"Huh?" Drake's thoughts were still sluggish.

"Shit, man. Lucky for you, your special, bestest friend ever is on the scene. You're not firing on all cylinders. Which lot is your car in?"

"Chicago Avenue. Assigned parking." As he answered he recognized two things.

He'd been subjected to shock and low oxygen and received antihistamines and high-dose steroids. The after-effects had left him spacey and giddy.

The second realization—his car.

Kip's thoughts had been ahead of Drake's.

He might owe the social misfit and brilliant pathologist for much more than just a ride.

Chapter 41

Town house, late afternoon

Rachelle pushed down and twisted the child-proof cap.

The kids were downstairs watching a Disney video. The outer doors were bolted and the alarm system on. The middle of the afternoon—all secure. Except nothing was.

Dr. Laura had said Drake's allergic reaction was serious. Rachelle knew what emergency doctors considered serious. It meant Drake had almost died. Somehow she hadn't fallen apart. She'd responded well—at first. But as the minutes and hours passed, her fear grew.

Yesterday she'd been worried about Drake losing the job that meant so much to him. Today brought the threat of him dying. Earlier, if not for the kids, she could have become hysterical.

Now it seemed Drake was doing better. She'd called the ER five minutes ago and Dr. Laura said she was surprised how quickly he was improving. Rachelle could tell he'd been bad. Even Dr. Laura said it had been a scary thing. The doctors that worked with Drake did not scare easily.

Rachelle hugged herself tight. *I do.*

She rolled one of the shiny red capsules around the palm of her hand. She could already imagine the drug slipping her into a warm bath of chemical numbness. A place where her head did not writhe with worry and the relentless images of past and possible nightmares were temporarily hidden in fog.

She'd first felt the escape chemicals offered as a child, starting in the hospital with the medications prescribed by doctors trying to help her deal with the physical and emotional trauma she'd suffered.

Medications had been a big part of her childhood and teen years. Concern had developed about her use of some meds. When she was thirteen years old, one doctor had said, "The drugs we give to help can also harm." She'd gone on to share, "Too much use causes dependence and stops people's emotional growth."

It became more and more important to Rachelle to have the medications. By her fifteenth birthday, her caregivers had recognized that dependence for her was more than a possibility. After meetings, counseling, and finally threats, the medical people had cut her off from the escape she craved.

After that, she used marijuana and street drugs every day for over three years while still working to scam prescriptions. A chance meeting leading to her first job—as a personal health caretaker for a patient with Down's syndrome—had ended her use of street drugs.

She still used prescription medications, but only occasionally and guiltily so. She knew that, for her, they were unhealthy. The doctors had warned her that the sedative medications she'd become dependent on did not cure anything. They only treated symptoms. Other than when she experienced a full-blown panic attack, they were an escape—a way to avoid her issues. They didn't help. The drugs prevented her from getting stronger and, when they wore off, they left her more messed up than before.

But sometimes, in the moment, the urge for escape could be overwhelming. Like now, when it felt as if worry and dread were holding her under water, drowning her. She needed air. Her nerves were a rubber band twisted to near the breaking point. *God, I am such a mess.*

The label of her only remaining prescription read, "Take one capsule each 6 hours as needed for anxiety/panic." Wouldn't anyone in her spot feel anxious? Her husband recovering from a near-fatal reaction and all the other issues they faced.

Wouldn't that be enough to justify anxiety even without the horrors of her recent and distant past?

This bottle had lasted much longer than those in the past. For the first weeks after the kidnapping, she'd been in the hospital dealing with her burns and skin grafts. She'd done well. Then they'd found Kaye. She'd stayed with them whenever Drake was gone—which was almost always.

The kids loved her. She laughed at things that would have had Rachelle hyperventilating. Kaye's competence and spare-the-drama attitude had been a gift—for Rachelle most of all.

Four days earlier, Kaye had been called out-of-state to care for a sick relative. Rachelle missed her.

Why can't I face things on my own?

In the last few days, her worries had grown. Despite recognizing much of what she faced was bad luck and misfortune, she felt she'd somehow brought it on herself. Karma? Did she deserve to suffer?

She'd done terrible things. And the way she'd manipulated Drake was the most calculated and deceitful of all.

Her husband, the father of their children—the best thing in her life—and their relationship was borne of a lie.

Her guilt, Drake's record, the threat to his career, his near-death reaction, their still-recovering kids, her egg-shell fragile emotions—the escape the medication offered called out to her. But she reminded herself it was not a true escape. It only allowed her to hide for a while with the fears returning, even more debilitating.

She had lots of experience playing the excuse game—her childhood, the recent traumatic events, her diagnoses of PTSD and anxiety, her virtual single parenthood, and more. She'd shared some of her litany with Kaye one day. The older woman had given her a quick hug. "Look at what you have—wonderful children and a good man. Focus on the good, honey. Keep busy and try not to worry so much."

Rachelle and Drake had not discussed any further what they'd shared after Faith's murder and the kidnapping. Maybe it was best he didn't know more. Things had been good between them. It seemed that for both of them the intimacy and release of lovemaking communicated something beyond what they could share otherwise.

Rachelle kept her guilt about the marriage hidden. Drake rarely shared his troubles and had told her little about his past. They both carried secrets but they reveled in one another.

Rachelle looked at the pink, thickened tissue of her hands and wrists. She'd gotten stronger. Scarred but functional. Several days earlier, she'd completed her first painting since the grafts. It had been one of her best works yet.

But now that calm had disappeared. Her mind thrashed like a blender on high. The red pill in her hand would bring the fuzzy disconnect she craved.

Tears trickled down her cheeks. She raised the pill and put it in her mouth.

She could hear Kaye's words, "...try not to worry so much."

Rachelle's response wailed in her mind. *I can't stop.*

She thought of her mother. Her stomach clenched and she placed a hand over the scar on her neck. *No!*

She spit the pill into her hand.

Chapter 42

Downtown Minneapolis

“It's this lot, Kip. Pull in.”

The open-air parking lot had an automated lift arm blocking entry.

“A pay lot?” Kip said.

“Right. Just hit the button and grab the ticket.”

“What's the minimum cost?”

“Whatever.” Drake's thoughts were on the events of the morning.

“Whatever? Screw you. I'm not paying,” Kip said.

Drake looked over at Kip. His expression proved him serious.

“I'll pay, Kip.” Holy crap, yet another weird trait.

“Hell yes, you will.” The medical examiner pushed the button and grabbed the ticket the machine spit out. “These lots aren't cheap.”

I just learned who is. Drake's thoughts flashed back to the morning. His throat went tight as he spied his Dodge. Whoever had picked it up for him had backed it into his assigned space.

“Right here, Kip. The old blue Dodge. The spot next to it is open.”

“Good God, man. You drive that? What a wreck.”

“Don't have a lot of cash, Kip. I'm still a resident and I have a mountain of debt. It's a dependable car. I'm glad to have it.”

Kip pulled his Humvee in next to the Dodge, leaving his door adjacent to the driver's side of Drake's car.

“Give me your keys. Keep your ass right there—understood?” Kip pulled latex gloves from his center console, then put them on. He opened the door of the Humvee and stepped out. He'd left his window open and the car running. He spoke through the window. “Do not get out of the car.”

Drake understood. He'd caught up with Kip's spot-on reasoning.

"Tell me exactly what you did from the time you touched this heap this morning." He inspected the Dodge's door handle.

"I unlocked and opened the door, slid into the seat, closed the door, put the keys in the ignition and started the engine."

Kip unlocked and opened the door, then bent and inspected the car's interior.

"Were the windows frosted?" Kip spoke louder and Drake heard him easily.

"Yes. I scraped the outside, then after the engine had run for a bit, I turned on the defroster." Drake's throat hurt with the effort of raising his voice. His voice sounded raw.

"Was there any frost on the inside? Did you use a scraper inside?"

"Yes, but the frost was light—I scraped it, then waited on the defroster."

Kip leaned into the car, his face just above the dash. He extended a gloved finger, trailed it across the dash, then peered at it.

"Did you have flour or chalk in your car?" Kip said.

"Flour or chalk? No way. I cleaned the inside of the car a couple of days ago. I even wiped the dash down."

"There is a very fine dusting of white powder on your dash. I thought it was frost, but it's not. You didn't notice anything on the dash this morning? It's miniscule and almost invisible."

Powder? Drake thought through his actions. Thick frost on the exterior window and light frost on the inside. He'd turned on the defroster—whoa. He remembered. The defroster blower had sent up a mini-flurry. He'd assumed it was frost crystals.

"I think powder blew out when I turned on the defroster fan."

"Stay there, Drake." Kip went to the back of the Humvee and opened the gate. He returned to the Dodge with a plastic case that looked like a large tackle box. He opened it and removed a tiny specimen envelope, a plastic bag, and a tiny brush. He bent into the Dodge and brushed the surface of the dash. He directed the contents into the envelope, closed it, then placed it in the bag.

"I'm going to get rid of these gloves, use the wipes I have in the back to clean my hands, and take off my coat and gloves and leave them in the back. You cannot get in your car. Until I wipe myself down, you will have to try and restrain your likely overwhelming urges to touch me. I'll give you a ride where you need to go and then I'm taking what I collected to the lab."

"I appreciate it, Kip." *What would have happened if I'd climbed into my car?* It was an experiment Drake was glad to have skipped. "Penicillin is the drug I'm allergic to. Almost has to be it."

"10-4, ER. That's my bet as well. It all fits together." He shook his head and smiled. "But I don't bet. I prove. It's likely I'm a hero again, but we'll have to wait for confirmation."

"You're the best, Kip."

"I know," he said, his voice coming through from the now-open tailgate. "It's actually quite cool being brilliant. But if I'm right, and I'm always right," he snapped his case closed, "someone wants you dead."

Chapter 43

Chicago Avenue parking lot, afternoon

Farley pulled the Crown Vic up behind the Humvee. His partner, Detective Aki Yamada, nodded toward the vehicle and its "IC-DEAD" license plate. The idling, orange Humvee's exhaust rose like white smoke in the frigid parking lot.

"Now we know who called 9-1-1 and requested us. It's Dr. Death. Kip Dronen."

"I've never met him in person. His smarts sure helped in the Faith Reinhorst Malar murder." Farley remembered the excited, squeaky voice on the phone in the midst of the murder investigation. The doctor clearly got into his work.

"Partner, I'll warn you. He's a genius, but he's been the *assistant* medical examiner for more than a decade because he's incredibly weird." Aki undid the seatbelt. "His ego blocks out the sun and he's got a black belt in attitude." Aki frowned. "He's always worth listening to but for some reason he loves to give me shit." He opened his door. "And he's damn good at it."

The detectives stood by the Humvee's driver's door. Aki tapped on the tinted window. It slid down an inch.

"Are your shoes clean?" came the shrill voice of Kip Dronen. "I've got Drake Cody here. If you don't dirty my car, I'll let you sit in the back." The locks popped.

Aki got in behind Kip, and Farley went around and climbed in the other back door.

***

The icy air chilled Drake as Detectives Yamada and Farley climbed into the back seat of Kip's vehicle.

"Close the damn doors. It's ass-freezing cold out there," Kip whined.

Drake had not seen Aki since the day after Rachelle and the kids were saved. Drake vaguely remembered being questioned immediately after the surgery for the gunshot wound to his shoulder. He'd figured out from Farley's earlier phone call about Dan Ogren that he'd been there, but he wouldn't have recognized the baby-faced detective if not for the media pictures following the shoot-out.

"Good afternoon, assistant medical examiner. It's nice to see you, too." Aki said. "Doc Cody, it actually *is* nice to see you. I—geez, are you okay, doc? You don't look so good."

"A rough day so far," Drake said. "Thanks for coming. I want to thank both of you for helping me and my family."

"Doc," Aki said with a big smile, "you thanked us like one hundred times when we were at the hospital."

Farley nodded.

Drake thought about all that had gone on back then. Faith Reinhorst Malar's murder, Jon's near death, Rizz's paralysis, and the nightmare Rachelle and the kids had endured. Without the detectives, things would have been even worse.

"Excuse me, old ladies," Kip said. "How about saving this blah-blah shit for your Christmas cards?" He frowned. "I called you because I suspect an attempted murder went down. Want to try investigating? Maybe this time I won't have to provide *all* the answers. The crime scene is the beat-to-shit junker parked next to us."

"That car was the scene of an attempted murder?" Aki said.

"Yes. Drake barely survived an episode of anaphylactic shock this morning. I believe it was triggered by material planted in his car."

"Ana—what?" Aki said.

"I'm deathly allergic to penicillin," Drake said. "This morning when I left work and started to drive home, I had a severe allergic reaction—anaphylaxis is the medical term. I couldn't breathe, swelled up, and went into shock. The paramedics saved me." Drake pointed to his face. "I look nasty due to the swelling and other issues I had. I came very close to ending up on a slab at Kip's place of work." Drake's throat still hurt and he felt a fatigue so deep he ached. He needed to get home.

"It would have been an easy cause-of-death determination," Kip said. "The widespread tissue edema, vascular collapse, airway obstruction—a slam dunk for me. I'd have determined anaphylaxis in minutes. The only issue would have been finding the trigger. It would have been fun!"

For a moment they all stared in silence at the inappropriate cheerleader of death.

"Aki, Detective Farley—Kip just recovered what looks like the trigger. When I started my car this morning, I turned on the defroster. The fan blew out a cloud of what I thought was frost." Aki and Farley nodded. "It wasn't. Kip found traces of a white powder on my dash. I had to have breathed some in. The odds are we'll find it to be powdered penicillin."

Aki pulled out his phone but craned around toward Kip. "How long until you can identify the stuff?"

"It could take several hours."

"Could it be an accident?" Farley said.

"Hard to imagine," Kip said. "It's theoretically possible someone very stupid would think it was a clever prank. The range of allergic reactions is large. The vast majority are not life-threatening, but with Drake's previous history, an informed person would know the likelihood of death was high."

"Okay," Aki said. "We need to tow the car to police impound and work it." He turned to Kip. "Did you touch anything inside when you collected the powder?"

Kip shot Aki a look that would wither a redwood. His voice started shrill and rose as his volume climbed. "Yes. First I got naked and thrashed around the front and back seats, touched every surface with my bare hands and then launched body fluids." He shook his head. "Shit! I'm a medical examiner and probably the top forensic pathologist in the world. You dare question how I managed the crime scene?"

Aki rocked back in the face of the outburst then collected himself. "I'll take that as a 'no'."

Kip muttered while Aki turned to Drake.

"Doc, the obvious question. Who wants you dead?"

Drake paused. The question may have been obvious, but the answer was not. And not because there were no candidates. As the news reports had made widely known, his history included violence, incarceration, and secrets far different than other physicians. Much had happened that should not have. His conscience was not clear. Had the news reports allowed someone from his past to find him?

In a moment of self-pity less than twenty-four hours earlier, he'd wondered how things in his life could be worse. Today he had an answer.

Someone wants me dead.

***

I-394

The blue 1970 Buick Skylark rode like a dream. Drake had never driven a car anything like it—ancient but in perfect condition. Six p.m. and it had been dark for over an hour already. A chemical pine-scent came from the skull-shaped air freshener product which hung from the rearview mirror. Kip had interrogated Drake on his driving skills and delivered detailed instructions on appropriate care of one of his “babies” before handing over the keys. Drake was touched by the generosity of Kip's loan.

Drake's old Dodge had been towed to the police garage for forensic examination and an exhaustive cleanup. The thought of ever climbing in the Dodge again left him uneasy.

Only five minutes to the townhouse. Should he tell Rachelle his near-death reaction had likely been a murder attempt?

The burns of her wrist and hands were healed, but the drug-and-greed-crazed kidnapper had injured more than Rachelle's body. She didn't see herself as strong or brave, despite having proved herself to be both.

She'd been dealing well with things until the catastrophes of the past few days.

Now someone wanted him dead. Could she handle that?

The ER and the research still kept him away too much. Hell, other than in the hospital after they'd almost lost everything, they hadn't talked much. Drake busy. Rachelle quiet. Both plagued by their pasts and hesitant. Physically they came together often and desperately. Their hunger for each other greater than ever. But...

Drake squeezed the steering wheel. The swelling of his hands and fingers was gone. He craned his neck and glanced in the rearview mirror. Bags under his eyes, but otherwise he didn't look too bad.

Just eleven hours earlier someone had tried to kill him. They'd come within seconds of taking him from those who needed him. The thought fanned the embers of who he'd been when locked up with violent offenders.

That person knew violence. Knew rage. Knew how to hurt and kill.

A primitive part of himself had surfaced when he'd dealt with the drug-seeking ER patient who'd struck Patti. That same part had taken over when the deranged woman had kidnapped and brutalized Rachelle and his children. It was the part he wanted to turn loose on Dan Ogren and the abusive jerk neighbor who'd bullied Shane.

Drake knew violence and death—those were facts of his life.

Something beyond the facts caused him worry. A fear that slunk among the shadows of his mind.

Fear that not only did he have the capacity for violence—but that he liked it.

Chapter 44

Ogren Automotive, Bloomington dealership

Dan shut the door to his office at the west Bloomington dealership, the newest of the Ogren lots, located right off 494 in one of the most prestigious areas of the Twin Cities. After his father had become too messed up to work, Dan took the dealership as the site for his executive office.

Dan put his personal stamp on the lot. He hand-picked all the new employees. He'd made sure there were none of the old fart mechanics or salesmen who couldn't shut up about how Big Dan would do things. As if Dan cared.

He had things set up with a small but deluxe apartment that had a separate outside entrance and was also accessible from his office through a private door. He couldn't count the number of women he'd already banged there.

Dan could see from his office cameras when lone women came looking for a car. He would visit the sales floor or outside lot, check them out, and when he sensed a hot, hungry one—he could usually tell in a glance—he'd invite them to his office. Very often the women—whether married or single—accepted. They knew what his offer meant. Sometimes he even sold them a car.

Hot damn, he had a hell of a life going.

He made his way to the desktop computer. Mesh's text message had said: Please review email communication immediately. Maintain secure handling as I've instructed. Situation grim. Follow recommendations.

Mesh—one freaky smart little guy. Law degree and CPA. Knew everything about everything. He made sense of the business stuff for Dan. Like the CliffsNotes he'd used once or twice in college before he'd dropped out. Why read the whole book when you could get the answers in a few pages? Mesh's summaries were a good thing, because numbers, balance sheets, and business details bored him. How had his father, even with Mesh's help, managed all this? The big hick hadn't even completed high school.

So many things about his father made no sense. His success was the result of unbelievable luck. A rube from the wilds of northern Minnesota discharged from the army and staying with a friend in the Twin Cities. Life on a farm and motor pool duty in the Army helped him develop a skill—he could fix anything that had a motor.

His father started buying damaged cars, repairing and then selling them. Although his dad had zero sales savvy, permanently grease-stained knuckles, and an accent like something from an Ole and Lena joke, Ogren Automotive grew to be the most successful operation in five states. Just a grease monkey who'd been in the right place at the right time. And everyone acted like he was the second coming.

Dan's father's shadow loomed over everything in his life. Even the "Big Dan" moniker didn't die, despite Dan growing to be five inches taller than his father. Dan made it known that if anyone ever called him "Little Dan," they'd be looking for a new job.

Dan sat at his office desk, then pulled up Mesh's password-protected, encrypted email. He scanned the "operational position statement" Mesh had written.

As he did with virtually all business-related documents, Dan skipped straight to the summary:

The six Ogren dealerships, independent lease operations, finance operation, and repair and body work spin-offs are all under the ownership of Dan, Senior. Due to his failing health, you have power of attorney. This has allowed you to carry on business, access funds, and enter into debt agreements using the assets of Ogren Automotive as collateral.

Your personal withdrawals, losses, and fund transfers have placed the Ogren automotive enterprise in a severely compromised position. Several of your actions are, as I advised you at the time, criminal. The funds shown on the books are not the funds that actually exist.

They are shown as existing in different branches simultaneously.

Two major notes are due in approximately six months (June). You now have each of the separate Ogren operations using the others as collateral. Failure on either of the two major notes will trigger a domino-effect collapse of all. Bankruptcy, investigation, and criminal charges would quickly follow.

There's no potential for a bridge loan or bank bail-out.

It is my considered opinion that you would be convicted of financial crimes and have to serve time.

The notes must be paid by June, and the funds you've embezzled need to be replaced (i.e. balance the books). We may be able to do this if no new claims on your personal wealth are made. Who else do you owe? Have you told me all?

This brings me to the most pressing of the threats—your criminal case and Beth. If Beth divorces you under the terms of the prenuptial agreement, we could still pay off the loans and keep your financial crimes hidden.

If she divorces after a domestic violence conviction—even a misdemeanor—the prenuptial is void and we can't cover the loans or hide your crimes.

In layman's terms: if you are convicted of domestic violence and Beth files for divorce, the company will go bankrupt, and you'll end up broke and in jail.

That's the story. You've ignored virtually all of my advice, but you must listen to me now. I don't see any way you can avoid an abuse conviction, so you must somehow convince (beg/plead) Beth not to divorce you. If you don't, you will be ruined."

Dan slid back from the desk. Mesh had earlier said this was big trouble, but Dan had still held out hope. Mesh's message was doom.

Elbows on the arms of the chair, Dan supported his bent head on his fingers. His chest tightened. Son of a bitch.

Mesh's recommendations: Avoid conviction—though he says that is hopeless. Convince Beth not to divorce you. How?

Thanks loads for the worthless advice, Mesh.

At least Dan and Clara had tried to head off an abuse conviction—and a hell of a try at that. What had Mesh done other than piss and moan?

So many times before in his life, Dan had been caught going too far but had gotten away with it. He only truly got nailed the one time—and most said he'd got off easy on that one, too.

It had been his second year at the U. He'd had the world by the tits. Playing hockey, partying, and slamming chicks like a rock star. Hell—getting more prime than a rock star. Then little Miss "Boo-hoo, I said no." Women did not did not say "no" to Dan.

The University police had come to the frat house and taken him to their half-ass station off Oak Street on campus. Miss "No" in the hallway with cry-baby tears and her Mommy and Daddy.

The campus cops had asked him questions. Dan had his role scripted in an instant—he'd acted hurt and surprised. He'd had no idea the girl had felt that way.

He'd put on a good act. But not good enough.

He made his one phone call, then they put him in a cell in their cracker-box station. From there he'd watched the comings and goings of what had happened.

Big Dan arrived with a guy in a three-piece suit. His father had looked lost. Later his head hung—he never even looked at Dan. Didn't try to talk to him.

Meetings behind closed doors. An hour, then two. Police, her parents, more guys in suits. At five in the morning they unlocked the cell and the police escorted Dan and his father to the side door opening onto the parking lot.

It was February. Biting cold. The plowed snow from the near-empty lot formed a dirty, icy mountain next to his father's vehicle. A lone light shone from a utility pole. His father walked head down, silent. He arrived at the big Suburban.

"Hey, no worries, Dad," Dan had said. "It wasn't a big deal."

His father had Dan off his feet and slammed against the vehicle in a blink. The sturdy man's blocky fingers held Dan off the ground and pinned as if by the blades of a forklift. Dan had looked into his father's face anticipating anger.

He saw tears.

First silent, on a face twisted with pain. Then a single sob as he released Dan, letting him slide down the side of the vehicle. His father had stared into Dan's eyes, then buried his face in his hands as his massive shoulders quaked.

In that last look, Dan had seen what he knew his father had been trying to hide for a long time.

His father knew what Dan was.

And he was ashamed.

***

Dan skimmed the final paragraphs of Mesh's email summary a last time and then deleted it. "Broke and in jail," Mesh had projected.

Dan would do anything and everything necessary to ensure that didn't happen. He didn't trust that Mesh felt the same do-or-die commitment.

Dan's cell rung. He scanned the ID. Speak of the devil.

"Yeah, Mesh."

"We need to meet right now. I have bad news. We need to discuss it face-to-face." Mesh spoke fast and sounded tense.

"Okay. I just read your email. Don't panic."

"Where can we meet?"

"I was just going to go visit the old man at the nursing home."

"Really?" Surprise sounded in Mesh's voice. "Okay, I'll meet you at Noble Village in your dad's room. I'm leaving now."

Dan disconnected. He hoped Mesh was overreacting. What could be so bad they had to meet immediately?

Chapter 45

Noble Village

From the window of his father's room, Dan spotted Mesh pulling into the parking lot. They called the place a "senior community," but it was nothing more than a fancy nursing home in Dan's mind—a place to park oldsters until they died. Dan had given Mesh the late-model, luxury car—on the books it was Ogren Automotive but same thing. Hell, Dan paid the little guy well. The attorney climbed out of the car, his breath fogging. He hunched into his coat as he headed towards the entrance, his face a frown.

When Mesh had called Dan insistent they had to meet "right now," Noble Village made sense, since he needed to check the layout anyway.

His father had been here for almost three years. Briefly in an independent apartment but soon transferred to full nursing care as strokes and dementia left him helpless.

Even though it was only a ten-minute drive from his office at the Bloomington dealership, Dan rarely visited. The place bugged him. Old people, wheelchairs, the smell—how did anyone work here? The few times he did visit, the old man slept most of the time. Like he was now. If not for the noise of his open-mouthed, lolling-tongue breathing, you'd swear the sunken, gray man was a corpse.

The rare times Dan saw him awake, his father didn't seem to recognize him or, the times he did, he became red-faced or had tears run down his face.

His father— too feeble to talk, stand, or wipe his own ass but he could still show his disapproval of Dan. *Screw him.*

Mesh seemed intent on taking over the judgment role. He'd been bailing Dan out of trouble since before college, but his nagging had grown old. And the smart, usually kick-ass attorney wasn't coming up with any answers this time. His "if you get convicted of abuse and Beth divorces, you'll lose everything and go to jail" was stating the problem, not the solution.

Dan had the big picture. He needed money and he needed to avoid being convicted on the abuse charge. If convicted, he needed to avoid divorce. His situation in a nutshell—the CliffsNotes version.

He'd hear what Mesh had to say, but he was working on things himself—with Clara's help.

They'd tried to head off a conviction on the domestic abuse charge. It had been a hell of a plan and it almost worked. But "almost" didn't count for shit.

He looked around. His father's private room was very private—rarely anyone around. Dan's leather athletic bag lay on the floor next to the chair. He'd bring it again tomorrow. Damn if Clara had not come up with another plan. She just might be as smart as she constantly told him she was.

A nurse accompanied Mesh into the room.

"Here they are," she said, smiling.

"Thank you." Mesh practically bowed. "Have a good day."

For a smart guy, Mesh had never learned who it paid to be nice to and who it was best to command. Be nice to those who have power or something you need. Command the rest. Underlings may not like it, but they jump to take care of those who chew their ass if they don't. Nice guys get forgotten.

Mesh and his old man were both like that. They talked to waitresses, lawn care guys, and other nobodies like they mattered.

Mesh stood at the foot of Dan's father's bed and looked at the slack-jawed old man.

"Every time I see him he's smaller," Mesh whispered. "He looks so frail."

"What the hell are you whispering for?" Dan said. "He's out of it. He wouldn't know what's happening if you set him on fire."

"Please don't talk like that." Mesh shook his head. "Your dad is a special man."

"Whatever he might have been," Dan shrugged, "he ain't anymore. Lighten up, Mesh. He's way beyond having his feelings hurt."

Mesh's eyes flamed and his jaw clenched. For an instant Dan thought the little guy might lose it. Nope—wasn't gonna happen. Mesh never made a move without thinking it through.

Loyal, that's what Mesh was. Like a dog. He thought of Beth and the goofy mutt she worshipped.

For being so smart, Mesh sometimes couldn't see the obvious. Dan's attachment to Mesh went as far as Mesh's ability to keep him out of trouble or make him money. Beyond that, he was someone Dan tolerated.

"What did you need to tell me that you couldn't call or text me with?" Dan asked.

"It isn't good." Mesh sat in the chair facing Dan.

"You've said that—cool the drama. What is it?" *Why is he dragging this out?*

"A contact I have in the D.A.'s office shared some news. Beth filed for an order of protection against you. She amended her report to the police. She said she was afraid to tell the truth in the ER. She says you assaulted her."

"Damn!" Dan jumped to his feet. "Are you shitting me?" *That bitch! That effing bitch!*

"There's more."

"Well, spit it out."

"Beth contacted Nancy Dudley. That's who facilitated the protection order request and change in Beth's report. She's one of the best divorce lawyers in the Twin Cities."

"Contacted? Has she filed for divorce? Contacted might not mean shit." Dan knew what it meant but it felt as if Mesh was drawing things out—as if he enjoyed delivering the bad news.

Mesh raised both hands in a "calm down" fashion. Dan wanted to punch him.

"It wouldn't make sense for them to file now. They'll wait for the verdict of the abuse trial. With you convicted, the divorce becomes a slam dunk. The court will award her everything they can."

Dan's throat constricted, his stomach clenched. The bitch could ruin him. He rubbed his face with both hands. *Shit!*

Mesh stood.

"You said there was no way Beth would ever say you assaulted her—you were wrong. If you did hurt her that's sick, and I don't want to know. Whether you did or not, her claim changes everything. The case hinged on the ER doctor. That's not true now. If she testifies—and it's clear she plans to—you'll be convicted. I told you if you avoided conviction and divorce, we might be able to find a way for you to cover the June payments and avoid default. I don't see that happening now."

"You said if I inherited before June it looked good."

"Geez, Dan." Mesh turned toward the sleeping old person. "Have some respect."

"Respect?" Dan frowned. "Nothing means anything to him anymore. We're talking about *me* here. You said if I inherit before the payments are due it looks good."

Mesh sighed, then rocked his head back and closed his eyes.

"Well?" Dan said.

"I never said it looked good," Mesh spoke quietly. "I said if you inherit before June you have a few more options. Inheritance and return of ninety percent of the buy-in from this place might help you, but inheritance happens when it happens. It would improve your odds of staying out of jail in the short term, but if Beth divorces after an abuse conviction, your crimes would still be discovered in the end."

"News flash, Mesh. It's *our* crimes."

Mesh's jaw dropped. His color paled.

How could he be surprised? Had Mesh thought Dan wasn't serious about not going down alone?

"Even with this shit you created you'd do that to me? I counseled in the strongest possible terms against your handling of the company funds." Mesh shook his head. "I advised against those moves. I specifically mentioned criminal charges, conviction, and jail. You ignored me."

"Whatever." Dan leaned forward and stared into Mesh's eyes. "If I go down. You go down." Dan leaned back, his foot bumping the athletic bag on the floor. 'Broke and in jail' would mean the end of the sex, drinking, drugs, and quality lifestyle Dan had built.

No way would he give it up without a fight. No way he'd give it up, period.

“Mesh, old buddy.” Dan put a hand on Mesh's shoulder. The man flinched like he'd been touched by a branding iron. “We're in some very deep shit. Use those smarts of yours and get us out, my friend. If you don’t, we are both truly, royally, and forever screwed.”

Chapter 46

Townhouse

The solid mechanism of the deadbolt slid open as Drake unlocked the second of the front door locks. He stepped out of the cold and already dark Minnesota evening. The townhouse was the same Spackle-patched, low-rent dwelling it had been before the kidnapping, but the doors and windows were now security grade. Rachelle had overseen these changes and more. He entered the security code on the wall-mounted alarm panel.

"I'm home," he called out. He took off his jacket. The bone-deep exhaustion he felt lifted in the tide of his anticipation.

Footsteps rumbled up the basement stairs, then Shane and Kristin burst around the corner. Kristin jumped into his arms.

Shane pulled up short, his gaze fixed. "You don't look right." His worry was palpable.

Kristin leaned back and stared at Drake's face.

Drake crouched and set her down. He reached for Shane and put an arm around him.

"I'm okay." Drake smiled. He had checked himself before coming in and knew only mild changes were still visible. "Do I look like a saggy face? A friend said I looked like a Shar-Pei dog." The kids knew that breed and virtually every other as they regularly "dog-shopped," impatiently awaiting the day they lived someplace where they could have a pet.

"Are you all right, Daddy?" Kristin spoke hesitantly. Shane remained silent, his eyes locked.

"I'm fine, little guys."

He looked up from his crouch and found Rachelle standing above him near the bottom of the stairs. She held a hand to her mouth, her eyes wide.

“Hey there, lovely lady. How about you?” He tugged on the loose skin. “Do you like the look?”

She said nothing.

“I was a little sick this morning, kids. I still look a little funny, but everything will go back to normal. I'm fine.” He stood.

Rachelle launched herself toward him. He wrapped his arms around her as she dove into his arms. She pressed her head against him as they clenched each other fiercely. He felt her body quake and the wetness of her tears on his chest.

The kids came forward and clung to them. They stood in a family hug for some time. The last time they'd embraced like this had been in the burn unit when they'd finally been safe and together after the nightmare of the kidnapping and shootings.

Drake loved them so strongly that the thought of losing any of them caused a stab of fear that penetrated to the depths of his being.

His love for them and the fear of their loss were the two sides of a coin minted in the forge of his heart.

No matter how exhausted, hurt, or sick he might be, he was sure of one thing.

He knew what mattered most.

Chapter 47

The bedside clock flashed 6:50 a.m.

Drake had come awake like a switch had been flipped. He felt strong. He'd slept almost eleven hours. Incredible. That was more sleep than he often got in four days.

Less than twenty-one hours earlier he'd been near death. Now other than soreness of his mouth and deep in his throat, he felt reasonably okay. Once again he acknowledged the good fortune of his physical gifts. Perhaps he shared a little of the resilience the Captain had?

The parking lot light made the townhouse bedroom window shade glow and cast the room in faint light. He tilted the shade a crack. The neighbor-guy's Corvette was still absent. It hadn't been there yesterday either. Good.

Daylight was still almost an hour away in the seemingly endless darkness of Minnesota's December nights. Drake had collapsed into bed shortly after returning home. Hadn't even eaten. His passage to sleep had been like he'd hit an elevator's button for the ground level and been out before it descended two floors.

Rachelle often tossed and turned in fitful, disturbed sleep. Sometimes she lunged awake sweat-soaked and screaming. Now she breathed deep and even, her soft curves shrouded by the sheet, her hair fanned on the pillow. The scar started below her ear and extended down her neck, broadening and dying out at the point of her left shoulder. The tissue lay thick and cruelly twisted. In the faint light it looked like a darkened flow, as if of molten wax.

He could make out the new scars of her wrists and hands. Wounds she'd accepted in her effort to protect the children. He caressed the damaged tissue with a feather touch.

Why has this kind, beautiful person been visited by so much pain and sadness?

Drake's engagement with formal Catholicism had faded with his time behind bars, the death of his brother Kevin, and what had befallen their mother. The news of the pedophile priests and the institution's criminally inadequate response had sickened him.

The church as an institution had failed and Drake had fallen away, but his conscience and the teachings of a warm and loving God remained with him. He *wanted* to believe, but the tragedy and pain that he saw daily in the ER and that had visited those he loved strained his belief. How could a loving God allow such suffering?

He believed in God, but—and this made him fear for his soul—he oftentimes didn't like Him much.

Drake stepped out of the shower. For him showers were a tonic. When on call and without sleep for extended periods, he found a five-minute shower had the recuperative effect of an hour of sleep. As he toweled off, his cell phone pinged. The attorney Lloyd Anderson had responded within minutes to the text Drake had sent—impressive for seven in the morning.

The attorney's message read *Eight-fifteen at the Loring Park Grill?*

Drake return texted, *See you there*.

Could the lawyer Rizz found somehow keep the Medical Board from taking his license? Jim Torrins had said the state Board's action was "as good as done."

Drake had not had time to research the lawyer, but while in the ER he'd read an earlier text he'd missed from Rizz. *Lloyd is a bad-ass barrister. Trust him.*

Drake's problems trudged through his mind as he brushed his teeth. His life was a mess but he was not going to give up.

He would fight to save their dreams.

He slipped into the bedroom. Rachelle sat on the edge of the bed, her legs free of the sheets and the rest of her incredible, naked body exposed. Her eyes glistened black in the low light as she looked at him. Her olive skin seemed to glow.

His chest tightened as he absorbed her beauty. It was as if he might burst into flame.

He closed the door. With a six- and four-year-old, they joked about having to engage in "stealth" sex. Sometimes in their seismic bliss they would struggle to contain laughter as if they were children giggling in the classroom of a strict teacher—their laughter becoming all the more uncontrollable.

He moved to her, inhaling her dizzying scent, like leather, cinnamon, and rose. He rested his hands on her shoulders. Her skin was on fire. She reached up and raised her fingers to his chest. Their eyes locked as she slowly trailed her fingers down his body.

He closed his eyes and his head rolled back.

Magic.

Chapter 48

Downtown

The morning temperature still registered sub-zero, but the still snow-free roads and light traffic made Drake's trip to downtown's Loring Park area an easy drive. Kip's Skylark handled effortlessly and the heater's output wafted warm air against his face. He thought of his beat-up Dodge. Would he ever feel safe climbing into that car again? His throat still hurt when he swallowed or spoke.

He'd been able to drink some milk, then eat some ice cream and applesauce. A strange combination but the pain in his mouth and throat made swallowing anything else a no-go.

He'd be a bit late for the meeting with the attorney. The time with Rachelle was special and he'd hated to leave. He hoped the attorney had the skills Rizz said he did. Drake felt vaguely uncomfortable dressed in khaki pants and a long-sleeved shirt—for the past four years he'd practically lived in scrubs.

Leaving Rachelle and the kids after the events of the last twenty-four hours, he carried a keener awareness of the specialness of the life-dreams he wanted to salvage. Heck—a greater appreciation of life itself.

Whatever other problems they faced, he and Rachelle had their health, their children, and each other.

And, as of today, he still had his work. The ER and caring for the injured, sick, or dying provided a constant reminder of his good fortune. So many of the people he cared for had no one—loneliness worsening their suffering and fear.

Drake had the opportunity to help, or try to help, those who were so much less fortunate than he. And sometimes all it took to relieve some people's pain was a caring ear, kind words, or a human touch.

His throat tightened with recognition that his ER opportunities—both dramatic and commonplace—might be coming to an end.

Drake had tried an early morning call to Beth Ogren but again no answer. He hoped that with Aki and Detective Farley on the case she was safe.

He passed the green-patina dome of the Basilica, then turned onto Hennepin Avenue toward the Walker Art Center. He turned left at the light, then found a metered parking spot on the street alongside Loring Park. He parked, then cut across the park, walking past mature, leafless hardwoods and the almost black surface of the park's frozen pond toward the Loring Park Grill.

Drake's stomach churned. This meeting could change everything. He hoped so. Could attorney S. Lloyd Anderson do what he said he'd try to do—save Drake's ass?

The cafe breakfast crowd clinked and clattered silverware and servers hustled about. The smell of coffee and breakfast fare invited, but Drake's swallowing discomfort and the business at hand ruled it out. Lloyd Anderson stood and raised a hand from alongside a window booth. He wore a black suit and red tie. He definitely looked the part of the high-powered attorney Rizz claimed him to be.

A quick handshake. The attorney insisted Drake refer to him as "Lloyd" and he sat at the table upon which lay his briefcase and a scattering of papers. He closed the briefcase and set it to the side. His manner said "all business."

That attitude worked for Drake.

After their early a.m. stealth magic and laughter, Rachelle had drifted back to sleep while Drake's thoughts had come in a flurry. He'd considered strategies to survive whatever the state medical board and courts might do to him.

If they stripped him of his license and ended his medical career, he'd ask Rizz and Jon to agree to sell the D-44 research. He knew they'd say yes.

Considering that people had been willing to kill for D-44, even with the Swiss firm contesting ownership, Drake figured he'd get enough money to pay his debts. There'd hopefully be enough to take care of all who depended on him—at least until he replaced his dream of working as an emergency medicine physician with a regular "job." His thoughts were grim but practical.

The prospect of not working as an ER physician made his mouth go dry.

Lloyd organized the papers. He looked at Drake, then glanced away. He cleared his throat.

"We're behind the eight ball on almost everything, and something bad happened." Lloyd looked toward the door. "Rizz was going to try and be here. He wanted to be the one to tell you, but we can't wait." Lloyd, the man who'd seemed unshakable, looked stressed.

Drake's chest tightened. This was not a good start. "If reassurance is a part of your professional style, I'm not feeling it," he said.

"Trust me." The graying man's eyes were unflinching. "I'm an attorney. You're my client. I'll give you all I have." He took a big breath. "Yesterday morning, while you nearly died, the university seized the contents of your laboratory."

What? Drake's stomach sank.

"They've claimed D-44 as the intellectual property of the university. You, Rizz, and Dr. Malar are part of a university-affiliated training program. The laboratory is university-owned property. Rizz and Dr. Malar have been receiving educational credit for their research work with you. The university has a case."

"But we registered as an independent business. We—"

"Drake," Lloyd shook his head, "you thought you had. Faith Reinhorst Malar was your attorney. As you know, she betrayed you. I've checked into the documentation. She didn't put in place the intellectual property protective measures she told you she had. The documentation she filed identified her as the owner. Before her murder, she accepted partial payment and signed a contract selling D-44 to Ingersen Pharmaceutical. They've filed a claim." He leaned forward and lowered his voice. "Legal ownership of D-44 and your research is a greased pig. You, the university, and Ingersen all have claims. Given the potential value, it's going to be a war. The university made the smart move." He grimaced. "I'm sorry, but I was still getting up to speed on everything. I should have seen this coming. Rizz and I got to the lab in time to grab a few things, but the university cleaned the place out. We did all we could."

The world dropped out from under Drake. His mind spun but thoughts would not track.

The research. His records. The last of his D-44 supply. *God, no!* The last of Rizz's supply. Drake felt nauseated.

Selling D-44 had been his survival plan—the way to take care of those who depended on him. *No!*

He reached a hand to Lloyd's forearm. "The animals. Did you—"

"We got the little black-and-white one—the pet. That cat, some animal care stuff, and personal stuff that Rizz wanted. Nothing of value, as far as I could tell."

Drake sat as dazed as if a stun grenade had gone off.

"They have possession, but your claim is strong," Lloyd said. "This is just the start. I'll file a counter-claim today. We'll fight this all the way."

Drake could only nod.

Without D-44, he had nothing. He faced the loss of his medical license, the end of his career, a civil suit, a mountain of debt, and now the theft of his breakthrough research.

"I do have some good news," Lloyd said. "I met yesterday with the judge and plaintiff's attorney in your civil discrimination and assault suit. It's been dropped. The security video blew the case out of the water. The bad guy's attorney cried 'victim' and 'racist' before he even checked the evidence. Sloppy legal work and ethically suspect."

Q. Jackson, the huge drug-seeker who'd struck Patti. It was good that the circus of a trial had been averted.

Q had said he'd make Drake pay. Could he have been behind yesterday's attempt on his life?

"Drake?" Lloyd held papers and a pen outstretched. "I need a signature for your counterclaim for the research."

"Huh? I have to file a counterclaim to the research they stole from me?" His thoughts were racing—more shocked than angry. The documents helped him focus. He had to save his research. It was his lifeline, and D-44 gave Rizz his best chance to ever walk again. And the university had stolen it. *So wrong.*

"Do your best," Drake said. He signed the pages. "The research is my only chance. We need D-44." He got up and started to walk away. He stopped and turned. "Lloyd."

The attorney looked up from the documents. "Good job on getting rid of the drug dealer's suit. Thank you."

***

Drake walked back across Loring Park. He stopped alongside Kip's classic Buick and looked over the still snowless park and the dark, frozen pond. Seventy-five yards to the west, morning traffic surged along the multi-lane thoroughfare of the Hennepin Avenue–Lyndale Avenue freeway interchange. The green patina of the Basilica's copper-plated dome rose to the north. His phone rang.

"Drake, this is Aki Yamada, Homicide/Major crimes."

Aki sounded formal—as if he and Drake were strangers.

"Yes, Aki."

"Our forensics crew confirmed that the powder in your car was penicillin. They referred to it as 'dust'. It had been put in the fan intake. Someone knew that when you turned on the defroster it would blow into your car's interior. It was definitely intentional."

"I figured Kip was right." The cocky pathologist always was. "I've been trying to think who it might be."

"We need to meet. Can you come to the station now?" Aki said.

"I need to meet someone else right now. Can I call you after that?"

"As soon as possible. Someone wants you hurt—or dead."

Drake clicked off.

He had to call Rachelle. And he needed to see Rizz as soon as possible. What must he be feeling right now?

Without the lab materials, Drake would not be able to produce more D-44 for a long time.

He leaned against the car and rubbed his face with both hands. Too much bad stuff going on. How could things be put right?

All the trouble had started with the betrayal by Jon's wife—Faith Reinhorst Malar. It was bad to wish ill of the dead, but...

Damn you, Faith. Damn you to hell.

Chapter 49

Duluth, MN

Jon pushed the button for the automated exit door from St. John's rehabilitation services building. He stepped onto the sidewalk and took a deep breath. Icy air filled his lungs. No pain and no cough—the wounds he'd suffered from the two gunshots to the chest continued to heal.

A biting wind came from the Duluth harbor. Even when covered in ice, Lake Superior dominated the city.

The door opened behind him, and one of the therapists exited, walking fast toward the parking ramp. "Have a good day, Dr. Malar," she said. "Great effort."

"Please call me Jon," he said as she hurried past. "Thanks for your help."

Being a patient and not working felt wrong. As if he were being lazy or a quitter.

Everybody working in emergency care had to be tough-minded. It was never okay to quit. It had nothing to do with status. Jon kept his "MD" hidden when not at work. Like Drake, he never introduced himself as a doctor unless he was working.

Jon turned downhill, facing the icy expanse that extended to the horizon far beyond Superior Avenue.

His strength continued to improve.

It was his brain that hadn't recovered. He didn't remember things. Not just little forgot-to-turn-off-the-light stuff, but leaving the door to the subzero outdoors open or getting lost in the neighborhood he grew up in. Things like forgetting his friend being paralyzed and in a wheelchair.

He'd seen the diagnoses in the therapists' paperwork. *Cognitively impaired. Post-anoxic encephalopathy. Emotional instability.* And perhaps worst of all, *situational depression.* They told him he shouldn't feel shame for being depressed. As a doctor, he knew he shouldn't blame himself. But he did.

Only he knew what he'd done.

He didn't like himself—with good reason. His parents were supportive and perfectly understanding. Yet he blew up at them. Anger splashed out of him like a tipped bucket. He'd never raised his voice to his parents ever before. Why would he?

He could see their worry. His tears could come at any moment. His anger flared over next to nothing. He wasn't who he'd been.

He reached into his pocket and removed the plastic card the therapist had made for him. He fought to slow his breathing as he read:

I'm Jon Malar. I'm an emergency medicine doctor.

I was shot and suffered shock, which injured my brain. I'm healing and can recover completely. The injury can make my emotions flare.

My body and brain are healing.

Things will get better.

A big guy in a ski jacket approached. He avoided Jon's eyes, walked faster, then moved to the edge of the sidewalk as he passed.

Jon recognized he'd been talking aloud.

As he stopped and raised his head, the wintry harbor breeze chilled his cheeks where he felt tears running.

Why am I crying?

He looked at the therapist's note card. His brain had been injured. That must be it.

Then as if in the flash of a photographer's strobe, his memory flickered. Glimmers of betrayal and death. Faith naked—so beautiful, so cruel. What he'd done. *No, God in heaven, no!*

His heart froze

How could he have?

Surely he was damned.

Chapter 50

Rizz's apartment, a.m.

Drake knocked at the door to Riverloft Apartments 4C.

"It's open," Rizz's voice carried through the door.

Drake opened it and walked in.

Rizz backed and spun his wheelchair from in front of his computer. He wore Memorial Hospital scrubs. Unblemished white sneakers with Velcro straps encased his feet, which sat on the foot rests of his wheelchair. The apartment had the clean and organized look he'd been known for since his days as a paramedic. A near-full case of Ketel One vodka sat alongside the computer desk.

"I couldn't make the meeting with Lloyd. Did he tell you where we stand?"

"Where we stand?" Drake stared at Rizz. "He told me the university ripped us off. We're screwed."

"It's all about big money. Big money makes for big greed. I guess I shouldn't be surprised, but I'm disappointed they pulled a sneak attack to clean us out. " Rizz shook his head. "Hold on a minute. I'll be right back." He rolled himself through the bedroom door.

Rizz didn't seem anywhere near as crazed as Drake expected. He wouldn't have been surprised to find his friend with a shotgun on his lap ready to storm the university to recover the D-44.

Drake moved to the windows. Rizz had a great place with incredible Mississippi River views. Out the east windows, the tumult of St. Anthony Falls and the Stone Arch Bridge spanned the river. The river ice opened about fifty yards above the falls, and blocks of ice as big as Drake bobbed in the water near the crest. The plunging falls and two hundred yard wide expanse of surging water gave rise to clouds of mist in the sub-zero air.

Rizz wheeled back into the room. He now had a red blanket across his lap.

"Yeah, the bastards pulled a sneak attack at dawn and tried to clean us out. But they didn't get everything." Rizz flipped the blanket aside and smiled. The little black-and-white cat lay curled on his lap.

Drake crossed to the cat. FloJo—the miracle. Drake remembered the night several months back when the undersized, spinal-cord-injured cat had first shown movement. He stroked the fur between the little cat's ears. She pushed up against his fingers and wriggled. "I'm glad you got FloJo. But if they have D-44 and the synthesis information, nothing else matters."

"I got to the lab just before they started to load our stuff into trucks," Rizz said. "Lloyd showed up a few minutes later. I gave him a list of what I said was personal property. I told them FloJo was a pet. Lloyd stood on the loading dock and lit them up with lawyerly outrage. He threatened to call Minneapolis PD, then broke out his smart phone and started filming. They backed off a bit and we salvaged a few things."

"He said all you got was your booze and junky stuff."

"Lloyd thought I was nuts," Rizz said.

"What are you saying?"

"Oh, ye of little faith." Rizz shook his head, smiling.

Drake recognized when his friend was feeling smug. He'd seen the look hundreds of times but not for some time. Rizz pointed toward his bedroom. "Take a look."

Drake stepped to the doorway. The familiar odor of cedar wafted. FloJo's kennel sat on the floor flanked by two large brown plastic drums—one filled with cedar shavings, the other with animal chow. Drake pointed. "Are those—"

Rizz grinned. "Removed undisturbed from our laboratory."

Drake put a hand to his chest and his jaw dropped. The flash drive containing the molecular identity and synthesis information for D-44 was hidden under a false bottom in the drum filled with cedar shavings.

"It was a good enough spot that I couldn't find it before—I figured we had a chance."

"Yes!" Drake hadn't even dared dream. "Hell, yes."

"Now look in the refrigerator. The upper shelf," Rizz said.

Drake moved to the kitchen then swung the refrigerator door open. The top shelf stood empty other than a single vial.

The administration vial Drake had prepared only two days earlier had taken the last of their D-44 stores. The printed label he'd applied, “Michael Rizzini – testosterone, administer as directed,” had been a joke, but he’d used an official prescription template, which clearly identified the contents as personal.

Beyond that, the university personnel could not have suspected anyone would administer an experimental, untested drug to a human.

Drake collapsed onto a chair. *Unbelievable!*

“Thank God you finally came around,” Rizz said. “I knew you'd do the right thing. And very funny labeling it as testosterone. Hell, I've got more of that stuff in my left nut than some countries.” Rizz's smile was huge.

Rizz's quick thinking and Lloyd's bravado had rescued FloJo, recovered the only remaining supply of the breakthrough drug, and kept D-44's molecular identity and synthesis pathway out of the university's hands. The university didn't have it and they couldn't make it.

The effort to rip them off had failed. The university had stolen lots of data, a supply of test drugs that had not worked, and four cats that would likely continue to improve. They'd emptied the lab but missed the drug and its synthesis formula.

The challenged ownership remained, but if the university had successfully seized D-44 or its formula, there’d have been little hope. The university had tried to throw a knockout punch, but the rightful owners were still on their feet.

Drake felt as if he might float into the air. Such relief. What must Rizz be feeling?

“I thought we’d lost everything,” Drake said.

“We owe Jim Torrins,” Rizz said. “He called and warned me about the seizure while you were in the Crash Room trying to die. Lloyd and I handled it from there.”

Although stuck in a wheelchair, some of the old Rizz swagger showed. This was the colleague and friend who’d thrown himself in front of a bullet meant for Drake's family.

“I've kept Lloyd in the dark on this,” Rizz said. “That's why I skipped the meeting with you two. I think he'll represent us most convincingly if he believes we lost the drug. The university won't know they didn't get D-44 for some time. They'll have to evaluate all the test drugs they stole, and they still won't be sure what they have. It's to our advantage to let them think they have it."

Drake's feelings surged. When he'd believed the university had seized everything, he'd had little hope. Though they weren't any better off than they had been yesterday, maintaining possession of the drug gave him hope.

D-44 still might provide a way for him to take care of those who needed him while the rest of his medical career collapsed.

"Now that you're up to speed, I have a job for you." Rizz said.

"A job?" What else could the morning bring? Rizz looked serious. "What is it?" Drake said.

"You're going to break the law and endanger my life."

Chapter 51

"Break the law? Risk your life?" Drake frowned at Rizz. "What are you talking about?"

"You wrestled with bringing D-44 to me when I was in the ICU," Rizz said. "Besides being illegal to give an experimental drug to a human, it's quite possible a serious reaction could occur. I could die." He shrugged. "I know the risks."

"You want me to administer you the drug right now?"

"Carpe diem, amigo. It's been eight weeks, actually fifty-three days, and I've got nothing. No movement and no feeling." He put his hands under FloJo and raised her gently. "This little mouse-catcher showed signs of recovery at forty-eight days." He set FloJo on the blanket on his lap. "I tolerated the first dose. I'm ready for more."

Drake's chest tightened. He'd known this was coming.

Rizz had tolerated the drug without evident problems, but it was still early and the risk of adverse effects more than doubled with repeating the D-44. They'd not yet even tried that with a cat. Adverse effects might take months to appear.

Drake started to open his mouth but stopped. Rizz was aware of all the risks. He looked into his friend's face. Rizz's eyes were clear, and his jaw set.

Rizz knew his mind, he knew the risks—he wanted to make the gamble.

"It scares me, but it's your call."

"Open that fourth drawer." Rizz pointed to the bureau next to the case of vodka.

Drake slid open the drawer. A 150-milliliter bag of normal saline and IV materials came into view. Even though he'd decided days ago to provide Rizz the drug, it felt different as he readied to go through with it.

It could kill his friend.

"I've got a med kit in the closet with epinephrine and emergency drugs if we need it. You can reconstitute the D-44, start an IV on me, run it in, and *voilà!*" Rizz said.

"Voilà?" Drake shook his head. "Perhaps you did have a reaction to the first dose. You've become French."

Rizz beamed. Drake knew it wasn't because of his lame joke. It was the hope of what D-44 offered that lit Rizz up.

"Becoming French wouldn't be an adverse reaction," Rizz said. "The French have their act together. Wine, beautiful women—I could deal with that."

Drake opened the third drawer and found epinephrine and other resuscitation drugs and instruments. Many adverse reactions, especially anaphylaxis, were much more likely the second time someone received a drug.

He used a needle and syringe to withdraw some fluid from the saline bag, then added it to the D-44 vial. He shook it, determined it had gone into solution, then used the needle-syringe to withdraw the D-44 solution. He injected the mixture into the bag of saline.

He pulled a chair next to Rizz's wheelchair, set his supplies on the table. "Let me put FloJo in her kennel."

"Not a chance. She's my good luck charm." Rizz petted her with one hand and extended the other arm to Drake.

Rizz had the kind of veins any nurse would drool over. Drake could put in an IV with his eyes closed. He pulled on the gloves, used an alcohol swab to clean Rizz's forearm, then slipped the IV needle through the skin. The flash of blood appeared in the chamber and Drake advanced the needle into the vein. He secured it, then cleared the IV line of air.

Drake connected the D-44 fluid line's port to the IV. He hung the fluid bag on the knob of one of the higher bureau drawers.

"Last chance to reconsider. Are you certain, Rizz?"

"Never been more sure of anything."

Drake opened the flow control and the D-44 solution began to drip in.

"Speak up if you get itching, trouble breathing, nausea, anything—got that?"

"Yes, doctor," Rizz said in a girlish falsetto.

"This is serious."

"Serious as paralysis, amigo," Rizz said.

The list of potential devastating adverse effects scrolled through Drake's mind.

Rizz's eyes tracked the fluid moving through the IV line, his excitement evident. FloJo nudged Rizz's hand then mewed. The astringent odor of the alcohol swab wafted. They watched in silence as their shared hope flowed into Rizz's arm.

When the last of the fluid ran in, Drake removed the needle. He held pressure on the site.

"Feeling okay?"

Rizz stared blankly then raised his free arm, waving it about, his palm finding Drake's face then groping it. "Ma? Is that you, Ma? I can't see."

"You are such a jerk." Drake shook his head as Rizz grinned.

Rizz put a hand on Drake's forearm and squeezed. His smile left. "Thanks, partner. You made the right call."

"God almighty, I hope so." It was a high-stakes gamble—the highest.

"Now that we've doubled down on D-44, we've got someone else to worry about." Rizz's tone was grave.

What now? Rizz had been in contact with Jon. His battered, kind-hearted friend had been struggling. "Did something happen to Jon?"

"No. He's messed up, but it's not Jon." Rizz paused. "How about worrying about yourself?"

"What do you mean?"

"Drake, I know Yamada told you they confirmed it was penicillin in your car. I talked with them."

"Right. They want to meet with me." Did Rizz think this had slipped his mind?

"Hell yes, they do. Yesterday morning you were at the side of the road jamming an endotracheal tube between your own vocal cords to keep from dying." He paused. "Someone tried to kill you. Next time you might not be so lucky. We need to find out who. And fast."

Chapter 52

Townhouse

“Kaye, are you sure?” Rachelle said.

“Positive, honey,” Kaye said. “My keys are on the table next to you. We'll be fine.”

Shane and Kristin leaned against the sturdy sixty-some-year-old. Both kids were smiling.

Kaye had returned home to Minneapolis earlier than expected. Her phone call had thrilled the kids as much as it had relieved Rachelle.

Once more the unshakable woman had appeared when Rachelle needed her most.

After making love with Drake in the predawn, Rachelle had slept.

When she awoke, the back of her right thigh where the skin had been taken for her graft hurt. The burn surgeons had taken skin from the thigh for the full thickness grafts they'd used to repair the burns of her wrists and hands.

The graft had been done weeks ago, and things had healed and been trouble-free for a while.

Two days earlier at the Y’s self-defense class, Rachelle had soreness in the same area of her thigh. She'd used moisturizing lotion and the pain had disappeared. Yesterday morning the area had been tender again but had improved by evening.

Now it flat-out hurt, and in the past hour she'd started to feel achy all over.

She'd called the Burn Care clinic at the hospital, and one of the nurses told her to come straight in to be seen.

Kaye's early homecoming call had been only minutes after that, like the intervention of a guardian angel. Kaye had volunteered to watch the kids and insisted Rachelle use her car.

"Kaye, you're the best. Call me if you have any trouble—"

"Oh, goodness, honey." She rolled her eyes. "This is good times for me." Kaye gave her an appraising look. "You look a bit flushed. Go get yourself checked out. Don't worry about us."

Rachelle closed the door and made her way to Kaye's little Toyota. As she climbed in her phone rang.

It was Drake.

"Rachelle, I just found out something that I need to share with you."

"Are you okay?" Yesterday he'd almost died. This morning he'd headed out before dawn. He thought he was indestructible.

"I'm fine. Are you sitting down?"

"Yes." Her throat tightened. "You're scaring me."

"Aki Yamada called me. The detective."

"Yes." Her mouth went dry. As if she'd forget the man who'd helped save their lives.

"My reaction yesterday—the police found someone put the penicillin in my car."

"What?"

"Someone purposely exposed me to penicillin. They put it in my car.

"Someone did that to you?" *God, no!* "Are they sure?"

"It looks like it. Aki and Detective Farley are investigating." He paused. "Let's keep the kids home. Be careful but please try not to worry." He paused. "They took me off the ER schedule for today. Makes me sick to think they're working short-staffed—"

"Screw the ER!" The fire in her outburst surprised her. Sometimes he was just so incredibly dumb! "You need to take care of your own health and your family's safety before you worry about the damn ER."

"You're right. I will. But if no one can cover for me, they'll be a doc short. Makes it rougher on everyone. I feel like I'm letting people down."

"That's crazy, Drake. You almost died." As she said it, the reality set in. Not an accident—*someone tried to kill him.*

She expected panic but felt anger. Who had done this? Anyone who threatened her family would have to face her—a pissed-off woman—not a panicky, drugged rabbit.

Drake cut into her thoughts. "I'm going to try and get home early. I have to meet with the detectives and do some things at the hospital. I'm fighting to save my license and career."

Her thigh throbbed and she felt drained. Was it from her leg or the weight of all that was happening? Hearing Drake talking about fighting boosted her spirits.

"Kaye is back in town. She's with the kids now. She loaned me her car. I'm just leaving to be seen at the Burn Clinic."

"Kaye? That's great. Wait. Did you say Burn Clinic?"

"I'm sore where they took the skin graft from my leg. It hurt the other day but then got better. It's worse again this morning."

"Did I hurt you this morning?"

She heard the concern in his voice. She smiled. "No, Drake. You definitely did not hurt me."

"Do you have a fever?

"Not earlier, but I'm feeling crummy now."

"Please ask someone from the clinic to call me after they've seen you. Infection is the worry."

"Go see Detective Yamada and do what he says. I'll be okay. A sore leg is not high up on our problem list."

"Let the experts decide how much of a problem your leg is. I'll call Kaye. You get to the clinic. I love you."

"Be careful, Drake. Love you."

Infection. Drake rarely talked about his job but he'd talked about infection. He feared it. Said it was like fire—could usually be handled if caught early and small, but it could spread like a forest fire in the wind—deadly.

She started the Toyota, her mind spinning with all they were dealing with. The kids still recovering from the kidnapping and she from her burns, Drake being sued by some jerk from the ER, the burden of their huge debt, and Drake's medical career in jeopardy. On top of all that, the allergic reaction that had nearly killed Drake was not an accident. *Why does Drake attract such insanity?*

She exited the parking lot. Her thigh ached. She felt flushed and clammy.

Didn't they have enough problems?

Chapter 53

River Loft, apartment 4C

A knock sounded on Rizz's door.

"You expecting someone?" Drake asked.

"I saved you a trip, amigo." Rizz raised his voice, "Come in."

The door swung open. Aki Yamada and Newton Farley entered. Both wore overcoats.

"Thanks for coming. Take off your coats and have a seat." Rizz pointed toward the couch by the windows. FloJo remained curled on his lap.

He pivoted his chair so he faced Drake. "We all needed to talk to you. They were nice enough to drop by."

Rizz had arranged this meeting, a flash of the old take-charge Rizz.

Drake shook hands with each of the detectives.

Coats were removed and all sat. Rizz rolled his chair so that he and Drake faced the detectives on the couch.

"Drake's reaction was not an accident," Rizz said. "Someone tried to kill him."

"Looks that way," Aki said. "The department has not released anything to the press. Other than my chief, the M.E., you two, and anyone you may have told, no one else knows that what happened to you was anything other than a medical thing. Let's keep it that way." He turned to Drake. "Can you get your buddy the M.E. to keep his mouth shut? That guy loves media attention."

"I'll talk to Kip," Drake said. "I just got off the phone from telling Rachelle. Do you think she or my children could be in danger?"

Aki looked at Farley, then back to Drake.

"Is there something you haven't told us that raises that concern?"

"I don't know who tried to get rid of me or why. After what Rachelle and the kids have gone through, I'm paranoid."

"Can you assign someone to them?" Rizz asked.

"TV and movies show stuff like that, but we can't even assign anyone to Drake." Aki said, then turned to Drake. "There's no authorization for us to do anything beyond investigate." He paused. "If you get any hint your family is at risk, call me or Farley immediately. Any hint whatsoever."

"I appreciate it. Thank you," Drake said.

"The obvious question," Aki said. "Who wants you dead?"

It had been in the back of Drake's mind off and on ever since Kip discovered the powder. Drake stood, memories making him restless. He looked out the window at the falls. Blocks of ice caught at the crest of the falls, then tumbled over. Clouds of vapor rose into the air above the churning water.

"D-44 is worth big money," Drake said. "But Faith's manipulation of our paperwork has left our ownership legally vulnerable. Yesterday, the university raided our lab and seized everything. They're claiming D-44 as their own. There's also a Swiss pharmaceutical corporation with a claim. We're headed for a court fight. Our new attorney says my claim is much stronger than Rizz's or Jon's, so if I were out of the picture we'd almost certainly lose." No one spoke.

Drake checked the time. No call from Rachelle or the Burn Clinic yet. His unease grew.

"There are other possibilities," Drake said. "Quentin Jackson, the guy who assaulted Patti in the ER, is not a fan of mine. And I just learned all his lawsuits were dropped."

"I'm familiar with Q," Aki said. "He was arrested for assaulting the ER nurse, but the charges were dropped—"

"And that's total bullshit," Rizz said. "Why the hell wasn't he prosecuted."

"It was the DA's call," Ali said.

"Well it pisses me off." Rizz leaned forward, his hands gripping the armrests. "This has been going on forever. Once people get into an ambulance or ER it's like they can do anything. Shit that would get them prosecuted on the outside is overlooked when it's just medics, nurses, and hospital folks getting victimized. We're sick of getting threatened, verbally abused, spit on, punched, and worse. Hospital administration worries about bad PR and marketing, and the DA's office acts like crimes against us don't matter. Meanwhile drunks, drugged up jerks, and criminal assholes are abusing healthcare workers with no consequences."

Rizz settled back in his chair. "I know it's not your fault but I had to get that off my chest."

"I hear what you're saying." Aki nodded. "But now we need to get back to Drake's situation. It's true Q is bad news. He's done time and is still a big dealer. Having his lawsuits dropped had to piss him off. That and the way Drake handled him after he hit the nurse—bad for his reputation. I know he threatened you at the time. Anything since then?"

"No, nothing from him." Drake looked out over the river again. "You guys know about Dan Ogren."

They nodded.

"When I told him I'd reported him for suspected domestic violence, he tried to buy me off. When that didn't work, he threatened me. Said I was 'history'."

"I know about Ogren from way back," Rizz said. "Back when I hit legal age, his bar was one of my prime spots."

"Bar?" Drake said.

"For years he had a bar off Cedar Avenue called The Penalty Box. Wasn't married then. Always lots of women around. The guy partied round-the-clock. Ex-jock. He played hockey for the U back when I was a kid. Got kicked off the team—I think all that was ever said was a 'violation of team rules'."

"Now he's a high-profile, wealthy guy with a lot of connections," Aki said. "Getting him convicted is going to be tough." He nodded to Drake. "The arresting officers agreed with you. They think he beat her. The wife denied it. Frustrating but common in these cases. His lawyer had him out of lock-up in about an hour. Ogren has money and influence. His father was a good guy, and the son still does some of the family charity stuff so he has some goodwill in the community. There's big-time push-back on the domestic case. Not sure where it will go."

Farley spoke up. "Ogren has a couple of DUI's. He's got a long record of trouble but no other convictions. Several arrests, and he's been questioned on a number of incidents through the years—accusations of rape, underage women, reports of assault, lots of alcohol and drug use. Either there's not enough to make an arrest or the charges get dropped."

"Fits what I know," Rizz said. "The bar he bought had been a gay bar. Shortly after Ogren took it over, one of the old patrons showed up, drunk and flamboyant. Someone I know heard Ogren tell the story and brag about leaving the guy bleeding and crying on the curb waiting for an ambulance. He laughed about it. Seriously sick stuff."

Once more silence.

"If he walks away without a domestic violence conviction, it'll be a travesty." Drake said.

"Latest report is his wife's got an attorney now and filed for a restraining order. She's scheduled to give an amended follow-up report on what really happened. Her attorney says she'll testify he beat her. Looks like she's trying to get herself safe," Aki said.

Drake had called the number she'd given in the ER and been unable to get a hold of her. The report of her getting clear eased his mind a bit.

"As far as him being a suspect for the attempt on you, I don't see where your death would do him much good," Aki said.

"Drake's death might decrease his chance of conviction on the domestic," Farley said.

"True," Aki said, "but his reputation has already taken the hit. And even if his wife testifies, she's already hurt her credibility in court. Sad to say, but with his money and lawyers, he'll probably get a misdemeanor at the worst. These bastards usually get some anger management courses and counseling—lightweight stuff. So why would he attempt murder?"

No one answered.

Drake spoke up again.

"One last possibility. I had a problem with a neighbor the other night. My son's tennis ball hit the guy's parked car—a Corvette. The guy ran out, grabbed Shane, swore at him, and threatened him." Drake looked down. His fists were clenched. "When I found out, I put hands on him and warned him. I think he's just a cowardly punk, but it's nagging at me that he could be a threat." He shook his head. "I don't know anything about him other than he's an asshole."

"Damn it, Doc," Aki said, "You can't do that shit. Call the police."

"And what could they have done?"

Aki and Farley were silent.

"We need the neighbor's name and address," Aki said. "Any others?"

"That's it," Drake said.

"We've been talking motive, but what about means?" Farley said. "Whoever did this had to know about your allergy. Who has access to that?"

"It's definitely in the hospital's medical and pharmacy records," Rizz said.

"Figuring out who has access sounds like a good place to start," Aki said.

Drake's phone sounded. He snatched it, noting it displayed the hospital's number. He got up quickly and stepped into Rizz's bedroom.

"Drake Cody here."

"Drake, hi. Gail Carlson of the Burn Unit calling. I just saw Rachelle."

Dr. Carlson had overseen all of Rachelle's burn care and performed her skin grafts.

"How is she?" He held his breath.

"Not good, Drake. Infection. It's moving fast. She needs to be hospitalized."

Chapter 54

The burn surgeon's words made Drake feel as if he'd been punched in the gut. He almost dropped the phone. "Please hold a second."

Pull yourself together.

He regained his breath. He covered the phone, turned, and stepped into Rizz's main room. He spoke to Rizz and the detectives as he moved toward the door. "Rachelle is at the hospital. She's sick. I'm gone. Call if you need me."

He vaguely heard good wishes as he grabbed his coat. He continued with the burn surgeon as he went out the door. "Thanks for holding. What did you find?"

"Her temp at check-in was 103 degrees. She developed chills and aches as she drove here. Her heart rate is elevated but her blood pressure is okay. The donor site on her right thigh is tender, hot, red and swollen—definitely infected. She needs to be treated aggressively and watched closely. Sounds like it developed quickly."

It sure as hell had. The queasy foreboding that had gripped him since Rachelle's earlier call grew stronger.

"She won't want to be away from the kids." Drake said.

"She's sick enough to be okay with staying. She spoke to your babysitter ten minutes ago. I told her I'd be talking with you. "

"Where is she now?" Rachelle's acceptance of admission meant she felt really sick. Drake's mouth had gone dry. She had to be scared. He certainly was.

He entered the stairwell of Rizz's building.

"I talked to Laura Vonser in the ER," the surgeon said "I sent Rachelle down there for Laura to evaluate and start treatment. We thought an admission with Dr. Peter Kelly as primary made sense."

The hospital's ER was the best place for fast, in-depth evaluation and getting the most done in the least amount of time. His partner, Dr. Laura Vonser, had cared for him there yesterday—today her skills were needed by Rachelle. Pete Kelly was a gifted physician. He'd stepped up huge when Jon Malar fought for his life.

"Sounds like a good plan," Drake said.

He wished top-notch doctors and nurses guaranteed good results, but he knew infection could overwhelm the best of care. He raced down the steps of Rizz's building. He'd had a queasy fear from the first moment Rachelle mentioned her symptoms. In the ER he sometimes made rapid and startling diagnoses on little information. Intuition probably played a role, but more likely he unconsciously picked up clues that triggered recognition.

The diagnoses impressed medical colleagues, but the patients' condition were such that he usually wished he was wrong. These diagnoses were rarely good news.

He had that feeling about Rachelle right now. His guts had gone to ice.

"I'll be at the ER in fifteen minutes. Thank you." Drake exited the stairwell.

"Laura and Pete will do the heavy lifting," Dr. Carlson said. "I'll follow her graft closely and do what I can to prevent scarring, but right now her issues are far greater than that."

Rachelle's scars. Her neck and shoulder from childhood tragedy. Her hands and wrists from fighting to save the children. The patches on the thigh from the graft harvest.

Wounded inside and out both as a child and as a mother protecting her children. And now in the grips of a serious infection.

Dr. Carlson was right—scars meant nothing in light of the threat to Rachelle that infection posed.

A sickening fear gripped him.

***

Clara stood behind the tech performing the microbiology assays. Each step was technical and challenging—any slip-up could be devastating.

The specimens were often obtained from the patients via difficult or one-time procedures such as spinal taps, radiologically guided needle aspirations from deep in the body, surgery, or blood draws from premature babies with vessels the size of thread. The results directed treatment of major infections. Microbiology errors could kill.

Most hospital lab results were crucial. Errors in the most common of tests could miss or errantly suggest lethal conditions. The medical significance and need for accuracy were what had drawn Clara to laboratory science.

Her overall excellence in all aspects, including her microbiology knowledge, made her tops in her field. This was not conceit—just fact. And she knew it.

Clara moved about the lab, kept an expression like a judge at a dog show, and said nothing. She often did this to the laboratory staff. She knew it intimidated.

She demanded her staff do their job—and do it perfectly. She didn't want to be their friend. Many disliked her. Several had quit over the years, but there were always plenty of applicants. Laboratory work attracted perfectionists. The Memorial Hospital lab staff performed at the highest level.

But she would never tell them that.

Intimidation got more out of them.

Her phone beeped—an incoming text.

It was from Dan. *urgent meeting w mesh. bad news. c u later.*

She avoided any expression but inside she flushed. He never used to text her other than to inform her he was interested and how long it would be till he got to her place. Now things were different. He shared more. Trusted her. Valued her. It made her want him. Her true partner—the one meant to be.

She pivoted and, without a word to the tech, made for her office. At her desk she finally let the smile out. Dan Ogren—handsome, virile, strong, and he needed her. Dan wasn't an intellectual—but that didn't matter. He was clever. She had more than enough smarts for both of them. *He's a magic man, Momma!*

Her smile grew. She wanted him right now.

An emergency meeting with his attorney? It had to be bad news.

Clara turned to her keyboard and displays. Her fingers danced and Drake Cody's medical record appeared. News of his critical care ER visit from the day before had spread through the hospital in a flash. She scanned the electronic medical record for at least the fifth time:

Level of visit: critical care. Primary Diagnosis: acute anaphylaxis. Secondary diagnoses: i) shock, ii) respiratory failure, iii) airway obstruction.

She reviewed the paramedics' record and ER care. No way should Drake Cody have survived. The doctor who threatened her man should have died. Damn!

Clara had earlier reviewed the ER record of Beth Ogren's visit. The bitch had some injuries but had deserved more. Dan needed to be rid of her. Clara knew he'd divorce Beth to be with her, but Dr. Drake Cody's report of suspected abuse had complicated everything.

Ogren Automotive would be Dan's soon. How could Dan be rid of his wife without losing the company and wealth that was his birthright?

She pictured herself on Dan's arm at gala events. She'd finally get the respect she deserved. Wealth demanded respect.

A magic man who worshipped her, wealth, and respect—she would have it all. She smiled.

It wouldn't be easy but she'd make it happen.

Chapter 55

Memorial Hospital

“Thank you, Kaye. I'll call you later with an update. I'm just getting to the hospital now,” Drake said. “Call me anytime if you need anything or if the kids want to talk again. You're an angel.” He disconnected.

Kaye hadn't hesitated when he'd asked her to care for the kids overnight. She'd reacted as if he'd asked her to water a houseplant. “No worries, Drake. I'll take the kids to my house for a sleepover. We'll have fun. Rachelle used my car so I'll just cab us over.”

Kaye—a miracle.

Drake parked the Skylark in his assigned parking spot in the Chicago Avenue lot. He climbed out of the warm car into the bitter cold and looked around the tough downtown neighborhood. If Kip knew his vehicle would be parked here, he would hyperventilate.

The Minneapolis sidewalks leading from the parking lot to the hospital were nearly empty. The near-zero temps and wind kept people indoors or using the skyway system. Drake reached the hospital and moved past a few freezing smokers huddled outside the ER entrance.

He entered. The ER waiting room was quiet and less than half full. The triage nurse attended to a lone new patient. Drake nodded at the security guard seated behind the plate glass. The guard hit the access button and the inner ER doors slid open.

Drake entered and the bustle, noise, and disinfectant-tinged smell greeted him. A glance at the patient assignment board showed him where Rachelle had been placed. Room 25—the same room Beth Ogren had been in.

Rachelle in the ER triggered both comfort and worry. Concern for her illness and comfort that the ER was the best place for her to be right now.

He spied Laura Vonser as she exited a patient cubicle while draping her stethoscope about her neck. A comfort to have Laura involved.

"Laura," he said.

She turned.

"Hey, Drake. I hoped you'd get here before we got Rachelle upstairs. Did the burn surgeon talk with you?"

"Yes. I'm worried."

Laura nodded. "At a minimum, it's a nasty cellulitis. Her temp was 103.4 degrees. That leg is tender, red and hot. Her white count is seventeen thousand. Pulse was 110. Her blood pressure is ninety over sixty, but she says she runs low. I'm hitting her with a couple of liters of IV fluid. We're hoping this is a non-hospital-acquired bug, but as you know, we're seeing a lot of nasty staph in the community. First dose of antibiotic should be about in." Laura sighed. "Yesterday I take care of you. Today Rachelle." She put a hand on Drake's arm. "How are you doing?"

"Physically I'm fine. Worried about Rachelle." He was scared sick. "Thanks for taking care of her. Did you have to double back to cover my shift today?"

"Yes, you slacker. We all know you intubated yourself just to get off work." She smiled. "But no worries, you know how it goes—if you only work ninety percent of the time, you miss ten percent of the interesting cases. Touch base with me after you see her. Any thoughts or suggestions, just let me know." She hurried off.

Drake moved down the hall, then pulled back the curtain at the doorway to room 25. His breath caught. *Oh God!*

Rachelle's eyes were closed, her color ashen, sweat wetting her temples. A liter bag of normal saline with a second smaller bag hung connected to IV tubing, the glistening column of fluid running into her left arm.

His throat clenched. She looked so drastically different from when he'd left her only hours ago. His reflex at-a-glance physician's assessment of "sick—not sick" buried in the "sick" range. She looked even more ill than he'd feared.

Every experienced medical caregiver feared infection and the prospect of septic shock. Drake had too much experience not to be worried. Infection is like fire—it can often be controlled by the body's defenses and medical care, but it sometimes takes off like flames in the wind. Too often, despite treatment, it rages out of control. The crashing blood pressure and multiple organ failure of shock could kill any patient with terrifying speed. Ensuring that the flames of a localized infection would not spread and engulf a patient was impossible.

Rachelle, who had been burned so badly before, now faced a different, but every bit as deadly type of fire.

He moved to her side. “Rachelle?” She did not stir. “Rachelle.” He put a hand on her shoulder.

Her eyes opened. Her pallor stood out in contrast to her big brown eyes. The twisted tissue of her scarred neck and shoulder lay exposed, something she would never allow to happen normally. Beads of sweat dotted her forehead.

“How are you feeling, babe?”

“Drake. Oh.” She looked lost. “Do you have the kids?” She clutched his arm and tried to raise herself.

“The kids are fine. They're with Kaye. Remember?”

“Kaye?” She blinked rapidly. “Yeah. Kaye.” She collapsed back. “I'm feeling fuzzy.”

“They gave you some medication.”

“Oh. Ask them not to do that anymore. I can't think straight.”

Drake bent over her with a dry cloth from the bedside and gently dabbed the sweat off her face. “You're sick, pretty lady. Infection. It hit you fast.”

She nodded, her breathing heavy. “I'm scared.” She clutched his hand. Tears welled.

“You're in the right place and antibiotics to help you get better are running into you now. The kids are safe. I'm safe. You're going to get well.” He squeezed her hand, wishing he could absorb her fear.

She looked into his eyes. A look he'd seen before in other seriously ill patients. A deep apprehension. Her brow already glistened again with sweat.

“I love you, Drake.”

He tried to respond but could not get the words out. It was not his injured throat that choked him mute but the thundering fear that stampeded his heart. He bent his head, touching his forehead to her shoulder. *What did she ever do to deserve this?*

"I feel so tired. Weak. Need to rest." Her eyes closed.

His words came out a cracked whisper. "I love you, Rachelle."

Chapter 56

University, St. Paul Campus

"Not here? Check again. It has to be here." Memorial Hospital CEO Stuart Kline could not believe what the pharmacology researcher said. He scanned the laboratory tables, glassware, and analytic equipment as if he might spot the D-44 information himself.

Dev Patek, PhD, the university's drug development research coordinator, looked at Kline with his head cocked. "You requested that I check the materials for the research drug's molecular identity and synthesis information. You asked me to review the contents of the refrigerator and cabinet for a sample of the experimental medication." The lean, graying scientist shrugged his shoulders. "I did that."

"You found nothing?" Kline's voice broke. *It can't be!*

"I found chemical reagents—the materials from which drugs can be created. I reviewed the data you supplied." He pointed to three large leather-bound volumes, a set of smaller notebooks, and a laptop computer. "I found procedure and results data." He nodded to the four cages housing cats along the wall. "I see four animals and a record of their neurological exams. One animal is missing, the one that responded, which is not critical." He shrugged. "What is critical is that I'm not able to find any description of the molecular identification of D-44, no synthesis information, and no sample of any specimen labeled as D-44."

"But the drug and the formula have to be here," Kline said. The researcher looked at him with his brow furrowed.

"It may be, but I have not found it. It may be labeled incorrectly. These drugs," he waved toward a rack in which a few dozen vials sat, "are labeled as experimental medications but according to the notes, their use produced no improvement. The drug identified in the records as having produced improvement—D-44— is not here. No identified sample, no molecular identity, no synthesis information."

"It *has* to be here." Kline recognized he was whining.

"Possibly, but we will have to test each one, essentially repeat the animal experiments, to know." The white-coated man shrugged. "Without a sample of D-44, a molecular identification formula, or synthesis instructions, there is no way for me to identify D-44."

Kline stood open-mouthed.

"I recommend you check with your original researcher." The scientist looked puzzled. "Please just ask whoever did the work. Their documentation is good. I'm sure whoever you obtained these materials from knows where the information is. Now I must get back to my own work." He walked out of the lab.

Kline's guts were in knots. How could— Shit! Could the doctors have removed drug D-44 and its formula? But how? The seizure of the lab contents had been kept secret. During the seizure, Drake Cody was in the ER as a patient, Dr. Malar was in Duluth undergoing rehab, and wise-ass Dr. Rizzini was stuck in a wheelchair. A university attorney was on-site to oversee seizure of the lab contents. What could have gone wrong?

Kline whipped out his phone and clicked on his contacts. He fought panic as he waited for the connection.

"Counsel Afton Tait here," answered the university attorney.

"Afton, this is Stuart Kline. You were on site for the seizure at the lab yesterday, right?"

"Yes."

"Did you get everything?"

"Yes."

"Absolutely everything?"

"Er, well, yes. Other than their personal property."

"Whose personal property?" Kline's sick feeling worsened.

"A Dr. Rizzini and an attorney showed up while we were loading. They made threats but I steamrolled them." Tait sounded smug.

"I'm in the university St. Paul campus lab facility right now. Our top research guy has gone through everything and says neither the drug nor any of the key drug information is here. What was the personal property you're talking about?" How had Rizzini and their attorney known to be there? The seizure had been kept strictly need-to-know and executed around dawn.

"Some personal property, nothing more. A bottle of booze. One of the cats—they said it was a pet. A cage. Big drums of cat food and shavings. They took one medication vial, but it was clearly labeled as for Michael Rizzini. The guy is in a wheelchair. We couldn't take his personal medication. Their attorney was all over us. Lloyd Anderson, a guy I know by reputation—he's tough. He threatened to call the cops with a claim of theft, but I flashed copies of the university's deed for the building and the residency agreements of the doctors. He backed down. They only took the one cat and the other junk. Nothing of value."

"Nothing of value, huh?" Kline's gut was an elevator going down. "Possibly just a breakthrough drug and its formula that may be worth billions." He felt sick. Had Rizzini and his attorney pulled a fast one? How could they have known?

"What time did Rizzini and his attorney confront you?" Kline asked

"They showed up just before the guys started to load the trucks. Sometime around eight o'clock. No one was there when we got there just after seven."

"You may have blown this deal, Tait. Don't hold your breath waiting for any money from me. Say nothing about this to anyone else." He disconnected. *Shit! How did this get messed up?*

The answer popped into his head. *Torrins.* It had to be Torrins.

Kline knew with an urge-to-vomit certainty that he'd messed up.

In the morning when he'd called to check on Drake Cody, he'd told Torrins they were seizing the research. Torrins must have warned the doctors.

That self-righteous asshole. Shit!

Without possession of the drug, his plan was in trouble. He looked around the St. Paul lab. Room fans and refrigerators hummed. A scent like lighter fluid hung in the air. The lab tables lay covered with complex glassware, burners, scales, and elements Kline couldn't identify. He knew nothing of science. Science mattered, but this deal was about money.

He had calls to make. People would be worried—powerful people. Everything should be in hand by now. He'd assured them it would be.

With possession of the drug, they'd planned to collude with the Swiss pharmaceutical firm. The skids had been greased. Money would flow like the Mississippi passing over St. Anthony's Falls. Plenty for the university—and plenty for Ingersen Pharmaceutical. Most importantly, two large streams of dollars would flow to a certain special consultant named Stuart Kline.

Drs. Cody, Malar, and Rizzini should have been left with a shaky legal claim and nothing more. The university legal department wolves had said that with possession of the drug, the university would be able to close a deal with Ingersen Pharmaceutical in short order.

The doctors would spend years after the fact trying to get a piece of the action. Too bad for them—in the beginning they'd used their partner's wife as their attorney and she was crooked. They didn't have their shit together and she sold them out. Too bad, so sad.

If all went as planned, Kline, his university collaborators, the university, and the Swiss firm would be swimming in money long before the courts made any decision. If the drug held even a fraction of the potential the science guys believed it did, there'd be plenty to pay off the doctors if the courts eventually ruled they deserved a cut.

If it ended up that the drug or its formula were not in the materials they'd seized, all was not lost.

In the worst-case scenario, they'd have to negotiate with the doctors. That shouldn't be too rough. Malar was a wreck, Rizzini a cripple who might never work again, and Drake Cody a criminal whose license to practice was as good as gone. No matter what had happened yesterday, in the end the deal would go through.

He, the university, and the Swiss firm still held the winning cards.

Hmmm. Things were messed up, but his wheels never stopped turning. Dan Ogren had once told him admiringly that he was "a sneaky bastard." Ha! What Dan meant was that he, Stuart Kline, had the smarts to always come out on top. He knew how to make things happen.

He was going to be one very rich man.

Chapter 57

"Rachelle looks like early sepsis to me," Drake said. "She's deteriorating fast." The worrisome clinical terms couldn't match the sickening dread in Drake's gut.

Dr. Laura Vonser nodded. "The labs are pointing that way. Her lactate is elevated. I just talked with Dr. Kelly. We're using the sepsis protocol and admitting her to the ICU." She paused. "Hopefully we can get on top of this fast. Is there anything else you'd recommend?"

"Rachelle asked me to let you know she wants to avoid pain meds or sedatives," Drake said.

"She said the same to me but I persuaded her to let me use some Ativan. The sedation seemed to help. She's getting two liters of saline, antibiotics are running in, and she's gotten Tylenol. I've marked the margins of the cellulitis so we can track any progression. There's no evidence of a pus collection."

Drake nodded. A line made with a surgical marker tracing the reddened margins of the infection on the skin provided a low-tech but sometimes useful indicator.

The antibiotic being administered to Rachelle was front line, but in the modern world, resistant bacteria were always a threat. Some of the killer bugs could swim in antibiotics. Choosing the right drug was a guess informed by knowledge and experience. Giving multiple or certain specific antibiotics could harm Rachelle and set her up for other life-threatening problems. The drugs were a two-edged sword. For every desired benefit, there was a horde of risks.

He made these critical treatment decisions every day—but not when the patient was the mother of his children and the person he loved most in the world. His mind twisted and spun. His hands were numb. He stared at his fingers as he opened and closed them. A sense of panic rose. He was drowning in helplessness.

Laura put a hand on each of Drake's shoulders and her eyes bore into his. “Partner, listen to me for a moment. You were raced into the Crash Room a little over twenty-four hours ago critically ill. Rizz told me about some of the other stuff you have going on. Things have not let you take it easy like your wise emergency doctor advised.” She gave a small smile. “Seriously, Drake, you need to take care of yourself. You know Pete and the ICU nurses will watch Rachelle like hawks—medically expert hawks. Let them do their job. You're not Rachelle's doctor. Try and get some rest.”

Get some rest? He'd likely advise the same if situations were reversed—but no way could he rest.

Laura's concern touched him. From the moment he'd walked into the department, he felt the support of the ER. His coworkers understood the stakes. Their nods and caring eyes could not be more eloquent.

Laura was right. Rachelle would be well cared for. The medications would ease her discomfort and help her fight the infection. Pete Kelly and the ICU nurses would provide the best of care. But—and Laura knew this—when you are a doctor you can't turn it off. He would oversee and evaluate every aspect of Rachelle's care. It was a responsibility that he couldn't free himself of—

“She's nail-tough, brother.”

Drake turned and found Rizz had rolled up behind him.

“Are you feeling okay, Rizz?” Rizz, now hours after his second dose of D-44, looked okay.

“I'm fine,” Rizz said. “Been here a couple of minutes. Laura updated me. So sorry Rachelle is so sick, but what I said is true. Rachelle has proved she's hardcore tough. She's going to be okay.”

“I hope you’re right. I'm standing here with my head spinning and my heart in my throat. I don't know what to do.”

“She’s in good hands. You know that.” Rizz lowered his voice. “It sucks, but you and I have another issue. Someone tried to kill you. We don't know who or why. We need to do some looking and I know where to start.”

“Right now, all I can think about is Rachelle and the kids.” The threat to him did not seem pressing.

"Of course." Rizz nodded. "Taking care of Rachelle and the kids comes before anything else." His expression hardened. "But you're no good to them if you're dead."

Chapter 58

Homicide Office, early afternoon

"Any luck?" Aki leaned back in his chair as Farley dropped a fast-food bag on the adjoining desk, then sat down. Farley had made a food stop—no surprise. Aki suspected his fleshy, young partner spent half his paycheck on fast food.

Farley fished in his pocket, then held up a flash drive. He stepped to Aki's side, took the stick, and plugged it into Aki's desktop computer. He leaned forward and his fingers sped across the keys.

"This is from an outside security camera mounted on the third level of the parking ramp across the street. I screened the entire night and found this. It's already been enhanced by the tech guys. No other surveillance cameras in the area. It's all we have." His fingers sped across the keys. "Just click 'play'."

Aki did, and a grainy, overhead view of a stairwell entrance, sidewalk, and parking ramp entry/exit showed. Across the street, the Chicago Avenue open air parking lot could be seen. A time cursor read 2:37 a.m. The old Dodge was one of only a few cars on the lot. The view was distant and blurry.

"The tech guys say the lens was frost-covered. No way to improve it," Farley said.

An indistinct figure moved onto the lot. A large man wearing a heavy coat, a dark hat, and with a satchel on a shoulder strap strode directly to the doctor's car. He paused at the driver's door, then reached into the bag and pulled something out. He set the bag down, took a step forward, and leaned over the windshield as if checking the wipers on the driver's side. Aki could see the man's arms move, but no detail was visible. After less than a minute, the man straightened, turned, picked up the bag, and walked back in the direction he came. Neither his face nor his skin color were discernible. The image stunk.

"What do you think?" Farley said.

"Technically it's lousy, but it confirms our theory," Aki said. "That's our guy. He leans over where the fan intake is. On an old car like the doc's, he can get at it from the outside. Can't prove it, but it's clear we just saw him put the antibiotic powder in the fan intake. The guy is big judging his size relative to the car. I can't make out anything else. Can we have somebody in forensics see if they can tell us more? Maybe a height estimate or something about the clothes or that bag? Can they tell if it's a white guy?" Aki said.

"They have a copy and are going over it now. The guy wore one of those face-mask stocking caps. No doubt he was intentionally keeping his face covered." Farley said. He sat at his desk, then reached into his fast-food bag and pulled out a large order of fries. He dumped the bag, and four wrapped burgers and a couple of ketchup packets tumbled out. He looked at Aki.

"Um, er, do you want some of this?"

"No thanks."

Farley looked relieved as he grabbed fries with one hand and pulled a burger close with the other.

"It tells us a lot," Aki said. "It's a big guy who somehow knew Doc Cody's car, knew its location, and knew the doc's schedule. Most significant of all, he knew of his deadly allergy and understood how to expose him using the car. Very clever, but it gives us a lot to work with."

"Definitely." Farley nodded then loaded in a mouthful of fries.

"Dan Ogren is a really big guy. Q Jackson is at least six-four," Aki said. "I think the neighbor guy Drake had a problem with is tall."

"Listed as six-three on his driver's license," Farley said while chewing.

"With that hat and heavy coat, it could have been any of them in the parking lot." Aki paused. "But does it really make sense that any of them would try and kill Doc Cody like this? Look at motive. Who has enough? Basically Drake just pissed them off. He's not really an ongoing threat—is he? What would they gain? Is pissing them off enough of a motive?"

Farley swallowed. "I've been trying to zero in on what we discussed earlier. Who could know of his penicillin allergy and also have the medical sophistication to pull this off? I've started probing the hospital's computer system, it's well-protected from outside threat but there are thousands of caregivers on the hospital staff. I also learned that all the out-patient clinics are part of the network. Access is tough but not as limited as I'd hoped." He took a bite of a hamburger.

Farley's computer and hacking skills had proved to be game-changing in an earlier case.

"Do your thing, partner." Farley was a rookie with a lot to learn, but Aki believed the young detective's combination of technical knowledge and deductive skills had him on track to becoming an exceptional detective.

"As I think about what happened, something occurred to me," Farley said. "If Dr. Cody had died the other morning, and by all reports he should have, there'd have been no suspicion. Everyone would have figured an inadvertent contact with the antibiotic at the hospital and a reaction right after he left. No one would have examined the car as closely as the ME did." He started to unwrap another burger.

"It would have gone down as an accidental death. If not for Dr. Cody surviving and Dr. Dronen discovering the antibiotic dust, no one would have recognized that the exposure was intentional. Am I right?" He took a bite of the burger.

Aki frowned. The realization that someone could have gotten away with murder in his town pissed him off. The fact that the near-victim was a man he knew and cared for made it personal.

"You're right." He nodded toward the screen. "Let's track this bastard down and put him away before he tries again. We may not be as lucky next time."

Chapter 59

Memorial Hospital, Security office

"I called hospital security and tried to weasel info out of them," Rizz said. "I told them I was a windshield repair service guy. Tried to get my parking lot assignment out of him. The guy gave me nothing. Said 'no personal info on any employee' and it was clear he meant it."

Drake nodded. They'd just exited the elevator. The security office was tucked away in the deepest section of the hospital. Engineering, utilities, and storage occupied most of the basement level. Folks came down here to get new photo IDs or keycards. Otherwise, the security office did not get much foot traffic. Drake opened the door under a simple Security sign that jutted out from the wall. He held the door as Rizz wheeled in.

A dark-haired, forty-something guy with a massive chest and arms looked up from behind a low counter.

He and Rizz scanned each other, both men seeing eye-to-eye from their respective wheelchairs. Rizz paused a beat before speaking.

"You Joe? I'm Dr. Rizzini. I tried giving you the bogus windshield repair story five minutes ago."

"Yeah." The guy cocked his head. "What was that about?"

Drake stepped forward, extending his hand over the counter.

"Dr. Drake Cody. I work in the ER."

"Joe Mentum." They shook. "I know who both of you are. I do communication and oversee most of our security cameras. We also do keycard access and IDs, so I have a handle on most everyone." He shrugged his big shoulders. "I was working during the attempt on Dr. Malar's life in the ICU and the following lockdown and pursuit. You guys and Dr. Malar are well-known to us."

"We appreciate you and your crew looking out for us," Rizz said.

"What can I do for you? Your windshield repair ploy has me curious."

"The other morning I was a crime victim," Drake said. "I can't give you details right now, but whoever did it had information on me. We're trying to track how they got it."

"So the call was a test?" Joe said.

"Yeah, no offense," Drake said. "We're trying to figure out who could have learned what kind of car I drive, my parking assignment, my work schedule, and maybe even my medical record. Do you have access to all that?"

Joe pivoted his chair to a desktop computer. He keyed in some entries. "You have a 2002 Dodge, I have the license plate number. You're assigned to the Chicago Avenue open lot, parking space G-25, for which you are charged monthly. That information is in our security files, but only personnel with a password can access it. I suspect there's a physician work schedule for the ER, but that wouldn't be accessible to me or anyone else who does not have the right sign-in and password. And your personal medical information is totally separate and HIPAA protected, so that would be harder yet."

"Are you sure no one in security could have been fooled into giving out my car and parking info?" Drake said.

"Unlikely," Joe said. "We don't cut corners. Heck, what happened just a couple of months ago proved how critical our job is."

"So to get the info through the hospital system, it would have to be someone with access to one or more passwords."

"A log-in and a password—yes. I'm not in the know on all the safeguards for medical records. There are hundreds of doctors, a couple of thousand nurses, and other caregivers that use the network. Computer security isn't handled by our department but I know it's well protected against outside intrusion," Joe said.

"Understood," Drake said. "Thanks for the info."

"Yeah, thanks," Rizz said. He pivoted his chair toward the door as Drake opened it.

"Hey, Doctor Rizzini," Joe said.

Rizz stopped and turned his head."Yeah?"

"I heard you were riding a chair." Joe shrugged. "I've been on wheels since Desert Storm. I was a wreck in the beginning, but my life is good now." He paused. "Call me anytime if you have any questions or think I might be able to help."

Rizz shrugged. "Yeah, er, sure,"

"I mean it."

"Got it, thanks." Rizz rolled out the door.

In the hall Rizz stopped.

"Drake, he's right that it wouldn't be too hard to figure out your car and parking spot. Even your work schedule could probably be found out with a phone call."

"Agreed."

"But somebody knew about your penicillin allergy and previous reaction. Medical records are not easy to access. Hate to think it, but it makes hospital personnel the most likely. You reading me?" Rizz said.

"All Memorial Hospital caregivers have sign-ins and passwords to access medical records. It could be a doctor or nurse."

"Whoever it was had to know of your allergy and have the medical knowledge to use it," Rizz said.

"It freaks me out to think it could be someone I know," Drake said. "What did you think of Joe's offer?"

"Huh?"

"You know, talking with a guy who's been where you are."

Rizz stopped and looked at Drake with a frown. "A nice guy, but his deal is different. I'm not staying in this chair." He resumed wheeling.

Drake followed Rizz toward the elevators. He'd learned two things: One, whoever had tried to kill him might very well work in the hospital; and two, Rizz was not prepared for anything less than the miracle of complete recovery.

Both thoughts were unsettling yet paled under the weight of his worry for Rachelle.

Chapter 60

Noble Village, nursing wing

Every minute Dan spent at Noble Village felt like forever.

They kept the temp somewhere near eighty. The halls smelled like Lysol, but as he passed some rooms he caught odors like bad meat, ammonia, or wet hay. With meeting Mesh here yesterday, this made it the first time he'd been here twice in less than three weeks.

Back-to-back days made it a record that would never be beaten.

The area they called the "activity" room was anything but. Gray and withered residents sat propped in wheelchairs like drying husks in front of a droning TV. Most dozed with mouths hanging open and heads drooped.

The alert ones' eyes tracked Dan as he walked past. He knew they were judging him. Was he a good son? They freaked him out. Did they sense his true self? Could their rheumy eyes and damaged minds see through his act?

He escaped into room B-21. His father lay tucked among the blankets and white sheets. Dan pulled a chair close—something he never did. The soft light of the freezing, overcast day lit the room. The bedside table held a single photo in a simple frame. A picture of his mother. Dan must have been eleven when it was taken, shortly before she got sick. His mother—the kind of beautiful that out-of-date fashion and a faded photo could not hide. He looked away.

The cancer and surgery had made her someone else. When he saw her near the end, she'd wanted to give him a hug. He'd stayed clear. That was not his mother.

Dan eyed the gaunt, shrunken man breathing deeply with his mouth gaping open. His father, Big Dan. The old man's hands lay on top of the sheets—too large for the shriveled body but the flesh so wasted they looked skeletal. The stubborn grease stains that he couldn't scrub away during his working years were finally gone.

The minutes dragged. God, he hated being here.

Dan checked his smart phone. The market was down again. His investments further in the tank. Damn! He needed cash. He needed to avoid conviction. He needed to somehow avoid divorce.

Mesh's input made it clear Dan had nothing to lose by swinging for the fences. He either knocked it out of the park or he was toast.

He nudged his foot against the unyielding weight of the leather satchel alongside his chair. Heavy, but as he'd learned from yesterday's visit, easy for him to make it appear weightless when slung over his shoulder. On both visits he'd noted how the nurses and aides had given him big smiles. Dan could read their minds. *"So nice to see him finally spending time with his father."*

The old people judged him, the nurses and aides judged him. It was fitting. He looked at the rise and fall of the old man's chest—here lay his lifelong judge. The man who from Dan's teen years onward could not hide his disapproval. His father had tried. He'd tried to act warm. But his father had none of the acting skills Dan had. Dan had seen the wariness grow in his father's face. He'd felt his father's arms hesitate and lock when he'd tried to hug him. Probably his father loved him—Dan had no way to recognize the phenomenon.

He wasn't sure love really existed. He considered it possible that it was a fiction. One that "regular" people desperately wanted to convince themselves was real. A delusion people talked themselves into believing

Dan knew that the medical people his father had taken him to as a teenager were correct. It had been funny to see the psychologists, therapists, and doctors trip over their words trying not to upset Dan or his father as they shared their professional assessments.

Dan knew what they were saying and could not have cared less. Amusingly to him, a Readers' Digest article had confirmed for him the experts' diagnosis—Dan had scored eighteen out of twenty in the sociopathic trait test the magazine had published.

Dan didn't feel what others felt. Early on he recognized he really did not feel emotions much at all. He definitely didn't feel like others did. It had taken him no time at all to be okay with that.

He felt the shuddering rush of getting his rocks off, the brain rocket of a good buzz, and the primal satisfaction of physically dominating others. Those and the indulgences that money could buy worked for him. He did not yearn to be like others—that was another of their great arrogances.

He checked the time again—it had been long enough. His father's deep rasping breaths continued, mouth open, teeth and gums so dry they were covered in a whitish film. The old man smelled like a bundle of straw with a hint of cat-box. Dan got up, walked to the door, then peered out. No one in sight. He closed the door.

Dan moved to his chair and slid the leather bag directly beneath him. He unzipped it a few inches. A green tank. Nitrogen gas. Recently the rage for inflating car tires.

He took hold of the plastic breathing mask and freed the clear tubing that connected it to the tank. He unfurled enough of the tubing so the mask would readily reach.

Clara had explained it all. Nitrogen was a gas. Breathing it eliminated all oxygen but did not make the person feel short of breath. She'd explained with science-talk about carbon dioxide, respiratory drive, and other things Dan did not understand—whatever. It meant no oxygen and no struggle. People blacked out in as little as seconds and died in less than four minutes. Clara didn't just know things, she was super smart—maybe as smart as Mesh.

No pain—hell, practically a blessing. It couldn't matter to his father when he died.

It mattered to Dan—big time.

Dan held the mask and stretched the elastic strap to fit around his father's head, but it caught and pulled on the thin white hair.

"Big Dan's" eyes blinked open. The pupils shone large. Recognition flared as they locked on Dan. The old man's face twisted. He struggled as he tried to rise up. The warmth of the old man's gasping breaths registered on Dan's forearms. Just seeing Dan had been enough to provoke the old man's stroked-out remnant of a brain.

Dan turned the tank's knob and hissing sounded from the mask. He held the mask over his father's face, easily overwhelming the resistance of the large but feeble hands. The bony fingers locked onto Dan's wrists like talons. His father's eyes did not leave Dan's. With each breath the grip weakened.

As the body went limp, the last glint of his father's eyes showed what Dan had first seen there so long ago.

Recognition of what Dan was.

Chapter 61

Dan stood over his father's body as the flow of nitrogen gas hissed in the plastic respiratory mask. His eyes trailed across the framed picture of his mother on the bedside table. He bent, slipped the elastic band from around the motionless gray head, and removed the delivery mask. Dead, unblinking eyes pointed unseeing at the ceiling. Dan turned the tank's regulator knob and the hissing stopped. Silence. The faint musk of the last of the old man's last breaths lingered in the air.

Dan quickly tucked the tubing and mask back into the satchel, then zipped it tight. Mission accomplished. Clara's medical smarts confirmed. His father ended. Ninety percent of the Noble Village buy-in dollars would come to Dan—it was a significant amount. Mesh said it wouldn't be enough, but Dan knew money helped everything.

He checked the time.

There were different ways to play this. Run out and get the nurses' attention right now? Or simply leave and let them discover the body later? Hmmm. Easiest to get it done with now. He definitely didn't want to have to come back to this place.

He slipped on his coat, slung the strap of the bag over his shoulder, and went to the door. The empty hallway led to the wing's side door opening to the parking lot.

***

Dan came back into the facility through the front door. The athletic bag now lay locked in his trunk. As he passed the nurses' station and the gauntlet of judging eyes in the activity room, he felt a surge of satisfaction. No more living in the shadow of his father's disapproval. He guarded his smile and resisted the urge to jump in the air and rack a fist-pump in front of the old folks and their caregivers.

A final bit of acting and this step was done.

He entered his father's room. The scent of old man hung. Had the odor already faded? When hunting with a guy who had a champion pointing dog, he'd learned that dogs picked up the smell of the bird's breath in the air—dead birds were harder to find. Dan used his thumb and index finger to close the lids of his father's open, already cloudy eyes. His breathing days were over.

He pulled the bedside chair over near the window and sat down. He used his cell phone to start reviewing his texts and email. It wouldn't be too long before a nurse or aide came in. He had several possible reactions mapped out in his mind. Throughout his life he'd learned that in order to get what he wanted, he sometimes needed to act in the way people felt was appropriate so as not to reveal his true self. His upcoming scene would mark the removal of his father from the script and free Dan from the role of caring son.

The threats to the life he'd built demanded he take bold steps.

He'd not anticipated that doing so would feel so satisfying. He'd do whatever it took.

***

Dan's phone trilled as he climbed into his car in the Noble Village parking lot. The wind had picked up. Son of a bitch, it was cold.

"Dan Ogren." He started his car then double-checked that the seat warmer and thermostat were set.

"I've called you ten times in the past two hours. Where are you?" Mesh said.

Jesus, first words out of his mouth and he's already whining.

"Just leaving Noble Village. I went to see my Dad."

"Good for you," Mesh said. The unspoken surprise of "way to go, you ingrate son" sounded in his voice.

Why did Mesh think Dan cared if he approved?

"We need to meet right now," Mesh said. "Something important."

"My dad is dead," Dan said. *Judge that, Mesh.*

"What?"

"He's dead."

"I'm so sorry."

"Whatever. It was his time."

A pause.

"You went to visit and he'd passed?" Mesh said.

"He died while I was in the room."

Silence.

"He stopped breathing," Dan said. That was the absolute truth.

Another long pause.

"My condolences," Mesh said. "He was a very good man."

Dan wondered if Mesh's eyes were misty with the news. His father had liked Mesh more than Dan. For sure Mesh cared more than Dan about Big Dan being gone.

"Why do we need to meet?" Dan said.

"How about the parking lot at the Lake Harriet bandstand in fifteen minutes? Please. It's critical. It may be a very good thing."

Mesh hadn't mentioned anything as remotely good for days. Everything had been doom and gloom.

"I'll head there directly." Dan opened his briefcase and removed a silver flask. The car already felt toasty warm.

"Again, so sorry about your dad." Mesh disconnected.

Dan uncapped the flask. Yep—his dad was gone. The Noble Village apartment buy-in money would be coming his way. Mesh had good news. Later Dan would let Clara work his pole in thanks for her awesome smarts.

He tipped the flask, letting the heat of Johnny Walker Black slide down his throat.

His day was getting better and better.

***

Lake Harriet

Dan rolled across the trolley tracks as he approached Lake Harriet from the Linden Hills neighborhood. As he came down the hill he looked east and south over the expanse of ice. No sun. The sky looked like wet cement.

Darkness nearing. The ice smooth and black. The woods and trees surrounding the lake stood leafless and without color.

Still no snow.

Wind gusts bucked his car. The usually well-used running and hiking paths were deserted. Minnesotans could feel when hard weather was headed their way. Mesh's vehicle stood alone in the large lot parked near the closed-for-the season concession building, the white of its exhaust barely visible as the wind whipped it away.

As Dan parked, Mesh climbed out of his car and waved for Dan to do likewise. Dan lowered his window.

“It's freezing ass cold. Get in my car,” Dan said.

Mesh came to the window.

“You need to get out.” Mesh pulled up the collar of his coat, buried his hands in its pockets, then backed away.

What the hell? Dan zipped his jacket tight. As he climbed out of his car, a gust almost ripped the door from his hand.

“This is nuts, Mesh. A storm is coming and it's freezing.” As Dan said the words, the long-overdue, first snowflakes of the year whipped sideways from the north.

“Come over here. Please.” Mesh moved toward the lee of the closed-for-the-season, wooden concession building. Dan followed. They tucked out of the wind behind the small building's south side.

“Where's your phone?” Mesh said.

“In the car. What do you care?” Dan said.

“I've found a way to save you, but I'm not going to let you blackmail me again.” Mesh patted Dan's coat pockets. “I know I can't trust you. No recordings. You say nothing to anybody and I'm not a part of it. Open your pockets. Show me.”

“Lighten up. I'm not recording anything.” Dan opened his coat, showed his pockets, then zipped tight once again. “What do you mean a 'way to save me'?” *Did he come through for me again?*

“If you can keep your act together and do what I say, you can stay out of jail and save Ogren Automotive.”

“Ha! I knew you'd come up with something.” The brilliant little shit was magic. Relief coursed through him like a hit of cocaine.

"Don't get carried away. It's going to cost you. And it's set to happen tonight." Mesh frowned. "Are you drunk? High on drugs?"

"I'm fine." Dan had nothing more than a walking-around buzz on. "What do I have to do, and what is it going to cost me?"

"You need to meet with Beth and her attorney. Don't cause trouble. Sign some documents."

"I knew she'd hang with me." Dan felt another rush. No matter how she'd messed with him he still wanted her. He'd forgive.

"Are you insane? She doesn't want anything to do with you. Part of the deal is you stay away from her forever after the papers are signed. You're meeting to sign a deal to pay Beth off. This is an under-the-table deal. I've convinced Beth and her attorney that divorce will leave them with little to nothing—which is the truth. I presented them with an alternative. This is your only shot. Her attorney insisted you sign in person and be recorded doing so—it protects them from you trying to renege. The deal is ethically questionable but legally solid. It will hold up."

Mesh's opinion on legal matters was never wrong.

"What's it going to cost me?"

"Half of everything plus the house. Specifically, it includes half of Ogren Automotive."

"You can't be serious. No way. It's too much."

A gust of wind ripped around the building. Snow swirled around them. The lake's expanse faded in the growing blizzard. Mesh shook his head, staring at Dan in disbelief.

"Can't you connect the dots? You're a slam-dunk to be convicted of domestic violence. Beth has retained a shark of a divorce lawyer. Divorce actions without a prenuptial mandate a full audit to establish property owned. The audit will include Ogren Automotive. You've stolen so much from the company there's no way to come anywhere near balancing the books, even with the nursing home funds. You'll be convicted of financial mismanagement." Mesh paused.

"If you don't take this deal, Ogren Automotive goes bankrupt, you go broke, and you spend the next several years behind bars. That's the best case." Mesh paused. Snowflakes swirled around them. He spoke, his voice raised over the increasingly noisy wind. "You still think it's too much?"

"There has to be a better way." Dan shook his head.

"That's it. I'm done with you. You're insane. Flat-out stupidity. I'm done worrying about you." Red-faced, Mesh turned and started to walk away. After two steps, he halted and turned back. "I've saved your ass dozens of times and how did you repay me? You set me up with a bullshit recording and threatened to have me convicted. I advised you not to take those funds. Told you what you were doing was wrong and illegal. Right? Well, you're on your own. I'm done. I'll take my chances in court." He turned toward his car.

"Wait," Dan said. "Give me a minute." An idea had popped into his head.

Mesh stopped, then turned to listen, a huge gust causing him to squint.

"I had to make it look like you were guilty, too." Dan said. "I had no choice. You're the guy who keeps me out of trouble. I can't risk losing you."

"Is that supposed to make me feel better?" Mesh stood jaw-clenched and staring as snowflakes accumulated on his clothes and hair.

Dan's mind spun. Bold steps. Whatever it takes.

"I'm sorry, Mesh. What I did sucked. It was wrong," He put on the sad expression he'd used to bullshit Beth so many times. "I need you. This deal is a lot to get my head around."

"You are a total asshole," Mesh shook his head, "and I'm a fool to keep helping you." His expression showed he'd bought Dan's act.

"Thanks, Mesh. I don't like it but I'll do the deal."

"It's the right move."

"Where will I meet with Beth and her lawyer?"

"You won't believe it." Mesh turned toward his car and waved his arm. "I'm freezing. Get in my car and I'll give you the details."

Chapter 62

Drake entered the ICU. Rachelle's name was written in marker on the assignment board. She'd been assigned to ICU bay four, the same bed where Jon Malar had almost died. Bad memories flashed. A nurse stood at the foot of the bed with a chart in hand. Hidden from his view, at the center of the profusion of lines, monitors, and devices, lay the mother of his children—the woman he loved.

He took a step to the side. His breath stopped.

Rachelle's olive skin looked as pasty and lifeless as clay. Dark circles pooled beneath her closed eyes, her lashes seeming impossibly long. The racing beeps of the cardiac monitor revealed a heart battling hard. A central intravenous line had been inserted into her neck. Multiple fluid and medication bags dripped while IV pumps cycled and clicked. The odor of disinfectant mixed with the sickly sweet tinge of diseased flesh.

His heart sinking, Drake scanned the bank of monitors mounted above her bed. The vital signs, wave-forms, and other readings confirmed what her appearance had already told him. The bacteria within her raged out of control. The flames of infection had spread.

His throat clenched and his mouth went dry.

He moved to the bedside and placed a hand on her cheek—cool, clammy, and doughy. She did not respond. His fingers wavered as he withdrew his hand. A white noise hiss filled his head and dread raced through his mind like wind-whipped snow. Emptiness clawed at his guts. He crossed his arms over his stomach. The foreboding he'd felt was now a thundering avalanche of fear. He would lose her. *No!*

"Dr. Cody?"

He found himself sitting, the roar in his head fading. A hand on his shoulder. Phones, voices, and the chattering of a printer began to register.

"Are you okay?"

He looked up. Blond hair, caring eyes, a kind voice—Tracy. The same incredible nurse who'd taken care of Jon as they'd worked together to keep him alive.

"I barely got the chair under you," she said. "Let me get Dr. Kelly. He's on the unit. Please don't try and stand. And you should know Rachelle received sedation. She's out."

Drake could only nod. The racing beeps of Rachelle's heart monitor sounded impossibly loud in his head. He had to pull himself together.

"Drake." Pete Kelly stood before him in scrubs and a white coat. "Rachelle got sicker fast."

Drake nodded.

"Her blood pressure nose-dived and her pulse climbed. She's getting high-volume fluids, and I started pressors to maintain her blood pressure. It's septic shock, Drake."

Drake tried to get to his feet. Dr. Kelly put a restraining hand on his shoulder and crouched to Drake's level.

"Please just sit back for a second, Drake." His eyes found Drake's. "You don't need to do anything. Let me and the others take care of her. Okay?"

"She's real sick, Pete."

"As sick as they come." The physician nodded. "I've consulted the best we have and she's getting good care. I know it's hard, but let us make the medical decisions. It's better for everyone—including Rachelle."

Pete was right. The emotional impact and potential for guilt made maintaining a degree of separation from the care of a loved one good advice among physicians.

"I understand," Drake said. "But I need to know what's going on." Pete's cautions made sense, but Drake could no more turn off the medical problem-solving part of his mind or limit his sense of responsibility than stop his knee-jerk reflex.

"Absolutely, Drake." Pete straightened. "Infection at her skin graft site expanded to cellulitis and has now generalized. Probably streptococcus or resistant staph. Can't rule out pseudomonas or other gram negatives. It moved fast. A fast-moving, nasty organism for sure."

Pete had listed some of the murderer's row of bacteria that caused infections like Rachelle's. The educated and crucial guess as to which bacteria was involved determined which antibiotic to try. Microbiology lab results, if available in time, could identify if their guess and antibiotic choices were on target. The choice could be the difference between Rachelle living or dying.

Pete continued, "She has high-dose, broad-spectrum antibiotics on board and she'll be receiving more. The leg site doesn't show an abscess collection."

A pocket of pus known as an abscess could serve as a focal source of sepsis. Antibiotics could not penetrate such a pocket of pus. If Rachelle had such a collection, cutting into the pocket and draining the pus would be vital.

In a few sentences, Dr. Pete Kelly had summarized the essentials of Rachelle's medical status. And the knowledge identified the limited treatment options available.

All that could be done was being done.

Rachelle could rally and turn the corner, improving rapidly—possibly within hours.

Or she could "crash and burn." The unscientific but all too accurate term used by medical caregivers described vividly what happened when disease won out.

Many, many times Drake had fought to save patients who went 'code blue' in the hospital or presented to the ER crashing. Too often he'd been unable to make a difference.

Please, God, no!

Chapter 63

Interstate 494, on the outskirts of the Twin Cities

Dan whipped the wheel to the left, his car out of control on the highway ice. He steered into the spin, did not panic, and his vehicle regained traction before he entered the ditch. He'd almost spun out twice while heading north on 494 before accepting that he had to keep it under thirty miles per hour. He'd passed at least four cars in the ditch. With the worsening conditions he had to go even slower.

He uncapped his flask and took a generous pull of scotch. Bad driving conditions and a horseshit plan. Shit! Mesh's pushing this deal showed he'd become an incredible weakling.

The snow continued to fall in the blackness, and though it was only seven thirty p.m., the highway was almost deserted. Snow emergency warnings had been strident, and many businesses had closed several hours early. His wipers fought to maintain a window onto the road. His headlights lit but hardly penetrated the whirling, glittering, unremitting cloud of the blizzard dense flakes. Three huge highway department trucks raced three abreast on the southbound lanes, plowing the rapidly accumulating snow and applying road salt in a non-stop circuit. Dan hoped the recent northbound pass of the plows he was following would allow him to get to his turnoff.

What happened tonight would determine whether he lived life as a dickless loser or continued to live large. He was made to live large.

A fierce gusting crosswind shook his car like the close passage of a speeding semi-truck. The snow-blurred lights of Maple Grove's business district showed to his right. His exit lay only a few miles ahead. His destination was as improbable as his supposed mission.

Dan had not been back to his Kenwood home so he'd not noticed his recreational vehicle was gone. When Mesh had told him where he needed to go to meet Beth and her attorney to make this deal happen, he couldn't believe it.

She'd hated the sporting event parties and hadn't been in the RV for more than two years. That had worked out well for Dan, as the home-on-wheels vehicle had served as the site for countless episodes of drunken, naked, rocks-off fun. Every woman he could get to have a few drinks and be in the RV with him alone was there for one reason—whether she knew it or not.

He knew what he could get away with—he'd pushed the limit more than a few times. As long as the woman was legal age and drunk, and there were no witnesses, he could do whatever he wanted. It had always been that way and, despite the bullshit laws that had gotten passed, it still was.

Beth. She'd flipped out after the ER day. The damn doctor had started all the trouble. Dan had not succeeded in killing the bastard, but trying had been a rush. It had shown him what he could get away with.

Now Beth was the bigger problem. It probably hadn't been smart to smack her around, but she'd asked for it. Leaving the injuries had screwed him. You can't leave a mark.

The way Dan saw it the whole thing was sexist. Because she was a woman she should be able to get away with giving him shit? No way. He believed in equality. He'd treated her like he would a man. Actually better. If a guy pissed him off he'd stomp their heads into the ground. She'd earned every one of the punches and slaps he'd delivered through the years.

Ideally, he didn't want her gone. He wanted things the way they'd been.

Beth on his arm was great for his role as husband, business, and community guy. Beautiful and sweet—she legitimized him—like a great prop. And such an incredible piece of ass. Despite what had happened, he knew if he got her alone she'd respond. She bitched about the rough stuff. And had finally got wise to his out-and-about sport screwing. But despite all that, if he got the chance to put it to her again, he knew she'd like it. Like it a lot. No matter what she said.

And he'd never held out on money. He'd rarely even noticed what she spent. Or how she spent her time. His money and her position as his wife had helped her become a standout among the goody-goody, help-the-puppies and poor people crowd.

But he smacked her a few times and suddenly all that wasn't good enough. Shit.

His tires hit black ice and for a moment his car swung sideways. Once again he kept his cool and avoided overcorrecting. The car fishtailed but he avoided the ditch.

The blizzard might help him.

He slowed even more and took the unplowed County Road 30 exit. Not too much farther distance-wise, but the roads would be rugged. He turned west.

Mesh's plan. Dan to meet Beth and her shark of a lawyer alone. Dan to act like a punk and sign away damn near everything. *Yeah, sure thing, Mesh. Great plan. What next? Cut my nuts off?*

Mesh had overreacted. He'd made the deal sound reasonable, but Dan had a better idea.

Thoughts of Beth had him half-hard. He was not going to show up with his limp dick in his hand.

Dan Ogren was nobody's bitch. He lived life the way that worked for him. He wouldn't live any other way.

His car bucked over a ridge of ice. A clank sounded from the trunk.

Bold steps. Whatever it takes.

Chapter 64

ICU

Drake stood helplessly by while Rachelle teetered on an invisible cliff. Within her, a life-or-death war involving bacteria, cells, tissues, and chemicals raged. Tracy moved about the bedside, checking monitors, adjusting drips, and continuously supporting Rachelle in her fight.

Rachelle's appearance, vital signs, and test results showed the fierceness of the battle but could not predict how it would end.

Victory meant life. He and the children would not lose her.

Defeat would open a chasm of blackness and pain beyond anything Drake could imagine. His mind backed away from the thought of losing her, like someone deathly afraid of heights veering away from the edge of a cliff.

He'd almost lost her before. Her courage and selflessness had helped save the children and her from a fearsome woman crazed by greed, drugs, and madness. It was beyond cruel that now bacteria—microscopic organisms little more than mold—threatened to take her from them.

He wanted to believe she would be okay. He wanted to pray but feared his pleas could be turned against him. Would prayers be answered from a person whose heart raged against a God who allowed so much misery? Would this harsh and mysterious God, knowing the doubts in Drake's heart, punish him for his lack of faith?

A soft alarm beep sounded. Tracy reached over, adjusted an IV line, then keyed in information, silencing the pump. The ICU nurse's practiced skill and attentiveness reassured. All that could be done for Rachelle was being done.

Drake felt a desperate need to be busy—to somehow be useful. Activity had been his survival tool for a very long time. No one but he knew that his manic schedule was a form of cowardice. It helped him avoid dwelling on who he was or thinking about what he'd done or those he'd failed.

For a time in his past, drugs, alcohol, and anger had claimed him. He'd been on the road to a bad place.

The birth of his dream of becoming a doctor and doing research had put him on a better path. The wholly absorbing engagement in meaningful work that the ER and research provided was both passion and therapy.

When he'd found Rachelle and become a parent, it was as if he'd been made whole again.

Earlier Drake had gone down to the ER, the place he'd practically lived in for the past several years. He'd changed into scrubs.

He'd pressured his colleagues into letting him carry the flight beeper and take any helicopter runs that might arise. He'd told his colleagues that he was staying in the hospital anyway, and feeling as if he was helping out would make him feel better. Rescue flights were always short, and the blizzard might ground them altogether. They gave him the beeper. He'd grabbed his flight jacket and brought it to the ICU.

***

Rachelle lay motionless as the pumps clicked and whirred. The beeping of her heart monitor continued to race as if she were sprinting. The buzzing of phones, printers, and voices from the nursing unit came from the bay's entry. The smell of antiseptic and laundered sheets mixed with the nail-polish odor of ketones—the substance the body formed when forced to burn the last of its energy stores.

Drake now experienced the agony he'd observed in so many others. The people in ERs and hospitals who waited helplessly while desperately hoping for their loved ones' recovery.

Drake had to turn his mind elsewhere or drown.

He borrowed an iPad from one of the ICU nurses.

As he sat at Rachelle's bedside, the sound of the monitors, alarms, and pumps provided an indicator of her body's fierce struggle. Tracy hung a small intravenous bag, then performed an examination and check of each line and monitor, her movements deft. His thoughts flew. The prospect of losing Rachelle had crystallized for him what really mattered.

Whether it was faith or cowardice, he had to believe she would survive. He couldn't do anything to help her now, so he focused on the obstacles to their future.

He began to devise a battle plan to fight for their dreams.

Ideas came to him straight and clear. This was not medical care, but his mind engaged with the same total concentration he used in the ER. He typed out the strategies and instructions in detail.

When he looked up, he was startled to see how much time had passed. After a last review, he emailed his plan to Lloyd and Rizz. Just as when battling to save a dying patient in the ER, no one did it alone. He would need help to have any chance.

With his document sent, Drake stepped to the narrow window of ICU bay four. The lights of the surrounding skyscrapers were fuzzy in the wind-whipped, falling snow. Huge trucks with flashing lights powered down nearly deserted streets, their massive blades hurling tons of accumulated snow.

He looked at Rachelle, so fragile and sick. Knowing how easily infection could kill filled him with dread. Rizz said she was tough as nails.

Could she hang on?

Chapter 65

Drake had to escape the ICU. As he sat beside Rachelle's infection ravaged body his feelings of helplessness and desperation had threatened to explode. He put on his flight jacket, pocketed his phone and the flight beeper, and headed to the heli-pad.

The halogen lights of the eighth floor rooftop flight deck illuminated the sleek Agusta helicopter. The pilot tossed a wave at Drake, then continued a check of his craft. The pilots and crew treated their air rescue machines like thoroughbred racehorses. The skilled operators and finely tuned engines were ready to go whenever needed and conditions allowed.

Snow continued to fall. The wind had eased and huge flakes fell heavier than Drake had ever seen. The temperature had climbed and the crystals clung to his hair, eyelashes, and jacket. The lights of downtown's hulking buildings, the stadium, pockets of metro parkland, and Drake's view of the Mississippi were shrouded in the gauzy whiteness.

Drake had called and talked to Kaye and then the children. Kaye understood the life-or-death severity of septic shock. She assured him the kids were in good hands—and his certainty of that made him appreciate her beyond limits.

She'd put him on speaker and he'd lied to Shane and Kristin. He'd managed to keep his voice from breaking as he'd told them that Mom was “a little bit sick” and needed the hospital for a few days to get better. He'd finished up by telling them how much Mommy loved them and had disconnected before he broke down.

“A little bit sick”—he wished that were true.

He scanned the metro area from his eagle's perch. The snow limited his range, but he could glimpse parts of the sprawling Twin Cities area. Almost four million people, all of whom were vulnerable at any time to the heartless cruelty of illness or injury. His life's work was treating those visited by the emergent, unforeseen devastation of disease or trauma.

The ping of the elevator door opening behind him caused him to turn.

Julie Stone stepped out. Her breath fogged in the cold. She hugged herself in her scrubs and white coat.

"Tracy in ICU told me you were up here," the OB/GYN surgeon said.

"Julie, you must be freezing." Drake moved to step into the elevator. She took his arm stopping him.

"No. It's okay. I'm a Minnesota girl. I can handle the cold." She paused. "I heard about your wife. Scary stuff. I stopped by the ICU to wish you the best. Most people think being a medical person makes it easier to handle having a loved one who is sick." Her eyes met his—kind and genuine. "Just the opposite, in my opinion. We know too much."

"Thank you."

She took a step onto the deck and her head swiveled as she took in the view. "I've never been up here. And tonight with all the snow. My God, it's beautiful."

Drake could not help but notice with a twinge of guilt that so was she—strikingly beautiful.

"I come up here whenever I can," Drake said.

"Can't blame you," she said. "I have positive news for you. Tina Watt, our anchorwoman patient, is going home tomorrow. She learned what happened in the ER and is now a member of the Dr. Drake Cody fan club." She smiled.

"So great she's doing okay. Score one for the good guys." He stuck out his hand. "We rocked it, partner."

"We sure as heck did." She shook his hand then looked away. "I'll leave you now." She still held his hand. "I hope your wife gets better quick." She released his hand then stepped into the elevator. The doors pinged close.

Their patient was going home. What a thrill. The paramedics, ER team, OR, and Julie Stone had saved the life of a special young woman. And he'd been a part of it. *Nothing better.*

His thoughts jumped and his good feeling sank.

His time as a doctor threatened to be over forever within days. Would he ever again have the chance to do anything as meaningful as helping save

Tina Watt? Such special opportunities were a regular part of his life as a physician working in the ER.

He'd been given the gift of the best job on the planet. Stressful, exhausting, and hard, but he'd saved lives and stopped suffering. What could match that?

The downtown lights fuzzed. The ache in his stomach returned. Hollow and empty.

Rachelle scary sick, and the most worthwhile thing he'd ever done was coming to an end.

Chapter 66

RV campground

Beth looked out the windows of the RV for the tenth time in the last five minutes. She checked the clock. She took a deep breath. The meeting had been scheduled to start five minutes ago. She slid her tongue along the inside of her mouth, sensing the stitches and the coppery taste of her torn flesh. The storm had stopped travel for almost everyone else in the Twin Cities, but Dan was different. He would not be stopped.

The snow blanketed everything and continued to accumulate. The blizzard had eased briefly, so at times she could see though the falling snow down to the county road. She felt sure she'd be able to spot headlights. If Dan did make it this far, could his car make it up the unplowed campground road? He was sure to be driving a vehicle with four-wheel drive.

Nothing stopped Dan when his self-interest was involved.

Her face and mouth still ached. For the hundredth time, she ran her tongue over the stitches in her mouth. She'd quit looking in the mirror.

He'd hurt her physically so many times, but the damage inside was worse. Always afraid. Ashamed. Living a lie.

She deserved a life. A chance to live and love.

She'd taken the first steps. She'd left him. And retained a divorce lawyer. And filed a restraining order. After so long, so much abuse, she had to go through with the whole plan. Had to complete the steps that would make her free.

A plan to assure her enough money for the future and, most importantly, to be forever safe from Dan. To have a life. One final meeting and she'd be done with him.

In these last hours she recognized she would have to face him. Just days before, they'd lived in the same house. Shared a bedroom. But now everything was different. The thought of him terrified her. What had seemed a great plan now seemed a giant risk.

She could feel panic simmering. She wanted to disappear. To run away. God, what might he do? Could she keep from collapsing?

Am I strong enough?

Headlights! Her breath caught. It had to be him. She retched as if she might vomit.

Lord, no. Maybe he'd be stopped by the unplowed road and turn around. *Please!*

She couldn't do this.

She looked out the window. The vehicle had stopped on the county road near the start of the campground's narrow track. *Give up. Turn around.*

The car began to back up. *Yes! Thank God, yes!*

After about fifteen feet, it stopped and accelerated forward, swinging wide to enter the deep snow of the campground road with momentum. The vehicle lurched over the margin of plowed snow, then pushed through the deep snow of the campground road. The headlights fanned through the naked trees and swung towards the RV. *No!*

Beth looked around frantically while hearing her own gasping breaths. The RV now seemed impossibly small. The papers, pen, and legal folder were set out on the table with a chair on each side. Dan would be in this space with her. She wished she had an army with her, but on this blizzard-savaged night there would be only her—and him.

Fear thundered down on her like an avalanche. She put her face in her hands.

Panic surged. She considered locking the door. If the lock held she could climb into the bedroom and curl up on the floor until he left. The headlights bounced through the windows as the car climbed toward their meeting. He would not be stopped. *I can't do this!*

She ran toward the door, her head an echo chamber of shrieking alarms.

Just as she put her hand on the lock an image jumped into her mind. A memory so ugly it caused her heart to clench and her blood to freeze.

Dan standing over her, his expressionless eyes locked on her as her puppy hung from the leash at the end of his arm. Her loving dog's eyes bulging, his neck twisted and grotesquely stretched, his legs swimming in the air as he struggled for air. Dan had done that—and threatened he could do it to her.

He was a monster. She had to get free.

She pulled her trembling hand back from the lock.

She moved to the chair behind the table. She sat facing the door to the RV and positioned the paperwork in front of her, making ready.

She'd never been so afraid.

Chapter 67

County Road 116, minutes earlier

Without four-wheel drive, Dan would have had to turn back. The main roads had been plowed but already many inches of new snow had accumulated. Each turn he took brought him to worse road conditions and increasingly desolate country. Now on County Road 116, he penetrated deep, untracked snow, advancing at only ten miles per hour.

The Dayton area had been large farms and open country when Dan was young. Now horse estates, commercial operations with metal buildings, and scattered housing developments were mixed among the working farms.

The closer he came to the meeting site, the greater his certainty grew that signing away everything and paying off Beth was a loser's move. Mesh had got Dan to swear he would sign the papers and then leave. He'd warned that if Dan threatened or misbehaved, it could screw the deal. Not till then did he tell Dan when and where the meeting was.

There had to be a better way.

Mesh saw the payoff deal as a no-brainer, but the little lawyer played the game much differently than Dan. Dan had the balls to pull off moves that Mesh would never consider. The brilliant little guy always saw several moves ahead, but he always played within the rules. So limited.

I make my own rules.

He felt the heft and reassuring denseness of tempered steel in his coat pocket.

The GPS guidance said the campground Beth had chosen to hide out in was close. The falling, wind-blown snow limited visibility, but he made out an area of woodland ahead on the right. A farm field buttressed a cattail marsh, with higher ground and mature trees behind. He spotted a small sign and slowed to a stop. The turnoff was almost invisible, but there was no doubt this was it. Squinting, Dan made out the rectangular shape of the RV on the crest of the rise a few hundred yards in. The lights of the windows glowed through the falling snow.

His excitement grew. This was game time and opening night rolled into one.

According to Mesh, it might just be Beth and her attorney. Two women. He could easily overpower two women. But he couldn't leave a mark. That was where the pistol came in to play.

He hadn't talked to Clara on this one, but he was planning to use what he'd learned from her. No one but Mesh knew of the meeting. Dan had pulled the battery from his phone so if police tracked its location, it would show nothing.

There was uncertainty ahead and he didn't have the details worked out, but if conditions were right, he'd make it happen.

Mesh would suspect—hell, he'd know—but if Dan kept "plausible deniability" in play for the attorney, he could be handled. Dan could always handle Mesh. The smartest guy ever but a wimp. He liked to figure the angles and play the end-game, but he didn't have the balls to live large and risk it all.

Dan had the balls.

He wouldn't be stupid but everything was at stake. Bold moves would have a big payoff. He was eager to take care of business. He had a full nitrogen tank in his athletic bag. His heart pounded and he tingled in anticipation. A total rush!

He'd enter and act like a nutless wimp ready to sign away everything. Then he'd pull the gun.

He'd immobilize them. He had soft restraints in the bag. Very strong, but they would not cut or bruise. Then the nitrogen tank, the respiratory mask, a twist of a knob, and his problems would end.

They'd slip away just as his father had. Dead bodies without a mark on them. He'd shut down the RV, leave everything open, and they'd be frozen by morning.

No one could prove anything.

Bold steps. Whatever was necessary.

Chapter 68

Drake swiped his ID card through the reader at the entry to the ICU and the doors whooshed open. He entered the unit and immediately sensed the crackling atmosphere of alarm. A huddle of scrubs and white coats surrounded Rachelle like a resuscitation team attending a Crash Room patient. *No!*

He rushed forward.

"Stop, Drake." Dr. Pete Kelly stepped forward from behind the counter and grabbed Drake's forearm. "It's not as rugged as it looks. Rachelle is doing okay. Her blood pressure dropped and her breathing slowed. I felt it best to get her intubated. We can keep her sedated. The tube went in smooth. Her pressure came back. We're playing it safe." He looked towards the throng. "Respiratory Therapy is adjusting the ventilator. Tracy is at the bedside and radiology and lab are there."

The pounding in Drake's chest slowed. He put his face in his hands for a moment.

"I'm okay. I just need to see her," he said.

As Drake neared, a few of the techs moved from the bedside, leaving only Tracy and the respiratory therapist.

His stomach dropped.

Rachelle, impossibly pale, closed sunken eyes, and now with the endotracheal tube exiting her mouth and connected to the ventilator's hose-like tubing.

As frail and vulnerable as a child.

He placed a trembling hand on her shoulder.

The ventilator's *click-hiss-blow* cycled, causing her chest to rise and fall.

"She's heavily sedated, Drake." Tracy's sympathy-filled eyes looked at him from across the bed. "Her blood pressure is doing better."

Putting a tube into people's windpipe and breathing for them was something Drake did multiple times each week. Bad trauma, heart disease, emphysema, and many other circumstances called for supporting or taking over patients' breathing for them. It was the intervention that likely saved more patients than any other.

Medically, he understood it. Emotionally, it hit him like a speeding truck.

"I think she's holding her own, Drake." Tracy was at his side, a hand on his arm. "Nothing I can measure, but I think she's stabilized."

Drake looked at the bank of monitors, displays, and vital sign indicators. The beeps of the heart monitor, the cycling gasp of the ventilator, the wave forms of pressure readouts. The background scent of antiseptic, laundered sheets, and sickness was now joined by the unmistakable banana-like scent of the benzoin someone had used to secure surgical tape.

Tracy's nursing insight didn't have a printout or display screen, but it was as real as the cables connecting Rachelle to the heart monitor. The intubation had not been a panicked bailout but a strategic decision. Despite her scary appearance, the nightmarish plummet of Rachelle's condition may have stopped. She was still deathly ill, but perhaps the antibiotics and her defenses were holding their own.

"I hope you're right, Tracy." Drake couldn't imagine anyone better to help Rachelle in her fight.

"We've got her, Drake." She squeezed his shoulder. "Hang in there." She adjusted the blanket on Rachelle, then checked the IV site where it entered the scar tissue of her neck. She picked up an oversized clipboard from the bedside tray and continued her unending tasks.

Drake put a hand on Rachelle's brow. Perhaps not as clammy as earlier? He bent and whispered in her ear.

"Tons of new snow outside, and it's still falling. Think about how much fun Shane and Kristin are going to have playing in it. You're going to get better. Keep fighting."

He straightened. He shook his arms and shoulders like a fighter getting loose. When he'd come into the unit and seen the crowd around Rachelle, his fear had jumped to the level where he felt ill. Now it was down to a nine on a scale of ten.

Drake pulled up a bedside chair. A shrill continuous beep sounded and Drake looked at Rachelle's monitors in alarm. She looked unchanged. He scanned the machines for evidence of trouble before realizing the source of the sound.

The flight beeper's shrill wail ceased as Drake silenced it. An Air care rescue flight had been scrambled. He grabbed his flight jacket, the feeling of leaving her both familiar and uneasy.

He bent and kissed her cheek.

"I love you."

Chapter 69

The flight elevator doors pinged open to the deafening roar of the helicopter's engines.

Drake crouched and moved across the vibrating flight deck in a blizzard- and rotor-whipped storm of snow crystals. As he neared the open copilot door, the burning jet fuel smell and driving heat of the throbbing engines struck him.

He climbed aboard and nodded to the pilot, who sat poised with hands on the controls. Drake strapped in and put on his headphones. The pilot worked the controls, initiating the helicopter's power take-off.

Drake's stomach plunged, then rebounded as the craft dove from the flight deck, then accelerated forward and up. The lights of the downtown buildings flashed. The copter swung clear of the skyscrapers, then flared toward the Mississippi.

St. Anthony's Falls tumult surged in the snow-fuzzed lights of the Stone Arch Bridge. The copter climbed as they escaped downtown via the open corridor over the river. Clear of the tallest buildings, they turned northwest. The blizzard's fury buffeted the craft, causing it to pitch and drop like a boat in a squall. He'd never flown in conditions anywhere near this bad.

They continued to race into the storm. The Air Care dispatch operator's voice crackled through Drake's headphones. "Responding to call for one down in an RV at a campground. Dayton Fire/Rescue volunteers on scene by snowmobile. Gunshot wound to the throat. North ambulance en route but held up by the roads. No other details. Be safe."

Drake's vision went blank. His heart clenched. *She's hiding out in an RV in a campground.* That's what Aki Yamada had told Drake to reassure him that Beth Ogren was safe. Drake fought a rush of nausea.

It had to be her.

He reeled.

He'd land to find Beth Ogren fighting for her life. If not already dead. Gunshot to the throat—please, no.

Was she another person Drake had failed? Sadness and guilt flooded in.

He'd recognized what Dan Ogren was capable of—he'd sensed it.

Had Drake's reporting of Dan Ogren's abuse to the police led to this? What if he hadn't reported it?

A massive straight-line blast of wind struck them. The windows went white-out. The copter lurched. Drake flew upwards, was caught by the restraints, then slammed back into his seat. The copter yawed to the side, feeling like a boat overturning. Drake faced straight down. In a slight lessening of snow, he glimpsed a furrowed and frozen field below.

"We may have to put down." The pilot's voice somehow sounded calm and matter-of-fact over the headphones. Drake neared panic.

At that moment the turbulence eased. The craft righted. Visibility improved. They'd passed through the fiercest part of the storm.

"There they are," the pilot said. "Flares and lights ahead."

The light bar of a police jeep flashed from the edge of a road near a grove of trees. Two flares and a snowmobile sat on an open field clear of the trees and far enough from the road to avoid the adjacent power lines.

The pilot spiraled in, their approach steep, and the landing jolted Drake's teeth. The rotors blasted snow in a cyclone of white, blowing clear some of the ground beneath. Drake grabbed the resuscitation bag and jumped out. The pilot kept the rotor spinning and engine idling, ready for their return flight.

Drake crouched and ran toward the person who waved to him from the snowmobile. As Drake got clear of the blades, he hit snow up to his thighs.

"Climb on back, doctor. Please hurry." The snowmobile driver was a young guy wearing a camouflage parka and blaze-orange hunting cap.

Drake climbed on, freezing in his flight jacket without a hat or gloves. The machine lurched forward.

"Is it Beth Ogren?" Drake hollered into the back of the driver's head, his insides knotted in dread.

The young driver yelled over his shoulder. “The lady is messed up...” Drake missed words in the sound of engine and wind. “...so much blood.”

They roared around the edge of a snow-covered cattail marsh, then climbed through the edge of the woodland. A huge RV with deep snow on its roof stood at the crest of the rise. Two vehicles sat at the end of snow-cut tire tracks alongside the RV. A large-tired, jacked-up red pickup truck with “Dayton Volunteer Fire/Rescue” printed on the door idled with the doors hanging open. Its roof-mounted flood lights illuminated torn-up snow and a rescue sled beside the RV's door.

Drake fought through waist-high snow, the rescue bag in hand.

“Get the transport sled hooked up and ready to go,” Drake said to the driver of the snow machine. “We'll load her and get to the copter as fast as possible.” The young guy looked confused for a second then jumped off the machine and made for the sled.

Beth Ogren—in the ER Drake had been struck by how she looked like she could be Rachelle's sister. A report of gunshot to the throat, lots of blood. He dreaded what he would see inside the RV.

Rational or not, he felt responsible. *Please don't let her die.* He opened the door and climbed in.

Two large, parka-clad men, one on either side, were bent over at the head of a blanket-covered body on the floor. Blood covered the floor and some had sprayed on the furnishings of the opulently appointed RV. One of the men working near the head spoke. “Lots of bleeding. Been holding pressure and trying to keep the airway clear, Doc. That's all we could do. We lost the pulse. Might be too late.”

A sob sounded, followed by shuddering moans—the agony of panic and hysteria. Drake raised his head to the source of the distress. His breath caught, his throat locked, his mind blanked in shock.

Beth Ogren stood behind the struggling rescue workers, wild-eyed, hands on her face. Her eye still swollen and blackened, the stitches in her face evident, but otherwise upright and very much alive.

“I had to,” her voice cracked. “He was going to kill me.” Another racking sob.

One of the volunteer EMTs shifted position as Drake looked down. Dan Ogren's ashen-white face lay in a pool of crimson. The rescue volunteer held a gloved fistful of blood-soaked gauze jammed against the downed man's throat.

A cascade of thoughts and emotions swept over Drake.

The doctor in him tried to save every patient—regardless of who they were.

But never had he been so relieved to find out who it was who needed his skills.

Chapter 70

Manny's Steakhouse

The waiter set glasses of single malt scotch in front of Scott Lloyd Anderson and Rizz.

"Drake's email said to investigate a deal with the university," Rizz said. "What do you think of the timing?"

"I think Drake is up against a wall with debt and responsibility. He's looking to see what options he has. Makes sense to me," Lloyd said.

Rizz scanned the others seated in the bar area of Manny's Steakhouse. The oak and leather appointed restaurant attracted the who's who of the Twin Cities. The blizzard had resulted in a very thin dinner crowd. Rizz recognized a major league ballplayer lounging at the bar with a friend. A couple of older suits and gold ring types had nodded at S. Lloyd. They did not intrude.

Rizz sensed that Manny's was a place where serious negotiations were commonplace.

"Who set this up?" Rizz said. "And why Kline?" Rizz had received Lloyd's call less than twenty minutes after receiving Drake's startling and detailed email.

"I called Afton Tait, the university attorney who was at your lab when they seized the research. I told him my clients would listen to an offer for the intellectual property rights to the drug—the one the university had stolen. He gave me the 'D-44 rightfully belongs to the university' spiel, then said he'd get back to me. Called back in less than ten minutes and gave me a phone number. I dialed it. Kline answered." The graying attorney shrugged. "The university is keeping this at arm's length. Using Kline as their contact tells me he's in on this deal somehow. It's ethically borderline and very suspicious. What do you know of Kline?"

"Mainly chatter from the doctors' lounge at the hospital. The last CEO left due to illness. Kline stepped in from a university position in finance," Rizz said. "People were surprised when he got the job. The hospital has been losing money and the board must have been sold on his business background."

"Heard anything about him personally? The more we know the better."

"Nothing good. He walks around in two-thousand-dollar suits and treats nurses and doctors like he owns them. He's apparently one of those who think medical care is like McDonald's—patients are customers and the staff are fast-food workers. No awareness of what constitutes quality care—it's all about marketing and money. Drake said he's a jerk and Dan Ogren's buddy. Ogren is on the board. Could be Ogren helped him get the CEO job."

"I checked out his university history," Lloyd said. "He was head of patents and intellectual property activities. That includes pharmaceutical development and intellectual property revenues. Universities rarely bring the drugs they discover through the whole development process. Too expensive. They work out mega-buck deals with pharmaceutical companies upfront, with more payments downstream if and when the drug gets FDA approval. It can be astronomical money. The annual sales of top drugs is in the billions. Maybe they've had D-44 in their sights from the start? Kline's appointment to CEO may have been strategic."

"Scheming bastards." Rizz shook his head. "Based on the lack of class their snatch-and-grab at the lab demonstrated, I wouldn't doubt it."

"The university has the drug and a prima facie case," Lloyd said. "The Swiss firm also has a claim based on the contract they signed with Dr. Malar's wife. We'll have to fight both of them in court. And each organization has an army of lawyers and deep pockets. The university having possession of the drug and research puts them in the driver's seat. This could be in court for years and be very expensive. Things look tough, I'm not sure what kind of deal Drake expects me to be able to get."

Rizz recognized it was time to get Lloyd up-to-speed on the real situation.

"There's something Drake and I have not shared with you yet." Rizz looked down. "When the university raided the lab they failed. They didn't get D-44 or the formula for making it. Those were hidden in the materials I had you and Vang rescue that day at the lab. The last of the drug and its formula were in the 'personal' materials you and Vang recovered that day."

"You mean your booze, medicine, the kitty litter, and other junk?" He looked doubtful.

"Yes. Hidden and camouflaged. Drake had the last of the D-44 labeled as medication for me, and he had the drug composition and synthesis info hidden in the animal care supplies. The university stole our data and samples of all the test drugs that had failed, but they missed getting what really matters."

"You didn't think it important for me to know you had possession of the drug?" Lloyd looked both incredulous and pissed. After a few moments he nodded. "If they don't have it, our position is better but still tough. We're not in a real strong position to make a deal."

"He said to *investigate* a deal with the university. He didn't say to pull the trigger," Rizz said. "I'm sure he's thought it all through. He wants us to get the lay of the land. With Rachelle sick and everything else going on, he's got other worries right now."

Rizz had shared the seriousness of Rachelle's condition with Lloyd.

"Understood." Lloyd pulled his sleeve up and checked the Rolex on his furry wrist. "Kline should be here any minute—"

"Drake and I figured there was no reason to let the university know they didn't get D-44," Rizz said. "Chemically analyzing all the study drugs will take weeks, and they still won't know for sure what they have—or don't have."

"I like it," Lloyd said. He put a hand on Rizz's forearm. "We'll act as if we believe they have D-44. We play the ripped-off and pissed party and see what we learn. We'll commit to nothing."

"I'm sure Drake is looking for how to make things right. Overall, he's more of a justice than a money guy."

"Legally, it's his call. I'm all for justice," Lloyd said, raising his glass, "but I'm also a serious and unapologetic in-it-for-the-money guy."

Rizz raised and clinked his glass with Lloyd's.

"To money and justice," Rizz said.

Chapter 71

Manny's Steakhouse

Rizz nodded toward the entry vestibule to the bar area. “He's here.”

Kline had not yet spotted them. He wore an expensive-looking silk suit and had his nose in the air as he scanned the room. Rizz could see Kline did not give the maître de the courtesy of looking at him as the man approached. Kline’s manner screamed superiority and entitlement.

Rizz knew instantly that Kline was the kind of guy he loved to drill. Having Lloyd to keep the business on track left Rizz free to mess with Kline’s head. There were few things he enjoyed as much as making fools out of arrogant asses.

This guy treated nurses and doctors like shit, thought patient care was best judged by surveys, and was working to get Drake tossed out of the hospital.

The pomposity poster boy approached. Lloyd stood.

Stuart Kline, hospital CEO and illicit representative for the university, stood as if expecting Rizz to stand as well. *Even if I could stand I wouldn't.*

Kline did not extend a hand to either of them. Rizz saw Lloyd's eyebrow arch. They sat.

“I'm sure you don't remember me.” Rizz had his innocent look in place. “I'm one of the emergency medicine doctors who takes care of patients in the ER. Geez, Mr. Kline, that's a great suit. I saw one just like that at Kohl's. Did you get it there?”

Kline sniffed and rolled his eyes. He looked toward Lloyd.

Rizz sensed that Kline had dismissed him as “just a resident doctor” and identified the burly, older lawyer as the man in charge. Kline sat, facing Lloyd as if Rizz were not there.

“I am Stuart Kline, CEO of Memorial Hospital. I also represent the interests of the university in my capacity as a special consultant on patents and intellectual property.”

“I'm S. Lloyd Anderson, counsel for the physicians who created the research drug D-44 and own its intellectual property rights. The university appropriated the research in a grossly illegal fashion. Theft is an appropriate term. I do not know you. Do you have anything to confirm your identity and legitimize your role here?” Lloyd's brow furrowed.

Rizz smiled inside as Kline's sour-milk expression showed the first blow had found its mark.

“The research belongs to the univ—”

“Please answer my question.” Lloyd leaned back. Despite the relaxed posture his visage was steely. “You need to confirm for us who you are and that you represent the university. Otherwise you are wasting our time.”

“Do you expect me to show you ID?” Kline sneered.

“That would be a good first step. It leaves open whether or not you are acting as a representative for the university.” Lloyd had not shifted a muscle or changed his expression.

“I worked as head of university patents and intellectual property revenues up until I took over the Memorial Hospital CEO position. Do you expect me to have a notarized document showing my position as special consultant?” Kline's face had begun to redden.

“Dependent upon who it is signed by, that may suffice.” Lloyd nodded, still leaned back and expression bland.

“I've heard that he worked for the university as an accountant before coming to the hospital.” Rizz said it as if trying to be helpful. He feared he was laying on the clueless young doctor role a bit too heavy.

“Accountant? I have an accounting background, but I'm a former member of the university administration and currently a special consultant.” Kline's face had now fully reddened. “The research belongs to the university and the proceeds will go toward helping the citizens of the state.”

“Will the university attempt to develop the drug themselves, or will they enter into an agreement with a pharmaceutical firm?” Lloyd looked around the room appearing disinterested. “Do you know anything about their plans, or are you too far down the totem pole? I imagine you don't have experience with the higher-level decisions.”

Rizz became more impressed by Lloyd each minute. He was playing Kline like a fish.

"I'm involved in the decision-making at the highest level. I've been a part of the legal and administrative decisions from our first awareness of the research. The plan is for us to complete an agreement with a pharmaceutical firm. They have the funds, manpower, and regulatory pipeline to facilitate bringing drugs to market. We will develop a patent-use agreement that will deliver funds to the university initially and ensure a percentage take of future revenues if and when the drug gets to the market. It's standard. I've overseen several such agreements."

"You mean when you were an employee of the university?"

"Yes, er, well, I still am working for the university. Now I'm in a consultant role."

"And you've worked with pharmaceutical corporations before?"

"Many times."

"So now you're an independent consultant?" Lloyd said.

"Yes."

"Will you have to file a 1099 for both the university and Ingersen Pharmaceutical? Will you have to pay a Swiss tax also?"

"The Swiss don't have an income tax on foreigners. They—" He looked side to side. "Whatever. That's none of your business." Kline's attempt at a snarl came across as a pout.

Rizz continued to marvel. Lloyd was filleting Kline. This was definitely a heavyweight toying with a lightweight.

"You are mistaken," Lloyd said. "That is exactly my business—looking out for the interests of my clients. Now that you've convinced me that you are being paid by the university, no doubt including incentive bonuses, I'm persuaded that you are indeed working for the university. I think now we can address some substantive matters. Agreed?" Lloyd was now the picture of affable. "I'm sure you understand I needed to know you were legitimately representing the university. Working for the Swiss as well is interesting. I suspect it could put you in a tough spot. You are representing two masters who may end up at odds."

"Don't worry about that," Kline said.

Rizz felt steam building—the corrupt bastard. In less than five minutes, Lloyd had Kline unequivocally identify his role in a plan to pirate

D-44 while playing middle man to both the university and the Swiss pharmaceutical firm.

The plan made sense but ignored the fact that by all justice, the intellectual property rights belonged to Drake.

"Do you know Afton Tait, the lead university attorney on the lab and research seizure?" Lloyd said.

"Afton is not the lead. Actually, he's more of a gopher for the board and lead attorneys," Kline said. "I've been in regular communication with the lead counsel and key administrative people."

"I doubt you are aware, but in discussions with Afton, he shared with me the opinion that the D-44 legal claims of Dr. Rizzini," Lloyd nodded toward Rizz, "and Dr. Jon Malar are not enforceable."

"Exactly." Kline brightened and sat forward. "That was discussed in some detail. No one is worried about them."

"But Drake Cody, in contrast, has a very solid claim. In fact, Afton acknowledged that everything Drake Cody had done identified him as the lead investigator, that he took all good faith efforts to maintain the research as private, and that his claim was legitimate. Isn't that true?"

"There was talk of that."

"So it was understood that Drake had developed the drug and had not engaged in any effort to sell the drug? True?" Lloyd said. He picked up his scotch and sipped it.

"Yes," Kline said.

"And isn't it true that you and the university legal team investigated the legal documentation and found that, due to fraudulent actions by attorney Faith Reinhorst Malar, there was a possibility of successfully challenging Dr. Cody's ownership? Further, didn't they identify that if the university had the drug in their possession, regardless of true ownership, they would benefit?"

"It's a legal world. The truth is whatever the law says it is," Kline said. "You know that. Whoever's attorneys argue best decides what the truth is."

"I think you and the university lawyers know that the intellectual property rights to D-44 should stay with Drake," Lloyd said.

"Should? You mean like fair?" Kline sniffed and shook his head. "The university legal team thinks they can win in court. That's all that matters." Kline paused. "If you want to help these doctors, let them know they can't fight an organization this big and win. It could drag on for years and cost millions." He shrugged. "Maybe make a quick deal. Your clients agree to give up any claim. They get a few thousand dollars, and the university will help its citizens. You get some money. It's the best you can hope for. A court fight will be long and expensive, and you won't win."

"Maybe you're right," Lloyd said. He removed an envelope from his pocket. "If you bring the proposal in this envelope to the university personnel who have the authority to make a deal happen, this could be over in twenty-four hours. Can you assure me you are in contact with executive level administrators with the authority to make such a deal?"

"I assure you this will go to the very top. I'll present this personally to..." Kline named several administrators that were known publicly and pocketed the envelope.

Rizz had known Lloyd was good, but witnessing this was like seeing an All-Star athlete at the top of their game. He slipped another peek at the cell phone on his lap below the table top. The indicator on the phone's digital recorder continued to signal. Rizz had captured it all.

Kline had got to his feet and was primping at his sleeves and collar. The man did not have a clue that he'd just had his ass kicked.

"Geez, CEO Kline," Rizz loved emphasizing the undeserved title with Kline, who had no idea how many megatons of sarcasm were loaded in his words, "I'm still curious about that great suit. Macy's? It was probably Macy's, right?"

Kline looked at Rizz like he was a dolt and, without a word, spun on his heel and left.

Chapter 72

The crime scene was as blood-tracked and contaminated a mess as any Aki had worked.

His first shooting in an RV. Blood had mixed with the tracked-in snow, making it looked like a giant grisly snow cone had been dumped on the floor.

The Dayton and Maple Grove volunteer Fire/Rescue and police squads had been on site for a while by the time Aki had arrived. The road conditions made everything slow.

The first policeman on the scene had called Aki when Beth Ogren had informed him of the domestic violence case and shown Aki's card. The scene was in the Hennepin County Sheriff's jurisdiction but Aki and Farley had beaten them to the scene. A county deputy had just arrived and after Aki updated him on the history and pending action against Dan Ogren, the deputy had joined Farley in the other room attempting to get a statement from Beth Ogren.

When the lead crime scene investigator arrived, he'd looked at the snow- and blood-tracked mess and had just shaken his head.

They'd cleared out everyone except Beth Ogren, who remained in the bedroom with Farley and the deputy. She'd refused the offer of an ambulance transport to the ER.

She'd repeated the same thing several times between sobs.

"I had to. He was going to kill me."

Aki had known that Beth Ogren had been staying in the RV. Her attorney had filed for a restraining order on Dan Ogren, though it had yet to be served. It didn't look like it would be needed now.

The scene, contaminated as it was, told a story. A four-wheel drive vehicle registered to Ogren Automotive was parked outside the RV. From the location of the pool of blood it looked like he'd collapsed about ten feet from where he'd made his entry. The first responders had bagged the .38 caliber pistol they'd found next to Dan Ogren's body.

A nine-millimeter pistol had been found on the floor next to where first responders found Beth standing sobbing and hysterical when they arrived by snowmobile in response to her 911 call.

It looked pretty clear-cut.

But there was always a wrinkle. A metal tank had been found in a leather athletic bag next to Dan. It was labeled as containing nitrogen and had plastic tubing and a breathing mask attached to it. The crime scene investigator said breathing nitrogen would kill.

Dan Ogren carrying a nitrogen tank. What the hell?

Aki didn't have all the answers, but the big question looked to be answered without doubt. Beth Ogren had acted in self-defense.

Two of the other questions involved Dr. Drake Cody. One—had Dan Ogren been the one who tried to kill Drake? That question mattered.

Question two—and this one didn't much matter to Aki—would Drake be able to keep Ogren alive, making Beth's actions justifiable assault rather than justifiable homicide?

Aki really didn't give a shit if Ogren made it. He certainly wouldn't lose any sleep over it.

Was he cynical? Maybe.

One thing he was sure of—if Ogren died it meant no trial and one less asshole out there hurting people.

Chapter 73

ER

Drake stripped off his surgical gown and collapsed into a chair at the counter outside the Crash Room.

"Geez, Doc. Did you jump in the shower with your scrubs on?" An ER orderly carrying a stack of white towels stopped in front of him.

"What?" Drake asked.

"You're soaked." The young woman smiled. "Catch." She flipped him a towel.

"Thanks." Out in the blizzard and in the helicopter he'd been freezing. Now after his resuscitation efforts under the Crash Room lights, his hair and scrubs were drenched with sweat.

He buried his face in the soft, dry fabric. The fresh laundered scent was like perfume in contrast to the odor of blood and booze that still hung in the Crash room. There was no doubt Ogren had been drinking.

Drake toweled the perspiration off his neck and arms.

The surgeons had Ogren in the OR. His injuries were more than serious enough to have killed him by now.

Ogren demonstrated what police, rescue workers, and hospital staff knew to be a perverse natural law. The bigger the jerk, the more reprehensible the criminal, the more likely they were to stay alive. Even though everything in his care had gone flawlessly, the fact that he had not yet died defied all probability.

The bullet had passed through Dan's mouth and jaw and then entered his neck. It tore through his trachea and lodged deep in his spine.

When Drake had arrived at the RV, Dan Ogren had essentially been dead. As limp as a piece of meat—likely his spinal cord damaged. Cold to the touch. No pulse.

Kneeling on the blood- and snow-tracked carpet of the RV, Drake had passed an airway through the ravaged mouth and bloody tissues. He'd slipped an airway tube between the slack vocal cords and into the trachea. He'd advanced it beyond the hole the bullet had torn in the windpipe, establishing a path for air and a chance for life. He'd placed IVs and delivered blood and fluids while they transported the grievously wounded body via snowmobile sled and then helicopter.

The wife-abusing, attempted murderer had arrived in the ER alive.

Further stretching those odds, Dan Ogren had now made it to the OR.

Drake took a deep breath. Exhaustion pulled at him. He rubbed his face and looked around. The ER occupancy board showed a few empty beds—a rarity on evenings at this time. An overhead hospital-wide announcement sounded, advising personnel to avoid nonemergency travel. The storm continued.

Earlier, Drake had called Tracy in the ICU and got an update on Rachelle—she had not declined. He needed to dictate his Air Care and Crash Room report then get to the ICU to be with her. The helplessness and desperation he felt were not unique. He'd seen many people fight to hold themselves together as the lives of a loved one dangled out of control.

***

“Dr. Cody.”

Drake raised his head, feeling lost.

“Dr. Cody,” the station secretary repeated from behind the adjacent counter.

Unreal. He'd zoned out after completing his Crash Room dictation. He looked at the clock. It had only been a few minutes. No sleep and still recovering from his allergic reaction—fatigue so great he ached.

“Detective Yamada is calling from the Surgery waiting room wondering if he can come talk with you.”

“Sure. Fine.” Drake rubbed his face. “Please ask him to come right over.” His fuzzy-headedness began to clear.

Aki's work and the ER oftentimes went together—violent crime and medical care. Lately the link too often involved Drake and those he loved.

Had Aki been to the scene of the shooting? Must have.

Beth Ogren. Drake had not had time to talk with her. She'd look dazed. Her words, “I had to. He was going to kill me,” raw with anguish.

Thank God she'd stopped her husband.

Drake was exposed to a lot of death, and he knew a lot about how to keep people alive. Beyond that, he didn't have special access to any of life's mysteries. But he wondered.

He wanted to fully believe in a just God, but his spiritual teeter-totter went from abject doubt to a belief linked to an expectation of damnation. Scant comfort arose from anywhere on that spectrum.

An old saying claimed, “There are no atheists in foxholes.” Drake wondered how many who came to believe also feared they carried a ticket to hell?

He was too fatigued and emotionally stretched for theological pondering. He was ready to believe in anything that might help Rachelle.

Luck, science, divine intervention—fingers crossed, promises of good works, knocking on wood, praying—he'd embrace them all if they improved her chance of recovery.

He thought with appreciation of Kaye and her caring for the kids. Knowing the kids were with her made Drake certain that Shane and little Kristin were okay. That was one of few things he did not have to worry about.

His fear for Rachelle could overwhelm him.

The State Medical Board planned to strip him of his career.

The university and the giant pharmaceutical corporation were working to take his research.

Someone had tried to kill him.

Despite everything, he had to keep it together. All that could be done for Rachelle was being done. He needed to think about their future and what he could do to make it secure.

If Rachelle could get well, Drake knew that the family would get by. Things might be very different, but whatever else happened, if they were together and healthy they'd make it. Together and healthy were special gifts.

He hadn’t given up on his career or D-44, but his battle plans were risky and the odds were against him.

Had Lloyd and Rizz reached out to the university yet? A drug with the promise of D-44 was worth millions. If it proved to be safe and effective in humans, it could be billions. Did that leave him hope? Or did the size of the prize guarantee the maximum in cutthroat corporate and organizational greed?

In many forms of fighting, one could use an opponent's momentum against them. Drake knew how to fight. His and Rachelle's dreams were not lost yet.

Detectives Yamada and Farley rounded the secretary's station, their coats folded over their arms.

Drake turned toward them.

"You look tired, Doc," Aki said as they reached him. Farley nodded. They dumped their coats on the counter and took chairs facing him.

"We weren't able to talk to anyone from surgery. They moved Ogren to the ICU. We're not allowed in there yet. That RV looked like a slaughterhouse. What are his chances?" Aki said.

"Almost zero," Drake said. "Huge blood loss. A long time with no blood pressure. His carotid artery was hit. It's one of the main suppliers of blood to the brain, so he may have stroked out. In addition, the bullet probably nailed his spinal cord. He shouldn't have survived this long."

"Can't say I'm too broken up," Aki said. They were all silent for a moment.

"We have some good news for you, Doc," Aki said. "And also some questions we're hoping you can help us with."

"I'm with you," Drake said.

"First, the good news. Ogren had an athletic bag at the scene with him. Did you see it?"

"I saw a leather bag. On the couch, I think," Drake said.

"That's the one. Inside was a nitrogen tank and a breathing mask." Aki flipped a thumb towards Farley. "My partner remembered seeing the bag before."

"Okay," Drake said.

"It's leather, has handles and a strap. Our crime scene people just identified it as a," he read off his notepad, "*Vaqueta Leather Duffel Weekender*, and it sells for over four hundred bucks. Very unusual."

"Why does the bag matter?" Drake said.

"It matches the bag that was carried by the guy who dumped penicillin into your car's fan intake. We have it on a parking ramp security video from a couple of hours before your reaction. Everything fits—Ogren's size, movement, and now the bag. It wouldn't have been enough to convict, but it was him. Ogren is the one who tried to kill you."

Drake's still aching throat clenched as he flashbacked to being unable to breathe, certain he was going to die—a nightmare while fully awake.

Dan Ogren had done that to him.

"I don't think I'll have to worry about him anymore," Drake said.

"A good thing," Aki said. "I wanted to ask you about the tank. Our crime scene guy said breathing nitrogen could kill. Farley thinks Ogren planned to use it to kill his wife. Make sense to you?"

Drake thought for a moment. He sighed.

His instincts that first day in the ER had been right. Ogren was evil.

"Breathing nitrogen would kill," Drake said.

"Could it pass as a natural death?" Farley spoke for the first time. "Could he have got away with it?"

Farley seemed about Drake's age. What he'd done at the riverside shoot-out weeks back proved his fleshy, soft guy appearance did not reflect the inner man.

"I think it might," Drake said. "If it's important we need to ask Kip. Does it matter? He didn't pull it off."

"That's just it," Farley said. "I interviewed Ogren's right-hand man after the shooting. An attorney named Mesh. He was totally shocked. When I told him Ogren had showed up at his wife's with a gun, the guy went white and almost passed out. I mentioned the nitrogen. Turns out it's used for inflating car tires and is at all the dealerships. When I suggested it might be used to kill someone, he got real quiet." Farley paused.

"Tell him," Aki said.

"The attorney told me Ogren's father died at the nursing home yesterday. Supposedly the old guy just stopped breathing," Farley said. "Ogren was alone with him when it happened.

"We need to call Kip," Drake said. "He'll make it a ME case and be all over it." He imagined the twisted forensic pathologist's inappropriate glee at having such a diabolical death to investigate. "If anyone can find out if nitrogen killed Ogren's father, it's Kip."

"I figured we'd need him." Aki did not sound enthused.

Drake sat still while trying to process all that had gone on.

"What set Ogren off?" Drake said. "If we're right, within a five-day period, he beat his wife, tried to murder me, killed his father, then attempted to kill his wife."

Farley fidgeted and looked away.

"What?" Drake said.

"Ogren had a prenuptial agreement."

"How does that matter?" Drake said.

Farley seemed hesitant. "An element of the prenup said if he were convicted of domestic violence, the agreement would be void. Everything he owned would be in play in a divorce judgment. His attorney said the dealerships alone are worth over thirty million." Farley shrugged.

"Beating his wife was probably not rare for this asshole," Aki said. "But when you filed your report and got him arrested, it set him up to take a huge hit financially. He couldn't afford to be convicted of abuse and divorced. He probably tried to kill you to beat the conviction. When that failed and he learned his wife planned to divorce, he went after her directly." He shrugged. "Think about it. If he'd gotten away with killing you, it would've been very unlikely he'd get convicted on the domestic violence charge. If he'd gotten away with killing her—no divorce. Killing his father—inheritance. In a sick way it all makes sense—if you're totally twisted."

"The big irony is that the DA had decided not to prosecute him on the domestic violence charge," Farley said. "Ogren has a lot of pull, his attorney is super-sharp, and the case would be high-profile. The wife had repeatedly denied in the hospital that he'd abused her, then again later that night to police. A day later, she changed her story." Farley shook his head. "Based on the clause in the prenuptial, she had a lot to gain. Ogren's lawyer would destroy her credibility on the stand. The DA told us yesterday he didn't feel he could get a conviction."

The young detective paused. "It stinks, but if Ogren had waited out the legal process, he would have been safe. The DA was going to let him plead to a lesser, non-domestic violence charge. Make him attend some anger management classes."

Drake felt like he'd been kicked in the gut. *The legal process...*

Following the law had resulted in him almost being killed and Beth Ogren traumatized for life and lucky to be alive.

And most maddening of all, if Dan Ogren had "waited out the legal process," he'd have gotten off with a judgment barely above a traffic ticket. Drake pictured Ogren sitting in an anger management class leaned back in a chair with his hands behind his head and a smug look on his face. *Son of a bitch!*

He got to his feet, shoving his chair back. A bitter taste filled his mouth and he felt the urge to spit. The detectives looked at him open-mouthed, eyebrows raised.

Farley and Yamada were good men, but he had to get away from them. He couldn't stand to hear any more about how his doing the "right thing" had caused everything to go so horribly wrong.

"I'm sorry. I've got to get upstairs and see Rachelle." He turned and left the detectives sitting, their best wishes for Rachelle faintly penetrating the thundering roar in his head.

His blood boiled. Rage jolted through his exhaustion-fried nerves. His anger massed like gathering lightning but with nowhere to strike. Anger at the nameless, faceless, monolith that was the "system." A system that, over and over again, punished victims and let abusers go free.

A system that once again had taken Drake and made him a participant in a gross miscarriage of justice.

A system that had made Beth Ogren kill to survive and brought Drake within a breath of dying. A system that, left to its own, would have left Dan Ogren free, rich, and able to victimize again.

Chapter 74

Clara heard the report on the evening news. "A Twin Cities businessman shot in a metro area township. Dan Ogren, heir to the Ogren Automotive empire, whose father died only yesterday, was airlifted to Memorial Hospital level one trauma center. He is reported to be in critical condition. No further details available." Her breath caught. Dan shot. How? Why? Critical condition? *No!*

The news jackals brought up Dan's recent arrest and his pending domestic violence case. They tried to make it sound like Dan was a bad person.

She climbed into her car and drove through the dark in the worst snowstorm she'd ever seen. Almost got stuck four times, but she rocked the car out with her four-wheel drive. The trip that had taken her fifteen minutes before the storm took almost two hours. It wouldn't matter if she had to drive for two days—she needed to be as near Dan as she dared.

The hospital at night was the special domain of caregivers. Administrators were a rarity. Even though Clara wore a white coat and scrubs she stood out. She was not one of the chosen. Despite being a PhD in Clinical Laboratory Science and one of the most accomplished persons in the organization, she did not belong in the hospital at night. In particular, her role did not allow her to go to the bedside of Dan Ogren. The patient's bedside was a sacred place where, other than family or loved ones, only doctors, nurses and technicians were allowed. The Intensive Care Units were the holiest areas of all.

She could not reveal that she and Dan were partners in a love bond unlike any other. Especially now.

She could sit within the nurses' station and act as if checking labs and electronic medical record issues.

"Well, lookee here. It's the lab chief and computer nerd. You supervisors and administrative types don't belong in the hospital at night."

Clara winced at the bullhorn voice of the nearly seven-foot-tall medical school admissions mistake.

"Black Bart" Rainey sat leaned back on one chair with his legs stretched out and feet resting on a second. He wore sweat-marked scrubs and a soiled surgical cap with his OR foot-covers still in place. His mass took up much of the nurses' station. She could smell his body odor from ten feet away. His insufferable habits included always speaking so loud that everyone within one hundred feet could hear.

She ignored him and went to the station's farthest computer terminal.

"Did some of your test tubes need washing?" he asked. "One of your computers take a turn for the worse, *doctor*?" He laughed like the braying jackass he was, wearing an "aren't I clever" grin, oblivious to the unanimous distaste of all who heard him. He alone among the medical staff outwardly ridiculed her for her use of the title she'd earned with her PhD. "As long as you're here, why don't you make yourself useful and run down and make sure you have enough blood on hand for my patient."

Clara despised everything about Dr. Bart Rainey, though on this night she wished him total success. She'd already checked and double-checked all the lab and blood bank requirements his patient may have. It had shocked and sickened her to learn that Dan—who loved her more than anything—was in critical condition. Finding that Dr. Bart Rainey was the trauma surgeon taking care of him added to her burden.

She'd just come from her office, where she'd bypassed the privacy walls of the electronic medical record system and pored over the details of Dan's care. She'd read all the up-to-the-minute reports of what occurred pre-hospital, in the ER, and in the operating room.

He'd arrived by Air Care at nine seventeen p.m. He'd spent twenty-three minutes receiving care in the ER Crash Room before arriving in the OR. He'd been transfused two units of blood during helicopter rescue and transport, then more than twenty additional units of blood products in the ER and OR. As undeserving as Black Bart was to be a doctor, and as much as she truly hated him, the documentation suggested he'd operated with skill and speed.

How and why had Dan been shot? What had brought him to a campground on the edge of the metro area in the middle of a blizzard? The last she'd heard from Dan he'd told her he needed to meet with his lawyer.

Clara didn't know the details but she knew in her gut where it began. The one who'd started Dan's troubles.

The wife of the person responsible lay in ICU bay four. The thought of Dr. Drake Cody caused the blood to pound in her ears. A violent criminal who'd falsified his record. Another of the many undeserving applicants the corrupt medical establishment had chosen over her to become a doctor.

Drake Cody's report of "suspected" domestic violence had started the chain of events that led to Dan being near death. It had started it all.

The ER physician was as responsible for Dan's condition as if he had pulled the trigger.

Drake Cody's wife had a serious systemic infection. Clara had checked her records as well. The physician reports, nurses' notes, and extensive lab results showed she'd undergone rapid deterioration but had stabilized in the last hours.

Drake Cody had leapt past Black Bart on Clara's most hated list. The life-saving care he'd provided Dan in the field and ER did nothing to diminish her desire to make him suffer.

Clara had stolen multiple glances into ICU bay five. She could not go to his side. Their love must remain hidden.

Clara knew the odds. The amount of blood Dan had received—enough to replace his total blood volume five times over—and the injuries he'd suffered did not predict survival.

She prided herself on facing reality straight-up, however grim it might be. She could lose him.

As great as their love was, she had to think about herself. Dan would want it that way. Were there any tracks linking her to Dan and his attempt to kill Drake Cody? How she wished he had succeeded.

Did she need to worry about the police? Unless Dan had made a mistake that pointed her way, she should be safe.

No one knew of the magic bond she and Dan shared. She needed to keep it that way.

Clara moved to the counter nearest ICU five. She took her longest look at her man. His feathered and flowing blond hair looked untouched.

Beyond that, what she saw was a nightmare. Massive swelling, bruising, and a grotesquely deformed jaw made him unrecognizable. The airway tube protruded from the ugliness. Her incredible man, her Adonis, had been brutally defiled.

She slumped and cast her eyes downward as if she might somehow erase the horror her eyes had revealed. She put her face in her hands.

Whatever happened, whoever in addition to Drake Cody had done this—they wouldn't see it coming, but she would make them pay. And pay dearly.

Chapter 75

Hospital corridor

The white noise roar in Drake's head faded as he escaped down the hospital's empty corridor.

Aki and Farley had to have wondered about his reaction. He'd practically run out of the ER. He'd felt ready to explode. *The brutal and blind legal system...*

The law was supposed to deliver justice. It had failed again. The system was without conscience—it did not look back or make amends.

His license to practice medicine and his ownership of D-44 would likely end up being decided by the law. He trusted no institution less. It could take from him all that he had struggled so long and hard for—the work that was his passion and salvation.

Drake entered the corridor leading to the elevators, his shoes squeaking on the buffed floor. He noticed the Code Blue beeper clipped on his top pocket. He'd meant to hand it off in the ER as he had the Air Care beeper. He'd have to swing back and drop it off, as otherwise he was responsible for responding to any Code Blues occurring in the hospital.

He stopped and before he could turn, the door to the male physicians' locker room opened ahead of him. Neurosurgeon Gaylan Rockswald stepped out. He had a winter coat with gloves and hat in hand. It was clear he was heading out.

Drake couldn't help but wonder how many middle-of-the-night trips to the hospital and the rarefied arena of the OR the venerable head of neurosurgery had made. Drake approached him.

"Good evening, Dr. Rockswald," Drake said. Despite having known the surgeon for almost four years, Drake never considered calling him by his first name. The tall, gray-haired man was one of those who commanded respect without effort.

Dr. Rockswald stopped and turned.

"Dr. Cody. Good evening to you." His eyes found Drake's. "I heard of your wife's illness. So hard. I hope she recovers quickly."

"Thank you, sir."

"I scrubbed in on your gunshot patient," Dr. Rockswald said. The man afforded genuine recognition and collegiality to all. He showed respect to nurses, physicians-in-training, and everyone. His awareness that Drake had cared for Ogren pre-hospital and in the Crash Room was typical of him. "I'm sorry, but I do not believe he will survive."

No doubt the bullet to Ogren's spine and suspected spinal cord damage had prompted the trauma surgery to consult with the neurosurgeon. The highly regarded physician had been the one to take Rizz to the operating room after his gunshot wound.

"Was his cord destroyed?" Drake said. Ogren had shown no movement below the neck while in Drake's care.

"Injured but not destroyed. It looks like a contusion—his cord is bruised but not severed. If he were to live he'd be paralyzed, but it is the type of injury where there would be a slight chance of recovery."

"I wish that would have been the case for Rizz," Drake said.

Dr. Rockswald cocked his head. "What do you mean by that?" His gray eyes penetrated.

"Just that I wish Rizz's cord injury offered a better chance of recovery." Drake felt awkward, as if his discussing Rizz were inappropriate.

"I'm not sure I understand," the neurosurgeon said. "Dr. Rizzini's injury was remarkably similar to that of the patient I just treated."

Drake felt as if the floor had shifted beneath him. Had he misheard?

"Excuse me?" Drake said.

"I said Dr. Rizzini's cord injury was remarkably similar. Contused, definitely, but not severed. The type of injury that unfortunately most often causes lifelong paralysis, but which can sometimes recover fully."

"Michael Rizzini?"

"Of course." A frown flicked across Dr. Rockswald's face. "I remember these things."

The man was legendary for recalling everything about his patients. Drake felt a flush of embarrassment.

“I'm sorry, Dr. Rockswald. It's just that... well, er, I was misinformed. I thought his prognosis was virtual zero chance of recovery. I had the impression his cord was severed.” Drake felt like a babbling first-year medical student. Why had Rizz—

“The odds against your friend are high, but, as I told him after surgery—low hope is not no hope.” The stately man smiled. “Good luck to you and your wife. I live close by, so I'm going to brave the storm and try to get a couple hours sleep in my own bed before my first case.”

He strode toward the exit end of the corridor, pulling on his coat as he went.

Drake reeled. “Low hope is not no hope.”

That was nothing like what Rizz had told him. Rizz had said Rockswald told him his spinal cord was “trashed.” That there “wasn't any reason to expect he'd be getting anything back.” Drake's decision to take the huge risk of D-44 had been made easier because the prognosis had been so grim. Why had Rizz said—

The answer flashed like a neon sign. Rizz.

Drake's brilliant, messed up, and vice-laden friend had manipulated him.

Rizz faced a low probability of recovery and was willing to risk his life for the improved odds D-44 offered. He'd needed Drake to give him the drug so he’d lied.

Rizz had foreseen Drake's internal battle about the danger of using the untried-in-humans drug. He’d read Drake like a book and worked him like a puppet-master.

Perhaps he should be pissed but... Who wouldn't lie for an improved chance of recovery?

He shook his head. Rizz‘s combination of people-smarts and guile left Drake far behind. Only Rizz could lie to him, manipulate him, and put him at risk of a lifetime of guilt, yet leave Drake almost smiling.

Drake didn’t agree with a number of things that Rizz did or said, but in the end he loved the in-your-face, hedonistic, tortured, but strangely loyal bundle of conflicting parts.

The thrilling part of Dr. Rockswald's news was that Rizz's chance of recovery was much greater than Drake had believed.

The thought of Rizz no longer paralyzed was a rush. All good if no adverse reactions occurred—a big *if*.

A shrill alarm sounded, snapping Drake's thoughts. The code-blue alarm clipped to his scrub pocket shrilled again as at the same moment a paging announcement sounded from the speaker over his head.

"Code Blue, ICU. Code Blue, ICU. Code Blue, ICU."

Drake was running before his mind could react.

God in heaven, no! Rachelle...

Chapter 76

"...Code Blue, ICU."

Drake had covered thirty feet before he silenced the screeching beeper.

Four years of responding to code blues had taught him the fastest route to everywhere in the hospital. During the day, hospital traffic required he maintain a pace restrained enough to avoid collisions. On nights such as this, he sprinted through the empty halls as if on a fast break in a pickup basketball game.

He arrived at the stairwell, ripped open the door, then raced up the steps three at a time.

The elevator was not as fast as his legs for codes on floors one through five. For the ICU on floor six, the elevator held the edge. But not tonight. Not when it could be Rachelle whose heart may have stopped, breathing failed, or blood pressure plunged.

He rocketed up the stairs.

"Code Blue, ICU." The operator's page sounded in every corner of the hospital, summoning the response team to wherever the patient lay dying. In the ICU, highly skilled nurses would already be at the bedside, along with the crash cart that contained the resuscitation drugs and equipment needed.

Please, God, don't let it be Rachelle!

Theological pondering had vanished. His thoughts were a prayer—desperate and total.

He burst out of the sixth floor stairwell and banked toward the ICU. Despite the sprint up six flights of stairs and hours without sleep, neither fatigue nor shortness of breath existed for him. The automatic doors swung open. He spied the scrubs and white coats of the crowd massed around the nursing station near ICU bays four to eight.

Don't take her. Don't you dare take her! Fear invaded every inch of his body.

The not-so-tongue-in-cheek adage for doctors responding to code blues was, "When you get to the patient, first take your own pulse." If the doctor leading the life-saving effort lost their cool, the resuscitation could quickly become a disaster and assure a fatal outcome.

Could he keep it together when it meant everything?

He rushed into the unit. His heart hammered.

The crowd of techs, medical students, and nurses who'd responded to the code filled the unit outside the bays. They parted, opening a path for Drake.

Tracy stood at the head of the bed directing CPR, while the crash cart sat with several drawers open and used med containers strewn on the floor. A tech stood on a low riser bent over the bed with his arms executing the rhythmic piston-like chest compressions. The faces of others in the room showed the blank look of those witnessing a failed effort.

With the crowd parted and a chance to get his bearings, Drake looked upon the person in extremis and felt something inappropriate, possibly immoral, and certainly unprofessional. The patient whose life hung by a thread was not Rachelle. Bay five—not four. A two-ton weight lifted off Drake's chest.

As Dan Ogren approached death, Drake felt relief so profound it approached joy.

***

Drake could not believe Ogren had made it to the helicopter. And then he'd hung on so impossibly much longer. It had to be his athlete's strength and animal-like endurance that kept him alive. His collapse was overdue.

The sweat marking the scrubs of the aide performing compressions, the medication packaging strewn about, and the burned-flesh smell of earlier defibrillation attempts showed the team's resuscitation efforts had been extensive. A second aide relieved the first in performing chest compressions while Drake assessed for any last-ditch lifesaving interventions. Each second of effort confirmed the futility.

The resuscitation team had not cut any corners and they were experienced. Nothing had been overlooked. They knew what the final outcome would be as if it were a multiple choice question where all the answers were the same.

"Hold CPR," Drake said. Pausing the compressions allowed Drake to see the heart rhythm on the cardiac monitor. The wave-forms showed the impulses to be terminally slow and irregular. The last beats of a dying heart. There was no pulse.

Death would not be stopped. Drake smelled it amidst the fecund odor of damaged tissue, the coppery smell of blood, and the sour tang of sweat.

He moved nearer to check Ogren's pupils.

Drake's breath caught and he rocked back. *My God!*

Awareness burned in the eyes of the dying man! Drake leaned closer. Ogren's fierce and cruel eyes locked on Drake's—unblinking and red-tinged like those of an animal caught in a beam of light in the darkness.

The beeps of the monitor became one continuous note.

"He's flatline," Tracy said. All cardiac activity had ceased.

The hatred in Ogren's eyes flared, then faded like the last glow of a dying ember.

There were no more possible interventions.

The eyes no longer reacted or registered light. A fixed and unseeing dullness claimed them. The heart no longer beat. All signs of life were gone.

Whatever Dan Ogren had been—he was no more.

Drake wished he had never been.

Chapter 77

Drake stood in the ICU washroom. He rinsed his face and started to clean up. He scrubbed more aggressively than if he were prepping for surgery. He held his hands and forearms in near-scalding water and applied the harsh and pungent iodophor soap. After a one-minute scrub, he repeated the scrub using the brush.

He did not want to touch Rachelle with hands that had been contaminated by Dan Ogren.

He dried his hands on a paper towel.

Before Ogren's Code Blue, Drake had received a report that Rachelle was stable. Holding her own was good. He had to be realistic—as sick as she was, it would take time for her to get better. The code had kept him from her.

He'd not been to her bedside since the flight beeper had launched him into the blizzard.

As he approached bay four, Tracy looked up from Rachelle's bedside and smiled. She gave a thumbs-up.

His chest clutched. *Yes!*

He would check the electronic monitors, vital sign charts, blood gases, and lab results, but he trusted no lab test as much as he did the thumbs-up of his skilled nurse friend.

The smile stretched across his face felt foreign. In the past few days it had not been present often.

Rachelle's eyes were open. The breathing tube and ventilator were gone. Still groggy and drawn, she managed a flicker of a smile as Drake stood stunned at the bedside. Clearly still sick, but the change made him want to cheer. *Incredible.*

"She's so much better," Tracy said.

"Rachelle?" Drake put a hand on her arm and bent close. Her skin felt better—not clammy or doughy.

"Hi, Drake. Very tired. But better." The effort of speech seemed a challenge. "Was scared. The kids?"

Drake bent and put his face along her cheek. He gently squeezed her.

"I was scared, too. Real scared." Her improvement could not be more dramatic. She'd been intubated only hours ago. "The kids are fine. Having fun at Kaye's place."

Her eyes drooped. Exhaustion showed, but the fear had left.

"Rest now, my lovely lady. No worries," Drake said.

She closed her eyes and was out.

Drake straightened and looked at Tracy, open-mouthed.

"I know," she said. "Totally amazing. Her vitals improved, her temperature came down, and at that point she definitely did not like the ET tube. Dr. Kelly checked her, then had us pull the tube. She's done fine. Blood pressure and pulse improved. Sleepy but alert. I was just going to page you but then bed five went south and the Code Blue was called." She looked at Rachelle, whose eyes were closed and breathing appeared easy. "You must be so relieved."

Tears sprang to Drake's eyes. He tried to speak but couldn't.

Tracy looked at him, set down the chart, and opened her arms.

Drake stepped into her hug and held her. There were no words for what he felt.

"Oh, geez," he said gaining control and stepping back. He swiped a hand across his eyes. "I thought I was going to lose her."

Tracy nodded.

"I'm a wreck," Drake said. "Didn't feel that coming."

She smiled. The embarrassment he felt about his breakdown was instantly erased.

She pulled over a chair. "Sit down, Drake Cody. You're worn out."

"Thank you."

"Both of you need rest." She picked up her chart. "I'm going to keep the curtain open so I can keep an eye on Rachelle." She moved toward the nurses' station.

Drake noticed Clara Zeitman, the head of lab services, sitting at a computer console in the nurses' station. He felt as if she'd been looking at him, her mouth pinched, eyes narrowed. Why was she here in the middle of the night?

He leaned back on the chair. So tired. He looked at Rachelle—dark bags under her eyes, pale skin, and her scarred neck exposed. To him no one could be more beautiful.

His career, D-44, and their dreams in peril, but Rachelle looked safe.

Thank you, God, for not taking her. He'd been given much but wanted more. The future they'd worked for was worth fighting for.

He would rest for a bit then prepare. He'd have to be more together than he'd ever been.

Tomorrow would be big.

It would be their future.

Chapter 78

Clara had watched it all from her spot in the ICU. The death of the man who loved her more than anything. The one who would have been with her forever.

Before Dan died they'd let a man in to his bedside. She overheard a nurse say it was Dan's lawyer. Mesh, the attorney who had worked for Dan forever. She didn't know him but it seemed unfair that he got to be near Dan. That his words, not hers, had been the last her man had heard. She'd seen the intense-looking man speaking to Dan for only a minute or two before Dan's ventilator alarmed. A nurse entered and fixed it. Less than a minute later the attorney left. He'd never even touched Dan. Even as little contact as that, she envied.

Later Dan had started to crash. Everyone in the unit had been expecting it. It could not be stopped.

She'd sat at the computer console at the nurses' station only thirty feet away as they'd worked to save him. Might as well have been thirty miles.

She'd had to stay clear. She could not reveal what they meant to one another.

All her feelings had to remain hidden.

Including how she felt about the person who was to blame.

Drake Cody—the lying bastard. He should have never been allowed into medical school. She couldn't fault how he'd handled Dan's rescue or resuscitation. Nothing could bring him back when he'd gone Code Blue.

But despite Drake Cody's medical efforts, he was as guilty of Dan's death as the whiny, clinging bitch who'd shot him.

Drake Cody's reporting of Dan to the police had caused everything.

His self-righteous, illegitimate action had caused her to lose her perfect mate. He'd taken from her the incredible body and bliss that had been hers. He took from her the only person who'd ever loved her.

She would make Drake Cody pay.

The Code Blue personnel had left, and the remaining ICU nurses and aides were cleaning and preparing Dan's body for transfer to the morgue.

She resented their hands on him. He had been hers fully and completely. They were not worthy to lay hands on his magnificence.

Her eyes drifted to bay four. Drake Cody's wife ill with a major infection. The curtain was drawn back and Clara could see her plainly.

Clara was surprised to see the prominent scarring of her neck. Looked like an old burn. Damaged goods.

Sick as hell and badly scarred but pretty even so.

Drake Cody materialized at the bedside. Clara had not seen him reenter the unit. His hair was wet. He must have cleaned up after the resuscitation but he looked drained. Darkened circles under his eyes. Face gaunt.

When he looked at his wife, his face showed he did not see the scarred and sick woman as damaged goods.

Bastard!

Why should Drake Cody have someone to love?

He'd lied and cheated, stealing from a deserving person like her the chance to be a physician. And now he'd taken Dan from her.

The wheels turned in Clara's head.

She knew how to make things happen. The corrupt medical school admissions system had kept her out of their sacred club, but she knew more about medicine than all but the best of them.

It would be so easy for her to make the pretty little lady gone. Two strategies came to her within a minute.

She would make Drake Cody suffer...

Should she make him pay now or later? Either way, she would see that justice was served.

Chapter 79

Hospital

Drake woke to voices. It took a moment to get his bearings. He'd left Rachelle in Tracy's hands and taken one of the hospital's first-floor call rooms. He'd dropped to sleep like a rock. He checked the glowing digital clock in the dark of the windowless room. 6:30 a.m. Less than three hours' sleep. He ached a bit and his throat was sore, but given what he'd faced the past few days, his body had held up well.

The voices that had awakened him came from the hallway. Drake didn't mind the early hour. This would be a big day. He sat up and his gaze found the picture of their children hanging on the tubing of his stethoscope. With luck they would all be together soon.

If Rachelle had made a turn for the worse, Tracy would have called him. No news was good news, but he still needed to be cautious. Rachelle was not safe yet, but he had a good feeling.

The thought of how sick she'd been left him hollow. After a quick shower, he'd visit the ICU and hopefully find his good feeling was warranted.

Next would be his last-ditch efforts to save his career and maintain possession of D-44. The state medical board was scheduled to meet this evening, and stripping him of his medical career was on their agenda.

Drake had violated the rules by denying his criminal record when he'd applied to medical school. His conviction had been unjust. Nonetheless, his clear and repeated denials of its existence was grounds for loss of his license and the end of his career.

The bad publicity Drake had attracted due to the drug-seeker did not help, particularly with the board facing its own PR issues. Public sentiment and recent media articles suggested the medical board was lax and did not appropriately discipline physicians. Drake could serve as a high-profile example.

Additionally, the university and its medical school had members on the state medical board. Kline, as CEO of a university-affiliated teaching hospital, also had influence.

His situation in a nutshell? Grim, with a high likelihood he would lose everything. He took a deep breath. *Don't panic and keep focused.*

To continue the work he loved and take care of those who depended on him, he'd have to fight hard and without rules. He was not intimidated by the size or power of his adversaries. Screw them. Screw their flawed and corrupt methods.

Who was on his side?

Rizz was damaged physically and otherwise, but he was formidable. He was both a liar and brutally honest. Brilliant, fearless, and able to read people—both the good and bad—like no one else.

Jon had given the support he could. His recovery was still uphill.

S. Lloyd Anderson had shown himself to be the kind of legal warrior they needed. Just before sleep, Drake had read Rizz's text describing their meeting with Kline. Anyone who could impress Rizz that much was special.

Lloyd had texted as well and informed him that he'd passed on the envelope with Drake's conditions to the university representative. Drake's demand for a meeting with representatives of those in power would occur in a couple of hours.

Today would decide his future.

Chapter 80

Beth sat in the den of the Kenwood estate, her puppy on her lap, the morning sun making the snowy world bright though the window. Despite the kindness of the police and medics, a phone call of reassurance from her lawyer, and even the call from her mother, it was holding Kidder that had finally helped her to stop trembling.

She'd done it. She'd killed Dan.

People had questioned whether returning to the house she'd shared with him was a good idea.

Over the past years Dan had been here less and less.

She'd withdrawn, which the abuse counselor said was common. Other than her volunteer work at the animal shelter and other charity events, she'd hardly gone out. Despite this being the place where she'd suffered the most abuse, it felt safe.

She rubbed behind the ears of her pup and he snuggled against her. Impossible to think that in the beginning this was the way she'd been with Dan. He'd been the best-looking man she'd ever seen. Older, confident, and exciting. He'd seemed kind and generous. Physically she'd experienced pleasure beyond what she thought possible.

She'd been blind to so much.

Had he thought of her as a pet? It hadn't been long before he started to treat her like some had treated the abused and broken animals she cared for at the animal rescue center.

She'd learned that the incredibly handsome man was ugly—dark, cruel, and sick inside.

She'd suffered so much hurt. He'd injured her physically, but the damage inside was even greater. Her mind and spirit had wavered. She'd begun to feel she deserved what came her way.

Then she'd found one who cared. Who sensed what was happening to her and would not let it continue. One who reawakened her knowledge of who she was—and that she deserved more.

He'd convinced her that there was a way to be free.

She hadn't believed she could love again. But slowly it had happened. First just glances, and her recognizing his kindness. Even without sharing words, she could feel his concern and sensed his worry about her.

The surprise when he'd showed up at the animal care center, though he'd hardly said a word. Then a scheduled meeting which they'd both known was a date. An illicit, forbidden, yet exciting and life-awakening date. It had led to much more.

He had helped her face the reality of her life with Dan and understand where it led. He'd helped her commit to breaking free.

He'd been planning a way out.

But things had not all gone according to plan.

The day that Dan had taken her to the ER, she'd known what comparing him to his father would do. But she'd had to do it. What she'd said was the truth. Dan wasn't one-tenth the man his father had been. At some level he understood that—and it enraged him. She'd been so scared.

He'd hurt her badly and the injuries were obvious this time. He usually hurt her in ways that did not show. She'd succeeded, but she'd underestimated his cruelty and it had terrified her.

Then the ER and Dr. Cody.

The doctor knew the truth right away. She could tell he cared and had tried so hard to help her. The plan had been for her to reveal the abuse.

But she'd denied Dan did it. That was what abused and fearful women often did. And that evening she'd been no different. Dan's torture of her puppy and the fierceness of his attack had paralyzed her.

Her fear had almost ended things there.

But when the ER doctor reported Dan for domestic violence, despite her denial, it had kept the plan alive. As much as that had scared her, it proved things were possible. That she could get free.

In the ER, her fear had initially stopped her. Her emotions like a car with the brakes on full and the accelerator floored—stop or race for freedom?

Seeing the counselor and the police gave her a chance to face her fear and, in the end, it drove her on.

Getting safe. Getting to a place away from others. Limiting all contact.

But being hurt and alone in the RV at the campground had almost been too much. She'd never imagined the terror. Dan was in her head. Was she any different than Kidder hanging at the end of his leash?

She'd had no choice—she'd gone forward.

She hugged Kidder, recalling the nightmare of Dan's cruelty.

She'd called the attorney. Had her put the restraining order in place. She took the first steps suggesting divorce. She'd followed through the way she was supposed to, to make the plan work.

In the end, just her in the RV with the blizzard outside. Alone—no witnesses. That was the way it had to be. More isolated and afraid than she'd ever been. Waiting. Knowing Dan was coming.

She'd almost called the police when she saw the lights of his car—but by then it was too late. No one would be able to reach her in time.

Trying to convince herself that she had the courage to do her part. And knowing. Not just wondering or doubting but *knowing* she couldn't. That terror would forever haunt her...

***

The headlights bucked as the vehicle climbed up the narrow track through the deep snow. The snowflakes whipped sideways in the blizzard's gale. The RV shook, the gnarled limbs of the oak trees quaked.

She could not breathe, could not swallow, her mouth and throat dust-dry. Dan. It had to be him.

The meeting they'd arranged. The plan. A final meeting and then forever done with him.

What had seemed the only solution now was a nightmare. How had she believed she could go through with this?

The headlights grew close then stopped. *Oh, God!*

Just her alone with him.

Panic. I can't do this!

She ran to the door. Her hand on the lock.

Then the thought of Kidder. Hanging, choking, legs swimming in air—then limp.

Dan was a monster. She withdrew her trembling hand.

She had to free herself.

From somewhere she'd gathered herself enough to move to her spot. She made ready.

She sat behind the desk facing the entry to the RV.

The paperwork sat on the desk. Everything was ready. She thought through the moves.

As the door wrenched open, her heart tried to explode out of her chest.

A blast of cold air and blowing snow, then Dan came through the door.

He rose to floor level. Tall, muscular, in a fitted ski jacket, with an athletic bag over his shoulder. Snow crystals glistened in his hair and on his shoulders. The door slammed shut in the wind.

Fear clenched her insides. Air disappeared. She tried to keep her mind locked on what she needed to do.

"Hey, bitch," he said. His lip curled, his eyes narrowed and shone with a predator's focus.

The black of despair descended on her.

In that instant she knew she couldn't do it.

"This is wrong. Please just go." Her voice broke. "I don't want to do this."

"Where's your lawyer? No car out there. Is it just you and me?" His smile grew.

"Just go. You can have your damn money." His presence paralyzed her.

"Sorry, babe. You can't be trusted and you can mess up my life. You're great-looking, a good lay, and we had a good setup, but you blew that. I know you're gonna miss what I pounded into you. You're probably thinking about it right now."

"You're sick, Dan. Cruel and sick. You are missing something normal people have. You have no soul."

"Don't piss me off. I don't want to leave a mark on you." Her savaged face, aching head, and the torn flesh within her mouth caused her to recoil from his threat. The image of her gasping puppy flashed.

"What are you going to do?" How had she ever seen this creature as anything other than what he was?

"I'm not going to hurt you. I promise." He took the strap off his shoulder and lowered the bag to the floor. As he straightened, a black pistol appeared in his hand. "But I am going to kill you." He smiled as if it were actually funny.

Everything she'd ever thought, everything she'd been told, everything she'd feared about him had proved true.

He waved the pistol.

"This is to make sure you cooperate. I've got something for you to breathe. It's painless."

There was only one way to be free of him. She understood now why the need to go over things so many times. The practice. The rehearsal of what she needed to say and do before and after. The movements performed over and over until automatic. In these last days and minutes, her fear had overwhelmed her recognition that it had to be done.

In this moment, her fear was pushed aside by her commitment to survive.

He bent down and, still holding the pistol in one hand, began to unzip the leather bag with the other.

Now! She moved through her practiced steps. She brought her hand holding the pistol from under the table, locked it in the two-handed shooting grip with the other. She raised her arms and extended the weapon, looking over the sight at Dan's face. His jaw dropped open, his eyes wide.

She squeezed the trigger, as she'd practiced so many times before. His jaw exploded and his head whipped back as if hit by a thrown brick. Even though prepared the blast still stunned.

In the plan, she was to keep firing until there were no bullets left—but she could not.

Dan flopped on the floor and lay on his back. Wet, guttural sounds came from his face. Blood welled from his destroyed jaw and mouth.

Once as a child she'd seen a boy shoot a rat with a BB gun. The beast had writhed in a horrendous fashion, making ghastly sounds. She'd become ill and vowed she'd never hurt an animal.

She'd broken that vow. This animal had given her no choice.

Dan now lay still. Shallow, irregular, sloppy breathing sounds came from his body as it lay stretched out. A pool of crimson expanded underneath his head. Everything was more horrible than her worst imaginings.

Her body shook. She could not get enough air. She dropped the gun, falling back into the chair. She buried her face in her hands and began to sob. After some moments her thoughts returned.

There were still steps to take. It was over but not over. She picked up her phone. She'd known she would be in shock. She repeated the memorized words to herself like a mantra as she dialed: "I had to. He was going to kill me."

***

Now, Beth stroked her puppy's back. He wriggled but remained asleep. The big house was solid and quiet.

Earlier, Beth had received a call from the Japanese-American detective. He'd told her Dan had died. It confirmed what she'd known—from the moment she squeezed the trigger she'd known she'd done enough. She'd killed him.

Detective Yamada hadn't asked any questions. He said that the police position was self-defense, though he might need to do some follow-up later. She'd not been charged and there was nothing in his words or tone that suggested suspicion.

The way things had turned out, many of the precautions in the plan were excessive. But her partner had tried to consider every possibility and always looked several steps ahead. They'd misjudged some things but only in degree—their main decision had been proven beyond any doubt. Dan would never have allowed her to be free.

Dan needed to die.

A sound from the kitchen caught her ear. Was it the door opening? Kidder twisted awake and growled. Beth's throat clutched as footsteps sounded.

Kidder jumped to the floor then made his excited yowl, his tail wagging.

Mesh entered the room.

Chapter 81

Mesh closed and locked the Kenwood estate door behind him. He moved toward the sound of the puppy's claws on the hardwood floor, then heard his friendly yowl.

Mesh stepped into the den. Kidder made his tail-wagging approach. Beth was curled up on the couch, wearing a large sweatshirt with a blanket around her legs—she looked to be trying to disappear. Her face showed fear. It quickly bled away to something else. His heart clutched. She'd gone through so much.

Dan had been even sicker and more twisted than Mesh realized. He'd thought he had Dan set up perfectly. He'd believed he had Dan convinced the meeting and paying off Beth was his only way out.

He'd presumed to know what went on in Dan's mind. Thinking he could predict Dan's behavior had been a mistake—an error that had almost killed Beth.

They'd known there was risk, but Mesh's underestimation of Dan's ruthlessness had made the finale of their plan a life-threatening nightmare. *Will she forgive me?*

Mesh moved toward her but pulled up just short. He could not read the mix of expressions on her face. Her eyes had a haunted look. He dropped to his knees, looking at her, his hands extended.

"I'm so sorry. It must have been horrible." Their hands linked. This beautiful, kind, wonderful woman, had suffered so much at the hands of a man who had proved himself an animal. The police were investigating whether Dan had killed his father. What he'd planned for Beth was unthinkable. He looked up into her face. "Can you forgive me?"

She cupped his face in her hands. Her eyes welled with tears, yet something that was almost a smile showed. "It's all okay now, Mesh. You saved me. What happened, what I did, what I had to do—you were right. He would never have let me go. He would have killed me if I tried to break free." She closed her eyes and he imagined the horrific images she was seeing. He moved onto the couch and wrapped his arms around her.

"I love you, Beth. I love you more than anyone or anything ever. Holding you is a dream. Falling in love with you was like finding a new world that I never suspected existed. Knowing that you were being abused, the thought of Dan touching you was a cancer, eating at my guts every moment until I could free you from him."

"I love you, Mesh." She buried her face against him. His chest filled, his scalp tingled—was it possible to be happier than this? In her embrace he felt joy, desire fulfilled, and the beginning of their new and wonderful life together.

"I'm finally free," Beth said. "We're free. He can never hurt me again."

He wanted to hold her forever.

***

Ogren Automotive, Bloomington dealership, two hours later

"Please send them this way. Thank you." Mesh hung up, then moved to the office door and opened it just as the two detectives approached.

He nodded to them. "Toss your coats anywhere. Please have a seat." He indicated two chairs in front of what had been Dan Ogren's desk. "Thanks for coming to me."

"We just have a few questions," the older detective said. Yamada, Mesh recalled. They'd talked very briefly at the hospital before Dan had died. The younger bulky detective was named Farley. He 'd spoken with him as well. Very likable.

They both sat as Mesh moved behind the desk.

"I'll do my best to answer anything I can," Mesh said. "I'm shocked by all that happened."

"You've been his attorney for a long time, correct?" Yamada said.

“Technically, I was Big Dan's attorney primarily, but, yes, I've also represented Dan, junior. Most of my day-to-day work involves my role in operating the car business.”

“Do you have any idea why Ogren tried to kill his wife?” Yamada asked.

“I know there'd been trouble. You're aware of the ER and arrest. There was talk of divorce. But I was shocked to hear what happened. Dan was an impulsive guy but this was insane.” Mesh shook his head. He reminded himself not to say any more than necessary. “Have you learned anything more about his father's death?” He directed that to detective Farley as he'd been the one to share the news of Dan's nitrogen tank setup.

“The medical examiner called his report. Thanks for tipping me about Dan being present when Mr. Ogren died. It was murder. Nitrogen asphyxiation is what the ME calls it. It looks as if Dan planned the same for his wife.”

Mesh looked from one detective to the other. He shook his head, leaned back in the chair, and let his arms hang and shoulders droop. He made no attempt to hide his shock and disgust. He'd cared about Big Dan—a very good man cursed with a very sick son.

“I should show you this,” Mesh said. He held out the print-out he’d made the day before of the RV’s location from the vehicle's On Star-equipped location tracker. “I found this in his desk.”

Farley looked at it, then turned to Aki. “This answers how he knew where she was.”

Aki nodded. There was silence for a moment.

“What happens to the company?” Detective Yamada asked.

“With Big Dan’s passing and Dan's death, the heir is Mrs. Ogren. Other than some significant charity stipulations in Big Dan's will, everything will go to Beth Ogren.”

“Is the company in good shape?” Yamada said.

“Very good,” said Mesh. “Ogren Automotive is doing well.”

“Will you be staying on?”

“That's the way things are established. I'll continue as head of operations. Of course if Mrs. Ogren decides otherwise, it's her prerogative.

“Did Dan say anything to you to make you think he'd do what he did?”

Mesh took a big breath and blew it out. He rubbed his face. He did not have to pretend uncertainty. Dan had been ruthless and cruel. Had he thought Dan would murder his father and attempt to kill Beth? He knew he would get even with Beth if she divorced—possibly kill her. But he hadn't seen Dan's murder attempt at the RV coming.

Mesh had done everything he could to make Dan believe that Beth's attorney would be present for the meeting. A witness would eliminate any thought of criminal action for a rational person. Apparently Dan had planned to kill her, too. *Insanity!*

Mesh looked each of the detectives in the eye.

"He was totally selfish and used drugs and alcohol every day. He paid almost no attention to the business and cheated on his wife continuously. He was not a good person. Can I believe what he did, or tried to do? With what I know now—yes." He dropped his hands to the desk. "Did I see it coming? No, I did not."

And that error in judgment had almost cost him his everything. Beth, not just kind and beautiful, but brave and enough of a survivor to get Dan before he got her.

Thank you, God!

***

Hyland Park

Mesh climbed out of his car at the nature center. He put on sunglasses as the sun reflected blinding bright off the mountains of fresh snow. Blue sky and a temp near freezing, but with the warmth of the sunshine Mesh was comfortable in a jacket. Actually comfortable was not the word. When the detectives left, he'd felt an anxious uneasiness. He'd had to get out.

He walked along the newly plowed trail. Could everything be working out as well as it seemed? He didn't trust his luck.

Beth—lovely, amazing, incredible Beth. She'd done what needed to be done and seemed okay. Thinking about what it felt like to hold her in his arms this morning made him want to jump into the air and shout for joy.

All the planning. The hiding. The multiple secret sessions of rehearsing and shooting. His stolen time with her were the best moments of his life.

They'd set up Dan. Beth had found the courage to say the words she knew would trigger his rage, but he'd hurt her so bad it had made Mesh want to weep.

Her wounds had been necessary to provide evidence for the domestic violence charge. Mesh needed to persuade Dan that he was sure to be convicted.

Beth had followed the plan by signing with the divorce attorney and getting the restraining order against Dan.

Mesh's long-term manipulation of Ogren Automotive's business operations allowed him to make Dan believe that his financial crimes and losses were insurmountable.

Mesh had been able to convince him that a domestic violence conviction and divorce would guarantee he'd end up broke and in jail.

Everything Mesh and Beth did was aimed to get Dan, with his recent arrest for domestic violence and a restraining order, to show up where they wanted him. A place where there were no witnesses. A place he was forbidden to be. A place where his presence alone would convince any jury in the country that he represented a lethal threat.

The plan had required that Mesh stay away from Beth. They couldn't risk communicating or leaving any clue that they had a relationship. Ironic, as Dan traipsed about the Twin Cities drinking, doing drugs, and rutting. Worst of all was Mesh's worry for Beth's safety and the disgusting thoughts of Dan touching her.

He thought of his visit to Dan's bedside in the hospital. His face was a mangled mess, but it was him. Mesh had recognized the animal eyes...

***

ICU, Bay five

Mesh didn't like hospitals. The sounds, the sterile white and chrome, and the smells all made him uncomfortable. Only family and loved ones were allowed to visit patients in the ICU. Based on Mesh's talk with the detectives, Dan may have killed his father, which eliminated any family apart from Beth. Loved ones? Mesh did not believe Dan had ever loved anyone. No one had visited and they allowed Mesh, as his attorney, to Dan's bedside. The nurse left them their privacy. She'd told him Dan could not speak or move and he might not be able to hear or understand.

The alert eyes glinting out of the grotesquely injured face proved he was there. Mesh tried to ignore the wicked injuries. The smell of blood mixed with a Lysol-like tinge. The jaw had large stitches loosely closing torn flesh with a small tube draining from inside. The breathing machine cycled in a rhythmic, click-hiss-blow, with Dan's chest rising and then collapsing in sync.

Mesh kept his voice low. His eyes on Dan.

“It's me, Dan. Mesh, the guy who has covered your ass forever. The guy you lied to, insulted, and abused for all these years.” He paused. “I need to let you know a few things. I'll give it to you fast because the word is it’s a sure thing you're going to die soon.”

The eyes twitched.

“You hurt Beth. You abused her and treated her horribly. She is kind, gentle, beautiful, and loving.” Mesh felt tears well. “You did not deserve to be on the same planet with her.” His face felt flushed. “I know you think I'm a wimp and that I always play by the rules. Well, you're wrong. You're lying there a battered piece of meat waiting to die because I went outside the rules.”

Dan’s eyes locked on Mesh with a predator's intensity.

“You weren't going to be convicted of domestic violence. The prenuptial was never going to be voided. The company is not in any financial trouble at all. I moved funds around to make it look that way to a lazy jerk who never paid any attention to all that his father had given him. I lied to you about the criminal case and about you going broke and going to jail. I cashed in all the trust I'd earned by all the years of taking care of your crap. You didn't appreciate me, but you trusted me. Well here's the news—you shouldn't have.”

Dan's eyes jumped from side to side. The ventilator hitched and Dan's ravaged face reddened.

“I made up the meeting with Beth and her lawyer, Dan. There was never any payoff to Beth planned. Her lawyer knew nothing about it. The payoff is what you got. Beth waited for you and fired a bullet into your arrogant, brutal self. She's the one who killed you. You're not dead yet, but it's coming."

The eyes seemed to glow red, the pupils huge and boring into Dan.

"The detectives think you might have killed your father. I believe you did, though I know for all intents you killed him a long time ago. He recognized what you are. And as a decent man it destroyed him. He tried everything. He even paid me to try and help you."

The pupils had gone to pinpoint, the ventilator hitched once more.

"I'm in love with Beth. We've been lovers since last summer."

The ventilator alarm sounded. Dan's face was red, his eyes bulging. The nurse ran in and touched a control. The machine quieted. Dan's chest pumped fast.

"I put him on blow-by," she said. "He's breathing through the tube on his own now. I need to get him some medication. I'll be right back." She left.

"I'll talk fast. I want this clear in your mind as you die." Mesh said.

Dan's eyes burned like a welder's torch.

"Beth and I will be together forever. We have the company and all your money. We have everything you had but never deserved. We also have something you've never had. We have love. It's hard not to hate you Dan, but maybe I don't. I feel sorry for you. I've wondered if you have a soul." He leaned close. Dan's chest was heaving and his eyes were locked on Mesh's. "You better hope you don't, 'Little Dan,' because if you do, it will burn in hell forever."

Mesh stood, turned his back, and walked away.

Chapter 82

Farley climbed into the passenger seat. Aki already had the car started and was talking into the speaker phone.

"We're at Noble Village now," he said. "Farley and I just confirmed that Ogren had been alone with his father. Later, when the nurse came in, they found the old guy had died. Ogren claimed he thought his father was sleeping. Nobody suspected anything. What did the autopsy tell you?"

"Autopsies don't *tell* me anything," Dr. Kip Dronen said, sounding peeved. "The multi-level analysis, exhaustive gross and microscopic tissue examination, and deductive reasoning that I perform allows me to tell others what happened. Autopsies don't tell—*I* do."

Aki looked at Farley, making a "what the hell?" face. "Please tell me what you learned."

"Cause of death was asphyxiation with nitrogen gas."

"So it was murder, like we thought?"

"Brilliant deduction, Sherlock."

"Thanks. Please email the report." Aki clicked off quickly.

"He definitely likes to give you shit," Farley said.

"For sure. I have no idea why, but I'm not going to let it wreck today. Another case closed, partner." Aki flashed a big smile. "Lunch on me. Any fast food joint you want." He began to back out of their Noble Village parking spot.

"Thanks, Aki. I'm thinking I need a walk instead. It's nice out. Let's swing by Lake Calhoun."

The car braked hard and Farley turned to find Aki putting the car in park. He looked at Farley, wide-eyed.

"What?" Farley shrugged.

"Newton Farley turning down fast food?" Aki feigned alarm. "Are you okay?"

"Yes, I'm okay." *Am I really?* He should be feeling pumped up like Aki was.

"Good. Let's celebrate. We closed four cases today. It's a record. One," he counted on his fingers, "the Ogren domestic violence case. Two, the attempted murder of Dr. Drake Cody. Three, the shooting death of Dan, the dirtball, Ogren. And four, the murder, by said dirtball, of his father." He closed his fist and raised it like a champ. "Four cases off the docket. Done. No upcoming court bullshit, no questioning of people we know are lying, no risk of anyone else getting hurt." He smiled. "It doesn't get any better than this."

Farley took a big breath and looked at his lap. On the surface Aki was right, but Farley couldn't help but look beneath the surface.

"What gives, Mr. Rookie-of-the-year Detective? You've been part of closing more major cases in less time than anyone in department history. Be happy."

Farley hesitated. "I don't think my mother nursed me long enough."

"What?" Aki laughed.

"Probably I'm just a head case. To me it feels like we're forcing a cover on a Tupperware container and it doesn't quite fit. I want it to snap shut tight but it won't. There are unanswered questions. Faith Malar's murder had them as well."

"Every case has unanswered questions. That's the nature of things." Aki scratched his head, then sighed. He looked Farley in the eye. "Partner, what we do isn't science or math. A lot of the time things don't add up. People, especially killers, are messed up and defy explanation. We never know all the answers. But sometimes we get it right. We know who the assholes are. We know who did what to whom. And we nail them. That's all we can expect. These cases are righteous."

"I know you're right but things nag me. How does Ogren have the smarts to try to kill Drake with powdered penicillin? Where does he learn to use nitrogen? How did he know about Drake's allergy? I don't know the answers and never will. It bugs me. I guess I'm obsessive."

"It's probably part of what makes you so damn good. But you need to learn to say 'case closed' and let things go. There are always questions."

Aki patted him on the shoulder. "You had a good idea. It's nice out. Let's go walk around the lake. Maybe I can help you with your psychological problems. You don't have to lie on a couch and my price is right."

Farley nodded and came up with a smile. Aki was flying high and Farley didn't want to bring him down. He signaled a "thumbs up." Aki shifted the car into drive and accelerated.

Farley had a way to go in dealing with unanswered questions, and he hadn't shared the toughest one with Aki. Why, when in the RV with Beth Ogren after the shooting, had he ignored it when he found the small foam earplug floating in the toilet? The pinched and deformed configuration showed it had been recently used. She must have tried to flush them and one had remained.

They were the same kind many used at the practice range. They didn't stop you from hearing conversation, but they dampened the top-end blast of firearms. How had she had the time to put them in?

Just exactly what had happened in that RV?

Instinctively, part of him had decided some questions shouldn't be asked.

Maybe he had learned to say 'case closed'.

Chapter 83

As Drake approached Rachelle's bedside, he saw Tracy standing there with the oversized ICU chart in hand. Rachelle's eyes were closed. His spirits lifted at the sight of her much-improved color and general appearance. Her sleep looked restful, unlike the exhausted collapse of yesterday. He scanned the vital sign monitors.

Drake spoke softly. “Good morning, Tracy. Is she doing as well as she looks?”

Tracy turned. “Morning, Dr. Cody.” She smiled. “For Rachelle and you, it's a real good one. She had a great night. An hour ago she was awake. Totally alert. Asking about the children and worried about you.” She indicated the clipboard. “I'm just finishing my charting of how good she's doing, then I'm going to give report and go home.”

Drake had known Tracy was working a double and felt grateful. She'd been in Rachelle's corner throughout every minute of her ICU battle with the potentially fatal infection. Tracy's medical skills and huge heart had been key in Rachelle's recovery—and in preserving Drake's mental health.

Drake put a hand on her forearm. “I'm not sure Rachelle or I would have made it without you.”

She blushed. “Thanks for the kind words. Makes my day,” she looked at the clock, “or night. I'm not sure anymore.” She smiled. “A perfect shift. My sickest patient is now doing great. I've seen one of my friends smile for the first time in a long while. And I get to go home and go to sleep.”

“Thank you, Tracy. I mean it. Your care meant everything.”

“When a patient gets better, it makes it all worth it.” She patted his hand. “Being appreciated feels pretty good, too. I hope you have a great day.” She made her way to the nursing station.

A great day. He looked at Rachelle sleeping, her vital signs on the monitors all normal. The infection that had struck like lightning seemed to be in full retreat. Rachelle's recovery was miraculous.

Her eyelids fluttered open. Her huge brown eyes turned to him.

“Hey there, Drake Cody.” She smiled. “I feel better. Let's not ever do that again.”

He bent and kissed her forehead, his hand on her cheek. He looked into her eyes.

“I'm with you, lady. Never again, please.”

“The kids and Kaye?”

“I called and they're all fine.”

“Yesterday it was like I was sliding down a hill toward a cliff and I couldn't stop.” She looked away. “I was so weak and scared. Not just anxious, it was...” Her words trailed off.

“I thought I might lose you.” His throat clutched, thinking about how things had looked.

“Is today the day the state medical board meets?”

“This evening.”

“I'm feeling healthy enough to be very worried, Drake.”

He sat on the edge of the bed and faced her. He took both of her hands in his.

“I've got a meeting in a little bit with the people who hold my career and the future of the research in their hands. I've got some good people on my side and a plan. But whatever happens, they can't take what means the most to me. I love you. We have amazing children who love us. I'm going to fight like hell to keep our dreams alive, but we'll be okay no matter what happens. I promise you.”

He squeezed her hands. His stomach gnawed as he tried to avoid thinking about losing his work in the ER.

“You're fooling yourself, Drake.” She shook her head. “Some people have jobs. That's not you. The ER is what you love and it's what you're meant to do. It's why you're so good. And you care so much.” Her eyes brimmed with tears. “I know we'll survive, but if you lose the ER, I'm afraid you won't be okay.”

“I'm going to fight, but whatever happens I'll be okay.” He took her in his arms. “We'll be okay.”

She hugged him, her tears wetting his shoulder. He wanted to believe what he'd said to her. In his heart he truly didn't know.

Would today end with him losing the work that meant so much to him? Could he deal with that? Could he heal?

"When someone is wounded, a scar isn't the worst thing," Rachelle said. She leaned back and looked him in the eye with tears running down her cheeks. "The worst thing is a wound that never heals."

They held each other tight.

***

Memorial Hospital, Conference room

Drake sat in the dimly lit back row of the Morbidity and Mortality conference room. The room had theater-like seating and could hold as many as forty. Today's meeting would involve about half that number. Drake had left the lights low with a single spot directed at the podium positioned front and center below him.

Drake had participated in multiple highly charged discussions in this room. The Morbidity and Mortality conference brought physicians together for frank and hard-nosed assessment of patient-care cases where death or serious injury had resulted. This was the place to dissect what had occurred.

Sometimes the exchange highlighted what had been done well. Other times, in cases that had gone wrong, the discussion involved what could have been done better, with sometimes fractious finger-pointing suggesting blame. The debate surrounding opportunities missed or perceived errors was always intense and often contentious.

Audiovisual equipment allowed for presentation of labs, X-rays, and, in the worst cases, autopsy findings. In Drake's experience, it was primarily surgeons and emergency medicine specialists who participated in these honest, and sometimes harsh self-evaluations. In the end, the meetings were about getting it right, thereby making things better for future patients.

It had seemed to Drake to be the right environment for the meeting he had organized.

Lloyd entered the conference room and approached the podium. He carried his briefcase and wore a dark blue pinstriped suit with a crimson tie.

The big man was an imposing figure. Drake hoped his performance today would match his appearance.

"Hi, Lloyd. Do you know where Rizz is?" Drake called out.

Lloyd started, then squinted into the spotlight toward Drake.

"Good morning, Drake. Didn't see you there. How is your wife doing?"

"Much better. Amazingly well. Thanks." Drake stepped down to the front of the room. "Do you know where Rizz is? He should have been here by now."

"He didn't feel well last night," Lloyd said. "We were going to get together but instead we spent a bunch of time going over your plan on the phone. He hung in there, but I could tell he was under the weather."

"I called him thirty minutes ago and it went to message," Drake's worry needle buried in the red. Rizz had received his second dose of D-44 less than twenty-four hours earlier. "What kind of 'under the weather' was he?"

Lloyd set his briefcase on the table adjacent to the podium. "Huh? I don't know. Just didn't sound like himself." He opened the case and pulled out some papers.

"Did he—"

Drake's phone trilled. He snatched it out of his pocket. 'Rizz' was indicated on the display.

"Rizz, are you okay? Where are you?" Drake recognized he was wired and talking fast. *Whoa, get a grip.*

"I'm fine. I'm at the hospital. I'm going to be a little late." Rizz's voice sounded tight.

"If you're here, just come down to the Morbidity and Mortality conference room. Lloyd is here. We need to set up for this meeting."

"I'm not at Memorial Hospital. I'm at the University Veterinary Hospital." Rizz paused a long time. "It's FloJo. She's having grand mal seizures. It looks bad."

In the silence, Drake heard all that Rizz had not said. The worry. The fear. He didn't have to tell Drake it was terrifying news—maybe the worst. A key part of the research was observing how their animal patients tolerated D-44 long term. Seizures suggested an adverse neurologic effect—a high risk for a drug treating nerve injury.

If it happened to FloJo...

Drake checked the time. Kline, the state medical board representative, and executive administrators representing the medical school and the university were to arrive soon.

FloJo seizing—no.

"Do what you can, Rizz. See if you can get them to do a mega-workup. Full imaging, spinal fluid analysis, and full blood labs—tell them we'll pay." Drake paused. He wanted Rizz here for this meeting. They'd been side-by-side facing the onslaught of ER insanity for four years. There was no one Drake would rather have with him in today's fight.

"You know what, Drake? Apart from the D-44 concern, I'm worried sick about this cat. Totally sucks to see her hurting."

"FloJo is the best, partner. Get here when you can. Did you talk to our OB/GYN colleague?"

"Not yet but I will. Don't worry. When you need me I'll be there. I've saved your ass so many times it's second nature to me. I think you ought to tattoo my name on your butt cheeks."

"Geez, I was worried about adverse D-44 neurologic reactions. Too late. You're already demented." Drake's heart was not in his joke. FloJo's illness cast a dark shadow.

"Love you, too, brother. Later." Rizz clicked off.

Chapter 84

Clara had the loaded syringe hidden in the blood draw tray beneath the latex tourniquets. She stood outside the glass-enclosed bay of cardiac unit six, double-checking the labels on each of the five tubes of blood she'd just drawn from the patient there.

Her reflection showed clearly in the glass. White coat, scrubs, short hair—from the outside she looked the same. Inside everything had changed.

They'd killed her Dan. The one she'd come to believe she'd never find. The one who was everything and more than she'd ever dreamed possible. His love for her had been beyond a once-in-a-lifetime perfection. It had been all-consuming.

They'd taken him from her.

She went through the automatic doors heading for the next site of her scheduled blood draws—the ICU.

Earlier, she hadn't decided how and when she would make them pay. Drake Cody was first in line. Her rage called for immediate retribution, but patience and the potential for exacting greater payback down the line also had appeal.

Then the aftermath of the storm presented an opportunity. As if nature were helping Clara to deliver justice.

The road conditions prevented more than a third of the techs from getting to work on time for the morning blood draws. Clara's stepping in to help was reasonable and not without precedent. She assigned herself to draw blood for the intensive care and cardiac patients.

Fate had paved the way for her to take action now.

She knew how to make bad things happen in the hospital and had been doing so for several months. So far she hadn't done anything major, and none of the doctors suspected anything. She'd never killed anyone, though she'd devised a number of untraceable ways to do so. Today would be the day.

She slid her ID card through the reader, and the doors to the ICU whooshed open. For the patient in ICU bed four, Clara would check and double-check her wristband identification, make sure the patient's name and each of the multiple tests were appropriately indicated on the labels, and then draw blood into the appropriate tubes and correctly affix each label. She would execute the tasks perfectly, as her respect for the profession demanded.

In the midst of doing her job and barring any obstacles, she would do something else. Something special. Something no one else would ever know she'd done.

She'd slip the loaded syringe out of the tray and inject its contents into the IV. The substances were natural substances found in the body and thereby untraceable. The injection would place them at one thousand times their normal concentration. By the time Clara left the ICU with her blood tubes, Drake Cody's wife would be starting to crash.

They'd call a Code Blue, and Clara's greatest wish was for Drake Cody to respond. No matter how fast he arrived, no matter what he did, it would not be enough.

Drake Cody would lose the one he loved.

It would be the first of the ways she would make him pay.

***

Clara left ICU four for last. She wanted to be out of the unit when things started. What had to happen deserved to happen, but Clara did not care to see it occur.

Rachelle Cody, ICU bay four, was asleep or sedated. Her nurse had just moved to the unit's central desk. Clara made eye contact with the nurse, then held up her blood draw tray and pointed at bay four. The nurse nodded.

Clara moved to the bedside. The heart monitor beeped soft and at a moderate rate. The slim, dark-haired woman breathed easy. Unlike many patients' bays, no foul odor hung, only the Lysol-like tinge of disinfectant. The patient's left arm lay free. There was a capped IV in the forearm with nothing running to it. Clara could draw blood from the arm with the IV port totally accessible.

She slipped the loaded syringe out of the tray and placed it under the edge of the sheet alongside the arm. Everything lay ready.

"Lab. Blood draw here," Clara said.

The patient roused and turned trusting Bambi-eyes toward her.

"I'm from the Lab. I need to draw some blood. Can you tell me your name?" Clara checked the wristband.

"Oh, okay. I'm Rachelle Cody."

"Your doctors have ordered tests. I'll be quick."

"I understand. Thanks," she said. "But I don't like to watch. Please tell me when you're done." The pretty woman turned her head away.

Clara felt a twinge. The woman seemed so sweet. But Dan had been special, too. Things were setting up so perfectly this morning that it showed this payback was meant to be. She put on the tourniquet and then entered the vein with her first stick. Blood jetted into the tube. She deftly switched them filling five. She slipped the syringe from under the sheet, her breath coming fast. It would only take seconds to inject the powerful substances. Once inside the woman Drake Cody loved, no one would be able to stop her death.

Clara leaned to her left, shielding the IV on the forearm and connected the syringe to the IV hub. Her pulse raced. A sense of incredible power filled her. Drake Cody's wife lay with her head turned, the pose exposing the scarred tissue of her neck above the patient gown. *So helpless.*

A twinge of holdback flickered. Then a thought of Dan. Never would she be with him again. She positioned her fingers on the syringe and placed her thumb over the plunger. The holdback was no more. She committed—

"Hey!"

The deep voice exploded over her shoulder. Clara flinched. Adrenaline flooded. She plucked the syringe free, sliding it into the sleeve of her white coat.

"Look here, now the lab-lady is doing it all." The braying voice of Dr. Bart Rainey. She sensed his mass loom behind her. She almost gagged on his overpowering cologne as her throat clenched.

"Good morning, Mrs. Cody," he said in a voice loud enough to be heard on the next ward. "I'm Dr. Bart Rainey. I'm a surgical colleague of

Dr. Carlson of the Burn service. She's unable to get in due to the storm and asked me to check your burn."

Drake Cody's wife looked up at the surgeon. Clara kept her face averted, her heart a pounding hammer. Her hands trembled as she arranged the blood tubes. She could not breathe.

"I guess you must be a VIP—you have the boss vampire drawing your blood today. Did she do a good job?" No one joined in his hardy-har-har donkey laugh.

Clara put the tubes in the collection tray, nodded to Rachelle Cody, and exited.

***

The ICU doors whooshed shut behind her. Clara's heart remained in her throat, and her nerves felt as if superheated. She leaned against the wall and exhaled massively. She acted as if she were checking her lab sheet while her body recovered and her mind settled. *Too close!*

She'd been rash and careless. Hot-headed anger had almost cost her everything—so very nearly caught! And by the obnoxious surgeon, of all people. His megaphone voice had startled her more than anything in her life.

This was a lesson. She needed to be careful. Now was not the time to avenge her Dan.

Days, weeks, or even months—the time did not matter, but she would make those who took him from her pay. Perhaps harming Drake Cody's wife would be wrong—her scars showed she'd suffered. Clara knew some scars didn't show. She needed to think things through when the pain of losing Dan was not as raw.

Careful planning with no possibility of her getting caught. That's what her Dan would have wanted. He would be crushed if she suffered any further.

That was the kind of love they'd had.

Chapter 85

Conference Room

Drake remained in the darkened, back row of the conference room, his mind a whirl as Lloyd prepared at the podium. This meeting meant everything. The document Lloyd had passed to Kline for review by the university Board of Regents and the state Board of Medical Practice presented what Drake, in his dreams, hoped they might achieve.

Success would mean an agreement on the future of D-44 and, most important to Drake, his continued opportunity to practice medicine. The organizations he faced were huge and powerful, and the odds were against him, but he wasn't alone. Lloyd impressed Drake more each day, and Rizz was Rizz—there was no doubt he'd give his all.

Drake looked at the clock. Rizz had not shown yet and it was five minutes past the scheduled time for the meeting.

The clunk of the door mechanism sounded. Drake looked up with hope.

Kline entered at the front of the room. He wore a dark suit with wide, padded shoulders and small epaulets adorning the lapels. A lean, tall, silver-haired gentleman entered at the same time. Trailing Kline and appearing to struggle with a computer bag and a heavy-appearing valise was a short woman Drake recognized as one of the hospital's administrative assistants.

"This will do. Set up on this table," Kline said to the woman. "We'll sit at that one." He indicated the adjoining table where Lloyd's briefcase sat open. He turned toward Lloyd.

"I'll take the head of the table with Dr. Regid, representing the state Board of Medical Practice, on my right." Kline nodded toward the distinguished-looking man with the military bearing. "She," he indicated the administrative assistant, "will set up and manage the technical aspects."

Lloyd stepped forward from behind the podium.

"First off, let's skip the sophomoric control tactics about who sits where. I'll remind you my clients called this meeting. We—"

"I'll remind you," Kline said loudly, "this is my hospital—"

"No, Mr. Kline. It most definitely is not." Lloyd spoke softly but stepped closer to Kline. "You are currently CEO and serve at the discretion of the hospital board. The issues to be decided are significant. Let's not play games." He shook his head.

The administrative assistant had pulled a laptop from the computer bag and now removed a camera and tripod from the valise.

"Regardless," Lloyd continued, "this table won't accommodate all of us when the rest of your contingent arrives."

"I *am* our contingent." Kline puffed out his chest. "The university regents will participate via one-way electronic audio-video link. I will communicate with them via my phone," he indicated a Bluetooth earpiece, "and I'll relay their demands."

"You open the meeting with a false claim, try and play silly seating games, mention demands, and then tell me key parties in the negotiations will not be present—are you serious?" Lloyd's eyebrows arched and his forehead furrowed. The big man made Kline and his faux shoulders look like a stick figure. Drake sensed Lloyd would like to throttle the pretentious CEO. Kline shrunk back.

"This does not feel like a good faith effort." Lloyd shook his head. "It sets up a basis for later deniability. I'm going to recomm—"

"Lloyd." Drake said as he joined the group and stepped to the head of the table. "Please. Just a moment."

He turned to the older gentleman who'd been watching the exchange. Drake extended his hand. "Dr. Regid, thank you for coming. I'm Drake Cody. My apologies for the short notice and challenging nature of this meeting. A large amount of money and the hopes and dreams of me and my family are at stake."

"I understand." He shook Drake's hand, his grip firm and cool. "I represent the state Board of Medical Practice and am chair of the Licensure Review Committee." The ramrod-straight man met Drake's gaze. "I'm not here about money or your dreams. I'm here to enforce the rules of medical licensure and uphold the responsibilities of the Board in safeguarding the public."

"Of course, sir," Drake said. The thought "tough old bird" ran through his head. "I know that among the fourteen members of your board, there are four who also serve as university leadership. Is that correct?"

"Yes."

"Is what Kline has said about the regents true?"

"I'm not acquainted with Mr. Kline, but I've discussed this meeting with my colleagues. Their participation is in good faith. The telemeeting arrangement was suggested to protect against use of out-of-context images or audio. Public relations concerns are paramount for the university. Frankly, the same is true of my board."

"We wouldn't do anything like that, but I understand the concern." Drake paused, thinking without guilt that what he'd just said was a lie. He'd do anything short of harming innocent people to maintain his claim to D-44 and secure his dream of continuing to practice medicine. He turned to Lloyd. "I trust Dr. Regid's assurance. Let's get to the issues."

Lloyd nodded.

While they'd talked, the assistant had set up the tripod on the adjacent table with the computer connected and devices plugged in. Lloyd slid his briefcase over and took his place on one side of the table. He indicated the spot across the table for Kline.

Kline and the physician sat—Kline facing Lloyd and Dr. Regid across from Drake.

"Are you ready?"' Kline said to the assistant.

She nodded. "Audio and video clear."

Kline adjusted his coat and patted his blow-dried hair, then adjusted his earpiece. The CEO seemed a harmless jerk, but he posed a major threat to Drake's dreams.

Drake, Lloyd, and Rizz had discussed via phone their strategy for the negotiations. Drake had drafted the main elements of their plan while Rachelle battled infection in the ICU. He'd emailed it to Lloyd for translation into "legalese" and delivery to the university powers.

Drake checked the time—no word from Rizz. He held their ace in the hole. Was he coming? Drake started to sweat.

"Let's get our business started," Lloyd addressed the camera. "The communication Dr. Cody and I drafted and which I passed on to you through your representative," he nodded toward but did not look at Kline, "contains a fair and reasonable offer."

Kline leaned forward. "Fair and reasonable? Are you—"

"Mr. Kline, I was not addressing you." Lloyd's soft but crisp words shut up the arrogant CEO. "I'm asking for the response from the university Board of Regents." He nodded towards the camera. "When they have a response we want to hear it. Understood?"

Kline's face reddened.

Lloyd once more faced the camera. "Do you accept the offer on D-44 laid out in Dr. Cody's document? He will sign an agreement sharing intellectual property ownership of D-44 with the university. The university will make the initial payment identified in the document and agrees to future revenue payouts if and when the drug reaches the market. The structure of such payments is identified in the document. That is the offer in front of you."

Kline's face looked like he'd drunk sour milk, but Drake knew the annoying administrator's response mattered least. This decision would be made by the Board of Regents, the stewards of the university.

Lloyd had shown him the regents' charter and annual budget. Listed second among their responsibilities was "Accept fiduciary responsibility for the long-term welfare of the University." The school's annual budget was greater than $3.5 billion.

Did they want to go to court and battle to claim the whole prize? Or would they accept a deal and work with Drake?

Lloyd faced Kline, "Have they relayed you their answer?"

Kline jumped to his feet and moved toward the door, speaking rapidly into the Bluetooth. "Don't respond yet! You've got to listen to me..." He exited the door.

Silence. The faint smell of leather and cologne hung in the air. Kline's absence creating a vacuum. Drake's mouth went dry. His next effort meant more than anything to him, and he felt totally on his own. Somehow, his voice did not break as he addressed the imposing man across the table from him.

"Dr. Regid, I've been informed that the state medical board will terminate my medical license at tonight's meeting. I beg you to reconsider."

The doctor sat motionless, his unblinking eyes on Drake. Drake's chest clenched. The older doctor let the silence stretch.

"I falsified documents regarding my past. I hid my conviction and the time I spent locked up. I lied in answering questions and swore it was the truth. But—"

"I'm familiar with your clear and multiple misrepresentations." Dr. Regid's face was stone. "Let's call them what they are—lies. False statements on your application to medical school and every document thereafter—the facts are clear. The board and I will uphold our responsibility and enforce the rules we've been appointed to administer. I'm sorry." His manner, age, and intensity combined to give Dr. Regid a daunting presence. This was a man who would not compromise what he believed in. He believed in the rules. Drake's stomach sank.

He scanned the clock. *Get here, Rizz!* A bead of sweat trickled down Drake's back.

"Sir, I respect your commitment to protecting the public and safeguarding our profession. The questions on the medical school application and other documents are intended to identify those who might abuse their power or misuse their position for personal gain. My arrest and conviction were an injustice. They do not reflect my character. I am totally dedicated to the care of my patients and being the best physician possible. If you can hold off making a decision until you learn the facts—"

"What is undeniable," the older man's expression remained unchanged but his eyes flashed, "is that you flat-out lied. You acknowledge lying, which is unethical and unprofessional conduct. I'm sorry but the facts—"

A red folder splatted onto the table in front of the doctor. He and Drake snapped their heads to Lloyd. The big man held Dr. Regid in his gaze.

"With all due respect, sir," Lloyd said. "You need to know *all* the facts. Please reserve judgment until you've reviewed the material in the folder in front of you."

"I don't know the details of the criminal case, but it ended with a conviction. Nothing else is relevant. The repeated lies are a matter of record," the doctor said. "I'm not sure that—"

Lloyd's hand slapped the table, sounding like a rifle shot. They all flinched.

Lloyd looked embarrassed. "I apologize." He took a deep breath. "Doctor, please. As is evident by my loss of control, I've become invested in this young man. For decades, I've lived the messy task of trying to get justice done. I'm sure your role on the state board forces you to do the same. If you'll look at the material in that folder and consider Dr. Cody's character, you'll sleep better with your decision. Sometimes our rules say one thing, while justice demands another."

The two veteran professionals sat with eyes locked like two bull moose taking the measure of the other. Drake found himself holding his breath.

Lloyd continued, "As different as physicians and lawyers are, the best thing either of us can ever do in our work is to get it right. Please, sir. Examine the material in the folder. It will help get it right."

Dr. Regid put a hand on the red folder. His blue eyes were unflinching. His brow knitted. After a moment he nodded. "I'll review this." He patted the file. "But rest assured I will not compromise my responsibility."

Drake let out his breath.

Lloyd had struck a spark from the flint of the dignified board member. The faintest glimmer of hope kindled in Drake's heart.

The door clunked open and Kline reentered after his phone exchange with the regents. He sat. Drake could not read his expression.

"Do we have an agreement?" Lloyd said, facing the camera.

"Your clients are not in a position to offer anything." Kline said. "Dr. Cody's legal position is far from certain, and Drs. Rizzini and Malar have zero legitimate claim. You're asking the university to assume all the costs and risk for the expensive path to possible FDA acceptance. And I remind you that the contents of the laboratory are in the university's possession." Kline straightened his collar and held his head high.

Drake met Lloyd's eye. They'd considered the possibility of Kline or the university trying this bluff.

"We agreed we wouldn't play games," Lloyd said, now clearly facing the camera and slighting Kline. "I suspect this gambit was suggested by Mr. Kline and I urge you regents to disregard his contentious ploys. The initial payment and downstream dollars that our document identifies are more than fair. In fact, I have recommended against my clients entering into a contract that is so favorable to the university. But they believe that the poor faith shown in the seizure of their lab and subsequent developments are more the result of misguided representatives rather than the university itself." Lloyd swiveled and stared hard at Kline.

Drake's nerves were stretched hunting-bow tight. "I believe that the university is getting bad information. That's why I made this offer."

"No!" Kline jumped to his feet, his face flushed. He faced the camera. "There is no need to cut them in. We can win in court. They're broke and can't fight us. We have the advantage—they can't get the drug to the market without our agreement. I have had more than enough of these…these," he pointed at Drake, "damn doctors."

Lloyd rose and peered over his glasses, as if viewing a yapping puppy. "Kline, keep your mouth shut for a moment." He faced the camera. "What some of the regents may not be aware of is that the seizure of the contents of Dr. Cody's lab failed. You did not secure any D-44, nor its molecular composition, nor the formula for producing it. In short, despite what some may have communicated," he looked at Kline, "you have nothing."

Kline stood with his head hung. He raised a hand to the earpiece.

Drake caught Lloyd's eye and nodded. They'd hoped to have Rizz and another ally present, but Drake had heard nothing.

"Regents," Lloyd said, "we ask you to accept the terms identified on Dr. Cody's document. We'll accept your verbal agreement now. If we do not receive commitment today, the offer is withdrawn."

"You must listen to me," Kline was waving an arm and speaking into his Bluetooth. He turned to Lloyd. "I'll be right back. We've agreed to nothing!"

Drake, Lloyd, and Dr. Regid exchanged looks as Kline exited with the door again sounding a clunk.

Dr. Regid pursed his lips then spoke. "He's a right annoying twit, isn't he?"

Despite the fact that everything Drake had dreamed, worked, and bled for hung in the balance, he began to laugh. Lloyd gave a guffaw, and the distinguished Dr. Regid's head shook in a controlled chuckle.

The clunk of the door opening sounded. Kline's quick return was accompanied by a smug look. He sat down, then flicked an invisible piece of lint off the shoulder of his suit. “I was able to prevent a rash decision. I’m authorized to tell you as the representative of the university and the board of regents that—”

“Hold on!” The yell came from across the room as Rizz wheeled through the other door. A second wheelchair followed, with Dr. Julie Stone pushing a striking young woman dressed in red.

Kline stood open-mouthed.

“The camera is the university group?” Rizz asked.

Lloyd nodded.

“Dr. Michael Rizzini here.” Rizz faced the camera, “Sorry I’m late. I was taking care of a sick friend.” He reached into his lap bag. “Before any final decision, I need to share something with you all. First, I want to thank Dr. Torrins for getting through to me on the phone and updating me as to where things stand.” He nodded to the back of the room where a light went on in the audiovisual control room. Jim Torrins stood and waved a hand.

Even for Rizz, this entrance broke all records for drama.

“Regents and all concerned. This is a sampling of the contents of the meeting of university representative and Memorial Hospital CEO Stuart Kline with attorney S. Lloyd Anderson and me forty-eight hours ago.” He held the phone near the camera microphone. “I believe you’ll have no trouble recognizing the voices of CEO Kline and attorney S. Lloyd Anderson.

“I’m a former member of the university administration and currently a special consultant.” A click sounded. “The plan is for us to complete an agreement with a pharmaceutical firm.” A click. “The Swiss don’t have an income tax on foreigners.”

“Working for Ingersen as well is interesting. I suspect it could put you in a tough spot.” This was clearly Lloyd’s voice. “You are representing two masters who may end up at odds.”

“Don't worry about that,” Kline response. Click.

“Isn’t the reality that you and the university legal team,” Lloyd speaking, “investigated and found that, solely due to the fraudulent actions of Faith Reinhorst Malar, there was a technical basis for challenging ownership? Further, didn’t the university lawyers identify that if they had the drug in their possession their position would be stronger?”

"It's a legal world. The truth is whatever the law says it is," Kline's haughty-toned reply, "You know that. Whoever's attorneys argue best decides what the truth is."

"I think you and the university lawyers know that the intellectual property rights to D-44 should stay with Drake," Lloyd said.

"Should? You mean like fair?" Kline sniffed and shook his head. "The university legal team thinks they can win in court. That's all that matters."

Rizz turned it off.

Rizz nodded and Julie rolled the young black woman in front of the camera.

"I want to introduce a friend," Rizz said. "WCCY news anchor-person Tina Watt. Tina?"

"Thank you." She commanded the camera and the room, the picture of poise. "Members of the university administration, gentlemen," she nodded to Dr. Regid and the others, "I'm a reporter. I sense the possibility of a big story here."

"This is a private meeting!" Kline stood red-faced.

Dr. Regid spoke with the authority of one used to leading. "Kline, sit down. Now!"

Kline flinched as if slapped. He looked about and finding only disgust, melted back into his chair.

The doctor continued. "Ms. Watt, I apologize for the interruption. Please continue."

"Thank you, sir," She continued. "On one hand, I might be forced to share an ugly account of a gross transgression of justice. A story of public institutions abusing their power and robbing a committed, young physician of his calling. A story of unseemly manipulation of the legal system to steal a breakthrough medicine from a dedicated researcher and his colleagues." She paused. "If that regrettable outcome should come to pass, I would do everything in my power to make sure that story received the attention it should." She paused, her silence making the message clear.

"Conversely, I sense the possibility of sharing the story of collaboration between a young doctor and our great public university. A story of benefit to the citizens of this state, and potentially, miraculous gains for injured patients.

"I'm alive today and going to be discharged from the hospital now because of the skills and care of Dr. Drake Cody," she reached a hand back and clasped Julie's, "and Dr. Stone, and all the special people who make such miracles happen." She faced the camera. "I want to thank you for the opportunity to speak. I look forward to sharing the story that you have the power to make happen." She nodded and Julie spun the chair and rolled her out of the room.

Drake had to restrain his urge to applaud. What Tina Watt said was truth.

Lloyd spoke under his breath so that only Drake could hear. "One kickass lady." The attorney smiled but then stood.

"Regents, Dr. Regid, thirty minutes should be enough time for you to respond. Please do the right thing. You have my number. Thank you for participating."

Drake felt like a Thanksgiving float in a holiday parade. If no one held onto his lines he might rise into the sky. A weight had been lessened and his breath came easier than it had for days. Hope filled him.

Had life been breathed back into his dreams?

He wanted to believe.

Chapter 86

Thirty minutes later

Drake swiped his ID card at the hospital's sixth-floor access to the elevator.

"Are you sure it's okay to do this? I don't want you to get in trouble," Rachelle said from her IV-pole-accessorized wheelchair.

"Me get in trouble? What's the chance of that happening?" Their eyes met and they both laughed.

"We've had enough trouble for a while," she said.

He reached out and grasped her hand. Her touch was warm and vibrant—miraculous in that less than twenty-four hours earlier she'd been in the deadly grip of shock.

She moved his hand to her lips, kissed it, and held it to her cheek.

The elevator dinged and the doors slid open. Drake rolled the woman he loved more than anything into the elevator. He had multiple blankets wrapped about her and two more to position as needed. Rachelle had orders to be transferred to a regular unit and she'd said she wanted to breathe some outside air. Drake had got the okay to take her out of the ICU for a short time. He trusted she was out of the woods

There was a special place he wanted to share with her.

"Waiting to hear what they decided is torture," Rachelle said. "I feel like we're on death row waiting for a pardon from the governor."

Drake hit the button and the elevator doors slid closed. His weight shifted as the ascent began.

Death row—sounded harsh but it fit. If "they" decided wrong, it would end the passion that had given his life meaning and saved him from the blackness of loss.

He'd joined with other dedicated people who shared his commitment to helping those in need. The work he did—from the heroics of the Crash

Room, to helping a sick homeless or mentally ill person—really mattered. It might seem sappy to some, but it helped him feel good about himself. It was the best part of him.

His throat tightened. He took a deep breath and shook his arms like a fighter before the bell.

He'd deal with whatever happened.

The elevator dinged and he hit the "stop" button before the doors slid open. He ignored the buzzing of the elevator's stop signal as he made sure Rachelle was ready.

"Very few have seen the view from here, Rachelle. You'll love it." He adjusted the blankets around her. The background buzz of the elevator's stop signal continued.

His ringtone sounded and a vibration registered. His breath caught. Would this be *the* call? The one that would end their dreams?

He whipped out his phone. "Lloyd" showed on the screen. Rachelle met his eyes. He nodded. She clasped his free hand as he put the phone on speaker and bent so she could hear.

"I'm hoping you have good news, Lloyd. What have you heard?" The casualness of his comment underplayed his tension. His heart raced.

"I just had back-to-back calls from the chairman of the University Board of Regents and from Dr. Regid of the state Board of Medical Practice. What's that irritating sound I hear?"

"I'm in an elevator that I stopped. It's a buzzer." *What did they say?*

"What?"

"Please just ignore the sound. What did they say?" *Come on, man!*

"Are you in your house?" Lloyd said.

"I'm at the hospital. In an elevator. I don't have a house. We rent. None of that matters. Lloyd, please. What did they say?"

"You could have a house."

"This isn't about houses, Lloyd. Tell me what they said."

"With the Regents agreeing to joint ownership of D-44 and paying you the amount you asked for, I don't see any reason you can't get a house."

Drake froze. Had he heard correctly? Rachelle's gasp, her clench of his hand, and her megawatt smile answered his doubt.

His mind pinwheeled. Everything shifted.

His research would go forward. They'd pay off what they owed and have money. D-44 would be available for Rizz's care. He'd be able to take care of Rachelle, the kids, his mother—all who depended on him. Finally, he'd be able to provide for them in the way they deserved. He felt as if he were floating.

He leaned his back against the elevator wall, closed his eyes, and rocked his head back. Rachelle said, "Oh, Drake. Oh my God!" She squeezed his hand. Part of their dream had come true.

Lloyd's voice sounded from the phone's speaker. "I trust that is satisfactory news."

"Most satisfactory. Thank you, Lloyd." Drake laughed. "But I almost died with your dragged-out delivery."

"Wicked of me," Lloyd said, chuckling. "I couldn't resist. Besides, if you had almost died, you're in the right place. They have a pretty good ER there. I just received a call about one of the doctors."

Drake's throat clenched. Had Lloyd given him the good news first?

"What did Dr. Regid say?" He feared he knew what the leather-tough doctor's position was.

"Dr. Regid informed me the state Board of Medical Practice will be initiating a punitive action against you tonight."

Drake's breath caught. His elation gone in an instant.

He'd known it. From the day of his medical school application, from that first of many times denying his past, he'd believed this day was coming. *God, no!*

After what seemed like forever, Lloyd continued, "You, Dr. Drake Cody, will receive a reprimand from the board for 'unprofessional and unethical conduct'."

What? A reprimand?

"You will report to the ethics section of the board every three months for a period of one year, but will suffer no restriction of practice. No further action is anticipated."

Drake slid to the floor of the elevator. He buried his face in his hands.

Rachelle spoke, her voice quavering with uncertainty. "A reprimand? Does that mean he has his license and can continue his work?"

"He has his medical license and can continue his work." The smile in Lloyd's voice shone through as if he were in the elevator with them. "Dr.

Regid reviewed the file I gave him. In the last few days, I obtained statements from Cincinnati police, the justice advocacy group that got Drake released, and the judge who presided over his juvenile court proceeding. They agreed that Drake's arrest and conviction following the mistreatment of his brother had been a miscarriage of justice. Dr. Regid and the board did not want to be part of further injustice."

"Thank you, sir," Rachelle said, her voice breaking. "Thank you so much."

Drake could not speak. His hands tingled. He felt lightheaded and his mind would not engage. What he'd hoped for, what he'd dreamed of, but what he'd never truly believed could happen, had happened.

Since the TV broadcast, he'd been grieving for the loss of the work he loved. He'd known it would be taken from him.

But it had not. Tension bled from him like a burst dam.

"So Drake," Lloyd's baritone came from the phone's speaker, "how did I do?"

Drake laughed. "Not bad, sir. Not bad at all."

***

As the reality sank in, Drake's gratitude surged. Good people who cared about him had made this happen.

He and Rachelle hugged and laughed and kissed. And laughed some more, both elated about the possibilities of a future that hours earlier had looked lost to them. Instead of starting over, they were leaping forward.

"Let me show you my favorite place in the hospital. The hospital I work in." Saying that and knowing he would still be able to work made him smile. He adjusted her blankets and hit the elevator button.

The doors slid open to the bright light and chilled air of the flight deck. Drake rolled Rachelle out to the open area beyond the gleaming helicopter.

The city lay spread out around them. Intense sunshine in a rich blue sky had transformed the cityscape into a brilliant white fantasy land. Everything was draped in a thick sheath of glistening, cotton candy snow. The lakes visible were untouched plains of unblemished white. The frozen snow-covered Mississippi and the trees lining its banks stood in pristine contrast to the open black water downstream of St. Anthony's Falls.

"It's incredible," Rachelle said. "The snow is…" she shook her head speechless.

"Are you warm enough?" Drake said. It was near freezing, but with no wind, the sunshine warmed them.

"I'm fine," Rachelle said. "It's so beautiful."

Drake crouched and wrapped his arms around her. "And it's where we live. No more hiding. No more waiting to be found out." He looked into her eyes. "We'll find a house that you'll love. The kids can have a dog. You can paint. We'll have a home. We can live our dream."

Her eyes filled.

The ding of the elevator and the sound of its doors opening reached them. Rizz rolled onto the flight deck. "The nurses told me you headed up here."

"Did you hear the news?" Drake smiled raising a fist in the air.

Rizz held up his phone. "Just spoke with Lloyd. Piece of cake. I never had a doubt." He was straight-faced.

"What?"

Rizz smiled. "Bullshitting you, amigo. Great stuff. You scored on D-44 and kept your license. Excellent. I didn't want to have to break in another flunky."

"Hah! You're as surprised as I am, I know it. And it goes without saying, but I'll say it anyway—everything D-44 brings gets split three ways."

As he spoke Drake felt a flush of guilt. In the elation of the university agreement and maintaining his medical license, he hadn't tracked down the details of what had been found with FloJo.

"How is FloJo, Rizz? What do the veterinarians think?"

Rizz wheeled over next to Rachelle. He, like her, had a blanket over his lap. "Hey, beautiful. I bet you're glad the bum you married still has a job."

"I'm very relieved," Rachelle smiled, then put a hand on Rizz's forearm. "Thank you for all you did. Once more we owe you."

"No worries." Rizz seemed subdued. Drake's puzzlement grew.

"Rizz, how's FloJo?"

"Her seizures ended and she looked okay. I got them to do a big workup. They found something 'iffy' on her brain MRI, but they need a specialist to review it. Did you know there are veterinarians who specialize in neuroradiology?"

Rizz was concerned, but he seemed far less uptight then Drake would have expected. FloJo's condition was scary stuff. Had the other good news mellowed him out?

"Did they have any thoughts?"

"Like with some of our first-time seizure patients, there are unknowns—including why it occurred and whether it will happen again. Their concern with the MRI of the brain was lymphoma. That would suck."

And the implications for D-44 and Rizz would be terrifying. Yet he didn't seem terrified at all. Drake couldn't read his friend. Something had changed.

Rizz looked out over the incredible view. "Minnesota winter is brutal, but sometimes it's crazy beautiful. It's a hell of a place we live in, isn't it?" He reached into his lap bag.

It felt good for Drake to feel he really did live here—no longer just a temporary hideout. He took Rachelle's hand.

She squeezed.

"I want to make a toast." Rizz held up his silver flask and three small paper cups. Drake and Rachelle each held one as Rizz poured. He then held his cup up to them. "To Jon—may he get better soon—and especially to you two and your children. Welcome to your new home. I love you guys." He met their eyes and for once Drake saw no joking there.

"You too, Rizz. We're with you all the way, no matter what happens." Drake rested a hand on Rizz's shoulder. "Love you, brother."

They touched glasses and tossed down the amber heat. Rachelle coughed and her eyes watered.

"Geez, uncool of me to be giving an ICU patient booze," Rizz said.

"I'm okay, Michael. Thank you for the toast." Rachelle smiled. "I'm so happy. It's a dream come true. The only thing that could make it better is if you recover." She flushed and looked away.

"Drake, will you adjust the blanket by my feet?" Rizz said.

Drake bent and saw that Rizz only had socks on and the blanket had slid off to the side.

Rizz put his hands under his thigh and lifted his leg. "Put the blanket under and I'll set my foot on it. Then you can wrap it."

Drake placed the tail of the blanket below and behind Rizz's raised foot. Drake looked up, waiting. Rizz had both hands clasped behind his head and a big-as-the-sun smile on his face.

"I've never been so happy to have my feet feel cold." Rizz wiggled his toes, then lowered his foot.

The End

Thank you for investing your valuable reading time with Drake and company.

The third book in the Drake Cody series is titled *Blood Loss* and is targeted for 2017 release.

Visit the author's website, www.tom-combs.com, or find Tom Combs author on Facebook. Contact the author at tcombsauthor@gmail.com He attempts to respond to every communication.

Acknowledgments

I want to thank all those I worked with and learned from at three incredible institutions. Hennepin County Medical Center, the University of Cincinnati Hospital, and North Memorial Medical Center (eighteen years at this top-ranked level one trauma and medical facility). My special gratitude to the nurses, doctors, and many others at North Memorial Medical Center who were there for me when I needed them most.

Special thanks to Jodie Renner (www.JodieRennerEditing.com) who, once again, went far beyond the call of duty in helping me get this book to press—an outstanding editor and friend.

Thanks to Michael (Sears) Stanley, author of the award-winning Detective Kubu Mystery series, for his generous guidance. Thank you to Laura Childs, NYT bestselling author, for her incredibly generous support.

Big thanks to my friends, especially Tom Holker and Bruce Johnson, for their perceptive input and encouragement.

I want to acknowledge those who provided technical expertise and feedback on *Hard to Breathe*: Tim Combs (25-year police veteran), Scott Anderson (attorney/CPA), Donna Hirschman (ER/critical care nursing), Robert Daun (literary review/story consultant), John Molnar (ER medicine/healthcare administration knowledge), Anne Hutchinson Horn (flight nurse/critical care nursing), Jayne Klukas (laboratory technologist), Michael Morse (paramedic, fire/rescue) and more.

At times I compromised authenticity for the sake of drama. Any and all errors are mine.

Thank you to Mike Lance (Mike@theLances.info), whose formatting, design, and technical expertise ensured that the book and eBooks reached you in good form.

The cover concept was executed by Travis Miles.

Thank you to my wife, Michele, my son, Brian, and my daughter, Kristin, for their support.

I must also take the opportunity to apologize to healthcare providers and administrators. For the sake of storytelling, I omitted or altered details of some medical procedures and practices (e.g. Air Care flights without paramedics or flight nurses), and described negative behaviors unlike any I have witnessed.

Thank you, readers! I appreciate your time and am thrilled each and every time I hear that someone enjoyed my work. I love to get feedback and respond to all correspondence.

***

About the Author

Tom Combs' career as an ER physician provides the foundation for his unforgettable characters and riveting plots. His emotional engagement arises from twenty-five years of helping those facing illness, trauma, and tragedy.

Nerve Damage, book one of the Drake Cody series, immerses the reader in high-level intrigue and edge-of-your-seat suspense. The events are tomorrow's headlines, with surprises unfolding to the final page.

Book three in the series is titled "Blood Loss" and is scheduled for 2017 release.

Tom lives with his artist wife near family and friends in a suburb of Minneapolis/St. Paul. Visit his website at www.tom-combs.com or communicate via email at tcombsauthor@gmail.com.